DARK LIGHT
A Neo-Templar Timestorm

ALAN RICHARDSON

MY THIRTY SECONDS
OF FAME

TR

DARK LIGHT

A Neo-Templar Timestorm

Alan Richardson

LONDON

First published in 2013 by Mutus Liber
BM Mutus Liber
London WC1N 3XX

Copyright ©Alan Richardson 2013

The rights of Alan Richardson to be identified as author of this work has been asserted in accordance with the Copyright, Designs and Patents Act 1988.

A CIP catalogue record for this book is available from the British Library.

ISBN-13: 978-1-908097-06-4 (Paperback)
978-1-908097-07-1 (Kindle)

www.mutusliber.com

Dedications

to
Laura Jennings-Yorke, my soror mystica, who triggered all this off

to
Jo Barnes, my inspiratrice, who knows a cowboy when she sees one

to
Sean Martin, for having the faith and unfurling the Beausant

to
Margaret, for all the bestest things...

Thus the notion that Jesus [controlled the spirit of] the Baptist, was not, by ancient standards, an impossible explanation of his powers.

~ Professor Morton Smith
Jesus the Magician

Whoever owns the head of John the Baptist, has absolute power.

~ Lynn Picknett and Clive Prince
The Secret History of Lucifer

Severed heads, Templars, MI5, CIA, two Death Goddesses, one extra-terrestrial, some dirty dealings by the French, plus several Time Storms and a Mobile Library... What chaos. That was the year we all nearly got buggered. No-one knew where it would end.

~ Apollo Fuge
Remembrance of Last Things

CHAPTER 1

In the balmy days before she became a Death Goddess and marvelled at the severed head of John the Baptist on her lap, which constantly tried to do wicked things with its tongue, Lilith Love slept soundly in her large, ultra-modern house which overlooked the sea on Martha's Vineyard. The house was white, glistening white, with razor sharp angles to the roof and pitch-black window frames with red shutters, ebony doors, and the steel blue ocean sighing up to the curved silver beach. Sleeping deeply, snoring lightly, Lilith woke suddenly with the certain knowledge of what her next book would be about. She sat up in bed and pushed aside the silk covers patterned with stars.

"Light" she said, and there was voice-activated light. "Brighter!" she snapped, irritated by the stupidity of the gadget. The room brightened in response.

She ran her fingers through her long red hair as if to collect her thoughts, pushed her two Savannah cats off the covers and with a fine-tipped pen jotted down in black ink her first ideas in the little hand-made paper notebook that she normally used for her dreams. Lilith was aching to write something new, startling, having rested a little too long on her laurels after the runaway success of her self-help book *I'm a Jerk – You're a Jerk, Okay?*, which had been the synthesis of all her insight and experience as a psychoanalyst. Her follow-up, *Memories, Dreams and Dejections* went on to knock Dave Pelzer off the all-time best-seller lists for sheer therapeutic misery.

As a cult analyst and wannabe historian trying hard to impress everyone as a polymath – someone who knew everything – she had also branched into archaeology and native lore, bringing out well-received essays on – she was certain – the Templar colony in Newport, Rhode Island, founded by Henry Sinclair at the end of the 14th century. She had also funded and been (slightly) involved in archaeological work at Newport Harbor, looking more closely at the site of a tower built to the exact measurements of a Templar baptistery. She was only slightly involved because her long nails and aversion to dirt made actual digging difficult. Her essay on this had been supported by two others on the financial skulduggeries of Henry II of England and Philippe IV of France.

This time her book would be on 'Real Templars.' In fact, that would be the working title. She purred, and underlined the word

'Real' several times. This was because she had read all the modern crap and met many self-styled neo-Templars and to her, they were as near to the real thing as Roy Rogers was to real cowboys. Everybody and their Virgin Aunts were writing books on those guys now: she would write the definitive one.

Her excitement rousing by the second, little guessing that it was being stimulated by the rippling of occult forces half a world away, she vowed that this book would cut away the nonsense that had surrounded the Templars, and show them as ordinary souls, being more like politicians, or bank managers at a time of financial crisis – struggling to adapt, doing anything to win – rather than agents of chaos and old night. Or even, she mused, more like members of the CIA than anything else, if truth be told.

"Wow...." she said, dead impressed by her genius, though she attributed at least some of it to the little silver amulet of the goddess Sekhmet which had been sent by a wacky old admirer. Sekhmet, she had Googled, was the lion-headed Egyptian goddess who almost destroyed the world. Lilith felt a lot in common with her at times. "Okay, okay" she muttered, "come to me, come to me," meaning the ideas that were forming in her head like clouds.

Poor, poor Lilith: she little dreamed that in a short space of time she would discover Real Templars and Real Magick and the Real CIA, and would never have imagined that she would fall in love with the greatest Mobile Library manager of all time.

You see all her research so far had been done at her desk, Googling through the centuries, positively leaping on facts like a cat would leap on birds, toying with them like she had done with men, often scorning, but never quite discarding. Hours earlier, she had prowled the web and pounced on four actual figures – real Templars – who had lived in the county of Wiltshire, in England, in the 14th Century. The only four whose names have survived.

Reaching for her lap-top and tapping her long red nails on its case as she waited impatiently for it to boot up, she went straight to that piece which she felt was like a door to her future, and read it again and again. You can find the exact words yourself if you care to look, though be careful where these characters might take you:

No single preceptor is known to us by name, nor any event in the history of the house. The Order of the Templars was suppressed in

2

England in 1308, and in 1313 the keeper of their lands in Wiltshire was ordered to pay the Bishop of Salisbury for the maintenance of four Templars, John de Mohun, John de Egle, Robert de Hambledon, and Robert de Sautré, the only Wiltshire Templars whose names survive.

Their preceptory – headquarters – she noted, was at a place called Rockley, which was in a county called Wiltshire, in a country called England. That last was her little attempt at humour, for she had never been outside the States before, despite her wealth. So you can see, she just had to go there.

And even if she had known that her simple trip for simple research would take her into the realms of major political conspiracies, occult practitioners, bizarre sexual practices with Mobile Librarians, bringing hints of Eternal Love leading up to the End of the World…. then she would still have gone. Get There. Deal with it. Okay!

"Drapes!" she called and they whispered open. "Blinds!" and the slats opened, and sunlight punched into the room. "Time!" and a soft automated woman's voice floated down the ceiling telling her it was 14.30. She stood up and looked out of the window at the broad crescent of silver beach, and the waves smashing against the rocks. It was high tide out there, as well as in her head.

"Are you okay honey?" asked a sleepy man's voice from the far side of the large bed.

Lilith almost jumped: she had forgotten he was here. "I am not your honey. Now beat it."

"My money?"

She reached into a bedside cabinet and drew out a large bundle.

"I'm deducting 100 bucks for your nap."

The man shrugged. "C'est la vie," he said, though he had never been nearer France than some or French toast and some professional soixante-neuf.

As he got dressed he was already forgotten. She got onto her agent, Gloria Monday, almost shouting down the phone with the excitement. "There are Real Templars that I've found. The real thing. The head honchos. I'm gonna go there myself. By myself – sure, sure I can! I know exactly where to go…" And then Lilith called her PA, telling her to book the next flight out to England…

So there was Lilith, your classic American ball-breaker who, like many control freak ball-breakers, fancied she was just a frightened little girl inside, nicely ensconced in a 'super-first' suite on the Airbus A380, sprawling on the bed under her Givenchy duvet and zapping manically through the channels of her 23 inch TV.

"No I don't want any wine," she said to the attentive little man in the uniform who had had appeared at the door, probably hoping to receive a handsome tip or to give her his own tip and thus join the Mile High Club.

"Certainly madam. Hey... that's you! You're Lilith Love!" he said excitedly, pointing to the screen.

"Just leave me, okay?"

"Okay, okay... I'm a jerk, sure I am. I get up your ass."

The door closed and she was alone again. It was her of course. Episode 14 of her show *Jerk Off*, where she used actors to represent historical characters, each one of whom was submitted to The Process, as she called it, building up to the catch-phrase "You get up my ass. You are a Jerk! Now deal with it!!" That always had the audience whooping as only Americans can. Mind you, they were paid to whoop, so they took their money and whooped so hard the ratings went up through the roof for the first series.

She watched herself: power clothes and power make-up. Sometimes she wished she could escape from all that, and have a little softness, somewhere. The camera zoomed in on her stony power face, ready for the climax, and try as she might she couldn't see any flaws:

"Hey listen Mr Oscar 'I have nothing to declare but my genius' Wilde, the root of the problem is this: it's nothing to do with your mother, it's nothing to do with being gay. You really are just a paedophile. If you'd come before a jury in Alabama you'd have been lynched for what you did to those little boys in that hotel room, with darling Lord Alfred. You're a shit. You're a jerk. DEAL WITH IT!"

Whoop, holler, holler and whoop. More whoops and wilder hollers. The actor looked as if he might really fear for his life. The audience looked as if they might really want to lynch him.

Yep, that went well, and the huge angry response from the gay population meant – as far as she was concerned – that she must have been doing something right. Lilith zapped the screen into nothingness and closed her eyes, and sighed. Truth... she was really scared, snapping at everyone, and wondering what on earth she going to find in Merrie England, when she'd never before been anywhere more exotic than Maryland.

Tiredness got her and as she crashed toward sleep she wondered if she'd dare do Jesus on the next show, maybe opening with the words: "Look Jesus, hon, you got all these gifts, and whaddya got to show for it? Listen, try the American way why dontcha... 5 shekels for making the blind see; 10 for making the lame walk. Think 500 shekels for raising someone from the dead, but demand a 100 more if they're still alive in six months. And what's with this feeding 5000, huh? Charge 'em a shekel each for admission, get Mary and your mom to do some simple refreshments at modest prices, do two of your sermons in a month and you'll have your own temple within a year. Get real, Jeez!"

Sure, sure. Him next, maybe. The Big One. Cut all this crap about Meek inheriting Earths. In the meantime....

*

In the meantime, as Lilith was dropping off to sleep, a very different kind of woman on the other side of the Atlantic was about to cause all sorts of cosmic trouble by finding the legendary and talismanic head of the John the Baptist on what was her birthday, June 24th, and his Feast Day. Honestly, you couldn't get anyone further removed from Lilith than she was. If rich Lilith was largely brain with only a squidgy bit of heart, poor Jenny was all mushy heart but not much in the way of brains. Yet she, more than anyone else in this saga, brought the world into strange and terrifying days.

Occult historians would argue that it might never have happened if Jenny Djinn, on her 32nd birthday, hadn't decided to treat herself with a day out and travel from Trowbridge in Wiltshire, to the little town of Frome in Somerset, some 8 miles away. Once there, with the £30 she had won on the fruit machine in the pub, she bought herself a state-of-the-art see-through electric kettle from the Argos catalogue shop, and then went to the Black Swan café to have some carrot cake washed down with a big pot of Earl Grey tea.

So blame her. Because it all began when she stopped off for a pee behind a hedge at the glowering National Trust property of Cley Hill,

5

e her way home. Mind you, the concept of it being
ɔ 'fault' is perhaps not the right word either, where
ɔle cosmic outpourings are concerned. Yet the fact is if she
. t won that money, and hadn't decided to get out of town for a
. and go to nearby Frome to spend it, and hadn't drunk too much
ɪor her bladder, and hadn't stopped where she did when she did,
then that dreadful and hopeful spirit of the Baptist might never have
butted its way into her life.

This is how it happened. It was simple yet so awe-ful that the tale
should be preceded by something like:

In the Beginning was the Word, and the Word was... Bugger!

*

She chugged the oil-burning old Peugeot 104 she had borrowed
from her friend into the muddy parking area which led to the base of
Cley Hill, and parked hard up against a hedge, next to a sign which
warned *Watch Out For Thieves. Don't leave Valuables in Your Car.* She
leapt out and was going to squat by her car door but heard another
vehicle approaching so, absurdly, she clutched the kettle (still in its
box) and took it behind the hedge with her. She didn't want this
taken by Thieves. It was modern. It was a statement. It was like the
one she had admired in her weekly visits to the Job Centre. So it was
not just a kettle to her: it was a symbol that her luck was changing.

She was absolutely bursting. Should never have drunk so much
tea. As she pulled down her grey cotton elasticated slacks, squatted
and peed, clutching onto a sapling for balance which dripped rain
from the leaves onto her hair, she kept the prize safely in front of
her. Above and all around her the crows were incredibly loud, and
the cattle were lowing, making noises like the whale-song she had
heard on telly the previous night. *Aaaaaah*, she gasped, as her pee
steamed on the earth beneath. There was a breeze up her arse and
Cley Hill loomed in the near distance, a rounded surge under the
scudding grey clouds. The rich dark green of the fields, scattered
with daisies, faded out in stages like a brush unloading itself of paint,
so that the cloud-wreathed summit was pale olive and capped with
an ancient burial mound, like a nipple.

It was supposed to be hollow, that hill. The focus of a dozen ley
lines. Haunted by faeries, bogles and Templars, who once owned the

nearby village of Temple. Supposed to have a golden ram inside a cave. And also a homing beacon for UFOs. Actually she knew a little about all that because of the book she got from the Mobile Library which stopped near her block of flats once a month. Didn't really want the book – hardly read anything at all beyond the telly mags – but she fancied that nice and flirty young Jack Hobbes, the driver-librarian, and more or less took the first one she saw, from the tiny local history section. It was interesting though. Lots of black and white photos. One day, she vowed, she would come back to this hill and climb it. Preferably with him.

The other car – a large black Mercedes – turned awkwardly into the parking area, bouncing as it hit the pot-holes, skewing around as if it had made a mistake and was about to go straight out again. Pulling up her panties and then hunkering further back behind the hedge, she watched, not wanting to stand up until they had gone. She noticed it was left-hand drive and with foreign number plates.

Two very large men got out and spoke to someone sitting in the back seat. One of them walked over to her little car and looked inside, but didn't look beyond to see Jenny crouching behind the hedge. He started to come around but the other called to him:

"C'est ici?"

The man turned from Jenny's car and gave what was clearly a Gallic shrug, emanating from somewhere around his bottom lip and finding expression in his broad shoulders.

Both looked toward the hill, then down at a hand-held device of some sort. Peering between the leaves, curious despite her fear, Jenny saw the way they opened the back door of the car and clearly deferred to a third person sitting there. She curled even further into the hedge, as foetally as a girl could. The chill she suddenly felt radiated from her solar plexus, and was nothing to do with the cold breeze from the hill. The crows were suddenly silent, the cattle still.

Putchwee, Putchwee, Putchwee...

That's how she thought of the noise when she tried to tell the story later to an historian who scribbled down every detail. She thought at first it was a strange bird, such as she had seen at Hawk Conservatory in Andover, where she learned about their different calls and tried to mimic them.

Then when she saw the standing men fall back against the car, blood spurting from the chest of one and the back of the other, and the one inside slump backward so that his legs twitched out, she realised it was a silencer on a gun. She'd seen enough films to know that much.

And yet there was something else that happened too. For a brief second which was actually half an infinity she saw... knights. They weren't in armour or anything, but she knew that's what they were, and they riding on red-eyed horses with the sun glinting off their swords, and she also heard the twang of crossbows and saw men around a cart stagger back under the onslaught of small arrows, and the men at the rear being chopped down by a roughly dressed man whose face was covered in a crude mask... and... and... Then she was back behind the hedge looking at a very modern carnage, under the grey clouds of an English afternoon.

She should have panicked, but she didn't. Perhaps her life had been so dull and hopeless that this was something of a treat. She looked around but there was nothing and no-one, and she knew from the film *Lethal Weapon* the killer could have been over a mile away. So she stood up, still clutching her Argos box with the kettle in it, and was drawn toward the car and the twitching limbs in the back seat. As in a dream, she stepped over the dead guards – if that was what they were. This was too much like a movie, and she had been inured by so many of them over the years that scenes of gore had little power to shock. This surely wasn't real. She had often told her therapist, Dr McHaffee, about the weird dreams she had, and this was no worse, and was in fact considerably tamer. It was almost matter-of-fact, reality being far less exciting than the most humdrum murder you see on telly.

Jenny looked into the back of the car, slowly edging forward, looking around and still seeing nothing and no-one else. The third victim was a boy: late teens or early twenties. With pale skin getting paler by the second, as if he hadn't seen the light of day in years, a shock of golden curly hair, with silver-grey highlights, tumbling to his shoulders, sharp features and azure eyes which pleaded. There he was in his expensive suit – but once again, for a brief moment, he was in a kind of pure silk gown, the sort that altar-boys might wear in a holy ceremony – and just as suddenly, he was back in his suit again, with blood spreading from under his heart.

He was pleading. Yet what did he plead? Help me? Take me away? Let me die at last? Bizarrely, he too was clutching a box, but a

8

very different one to Jenny's. This one was slightly bigger, covered in ancient leather like an expensive briefcase, studded with what looked like jewels along the seams. It seemed to thrum. Jenny felt a bit stupid with her Argos box and its plastic kettle.

"Aidez moi," he gasped. "Prenez... prenez..."

Jenny turned to run. What did it matter to her? She would have done – if another figure hadn't risen from the very earth, camouflaged so completely with branches and twigs and leaves that he was hardly human, no sign of eyes or any hint of concern, yet focussing completely on the box. Not hers, of course, but the angel boy's.

The camouflaged assassin raised his rifle again, to finish Jenny and the boy off – both of them clutching their silly boxes – when a proper gun-shot made her jump, and she saw one of the downed bodyguards doing with his last breath what he was presumably paid to do. The assassin dropped to the ground, his face smacking into the mud, making brief bubbling noises before twitching into stillness.

"Ils viennent," the guard gasped his last, and it was only later that Jenny realised she had actually understood the French. *They are coming.*

"Bugger," Jenny said.

The boy's eyes widened with a sense of horror. "Non, pas la. Jamais!"

Which she understood clear as a bell meant *No, not that. Never!*, though she didn't learn until much later that "that" was one of the false accusations against the Templars when they were outlawed.

The boy seemed to go into spasm.

"Bugger," Jenny said again, but at least she knew what to do, having watched a dead good episode of *Holby City* the previous night, in which the paramedic talked someone through the resuscitation procedure. ABC. That was it. Airways, Breathing, Circulation.

"Airways..." and she leaned over him to check they were clear, pulling his jaw open and running her finger into his mouth to check for obstructions, just as the actor had done. "Breathing." She put her cheek against his nose and mouth but felt nothing, so she figured there wouldn't be time to go on the Circulation, and started the kiss of life.

His eyes opened at the touch of her lips. They seemed to glow. She carried on respirating, and then pushing down on his chest, then panting into his mouth again.

"Please," she said.

Something seemed to surge through him, up through his body and into her mouth, and down to her feet. For a moment she felt golden, glowing, as if his life force had left him and travelled through her entire body on its way to whatever heaven he believed in. The car shuddered on its springs. Or was it her?

"Bloody Mary," she swore, her being a lapsed Catholic an' all.

And that was it. There she was in the muddy little parking area with three dead Frenchmen, one dead Green Man, and it was if they were all sealed into a bell jar, it was so still.

She backed out of the Mercedes. Picked up her own box containing the precious kettle, not realising until much later that it was somewhat heavier than it had been, and scuttled into her old Peugeot. This time – for once – it started immediately. When she pulled away out onto the road it positively roared, and there was no cloud of burning oil. She touched 80 at one point on the road back, and the heap had never got to 50 before.

"Hmmmmm," Jenny said to herself, suspicious of both her car's sudden enthusiasm, and what she had just seen.

That evening there was nothing on local or national news. She checked and checked again. Had she imagined it all? Well, in truth, she had been seeing Dr McHaffee for a couple of years now, and he had stood up for her against all those who accused her of having – supposedly – bipolar schizophrenia. But she herself always knew what was real and what wasn't. Except that she was the sort of hopeful soul who often felt that merely saying something was so, made it so. Or as near as, dammit. It was not illness, just extreme optimism.

Still, after the strange events at Cley Hill, she could have had another downer, but she rallied: she still had her prize, after all. It might have been a poxy little electric kettle to others, but Dr McHaffee (doing some Cognitive Behavioural Therapy) would have told her to think of it as a change of luck, a symbol of better things to come. So, almost reverently, she put it on the table in her little flat, and started to open it...

Now, had she known what was happening at that very moment to the other box – the one that had been held so firmly by the angel-boy – she might have chuckled. In a large room in the heart of London, in a vast hall with black and white tiles on the floor and a five-pointed star on the blue and gilded ceiling, by the light of a thousand candles, men in sumptuous robes of many colours stood transfixed before the Sacred Casket. The walls were decorated with eyes, of every shape and hue: in the flickering light, they seemed uncannily alive.

In a crescent at the very back of the room, melting into the shadows, stood the tall, shimmering, strangely shaped hooded figures of the Nine Elders who were supposed to be the secret rulers of the world. The REAL rulers of the world. Their robes were in the nine colours of the spectrum from infra-red to ultra-violet, and you might have been forgiven for thinking they were mere holograms because their outlines were translucent, and their substance seemed to owe more to the aurora borealis than bone and flesh. None-one dared go near them.

And surrounding the Nine were their representatives from the various Orders, Lodges and Temples of every kind: Masons, Rosicrucians, Yogis, Lamas, Martinists, Taoists, Essenes, Hermeticists, Quantum Magicians... Plus all those secret cabals with political as well as mystical aims. There was every nationality represented, every occult society, and even a couple of highly esoteric Christians looking very uneasy and clutching their crucifixes.

Off in the background men chanted in low deep voices, like the sea. There were lighting effects and incense. There had never been anything like this before in the whole secret history of the world! All gathered to see the legendary, utterly powerful Sacred Head of St John the Baptist.

Only one of those present, Nyron Hughes, who was standing behind the Casket and ready to open it, knew of the near-disaster earlier that day and he was not about to blab. An incident caused by French negligence – not the first time – which he had put to rights by his prompt arrival with back-up and efficient disposal of the bodies, hardly believing his luck that the Holy Treasure was untouched.

He looked out on the crowd with some awe. There was even a broad-shouldered oddly Mexican-looking gent in a dark suit with dark glasses, who resolutely refused to wear one of the many robes offered, and who was rumoured to be from a different galaxy to ours. Alright, alright he had given his address as Colerne, which was a small village in Wiltshire with – as Hughes knew – very dodgy public toilets, but everyone could tell you that the RAF base there contained a crashed UFO. So everyone kept a certain distance from that fella. He seemed to leak energy like a crocked microwave.

Hughes was sooooo excited. Plus he was dressing up again and wearing his favourite robe, a nice light grey affair with spacious sleeves and deep hood so that he could see and not be seen, and look as mysterious as the rest of them out there. In fact this was probably the greatest moment of his life. Here in the Mother Lodge, where no women were allowed, much less mothers, were some of the most august figures in world politics, business and industry. There were Names, here, and you could more or less tell which were the Names because they kept themselves more robed and hooded and anonymous than anyone else. And there were also individuals whom you had to think of as Powers, and you could tell them because they looked quite normal, stood their ground, and just radiated.

Having a mortgage to pay, Hughes smiled benignly on all of them just in case. He was sure he saw his old headmaster there, Thrasher Chapman, in the blackest of black robes. In fact he wanted to giggle with nervousness and was thinking of his Plan B if a chortle slipped out. Judging from the Grand Master's mood, however, suicide would probably be the best option.

The Grand Master's plan had been simple: bring all the Orders together, all the spiritual disciplines. Combine all their resources, all their temporal and spiritual powers and get The Head to take them all to the next level. World Domination.

Hughes was in fact standing exactly behind the box, like a man in a Game Show, waiting for the extreme moment of tension within the rite to lift the flap and reveal St John the Baptist's severed head, the one that Jesus had used to secure his powers in that necromantic way he had had, as described in the Talmud, and which the Order now planned to use for themselves.

The chanting reached a climax. Bells were rung. A beam of light from a spot at the end of the room splayed on the Casket. A few people yawned, rather rudely he thought, and the alien from Colerne let rip with a very human fart. Thank the Great Architect of the Universe, then, that the room stank with frankincense: they wanted to make the Head feel at home, of course.

Hughes swallowed hard. He was waiting for his cue, the word 'Extension'. Then they'd gasp, commune, reverence, get some power and feel infernally smug. Afterward as they went to their rooms and talked into the night about how they'd use these powers, he would go to bed and sleep the sleep of the just, having done his job, ridden his luck, and not been branded by the Order for all time as the Man who Lost his Head.

"Konx om Pax," said the figure in the East.

"Khabs am Pekht," came a response from the West.

"Light... In... Extension!" said the Grand Master in that wonderfully deep voice of his.

There was the cue!

This was the apex of Nyron Hughes's life so far. He reached both arms around and lifted the flap. The Servers – for that is what they were known as within the Order, although none of them had ever served anyone but themselves – the Servers gasped, for they were in a semi-circle nearest. They groaned. A wave of collective shock flowed through the rest of room. None of them had seen anything like this! thought Hughes, who had glimpsed The Head twice before today and seen it wink, though not talk (as he knew it did).

Then silence.

"Are you taking the piss, sonny?" came a chilly voice from the back of the room.

"I came from Chicago to see this?"

"Qu'est-ce que c'est?"

"Was ist dast?...."

"That's not on the level, old chap..."

And other voices joined in, in all tongues; it could have Pentecost in that room. The great curtains wafted in the breezes of their outcry. Nyron was bewildered. It had never happened before in any of the discreet little unveilings they had had to highly select members of his own Order. Did these Outsiders think it was a fake?

"Master? I don't... I mean this is...."

He came around the double-cubed altar and looked into the Casket, and his knees almost buckled, he had to stop himself from fainting. Not because of awe, of course, but because the last thing he wanted to be looking at now, here, was the reflected faces of some of the most powerful men on the planet, curved around the glass walls of an electric kettle – and blaming him.

"It's from Argos," he said lamely, looking at the receipt taped to its side.

"I don't care if it's from Alpha Centauri," roared the bull-faced Grand Master. Even his nasal hair seemed to quiver. "I want to know what it's doing here, and where The Head has gone!!!" and spat in Hughes' face, a great viscous greeny wodge of phlegm.

As the room started to empty, an Honourable Member from a great and venerable Irish lodge sauntered up, looked at the item in the box and asked ingenuously:

"Does it whistle, laddy?" before following the rest, shaking his head.

Bugger, thought Hughes, leaving the Grand Master's phlegmmy gunge to trickle down over his lips and down off his chin onto his grey robes, not daring to wipe it off, not daring to make eye contact with anyone.

*

The Head itself had swapped places of course. The link she had made with the angel-boy enabled it to activate itself. Having been incarcerated in a variety of splendid containers of nearly two thousand years, it was quite happy to bide its time in the cardboard container which now rested on Jenny's table.

Jenny Djinn's world was very far indeed from that inhabited by Lilith Love. Jenny lived in a tatty little second floor flat near the centre of Trowbridge, a small town in the heart of Wiltshire that tends to wrap itself around people like an old coat. She was near a curry house (where the owners would give her regular free treats), a kebab hut, two pubs popular with the Moroccans, a Turkish take-away and a Polish deli. If that occult lodge in London was filled with the brightest, richest most secretive sparks of every nationality, then the street outside her grimy windows was at the very other end of the spectrum. And there were quite a few, who, when the pubs were closed, staggered along the pavements in a way that definitely wasn't human.

So that was where the Head was now, on the Formica top of her little table, pushed against a wall with rose-patterned paper peeling back from damp, and smelling of mould. It shared its spot with some dirty plates, mismatched cutlery, various items of food from the Pleistocene Era at the latest, an opened box of cold chicken nuggets, several free newspapers, a near empty ketchup bottle and an empty margarine tub.

The telly blared loudly in the corner and Jenny had finally persuaded herself, from constant study of the local news, that nothing actually had happened. Or nothing that would impinge upon her life in any way. Goodness me, but she would have been lost without that little white cube of a television, with its cigarette burns on the case: it was just as important to her as the Casket was to the Servers. Dr McHaffee and the key-worker he appointed, a young woman called Becky, once opined that Jenny would probably know nothing about the outside world at all if it hadn't been for that box. You can sneer, or tut, but it wasn't that far removed from Lilith who couldn't really function without her internet search engines.

No chanting in Jenny's little flat, just the theme music of Casualty. No exalted robed beings oozing testosterone, either.

She was gasping for a drink after all the excitement, although like everything else in her numbed life the potential for agony behind what she had seen at Cley Hill had just faded away. If indeed it had ever happened. Her work with Dr McHaffee was paying off. Having long and somewhat dirty nails, she was able to slice through the Sellotape on the box, lever up the cardboard flaps and... and...

"Jesus – oh Jesus!" she cried, staggering back, falling into the rickety armchair, one leg propped up with an unread, tea-stained copy of *The Da Vinci Code*.

"Oh please..." said the head chirpily, "Not him. Couldn't stand the lad. He couldn't stand me, come to think of it."

There was a huge silence. The clock on the wall seemed absurdly loud. She stared at it. It stared at her.

And then the head spoke again, in the softest of voices:

"Don't be afraid."

Suddenly she wasn't. Suddenly the room was warm and soft. Whatever the head was, it took away her fear, made it seem completely normal to be talking to a severed head.

"You speak English. You've got a Wiltshire accent!"

15

"I speak every language. I speak the sounds in your head."

"Who are you?"

"Well those bastards that had me before called me John the Baptist, so I suppose that'll do. Before all this happened, before my bloody cousin Yeshua – Jesus to you – started messing about with my cosmic fabrics, I was Yohanan Ha'Matbil. Known to his mates as Yahya."

"You look like Jim Morrison..."

The head closed its eyes, as if accessing this knowledge. It smiled, as if something had just lit its fires.

She released the breath she had been holding. "Why... why are you here?"

"Glad you asked that. I'll tell you later. I'm sick of hairy-arsed men asking me deep questions. But let me give you some awesome powers first, eh? That's what everyone wants from me. They're a lot better than Bingo."

Although the head was static, the eyes rolled all over the little room. Jenny felt suddenly embarrassed.

"This is only temporary," she lied.

"Now that I'm here, yes it will be. Soon as you've got your powers."

"I couldn't handle powers."

"Yes you can."

"What sort?"

"The best sort. I'll make you become what you are within yourself."

"Whaaaat?"

"But first I'll change your name."

"How do you know - ? What is it then, eh?"

"I know everything. You know how folk who lose limbs develop phantom limbs? Well I've got a phantom body. Most of me is in the Otherworld. I can do all sorts of things, know everything. Nearly everything."

"You're not shy, neither. So what's my name then?"

"You're known as Jenny Grey. And your National Insurance number is WY985173B. But that's not really you. I'm gonna call you Jenny Djinn, djinn being a fire spirit."

When he spoke she almost saw his words in her head, so she knew it wasn't the drink Gin he was talking about, but something else again. After a long moment her impassive face broke into an almost girlish smile.

"Jenny Djinn... Jenny Djinn... I like it!"

"You'll like it more when you become what you are."

"Which is what exactly?"

"That's up to you. Inside."

She sat up in the chair, pinched herself through the old cotton slacks she had bought from the Oxfam shop. She could still feel through them the scars where she had once self-harmed. The face was... beautiful. Long, long dark hair that tumbled down to the base of his neck. Heavy eyebrows which met in the middle above an aquiline nose, and electric blue eyes, like those things in the curry house which attracted and zapped flies.

"Really?" she said wonderly, like a little girl.

"*Vraiment*! I mean, really. Sorry 'bout the French. They had me a loooooong time."

"What do I do?"

"Close your eyes, let the world come through to you. Me and the Powers will make the links."

"I don't understand."

"Close your eyes. Peace, be still..."

So she closed her eyes and relaxed, and it felt as if she was floating in space, in light. From outside she smelt the vindaloo from the curry house, and the notes from the annoying muzak they played – sitars and reedy flutes, the latest hits from Mumbai – and she seemed to feel her chest heaving and then get very heavy, heaving and aching, and for a moment she feared she was having a heart attack and opened her eyes. The room was exactly the same at one level but it seemed brighter, somehow, as if she was seeing something behind it, or beyond it.

And he was still there, the Head. Yahya did he call himself?

She looked down at herself. The same old clothes. But she felt different.

"So what am I, Mr Head?" she asked, almost giggling, it was so absurd.

"Well," it mused, "I think you got fixated on certain olfactory and acoustic items, and so your innermost essence was up and running before I could step in. Which is no bad thing. That's why they kept me in sterile rooms in the past couple of millennia, so people like yourself wouldn't get carried with the unexpected. Which was so bloody boring if you ask me. So I reckon… all things considered, and looking at your spiritual essence rather than your corporeal… I'd say you were…"

"Who?!"

"Kali. The Death Goddess."

Jenny burst out laughing. "Me? Me?! Don't be so bleedin' daft. A Death Goddess? What's the fun in that? Couldn't I be, like, a Lurve Goddess eh? Eh?"

"No, Kali. Definitely Kali. And you don't need to read about her in Jack Hobbes' library van. You will become her."

Kali… she had seen pictures of her. A dancing lady with four arms. An old boyfriend had her tattooed on his left arm, above the word 'Death'.

"Four arms yeah," said the Head, reading her thought. "One arm to give, one to take. One arm carries a sword; the other a severed head. So it's partly my fault – that and the stink of curry from next door."

Jenny looked down at herself, and in the cracked full length mirror.

"Can't see it myself."

The Head sighed, smiled. "You soon will. And when you do, after I've proven my powers, I want you to do one favour for me. Something I've done without for nearly two thousand years…"

"Yeah?" she asked, fearful that sex would be involved in this somehow, as it was with all the other men who asked 'favours' from her. Not that she was agin sex, you understand, but when there's no body involved, it was probably gonna be difficult.

Her nipples felt itchy and sore, even though it wasn't her period. Maybe she just needed a new bra, or to wash the one she was wearing. She felt too embarrassed to scratch them with him watching.

"Jenny Djinn, I have been cooped up in a box for an exceedingly long time, even by the standards of someone who, like me, is Beyond Time. I've been worshipped, prayed to, implored, beseeched, but there's one thing those bloody Frenchmen never thought of…"

"Which is what?"

"I'd love to have my hair washed."

Jenny mused upon all this as she walked back from Tesco's after having got some food for herself, the *Wiltshire Times*, a small soft cushion and a large bottle of medicated shampoo for her unexpected guest. By this time it was cold, almost dark, and disgustingly wet. Wind moaned across Tesco's car park, making noises like a dinosaur in pain. Every few seconds squalls lashed wire bristles of rain into her face and threw her out of her stride. Her trainers were soaked through. Her jeans clung to her thin legs, and her old duffel coat was little more than a sodden blanket with wooden knobs attached. The hand that clutched the bulging carrier bag was raw from the cold and rain, and Jenny couldn't wait to get back to her flat. Most people try to make such places cozy with the help of IKEA, or MFI or even Habitat if they could afford it, but somehow that severed head on her table did the trick as nothing else could, as if it made her best wishes and hopes take on a reality that was greater than the outer world.

John the Frigging Baptist, Kali the Death Goddess... she had to laugh. Yet it was no more bizarre than some of the hallucinations she had had in previous years, and a lot more fun. And she hadn't had much of that in a long time.

A narrow pedestrian bridge connected the superstore with the park: a failed rainbow of grey concrete, arching above the dual carriageway, connecting the eternal wasted light of the superstore with the dark underworld of the town's park. She struggled up the steps, the cans in her bag bashing her ankles and making her swear. She took a deep breath and headed up the curved slope. It took her a while before she noticed the man who was intent on blocking her way. Jenny knew him by sight as someone who probably had more heroin coursing through his veins than most drug smugglers had ever stashed away up the rectums of their mules, and he swayed as much from this as from the gusts which roared down County Way.

"Gimme yer purse," he ordered, holding out a knife and waving it vaguely, roughly at the level of his dick.

"Lemme think about that," Jenny said, putting the index finger of her free hand to the side of her face. "Erm, how about, you go fuck yerself?"

Now you can say what you like about kung-fu, aikido, karate and the rest, but the fact is, once a man has been hit at force with the full metal jacket of several tins of Fray Bentos corned beef, his chances of remaining upright are slim. The man sprawled on the bridge, gurgling incoherently, surrounded by tins, bananas, a loaf of thinly-sliced white bread and the remains of the newspaper that Jenny had so looked forward to reading. The pages were split and gusted to the heavens before being pinned back down and made useless by nails of rain, but at least the medicated shampoo was intact. He made a noise which sounded oddly like *bloop bloop bloop*, completely unaware of Jenny's rage at the way these new eco-friendly carrier bags split open so easily.

But that wasn't what killed him. Had she left him there and then he would have been soon helped to his feet by some out-of-town Samaritan and taken to hospital to be treated for a smashed cheekbone and several broken teeth, only to assault the ward sister and raid the drugs cabinet when he had recovered. What killed him was the moment of compassion she felt as he rolled in narcotic agony, his shrivelled little aura like a burst balloon telling her that here was a man with no future, with no point to life, no possibility of ever climbing from the Horrible Hole that he had dug for himself.

This was her Damascus moment. Something seemed to open within her, unfolding at the level of her breasts. It felt like extra pair of arms, ethereal angel-arms. No-one else would have seen them, but they were there, and they were real. Something in her head was like music, something in her muscles like dance.

"Go," she said, touching his forehead, and he looked up, to the infinite darkness beyond Jenny's head, and she felt a depth of pity which was almost like love, even though he had almost ruined her evening. "Go," she said again, and after a couple of spasms, he went.

The wind dropped. The rain ceased. The clouds rolled back and there were stars.

Jenny did then what all true Death Goddess must always do when their work is done: she gathered together her corned beef and walked on by...

CHAPTER 2

The one person who would unite both Lilith and Jenny – though not in the ways they would have imagined – was sitting at the wheel of a large, high and fat Mobile Library van as it made its way to the next stop, feeling very proud in his new Wiltshire County Council uniform of grey stain-proof perma-crease trousers, and dark blue sweatshirt. You can see right off that if Lilith learned everything important from the internet, and Jenny via the telly, then young Jack Hobbes' entire knowledgebase lay among the 3,000 books in the back of the van he drove. The three of them were made for each other, really.

"Y'see Jo," Jack said to Joanna, his boss, who was out with him for the day to make sure he hadn't developed any bad habits in the three months since he'd started. "Y'see, to you this might just be a 7½ ton Mercedes Sprinter van with library terminal and internet access, but to me... this is a Magic Steed."

"The short version please Jack," she said, peeling a satsuma while reading the latest Lee Child thriller on her lap and not bothering to look up.

"To me this van is a magic beast up there with Bucephalus, Pegasus, Epona, and Bill the Pony – and where was Bill the Pony from Jo, eh? Eh?"

She gave a deep sigh and looked at him over the top of her gold-rimmed specs. "It's from *Lord of the Rings*, and belonged to the Hobbits. There. God you're a smug twat you are..." Joanna's language had the tones of the Ladies' College from Cheltenham and the substance of the submarine pens at Portsmouth. She rather liked the challenge of banter with Jack.

"Or, it could be Trigger, the Lone Ranger's horse. Or even Skippy."

"Which was a bush kangaroo," she said firmly. "I watched that programme before you were born."

"Just testing, just testing. Anyway, this badge I wear might say to the ordinary eye that I'm an employee of Wiltshire County Council, in the Library and Heritage Services, but to me this is like the badge worn by US Marshals. My job is to drive about righting wrongs and doing good, as well as issuing books to the elderly and housebound."

"Bollocks," Joanna said, not looking up, trying to get back into her book.

"Anyway to you, this is just Trowbridge, a battered old town with little charm and lots of dog-shit, but to me this is.. this is…"

"A demi-paradise?" she prompted.

"Yeah! If you've got eyes to see. This jewel set in a green sea, this demi-paradise, this sceptered–"

"Septic?"

"Gosh you librarians have got no soul, no vision. Did you know that Keith and Mike back at the depot are having fierce arguments as to whether I'm the – wait for it – The Greatest Mobile Library Manager in History, or merely The Greatest Mobile Library Manager in the Past Twenty Years. Wotcher think?"

"I don't even think you're The Greatest Mobile Library Manager in the Past Twenty Seconds of Pure Shite."

"Bah… How long before you retire now?"

"More than a month, less than an aeon. That's all you need to know. Just about the time that your probation ends, and we have to decide whether you're fit for the job. Hint hint."

Roadworks. The lights were red. He stopped and pulled on the air brakes with a hiss. As he waited for the lights to change, Jack Hobbes carefully combed his wavy golden locks in the rear-view mirror. Gosh he liked what he saw! Just to make sure he wound down his side window, angled the wing mirror upward and took it in from another angle.

"Am I not the most perfect and gifted Mobile Librarian ever, in the whole history of the world?" he asked Jo.

"Double Bollocks" she said, with great serenity.

"Phwaw!" he snorted, as the stink of the curry floated in over the dust of the road drill. He hated that, and wound up his window again, turned the knob on the dash that would seal them from the outside air. "Anyway, did you know that bollocks isn't actually a swear word? It doesn't mean testicles or anything like that, it was a speech given by medieval –"

"Triple bollocks. And the lights have changed. Home, James!"

"So did you know that 'Home, James' came from the time that Lord Montagu of Beaulieu hired a chauffeur named James Darling, and –"

"Jack, dearest… SHUT UP!"

The thing is, to Joanna's surprise, he did exactly that for the first time since she had known him. But it was not because she had shouted. Unbeknownst to her it was because Jack's van, splendidly illustrated with Wiltshire scenes of hills and happy readers and white horses, had come near Jenny Djinn's flat, and within range of the Head, and it was affecting him. The tawdry streets with all their roadworks and empty pizza boxes and broken beer bottles and general rubbish fell away. Jack saw empty fields of long grass which rippled in the wind and churned up the light, and distant oak trees which hunched together like old men, and instead of the library van, he sat on an old cart drawn by four old Shire Horses, and Jo wasn't wearing the regulation blue top, grey trousers and fleece, but a long dress which came to her ankles, her long hair fastened back in strange medieval ways.

"Jack," came a voice into his head – her voice. "The light has changed. You can go. Jack...?"

And it was the true: the light had changed. The light and the world itself.

"Jack... stop pissing about!" Jo said, wondering if he had had a petit mal, and relieved when he suddenly gave his golden grin and drove on, outwardly normal again, but inwardly wondering what the hell had just happened.

Jo gave the young man at the wheel a Look. Although Jack could issue and discharge books and do the stock rotation with the best of them, and looked like one of the girly young knights in pre-Raphaelite paintings, there were times when she felt he wasn't quite on this planet.

*

By this time, a certain transatlantic flight had touched down at Heathrow airport. Passengers had disembarked, the flight crew were making their weary ways home, while one woman among them all was experiencing her first contact with foreign soil and going ballistic.

Lilith in London was gonna kick ass, Lilith in London was Livid! It sounds like a nursery rhyme but it felt to her like a nightmare. She who had often complained loudly about the problems of living in a goldfish bowl, and of fans acting as if they had rights of ownership, was in a place where no-one recognised her, no-one gave a damn, and someone had stolen her luggage. The thought of having to cope without the Voice and Handwriting Recognition features on her laptop, not to mention the Wi-Fi connection, was a situation that brought her out in a sweat. What would she do without Google?! Lilith used the internet as means of bringing the universe to her, rather than going out there in flesh. Damn this country. She had been stupid to think of coming here. Why hadn't she visited via Google Earth?

More, she had been pulled aside by the Customs Officers and questioned at length about the reasons for her visit.

"I've told you, I'm here to do research. I'm Lilith Love. I'm big in the US of A. Look me up on Google, huh? Can't you go bust some drug smugglers? Look, just get me my lawyer and let me outta here."

Now Lilith was of the insular breed who regarded all Englishmen as under-functioning Americans. Or if not that, then they were gay, as this tall and handsome man questioning her undoubtedly was. Using all her training she sought the best ways to relate to him, without demeaning his sexual preferences or giving him a slapping.

This was Nyron Hughes, of course, who despite all his problems, felt rather good in that dark-blue uniform with natty little things on the collar expressing rank.

"Why me?" she asked petulantly.

The fact is, she had already entered certain radar screens by the funding work she had done – in all innocence – on the digs in Newport. And some of the neo-Templars she had dissed actually had more clout than she might have imagined. But the trigger was pulled when Lilith had phoned her agent and talked passionately about going to find Real Templars. As she spoke, her signal had been plucked out of the air by sophisticated listening equipment at GCHQ, in England. She didn't know the place existed – most English people didn't either – but had she Googled those letters she would have been amazed... (Try it yourself and see.)

Government Communications Headquarters (GCHQ) is an intelligence and security organisation. A Civil Service Department, we report to the Foreign Secretary and work closely with the UK's other intelligence agencies (commonly known as MI5 and MI6). Our primary customers are the Ministry of Defence, the Foreign and Commonwealth Office and law enforcement authorities, but we also serve a wide range of other Government Departments.

And so it happened that deep inside a shiny white and almost impregnable room, a quantum computer which kept track of all calls on cell phones across the world and which was programmed to activate by certain key words, heard two of them: *Templar* and *Head*. The computer then in turn notified certain persons, and they in turn notified certain figures in authority, and they in turn contacted certain counterparts in the US and France. *Lilith Love*, they muttered. *Who is Lilith Love? What does she know?* And although 'They' were fully paid-up members of the security forces of the Western world, and presumably on the side of Truth, Justice, and Various Other Highly Flexible Principles, yet there were groups within groups, secrets within mysteries, and before the engines of the A380 had whispered into silence, Hughes was waiting for her.

"What's your real name?" he asked, very polite but very steely.

Lilith, who had had lots of experience of men who say one thing in a certain tone but meant something completely different, paused. He was dressed as a Customs Officer, but he seemed to have more than that about him. She sniffed danger. Yet didn't know whether to keep her claws out or in. On the whole, she decided to retract them.

"My real name is Lilith Love. Legally and completely."

"It's not Ada Heimerdinger any more?"

"Not any more," she bristled.

"And you're here to look up... what was it?... Templars?" He said it so casually, as if the word was an unfamiliar one.

Really, she could have blasted him, gone for the jugular like she did on her TV shows. Then again, she reminded herself, those were actors she was dealing with, delivering lines she had scripted herself. This man was real, and they were in a room without windows, in a world whose rules she did not understand.

The conversation – for it was hardly an interrogation – went around in circles aimlessly for a few minutes. The man became vaguely charming, and although she knew it was a professional tool he was using, nevertheless she began to relax. The door opened and a young woman came in and nodded to Hughes. What the nod meant was that a variety of tracking devices had been placed in her belongings.

"Right then, Ms. Love, you can go now," Hughes said. "Oh and the good news is that your luggage has been found. Just pick it up in the usual place."

Lilith stood up so quickly the chair fell over. As she righted it she looked into his eyes. Very troubled eyes. Goddam, but she almost felt sorry for him. If he had been a client she would have done Good Things for his head. She thawed a little.

"Sorry to have troubled you Ms. Heimerdinger," he said in those smooth tones that had started to sound so cute. "Just a random check. Terrorism and all that."

"Terrorism..." she said, and then made the mistake of assuming that the rest of the world knew about her unusual analytical methods, and telling him: "You're a jerk. You get right up my ass."

It was a joke; anyone in the US would have known that right off. Yet Nyron Hughes, who had had a very bad day, and felt the entire hidden world of Secret Societies and Security Services breathing down on him with complete scorn, decided not to let this one pass.

"Actually... I think I'll take you at your word. WPC Smith here will do one last check on you in this respect."

The woman constable, who looked as if she might spend her leisure hours as front-row forward for the England Rugby team, smiled, and pulled out some rubber gloves...

*

Jenny Djinn, on the other hand, was leaning at her little table, elbows splayed and head in her hands, in a state of great pleasure. Facing her from the other end of the table was her new friend, perched neatly on the cushion she had bought from Tesco's, his hair shampooed and conditioned, splaying around like a lion's mane. It all felt so natural to her. Plus the little flat – although threadbare – was now spotless. And that was not down to the head's magic, but a scrubbing brush and some cheap disinfectant from the nearby discount store.

"I killed a man tonight," she said, not troubled at all.

"The man on the bridge."

"You saw? How?"

"My mind surfs the aethers."

That meant nothing to Jenny Djinn. She wasn't the brightest of souls. Truth was, she wasn't at all worried. "How did I kill him?" – *that* she was interested in.

"You became Kali. You became yourself. You loved him to death."

Jenny thought about this. Yes, she had felt for him. Then something happened within her and her nipples got itchy and then she felt as if she had sprouted arms – or the sense of arms – and the man died.

"Can I kill anyone?"

"Anyone. If you can make a link. If you love them first. Death Goddesses do it out of love."

"Are there a lot of them out there?"

The Baptist did things with his eyebrows to parallel a shrug. He was actually looking over her shoulder to the telly behind. After two thousand years in a box, opened only in sterile temples in times of tension and fear, the sight of *The X Factor* was enormously attractive to him. Far better than surfing aethers.

Jenny picked a custard cream off the table and nibbled at the corners, then suddenly thought: "Here, do you eat? What do you live on?"

"Food?" he asked absently, engrossed with the talent show. "Oh, erm, I live on the essences. Prana. Zero Point energy. Absolute Nothingness. Ain. Can you move me nearer the screen?"

Jenny picked him up. Although she had never (knowingly) carried a severed head before, he was heavier than she might have imagined.

"Sit on the couch with me" she offered, and put the head on the cushion so they could watch together.

"Do you mind if I smoke?" she asked, on her best behaviour.

"Only if I can try one too."

"It's bad for your lungs."

"I don't have any."

So they sat there, and Jenny was so deeply happy, her arm around the head of John the Baptist – known to his mates as Yahya.

"He'll win – that one – with the leather trousers. Good voice."

"Do you really know everything?"

"More or less."

"Am I Kali now?"

"You're Jenny Djinn. You're having a moment's peace, which passeth aaaaall understanding. You become Kali by loving your victim first, and pressing that little button at the bottom of your brain."

The smoke came out of his nostrils and from under his neck. They looked at the telly like an old married couple.

"This is dead good" she sighed. Then: "Can I really make anything die?"

"Whole worlds when you get the hang of it. There's lot of prophecies about it. About you."

"Could I make you die?"

The head turned its eyes and looked at her with deepest longing. "If only... Oh, if only. I can only be released by fire and air, and the sacrifice of someone's beloved. That's the deal. The thing is, I'm not actually alive, so you can't kill me."

"I'd never do anything to harm you," she said softly.

"That's what Salome said too."

"What a cow, eh?"

Yahya fell asleep as she stroked his now-lustrous hair. Carefully, tenderly, she put him back in the box for the lost kettle – a box which she had now lined with towels to make more comfortable – and dropped the flap gently, so no-one would see.

And then she went to the pub, coz she was absolutely dying to tell somebody.

*

It was getting dark. The street lights cast their orange glow onto the silver of the closed shop windows. Cars were parked on the double yellow lines so their owners could get kebabs from Chico Land. She pulled the hood of the duffel coat up against the cold and hurried on to The Old Malt, which had a little verandah off the main street that the hardened smokers used.

"Ey up!" said one of them, called Lazza, who had always baited her. There he sludged: thinning but slicked-back hair, old leather jacket that barely fitted and stank like an old football boot. "Elvis has just left the building luv. Think he's gone around to Wetherspoon's."

Jenny ignored him. In the past years she had seen a host of celebrities in or around the town: Nicholas Cage, Johnny Depp, Madonna, Tom Selleck, Van Morrison, the young lad who played Harry Potter and the huge fella who did Hagrid. She had seen them – with her own eyes – she really had! But no-one believed her, and when she pointed out to Dr McHaffee that these characters all had homes around there, or filmed around there, well he too had just given a knowing smile. Which, as far as she was concerned, didn't know anything at all.

The pub was packed. In the corner a hard group of men were watching England play on the large-screen telly, each one wearing his white shirt with a red cross, and waving his bottled lager in the air like a sword. The bar itself was heaving.

"Here Jenny!" she heard above the noise, "Over here!!"

Her two pals Tasha and Shaz were sitting against the wall, doing some scratch-cards, their bleached hair like starbursts. "Have you got a new fella?" asked Tasha, as Jenny pulled back a chair and sat down.

Sssssh, said a Head within her head. So: "No, why?"

"Only, since you borrowed me car it's been goin' like a bomb! I thought you mighta got some mechanic that you were shagging to have a go at it."

"Have you been got at by 'Them' yet?" asked Shaz, fiddling with her nose rings, totally ignoring the line taken by the other one. By 'Them' she meant those forces which were every bit as powerful in her eyes as the mysterious beings who ruled Nyron Hughes' world: in other words, Social Security.

"No, I'll still be kept on benefits. Dr McHaffee doesn't reckon I'm ready for a proper job yet."

"God I wish I had a doc like yours. I'd love to be signed off sick forever."

"Hey but you do look a bit odd," said Tasha. "Been havin' some more funny turns?"

Jenny grabbed her friend's glass and swigged. She had to tell somebody something. And while these were never great pals, certainly not even good pals, they at least tolerated some of her madness.

"Listen you two... I've got special powers."

"Is that a DVD?"

"No it's not a film – I mean real powers."

"What, like flying?"

"No! I can... I can make people die."

The two women looked at each other, and then at Jenny. The latter was fun, most of the time, but sometimes... They burst out laughing.

"Can I get you a lager?" asked Shaz.

"No, I'm serious, and I can prove it. I don't even have to move from my chair."

"Maybe a Pasquale's pizza?"

"NO!"

She looked around for a likely victim. At the next table, with its lead wrapped around a chair leg while its owner sat and shouted advice to the entire England midfield, was an old placid bull terrier.

"See that dog? Then watch?"

Jenny looked at the dog, looked into its sad eyes. As if sensing the attention, the power, it got up on all fours and weakly wagged the stump of its tail. Jenny thought of all the dogs she had known, and the pets she had wanted to own, and marvelled at what a loyal beast this one had been. She loved it, she really did, and then she did that thing at the base of her brain and she was Jenny no more and she was opening gates for it to Another Place, and the dog seemed to sigh and closed its eyes, and lay down, head on its paws.

"It's gone to sleep," said Shaz, as England scored a goal in a faraway land, and men showed their balls by roaring and thumping tables.

"No, it's dead."

They tutted, wouldn't have it. Tasha, who was called that by her husband instead of her proper name Natasha, because she had a slight – very slight – moustache, felt rather troubled for reasons she couldn't have said. She made a very crucial challenge then.

"Right then, Ms Grey... I'll give you fifty quid here and now – look, here in me purse, see! – if you can kill my old man out there. I hate the bastard. He's useless, and he smells. No, I'll tell you what, you can have the whole lot – that's nearly... ninety quid. All me housekeeping. If you can do it. Now."

Go on, said a Head in her head.

Jenny stood up and walked toward the verandah to look at Lazza from behind. He was loud, he was large, he was charmless... Could she love even him? Jenny couldn't – not after the cruel things he had had said over the years – but could The Other? The Kali Within? Even though he stank of lager and cigs and BO?

Then she saw the word *Mum* tattooed on the back of his neck, and that was what she needed. She saw him as a little boy, sitting on his mum's lap, curled up and comfy, watching *Dr Who*. All curly hair and clean, crisp and innocent, doting. Little boy in love with his Mum. Some mother's son. How could anyone not love him?

Amid the noise, the screams as the England team scored another vital goal, Lazza turned, as if something had touched him on the shoulder. In fact it was one of Kali's arms. He turned and he saw the face of what had just been Jenny, and his eyes widened as if the innermost Lazza – the best of him – had recognised someone or something else.

You can go now, said Kali, who was possessing her priestess, waving her aetheric arms as she did that strange dance which severed links with the mortal world, even though anyone watching would have seen nothing more than weird little Jenny Grey shifting the weight on her feet as she stood in the doorway.

Lazza smiled, sighed, and he leaned back in his chair and closed his eyes.

"Pissed again," said one of his cronies, grabbing the beer and cigs from him.

Jenny returned to her seat, still thrumming from what she had done, still hearing something of the death-dance music. She smiled brightly and showed what the other two thought was lipstick on her teeth.

"What did you-"

Tasha stopped. She saw her husband's reptilian mates shaking him, trying to get him to wake. She saw one of them dialling for an ambulance on his mobile, as Lazza's body slid off the chair onto the cold floor.

"Here Jen," said Shaz, "You know first aid. Shouldn't you do something?"

Jenny shook her head. She had just given him the kiss of death; it wouldn't be appropriate to try the kiss of life.

As the ambulance arrived quickly from just down the road, and the paramedics cleared a space in the crowd before doing what they could, and then asked Tasha – pointed out as his wife – if she would come in the ambulance with them, Jenny just sat there smugly.

"That was in-kuh-redible!! Jesus..." gasped Shaz, awed.

"No, not him. Nothing to do with him. Can't stand the lad," she said, echoing Yahya without understanding.

"Who the fuck are you? What are you?"

"I'm Kali, the Death Goddess."

31

"Who the fuck is Cally!?"

"You mustn't tell anyone. I'm telling you Shaz, you mustn't."

"Hell no. Hey but listen girl, whatever you did, however you did it, you could make a bleeding fortune from this!"

They caught a glimpse of Tasha's face just before the ambulance doors were closed. She was breathing heavily: looked as if she'd just won top prize on the Lotto. The man at the next table had just noticed that his dog was completely stiff, and was devastated.

"Come on," said Shaz, "you got ninety quid on you now. Get the next round in, then me and you have gotta talk...."

*

Nyron Hughes was in the basement of a hospital morgue in London, wearing one of the crisp white sterile outfits that are appropriate to autopsies, but which was slightly too small for him. He kept pulling at the elasticated cuffs to stop them disappearing up toward his elbows. He just didn't feel good in this at all, and looked positively absurd in the full-length mirror. Yet it was a serious business, this. If Jenny Djinn had created two corpses in the pub, then Nyron had twice as many on his own hands, though there was no doubt as to what had caused their collective demise. The bullet holes were a bit of a clue. Members of the French Secret Service, the DGSE, had taken the corpses of the angel boy and his two bodyguards, but he was still left with this one of the assassin.

Actually, the agents had presented themselves as DGSE, but he had rather suspected they were really from the GISS, which was the Belgian Secret Service. Everyone hated the French, while the French themselves loathed the Belgians. Still, let them have their own fights. Like John the Baptist, his head was on a plate, and he wasn't too sure where the bearer was going, or whether he was likely to be dropped. The Grand Master, who communed with Higher Powers through the most secretive societies, whose mortal name was Porteous and who lived in large technologically secure house in a small village near Box Hill in Surrey, was in a stinking mood, and he was steaming across at Hughes from the other side of the corpse.

"I've had the PM onto me, the heads of the CIA, NIS, SDU, the KGB, the–"

"FSB, sir. Not KGB any more. They call it the FSB now. It means–"

32

"I don't give a toss what it means, Hughes! I have had the most powerful men from the security services of the entire world asking me what is going on here. Plus I have had the REAL Rulers of this world – and you know we dare not speak Their names – giving me looks that make me piss myself. After what should have been a pivotal moment in the Inner History of the Secret World, in which all powers of all the Real Orders could be confirmed, enhanced and magnified, all I'm left with is this corpse and an electric kettle that came from Argos. I'm a bit unhappy, Hughes. Can you tell that I'm a bit unhappy?"

It was a good job Nyron's organisation had taught him a lot about body language, because Porteous's bloodshot eyes and the twitching muscles on his heavy shoulders gave him a few hints. Actually, Hughes found his boss strangely attractive when he got like that, which was often.

"There was nothing on the kettle at all sir, no prints, nothing. It hadn't been used or even touched, though we've got some clues from the receipt that will give us something. We know that the Head has, at several times in the historical past, apparently teleported itself short distances under certain circumstance – escaped if you like. We don't know why they stopped at Cley Hill."

"It's an old Templar site. Perhaps John told the angel-boy to stop and have a look. We've never used it. Go on..."

"Well, in the meantime what I can tell you about this fella here is that he's from the Indian sub-continent."

"What?!"

"Yes, Grand Master. We can also tell from the contents of his stomach and more particularly from analysing his hair that he has been at various sites throughout Western Europe in the past three months. At some of these sites, our Holy Casket has been based for the regular Lesser Revealings."

"So the bastard has been following us?"

"Following John?"

"That's all we bloody need. Is this exact science?"

"No. Not unless we want to stitch someone up in court."

"So what Order does he come from? Or is he just from the Indian Security Service?"

"Look at these marks here, in the crook of each elbow..."

The Grand Master put on his glasses and peered closely at what seemed to be a random splodge of lines which seemed to have been burnt in. "So?"

"We also found on him this silken scarf with this large heavy coin in it." Hughes mimed how the scarf could be flung around someone's neck, and used to strangle the victim. "There seems no doubt about it... the man was a Thuggee."

"Thuggee! I thought they died out two hundred years ago. What's a Thuggee doing over here? What possible interest would that cult want with us?"

"I don't yet know sir. Maybe they were just pissy because they didn't get an invite to our 'do'."

"It was not a 'do', Hughes."

"Of course not sir. But according to their traditions they often travelled large distances in company with, or following, their intended victims before a safe opportunity presented itself for carrying out their sacred murder. Then they would perform rites in honour of their goddess, Kali, and go on their way."

"Kali... what a bloody mess this is."

"But this is where it gets interesting... the follicles indicate that before he followed John around Europe, he might – just might – have spent at least a week in Tel Aviv."

The Grand Master, who sometimes felt like a little boy wading out of his depth into the ocean of night and wanted a nice warm mummy to bring him safely back home, groaned softly. "That's all we bloody need. Mossad getting somebody else to do their dirty work. Might have known. Same old story in the headlines: Jewish Conspiracy aiming for World Domination."

Hughes was almost sympathetic. Had never seen the Old Man, as the neophytes called him, show his human side.

"Hughes... you have to find the Head. I'm not sure you really understand what's at stake here, but you really have to find John. The last thing we want is Kali loose in the world."

"What would she do?"

The Grand Master gave a slightly theatrical sigh. In what was obviously a speech he had given several times before he said: "In late 1918 and throughout 1919, an epidemic of what they termed 'Spanish Flu' swept the world. It spread even to the Arctic and remote Pacific islands. Current estimates are that 50 million to 100 million people worldwide died, dwarfing the casualties of the First World War and possibly more than that taken by the Black Death. The most virulent strain, as they thought of it, emanated from Brest, in France. This was where The Head was staying at the time, and where it influenced a young man who had a certain fascination for the one of the Four Horsemen of the Apocalypse. The term 'flu' was a cover-up. If a new apocalypse is about to be loosed upon the world from the heart of Wiltshire, then I have to tell the Home Secretary to get his own cover-up ready, probably involving swine or bird-flu. Can you see why this is so important, Hughes? Can you see why we must find that bastard pissing head and its new keeper before we all end up crossing over?"

The younger man nodded, giving his superior his best look of steely efficiency. With a flourish he slid the drawer containing the corpse back into its vault, and clanged shut the heavy metal door.

"I'm onto it sir," Nyron said, peeling himself out of the silly suit and flinging it into a stainless steel bin. The Old Man looked wearily magnificent and oddly vulnerable at that moment. "Trust me sir."

"And Hughes... stop looking at me like that."

CHAPTER 3

Although Nyron never knew it at the time, the eventual focus of all these activities and energies was at that moment in the library depot trying to clean graffiti off the side of his van.

"Hmm," said Jo, as she strolled out from her office to see the overnight damage, radiant with the air of someone whose working life was coming to a happy end. "Interesting use of language. Powerful use of metaphors. 'BookBoy is a knobhead'. You are BookBoy, I presume. Sounds like one of the X Men. Is this one of your customers? Did you upset him? Fail to reserve something for him? Issued a Large Print instead of normal print? Hmm?"

"You taking the wee wee?" Jack said. "This is my van! Probably the most beautiful vehicle in the whole history of beautiful vehicles! This is a Spitfire, an F18 Hornet, the Starship Enterprise, or–"

"It was Bill the Pony yesterday."

"Ah come on Jo, it's what you need it to be. You gotta learn to see. There's a book in the non-fiction section by Castaneda which might help you."

Keith the Transport Manager and Mike who was Lord of the Stores came out from the loading area where massed crates of books were distributed countywide.

"Somebody doesn't like you, Master Hobbes," said Keith, a large man who was like a Thunder Lizard in the eyes of young Jack: tall, strong and scary, but a great big softy inside.

"Everybody likes him!" countered Mike, who was the library's version of a trickster-god, and who delighted in winding Keith up.

"Thank you, your Grace," said Jack, who treated them both like royalty.

"Here, try this," Mike added, offering him a spray specially designed to remove graffiti from walls. "You see, Keith, he's every old lady's favourite son. That's how he's able to spend all his time out in the wilds drinking their tea and eating their cakes."

"Hey listen, your highnesses, you might think my job is easy but it ain't... stuck out in the boonies, behind enemy lines, with a load of overdue books and regular life-threatening wedgies. I might be the greatest mobile library driver in history, but I earn my crust."

"Sure you do," said Keith chuckling, walking off to kick the tyres of the other vans as if it could tell him something. Mike went off to put out his big bollards, to stop people parking wherever they shouldn't, swinging them like Indian Clubs while singing 'Oh What a Beautiful Morning'.

Jack sprayed and scrubbed furiously. Jack's magnificent van was covered in large graphics showing a variety of readers – old and young – whose blissful faces showed that they each possessed current Wiltshire Library tickets, and knew how to use them. The graphics, which were simply huge photographic transfers, had bubbled up in ghastly places so that the large face of a benign elderly reader seemed to have leprosy.

"You're making it worse" Jo giggled, walking back to her office, a spring in her step like a young girl.

Time to go. Jack debated what tune to play on the CD as he left: 'Born to be Wild', 'Ride of the Valkyries', or 'The Dambusters'. In the end he settled for the random choice of the radio, determined to glean wisdom from whatever tune would come out at the press of a switch. The fact that it was 'Chirpy Chirpy Cheep Cheep' did make him gulp and say to himself – not for the first time – *I've gotta get a life!* Though little realising that before too long he would get a severed head instead, and have all of our lives in his hands.

"Calm down van" he said, when it sounded a bit rough on starting. "That's better, good van..." Outsiders thought he was a bit of a loony talking to things. But if you took the time to ask he would explain that, in his view, everything – no matter how apparently inert – had life and consciousness of its own kind. He had a book in the van about that too, called *The Changeling*, an autobiography, and he felt he was something of the sort.

Was he a changeling? A later biographer would describe him as being neither fish nor fowl, to use an old phrase, and that wasn't entirely untrue. You can see right off though, can't you, that he would make a perfect replacement for the angel-boy who had been murdered.

His boss came back out of her office and across the depot's loading bay, waving. He had forgotten the blue backpack which contained, among other things, the packed lunch his Mum had made.

"Nice tune!" Jo noted, as it surged out through the wound-down window. Handing him the bag, she asked: "Remind me where are you going today... Is it the Black Hills of Dakota? Apache country? Or just Lothlorien or Mordor?"

37

"Erm, Marlborough actually. You've really got no soul, Jo. There's no hope for you."

"Just don't get into bad habits, that's all I ask. Don't stamp the books as belonging to us when they clearly don't. Don't let the dust gather on the tops of the shelves. Don't have the books packed too tightly else little arthritic ladies will have problems getting at them. And make sure you discharge before issuing. Always, always! This is the Hammurabic Code as determined by the Libraries and Heritage Department – and moi!"

Jack smiled and chucked the bag onto the empty passenger seat, gave Jo a regal wave and pulled away, crunching up through the gears, heading for his first stop.

*

As he headed for that first stop, delivering a crate of books known as a Deposit Collection to an old peoples' home down Binyarn Street, he didn't realise that one of the most important women in his life was about to manifest. Having left his van parked on double yellows, and a sign on the window for traffic wardens saying: *Back in Five Minutes – Honest*, he took a discerning blend of large-print Romances, Mysteries, Non-Fiction and Biographies, plus five Westerns, into the home, put them neatly on the designated shelf after first removing the old ones, then made his way back to the locked van. Normally in his remote stops he could leave the doors open, but Binyarn Street, only around the corner from where Jenny lived, was Trowbridge's answer to the Gaza Strip.

"Hello Jack," said Jenny softly, coming up from behind as he undid the doors at the rear of the van.

He didn't recognise her. Gone were the elasticated cotton slacks, the old sweat shirt and duffel coat and greasy hair. The £90 from Tasha had bought her: a visit to the hairdressers, where her lank, mousy hair was cut, styled and dyed black; two visits to the Oxfam and Dorothy House charity shops where she got herself some dresses, skirts and two tops, so that she wore for him a charcoal grey outfit that any mother might have approved; a visit to the Factory Shop for some new underwear, cheap but new shoes, and some make-up. Instead of slouching as she usually did, she was now shoulders back and tits forward, straight as a die, confident at last.

You couldn't become a Death Goddess and not be confident, could you? Amazing what a new attitude, a bit of money, and a suddenly discovered talent for mass murder could do in terms of transforming a woman.

"Hello" she said again, and he still didn't know who she was until she held up the book she had borrowed last time. Disconcerted by her manner, wondering if she was on drugs because of the way she was staring, he quickly scanned her book to discharge it, and saw her details.

"Ah, Jenny Grey! You were my first weren't you?" he said with the merest hint of archness. "The first new-user library ticket I ever made. That was quite a time, eh?"

He remembered! She beamed. She loved him for what he said and even more for what he didn't say. She who had more or less let any man who asked shag her, just for a brief sense or pretence of companionship, wasn't used to this.

"That was a dead good book. I like things like that. Mysteries and things. But real ones."

That's what she said. But what she actually thought was something like: *Ooh you're lovely, you are. Do you fancy me too?*

"Well I've got lots more, if you're interested."

She was interested, of course she was. And he had, too. His predecessor had packed the shelves with train books and westerns, but Jack was slowly, covertly replacing these with stock on local history, folklore, mythology and a bit of philosophy. Not that the old dears in remote communities would have wanted anything other than Large Print Romances with titles like *The Latin Lover's Secret Child* and Large Print Thrillers lurid enough to take their minds off the arthritis, but Jack was being a bit selfish. He had plans of buying an old mini-bus, you see, and he hoped that one day soon he would do full-time tours of the sacred sites of Wiltshire, pitching it to rich Americans. For him, the Mobile Library was something of a stop-gap until he could get it all up and running.

"I've changed my name. It's Jenny Djinn now. Not 'gin' as you drink. 'Djinn' as in fire spirit."

Jack blinked. He knew exactly what a djinn was. It was surprising to hear someone down Binyarn Street using the term. And especially someone like her.

"Oh, erm, well... Nice name. Do you want me to change the name on the ticket?"

"Yeah," she said. "That would be good." Anything to keep him talking a bit longer.

He went back to the PC screen and clicked on BORROWER – ADD/MODIFY/DELETE. Another screen appeared which gave all her details: name (*Grey, Jennifer*), age (*25*), address (*14 Binyarn Close*), telephone number (*None*), occupation (*None*), ethnic origins (*I would prefer not to tell you*), language (*Hindi*)...

She had lied about her age of course, and that bit about the Hindi was down to a slip of the mouse which had them both laughing, and which he left as it was, and she didn't mind. Now... a few deft strokes of the keyboard later and she was suddenly, officially, Ms Jenny Djinn as far as the Library and Museums Service of Wiltshire was concerned. She felt strangely pleased seeing this in the PC screen: as if it made it all official.

Oh but she was dying to tell him about the dying.

Don't, said a Head within her head. *Not yet*. That last rider pleasing her no end.

"Okay here, what about this book, all about Wiltshire ghosts and local legends. I often think the author knew more than she dared say. Or this one: *The Secret Country*, all about magical places around Britain."

Jenny pointed to the latter. "I'll have this one with all the pictures."

He opened the book at the front, scanned the barcode and stamped the return date, and almost jumped when he looked up at her. For a moment, the merest nanosecond, she was 'other' than herself. It was as if she was surrounded by subtle fires of red and green, pulsing and waving, every particle of her body intense and dazzling.

"Dead good," she said, being arch herself this time. Then as Jack blinked, the vision ended as abruptly, and he was left alone in the van with a staring woman who seemed to feel herself a lot closer to him than he felt toward her. "You know you look just like that young lad in *The Emerald Forest* that was on telly last night." She had watched it with Yahya in fact, but didn't have to be told telepathically that it was best not to mention that. "Charley Boorman, that was his name."

40

Jack felt uneasy. He didn't like people getting close. Despite his flirty conversational skills, there was no predatory intent. "Right then," he said, ushering her toward the exit at the back of the van. "Don't wanna push you out, but the green hills of far-away Marlborough are calling me. See you soon!"

Jenny stood on the pavement as the automatic doors sushed together, clutching *The Secret Country* in one hand and giving a wave-cum-salute with the other. God he was such a gentleman! – so different to the other blokes in her circle who couldn't seem to get beyond the opening gambit of: 'ere, fancy a shag?, before they headed off to the bar.

Jack watched Jenny shrink in the wing mirror, seeing her pause at the door of the curry house, where an Indian lady gave her the take-away she had presumably ordered, and genuflected as she left. Trouble, he thought, vowing to have Jo come with him next time.

Cool, thought the fire lady, peeking at the vindaloo in the carrier bag, then watching him drive off. Dead cool…

*

Now Lilith Love was actually in Marlborough, a rambling town with a broad main street, posh college containing a mound that was supposedly Merlin's burial place, a small river, and some ancient buildings. She was staying in The Green Man Hotel, which she had Googled up herself and paid for on-line after doing the Virtual Tour that the web-site offered. Lilith, who had never been abroad before, was feeling pretty good about herself, though she wondered who she should contact to see about getting her show over here. Back home she had made a fuss about having no privacy because she was a celebrity. Here, she had the privacy of complete anonymity, but wished at least someone would recognise her.

Plus, she was horny as hell and wondering how and where and when she was gonna get laid. Not daring to take her sexual devices through the scanning machines at the airport, she hoped to find the real thing locally. So she had tapped "Wiltshire studs" into the Google search box but all she got was 103,000 entries about the breaking, pre-training, rest and rehabilitation, sales preparation and boarding for broodmares – whatever they were! They sure as hell liked their horses in this part of the world.

41

The site of the ancient Templar preceptory was a few miles away from Marlborough, but she quickly realised that without a car, without a guide, it might as well have been on another planet. So she did what she often did when she was bewildered: she sat down and rubbed her Sekhmet talisman and asked for inspiration. All she learned about Sekhmet was from her initial forays onto the Web, and that's all we need to learn for the nonce, too:

Sekhmet (Sakhmet) is one of the oldest known Egyptian deities. Her name is derived from the Egyptian word "Sekhem" (which means "power" or "might") and is often translated as the "Powerful One". She is depicted as a lion-headed woman, sometimes with the addition of a sun disc on her head.

Was she really powerful at that moment? No, not really. All hype and lots of noise, if truth be told. Take away the sun disk of her wealth and she was just another 32-year old with a lot of brains and a big mouth. Though it must be admitted that this would change, somewhat, when she met The Head.

Even so, something must have worked when she rubbed the talisman because as she stood on the broad high street (still carrying her ultra-slim laptop of course) looking up and down the ancient buildings, what should pull up in front of her but Jack's library van. She stepped back a bit and looked along the side at the graphics of the old man with apparent leprosy, and read the words 'Wiltshire… Serving Your Community' as well the traces of the graffiti about BookBoy and knobheads. It all seemed very charming and typically English. However she was completely undone then because the automatic doors at the rear sighed open and there was Jack Hobbes. She didn't know him from Adam of course. She just knew that there was the most beautiful young man she had ever seen. And you must believe she had seen a lot of them lately having Googled the images for the words: 'Beautiful Blonde Men', and been taken to a site that was bristling with them, including a certain Jonathan Rhys Meyers, as he had appeared in the movie *Titus*, as the character Chiron. This was just like the young man before her now.

"Hi," she said weakly.

"Oh hello," were his immortal words. "You can come on board if you want. I've just got to deliver this crate of books to that old peoples' home over there."

God, he sounded as good as he looked! The breeze caught his long hair and flicked it over his eyes. She wanted to brush it away but controlled herself. He hefted the heavy red crate filled with 30 large print books of various categories down the three steps and made his way toward the home. So strong, too!

"Please," she gasped to herself, invoking nameless powers of love and lust, looking at what was now known as an arse, instead of an ass, heading away from her across the sidewalk which was now a pavement, and rubbed her Sekhmet talisman between her forefinger and thumb for even more help. As with Jenny Djinn, she had to have him. The poor lad never stood a chance, did he?

"Did you want to join the library?" Jack asked when he came back on board with the old books.

"Is that possible?" she asked. He caught the accent.

"Well no, not really. You have to be local. Where are you from?"

She told him. She told him all about herself. She was a babbling brook – wet wet wet.

"You're Lilith Love? I've got one of your books in here. Here... here it is. *'You're a Jerk, I'm a Jerk, Okay?* Bantam Press. *No. 1 Bestseller!!*' it says. Haven't read it yet I'm afraid."

"Omigod, don't be afraid. It's just a piece of bubblegum."

The two of them did the small talk that people do in such circumstances: but for Jack it really was small talk, while for Lilith it was life-enhancing. As he took the books out of the crate and issued them for the old peoples' home at the next stop, not bothering to discharge them first as Jo has always insisted, he was completely unaware of the effect he was having. You must understand that he was born and bred in Trowbridge. Jack once figured, looking up name and word origins, that this was actually the bridge of trows, or trowles, or – as we would spell it – trolls. From the medieval Scandinavian influx, when wool was as big here as oil in Texas. So coming as he did from Trowbridge, where women seemed to prefer troll-like men who were only just on the evolutionary ladder, he had little idea of his attractiveness. Oh he knew he was beautiful but played up to it in a self-parodying English sort of way; in truth he was too wrapped up in the romance of ideas to get genuinely fixated upon his own looks.

"So what are you doing here?" he asked, over-riding the computer so he could Issue without Discharging first, which in Jo's eyes was something akin to Original Sin.

"I'm researching Templars. Real Templars. Do you know anything about them?"

"Well yes, yes I do."

Her heart almost burst. She had no doubt that, at last, she had found The One.

"I've got books here by Knight and Lomas, by Lynn Picknett and Clive Prince, and – oh this one's just come onto the van – *The Knights Templar*. Nice and glossy, lots of pix. Shame you can't borrow it."

"I'll buy it instead. I'll buy anything you recommend, Jack Hobbes." She knew his name because of the badge her wore. It sounded to her like the most perfect name in the world. "But now listen, do you know anything about Temple Rockley?"

"Never been. It's not far from here though. Off the Ridgeway. Often wanted to go."

Her heart smashed against her ribs. "Will you come with me? I mean, I'll pay you for your time."

That struck a chord. He might not be able to hear when a woman was gagging for it, but he knew the sound of cash registers alright.

"Okay… what about tomorrow, Saturday?"

"Could you not just drive me up there now, in this cute truck of yours?"

"Ha! I'm sure my boss would like that! Nice idea though."

"Ah come on…"

"I'd get sacked."

"I'm Lilith Love. I'm filthy rich. I'd see to things."

They shared looks. You can imagine what she read into his intense gaze, and what he failed to read into hers.

"How well would you see to things?"

"I'd cover your salary for a year."

Jack looked. He looked and looked. She changed before his very eyes from a wacky American tourist into a fabulous Gift Horse.

"Press that button there to close the doors, and come sit up front. Temple Rockley here we come – though I'm not sure the van will be up to it. Will you be up to it, Van?" he asked, leaning forward and turning his ear as if to listen. "Yes… yes I think it will."

"Yee hah!" she cried, feeling young again, and all zingy. And as the cumbersome library van pulled out into the traffic neither of them noticed the black car which followed them…

*

Back in Trowbridge, while Jenny was still thrumming with delight at her own meeting with Jack, Shaz and Tasha were taking her by the elbows to walk her away from the pub and toward the park. Their voices were rising to such an excited pitch as they talked that several times Jenny had to shush them, especially when they passed the police station. They turned into the park, skirted a group of drunken young men shouting Polish insults, and sat on a bench under the shade of a large chestnut tree.

"This fan-bloody-tastic," said Shaz, twirling one of her nose rings.

"You're not joking. I got rid of that bastard husband of mine, and got all that insurance money."

"In-kuh-redible."

"And you look so smart now, so pretty. Don't she look pretty now?"

"Yeah really Jen, you look lovely. New clothes, make-up – you're even walking differently."

Well she would, wouldn't she. Having an extra pair of arms – however invisible – had to affect the posture and gait.

Jenny smiled a shy smile. She was glowing inside, what with meeting Jack and all this praise.

"But you gotta promise Jenny…"

"Really really promise…."

"That you'll never 'do' us."

Jenny was startled. "I promise! You're my friends!!" Then she had a thought: "As long as you two promise never to ask me to explain how it's done."

Good thinking, said the Head inside her head.

"I don't think I wanna know," said Tasha.

"But we gotta make the most of it," added Shaz intensely. "It might go from you soon. We can use this to get rich. I've got it all worked out. I mean, can you kill anyone? Or anything?"

Jenny closed her eyes and thought. *Yes*, said the Head in her head. *Pretty much. If you know how.*

"Yes. Pretty much. I think I know how."

"Could you do those yobs drinking over there?" asked Tasha, who now had a taste for getting rid of men she considered were wastes of space.

"No!" cried the other two.

"I wasn't serious," Tasha lied.

"How about a tree?" suggested Shaz.

"I think I could do that."

"A tree would be good, yeah."

"That one there, then," said Shaz, pointing out a small birch near the bandstand.

So Jenny did that thing inside her which made her become Kali, and focussed all her attention, all her love, upon said tree from the roots upward.

"Bloody hell," said her two pals in near unison as the rich green of the leaves turned to brown and then black, curling into themselves and then flaking apart like burnt skin before falling off. A couple of the branches cracked and fell, and the drinkers near it stopped drinking and hurried away looking up at the sky as if silent lightning had struck.

"I saw that happen in a film with Johnny Depp in. *Sleepy Hollow* – yeah, that was it. Not bad eh?" This from Jenny, quietly proud of herself. Though it was a little unusual that she only regained her self-esteem by becoming a Death Goddess.

The three of them sat in silence, until Jenny also observed: "Didn't Jesus do that with a fig tree or something?"

Don't talk about that bastard, said a tetchy Head inside her head.

"Sod the fig tree," said Shaz. "Listen. Me and Tasha have a worked out a dead-easy way to get us all abso-luter-ly stinking rich..."

*

Later that day Jenny was sitting on the couch with The Head next to her, watching *The Outlaw Josey Wales*, and puffing heartily on a cigarette. If Lilith Love had been in Jenny's position, she would wonder why this fount of all knowledge liked Westerns so much, and then ask all sorts of deep and meaningful questions about life and its origins and destiny. But Jenny, bless her, took it all in a matter-of-fact way.

"This is good this next part, when he says 'Hell is coming to breakfast'."

"Don't spoil it for me!" said The Head indistinctly, the ciggy dangling on the corner of his lips.

If he had had any ribs to nudge affectionately she would have done.

"Ah... I thought you knew everything."

"I do! But only when it's time for me to know it. I still like surprises."

They sat quietly and watched as the sun went down and the neon light outside her window flared its sickly orange into the room, and the noise from the police sirens bounced off the walls.

"They're gonna make me rich. My pals I mean."

"I know. This always happens. One way or another someone uses me to get rich."

"Do you mind?"

"Not at all. Anyway, you'd be doing it yourself. Go ahead and enjoy yourself."

"Isn't there nothing you want?" she asked, tenderly taking the ciggy from him, peeling it gently from his dry lips.

The Head seemed to stare into infinity. He made a sighing noise, which is difficult to do properly when you don't have a chest.

"Yes," he said sadly. "But not yet. Things have to happen first..."

Jenny felt his sadness. She stroked his hair, and his eyes closed with pleasure like a cat. It never entered her head to ask him things. Besides, for the first time in two millennia, he was enjoying not being questioned.

"Hell is coming to breakfast..." said the Indian on the telly screen as the sun rose over the hill, and Yahya gave his own equivalent of a nod.

*

"So what have you got?" asked the Grand Master, throwing his bag of golf clubs into the corner and sitting down in Hughes' office, in Hughes' swivelling chair, leaving his underling to close the door upon them both.

47

"The kettle was bought in Argos in Frome, Somerset, which is–"

"I know where Frome is!" he snapped, having lost his virginity there in the back of a large Volvo estate, at the edge of the British Rail car park, many aeons before.

"Was bought in Frome, Somerset," Hughes persisted, used to such interruptions, "at 11am on June 24th – which as we know, is the Feast Day of Himself. And it was paid for in cash."

"CCTV records?"

"None. Their system wasn't working. No CCTV footage from any of the neighbouring shops or street cameras shows anything resembling someone carrying an electric kettle. It's only a small town, not more than–"

"I know how big it is. What about the car park at Cley Hill?"

"It's a popular place for walkers. Endless footprints, but none that we can get any clues from."

"Then it must have been a professional job. And someone who knows about the Templar connection with the hill."

"I agree sir. There is just that one possible suspect so far."

"The American woman."

"Lilith Love, yes. But she has just made contact with a young man from Trowbridge who claims to know all about the Templars. Jack Hobbes by name. No previous. Her laptop, which she carries everywhere, has been wired for sound and the conversations are – well, promising."

The Grand Master stared right through Hughes as if he didn't exist, stared right into other galaxies, into the oceans of worlds beyond the younger man's understanding.

"Do you know what our Chinese and Japanese brethren are doing now, Hughes? Have you any idea? Using the full 93° rituals, they are staring into that bloody glass kettle of yours as if it's a crystal ball, and – they claim – getting results."

"What kind of results?"

"They won't tell us, that's what upsets me."

"How can a mere kettle…"

"Do I look as if I knew? Can you imagine what this is doing to my normal peace of mind, Hughes? Maybe The Head left a resonance within the Sacred Casket, and the kettle – which as far as our Oriental brethren are concerned is rapidly becoming a bloody Sacred Kettle – maybe it's picking that up. I don't know, I just don't know." He plucked a mashie niblick out of his golf bag and twirled the shaft like a straw. "Or maybe they're just taking the piss, and don't see anything."

The Grand Master, who didn't like people knowing that his first name was Perry, glared across the desk, holding the golf club across his chest, like an axe. He despaired of the young men now coming up through the Order. It seemed no-one of any real quality wanted to join these days, and were all quite happy snorting their coke or playing with their on-line virtual reality games at home. Sometimes he felt like a dinosaur.

"You got that trouble with the lady-boys sorted didn't you?"

"I did sir."

"That's not mascara on your cheeks is it?"

"It's not sir," lied Hughes, turning his back to look in a mirror and rub briskly. "I just blush easily."

"Well don't blush at me. I know the sort of things that you lot in the 9° meetings get up to..."

*

Jack and Lilith left Marlborough and took the narrowest of roads north-west, hedges scraping the van's sides and its top being raked by overhanging trees, making Jack wince at the thought of damage.

"I'll pay for it," said Lilith, laughing. "Don't worry. I'll buy this whole damned vehicle for you if necessary!"

Assured of that, he relaxed, and they had a sort of a duel: him with his books and her with her opened lap-top. It was like a sort of 'Anything you can do I can do better' using different media:

Him: "I've got 'Wiltshire Place-Names – their origins and meanings' in the back of the van. Have a look at AAA.917."

Her: "It says here 'The name is derived from that of the former county town of Wilton, and was recorded as Wiltunscir in an 870 AD document. In comparison with many modern counties, it may therefore be regarded as a shortened form of Wiltonshire...'"

Him: "Now Rockley... I think you'll find that up there – see it? – in *The Place Names of Wiltshire*, which is technically a reference book, but I've relocated it here."

Her: "Got it... got it!" she squealed with excitement at how quickly she could Google, feeling like a gunfighter beating everyone to the draw. "Okay now listen: 'Despite its sarsen-littered setting the name derives from rooks, not rocks, and a local legend predicted that when the rooks leave Rockley the manor will fall.' Oh wow, how cool is that!"

It would have gone on more but the hands-free phone rang. He gestured Lilith to be quiet and pressed the green button.

"Jack..." came the crystal clear voice of his boss Jo. "Are you alright? Pensfield House have just rung complaining that you haven't turned up."

He took some paper and crunched it next to the mouthpiece. "Hello? Hello?! Sorry the [*crackle*] reception is very [*crackle*]... I'm not sure [*crackle crackle*] who this is.. Can you...[*crackle crackle crackle*]..."

Lilith laughed when he pressed the red button and hung up. Lilith Love was in love of course, just as much as Jenny Djinn, and they were both projecting onto him like mad, but you can see why can't you? If Robin Hood was no good without his Marion, then Kali needed her Shiva, while Sekhmet wasn't worth a shit without her Ptah.

Jack had no idea he had become an archetype, however. He just wanted to get on to the parking place his map showed, not far from the site of the preceptory.

"You are beautiful, you know that?" said Lilith Love, turning in her seat to look full at him. "Anyone ever tell you?"

He changed down a gear and pretended to concentrate very hard as he drove along the sort of very narrow lane that no library van should ever attempt. "Thank you," he muttered, frowning slightly, suddenly uneasy.

She gave a girly giggle: he was sooooo cute! "Hey don't be shy. I wrote a book about honesty once. I say what I mean and mean what I say – sometimes."

"'*The Healing Powers of Lying – Dare to Deceive*,'" he said. "Haven't read that either."

"Believe me Jack... you don't need to."

*

They could never have dreamed that as they talked every word was being recorded, and that Nyron Hughes was hunched in the back of a van bearing the logo of Wessex Water, listening in on them, ready to activate the Strike Team which had been following every inch of the way. In fact the library van parked right next to Hughes's, and he automatically held his breath as the couple got out. He watched them stroll into the distance, young Jack carrying a small rucksack which we know contained nothing more than the sandwiches and drinks his Mum had prepared (yet which could, as far as Hughes was concerned, have held a Head), and Lilith with the laptop to which she seemed surgically attached. "Keep your distance," he whispered to all the teams in the loop. "Wait for my word. Don't act on your own initiative."

Nyron got out of the back and stretched, then smoothed the wrinkles of his blue Wessex Water boiler suit – not his favourite uniform, admittedly, but one which made him feel vaguely sexy. He had to keep his distance because Lilith had already met him. The young man was an unknown, of course, and he really hoped that Jack wasn't a player because... because... Because that young man who was walking away across the green sward of a Wiltshire hilltop was probably the most beautiful and sexy young man he had ever seen in his own long and often sordid history of beautiful and sexy young men.

Take a deep breath here and see the potential for trouble: there was Lilith Love wanting a man who was very strong but inherently gentle; Jenny Djinn yearning for a man who was innately gentle but very strong; while Nyron Hughes was aching to find his soul mate, and wanted someone who was gently strong and strongly gentle and very very bendy. Between them, they were creating a sort of atom bomb.

*

Jack and Lilith arrived at the place marked on the Ordnance Survey map as the site of the former Templar preceptory. The old map, Jack was pleased to note, was far more useful than Lilith's Google Earth, which returned no more than a screen of smudges. There was nothing to show of the preceptory, of course. It had been pulled down over the centuries and the stone used for local buildings, much as they had done with some of the massive stones at the nearby Avebury circle. Even Lilith hadn't expected it to be intact. The sun

51

was warm, the deep grass rippled like wavelets in the breeze, and from their high vantage point, the green fields of England stretched away from them.

"Over there is Temple Farm, Temple Covert and we're in – I think – Temple Bottom."

"Beautiful," said Lilith, and she wasn't thinking of the man next to her for once. "Why live in such a remote place though?"

"Well," said Jack, going into his Tour Guide mode, "it wasn't like that then. That rough path back is the Ridgeway, once a major cross-country route for pilgrims and driving cattle. It was like one of your interstates. Being international bankers an' all, it was a perfect place for them."

Ooh, she loved his knowledge! Such a turn-on. All that info in that pretty head and yet it was going to waste. She couldn't wait to get him back State-side and make something of him, show him how it was done over there.

"Hey, er, Lilith, do you know the names of those four lost Templars you're looking for?"

She knew them by heart of course. "John de Mohun, John de Egle, Robert de Hambledon, and Robert de Sautré, Why?"

"Well… wouldn't it be nice to honour them now? Tell them that they're not forgotten? Here…" He took the flask of tea from the side pocket of his small backpack, poured some into the cup which he gave to Lilith, and prepared to drink out of the flask. "A toast! To….?"

And so for the first time in seven centuries the names of these men were said out loud, on the site where they had once lived, and if it was a simple enough little toast for Jack Hobbes, then to Lilith it was the most valid and magical thing she had ever done, and she knew beyond any doubt that she had to have this man at all costs.

"That was wonderful," she said.

"What the tea or the toast?"

"The tea was crap – full of caffeine, milk and sugar – yeuk! – but the idea was something else."

"Hmm… Only being polite. Us being uninvited guests and all that."

Any other fella on the planet could have sensed just then that she was gagging for it, and tried for a snog at least, but Jack just stepped back and checked his watch for the time in that timeless space.

Lilith took a deep breath and decided to show him the surprise she had prepared.

"What do you think it might have looked like here in 1308 Jack? Before the suppression of the Order, and them being imprisoned?"

Jack didn't have any real idea but he made valiant noises and invoked thick ivy-covered walls, small doorways, a round chapel, horse shit, woodsmoke, large hounds, various grey and thin servants, straw on the floors of every room.

Lilith did the *hmm* and *ah-ha* thing as he spoke, and in their imaginations at least, the walls arose from the grass and took on a hazy shape under the tools of their conversation. "Have I got something for you, here, in my little box of tricks." She squatted on her knees and switched on her laptop. "When this is opened," she said, meaning the programme, "you will not believe your eyes!"

The previous night, when she had not been climaxing herself in the hotel, she had used the latest software to create a Virtual Reality preceptory. Using the special glasses which connected with nerve-endings in her temples, then with a simple press of the OK button the whole thing – as it might have been – built itself rapidly on the screen but also around her, brick by brick, room by room, from ground level to fluttering flags bearing the cross-patte and beausant of the Templars.

"God," said Jack, but it wasn't the technological wizardry that had struck him, but the fact that he was having another 'wobbly', as his Mum would have termed it. Whatever was happening on the screen was being superseded by his own alternative reality.

Suddenly, he found himself in the yard of the preceptory, leaning back against a cold stone wall to keep out of the way of the large horse which ambled past to the stables, carrying a worried looking knight in a dirty white mantle, a large door creaking open and three other men bursting out and looking at him as if he might bring bad news. They were Templars, all four: all short-haired but heavily bearded. Only the rider wore the white mantle, the other three wore the brown of the sergeants. They all had red splayed crosses on their hearts. It was sunny, the air was still, the buildings were covered in ivy and there were neat rose bushes under the windows. Jack reached over and touched a rose and a thorn pricked him. Only the old horse seemed to be aware of his existence, and it glared with one red and bleary eye before snorting and moving on.

And then it stopped, and he was back in the 21st Century again, and there was only graphics on the screen of Lilith's laptop to fasten onto, which were pretty pathetic in comparison, although she thought he had been stunned by them.

"Amazing, huh?" she said, as he sucked at the tiny blood spot on his finger where the rose had pricked him. "Knocked you out, hey?"

Jack took a deep breath. These things were happening more and more frequently. Good job he had enough books in stock to explain such things, and not have to think he was going insane. To help him gather himself again he took the map out of his backpack and pointed to a place – not far from where they stood – marked as Man's Head. Now Lilith, because of her researches, knew something about the belief that the Templars had worshipped a sacred head, or heads, but her hormones were so active then that she wanted to tease. She was pretty sure that Jack was a virgin, and she had never had a virgin before. She bent over and looked at the map, and looked up at him. They were very close at this point.

Man's Head... Are you trying to tell me something?, she wondered, and gave him a smiley look which tried to ask that very question, testing his skills in non-verbal communication. Then – why not be bold! – "Do you want me to give you head? Is that what you want?"

Lots of things happened at that moment, on many levels. To understand one of the levels, think of the mere words the snooper Nyron Hughes heard them speak, and try and imagine what images he had built up: *Have I got something for you, here, in my little box of tricks... When this is opened you will not believe your eyes... God... Do you want me to give you head?*

It's a good job he was recording everything, because that played no small part in his defence later when the Grand Master and other Masters felt he should have been bollocked at least, and executed at best, for the cock-up that followed.

"GO GO GO!" cried Nyron Hughes from the control centre in the car park.

Not that Jack and Lilith on top of their hill heard that of course. All they knew was that four men who could have been Messrs Mohun, de Egle, de Hambledon, and de Sautré themselves, just popped into their space, appearing out of nowhere, grabbed them, slapped on the plasticuffs, and picked up the backpack as if it held the Holy Grail.

"Fucking Hell," said Jack.

"Jesus Fucking Christ!" screamed Lilith. Though that was just for starters.

Hughes sprinted toward them taking mental snapshots of the tableau, as he was trained to do: Lilith kicking out and yelling the sort of things that would never get her accepted into the Womens' Institute; Jack – the beautiful Jack! – standing there with his hands bound, like a bewildered St Sebastian waiting for the arrows; and an operative, who was also a neophyte, looking into the backpack with absolute horror.

"Talk to me, Hughes!" came the Grand Master's voice in his head, but this was not telepathy: it was coming through the earpiece. It's not easy to sprint and talk, but Hughes did his best: "I think sir... we've... we've... got it. Suspects secured. Spoffo's looking at the... in the...."

"What's in there?! Can you understand how anxious I am Hughes – WHAT'S IN THERE?"

The pain in Hughes' ear was immense. He had to stop and shake his head and remove the device for a second, massage his ear and replace said device, and then ask young Spoffo the same question, not sure whether to be reassured by his shocked expression or worried.

"Wh-what is it?" Nyron panted.

Spoffo, standing there like an elf with his black spiked hair and sharp features, peered again into the open bag, and then looked up with absolute horror.

"It's horrible. It's a crime against humanity, that's what it is sir."

Hughes took the bag carefully, like a new-born baby, and just as carefully looked into it. His stomach churned. Spoffo was right.

"HUGHES!" came the voice in his head, which was so not like the voice that Jenny Djinn would get in hers. "Talk to me sonny. Have you any idea how much I need to know...What's IN there?"

He had to take a deep breath to prepare himself for this. "Well sir, there's a burst bag of Cheezy Wotsits, a bottle of Coke Zero, and what looks like a prawn mayonnaise sandwich."

"With thin white sliced bread," said Spoffo in disgust, loving every second of this.

There was a long silence, broken only by the distant yelling of Lilith Love as she and Jack were carried off to the large black MPV that was parked next to the library van.

"Hughes," said a weary voice in his head. "Come home." And he couldn't have been sure if it was the Grand Master or his own inner self.

CHAPTER 4

Jenny, Tasha and Shaz drove around Trowbridge in the new-ish black BMW that Tasha had bought with the advance on her ex's life insurance payout. Shaz drove, Tasha read the manual and fiddled with various buttons which made her seat go up and down, forward and back, and Jenny sat centrally in the back feeling oddly queen-like. She had left The Head at home watching Jerry Springer, which he seemed to enjoy and said reminded him of the ding-dongs he had had with his cousin Jesus. Now they were on the look-out for a place to start a new religion.

And that's what it became, really. Although History has gone into a sort of plastic melt-down now because of what happened over the next few days, weeks and months, and its impact on the planes, those early days of the Head's empowerment marked the start of the best time in Jenny's personal life, and the beginning – or ending – of a new Age.

In practical terms this involved becoming very rich in a very short space of time, and Tasha and Shaz – disciples of a sort – made sure they got their full share. It was easily done, as The Head had intimated, coz Sex and Death are the two greatest powers and money-makers in the history of the Universe, even including Trowbridge.

With the help of her two friends, and a practical no-death no-payment contract which Shaz showed surprising acumen in creating, Jenny soon had a steady stream of disaffected women making discreet enquiries about the services offered.

As word spread with increasing speed about her unusual talents, she became in great demand, mainly from women wanting men put down for all sorts of reasons. Mind you, she had to explain in the brochures that they eventually created that she didn't do illnesses – she did straight Death, nothing slow. None of this *I want his balls to fester and drop orf*, which was the commonest request of that sort, usually by posh tarts from Gloucestershire. To Jenny Djinn mere illnesses were cruel, and she saw herself as something of a charity worker, taking each request on its merits. Her psychiatrist would have been proud of her, she felt. At first she had to be physically within sight of her patients, as she called them; as her powers developed, she only needed two photographs.

"You know," said Tasha as they drove down County Way looking for a suitable building to hire as their headquarters, "one day they'll put up a statue of you in Trowbridge Park."

"And they'll have to show all four arms!" chipped in Shaz, twirling a new platinum nose ring.

Tasha and Shaz had both looked up Kali on the internet, and were quite knowledgeable now. They didn't understand it, and had been told not to try, but they knew it was working and it was a lot more fun than spending the afternoon in The Mash Tun or Wetherspoon's. Of course, neither of them knew about The Head, who was still living quite happily in Jenny's flat, watching telly and then sleeping a lot, cheerful as anything – unless you mentioned Jesus – and no more trouble than having a budgie. Jenny Djinn loved him, purely and truly of course, and created a lavish box in her own head which she could shut up and thus keep her consciousness of him sealed away from other prying minds.

They passed under the footbridge that connected Tesco with the park, on which Jenny had performed her first killing. Actually, skipping forward a bit here, she quickly dropped the concept of killing people and preferred the term 'releasing' them. Not only did that sound better, but she felt it was closer to the spirit in which she worked. Life on earth was hell: she helped them to escape...

Of course, as far as Death Goddesses go, she was indeed a jolly little thing now. We've already seen how, before the full powers of the Kali descended upon her, she had been a sallow, hunched, loveless and unloved soul who enjoyed endless niggling illnesses, snuggled comfortably into her depressions, and drank rather too much cheap red wine than was good for her. Now that she was an avatar of the Kali – the very incarnation of Her spirit – she straightened, shone, bounced around like an aerobics teacher. She became straight and pert and sexy so that old acquaintances didn't recognise her. Bizarrely, she even seemed to have grown unusually long fingers and toes. In a brief period of time everyone wanted to know her, and be like her, even those put-upon but devoted women that Shaz would hire to knit those four-armed sweaters which sold so massively. That's what becoming a Death Goddess can do for you. Much better than Prozac; much better than HRT.

"What about this place?" asked Shaz, pointed to the cubical and massive unused mill building near Tesco's, riddled with the windows of empty rooms and made ragged by various aerial masts. She went twice around the roundabout and cut into the near-derelict yard surrounding it. "It'll be bri-lli-ant!"

"We'll never be able to afford that," said Tasha. "It's huge!"

Yes you will, said a Head inside Jenny's head. *Go for it.*

"Yes we will," said Jenny smugly. "Let's go for it."

Tasha and Shaz both blinked. Only a week or so ago Jenny was so passive that she had almost no personality. Now, she had an air of command.

"Okay," Tasha and Shaz said in unison.

*

How ironic, that even though Lilith Love had not yet met The Head, she was being affected by it every bit as much as Jenny Djinn. As the life of the young woman from Trowbridge rose like a rocket, that of the woman from New England was about to plummet like a stick.

A small black helicopter had landed on the hilltop, out of sight of the others. A large red Grand Master emerged and debriefed Hughes. The Grand Master went even redder. Hughes went paler, and you could have seen him shaking from a distance.

"You know what to do now," said Porteous.

The younger man reached for a tissue to remove the last of the eye-shadow he assumed the Grand Master was referring to. Then his brain clicked into gear.

"Damage limitation? *The Diana Option*? Or simple deportation?"

"Just make life difficult for her. She has to be part of this, whether she realises it or not. Sooner or later one of them will lead us to you-know-who, but remember that John has his own agenda. No-one, in two thousand years, has ever quite known what goes on inside John's head. For whatever reason he wants to be wherever he is now. Let them know we're there, but don't hurt them. And particularly watch out for that little poofter Hobbes."

Hughes winced. But at the inner levels in which he moved, the protections afforded in the outer world by political correctness were non-existent. He could hardly take the Grand Master to a tribunal and get him done for homophobia. In this odd world which existed between society and secret society, it was all grips, postures, passwords and initiations. The old days of getting to the top of the

British elite by theatre passes and deft buggery were long since gone.

"Right sir," he said briskly, mastering himself.

The Grand Master himself stared around at the gently rolling landscape, and sighed. His life used to be so simple. "You don't know what it's like being on top of a pyramid, Hughes. Then finding there are... Things... above you."

"Must be a lot of paperwork involved, sir."

The Grand Master glared, then gestured to the helicopter pilot to start up.

"Don't take the piss, sonny. You might be up there yourself someday."

*

And Lilith Love was furious again. Except by now she was so drained that she couldn't work up a proper rage, and the marks from the plasticuffs were still on her wrists, and it didn't make sense, none of it made sense. And here they were alone again, the assailants having disappeared as suddenly as they had come, taking with them that man who had recently been a Customs Officer and who was now some sort of plumber, and they had left without explanation or apology and now Jack had to drive the library van back into Marlborough.

"Did that really happen?" she asked, looking at the marks on her wrists as if they were stigmata.

"It did. So who are you?" he asked, throwing his little backpack into the back of the van.

"I'm Lilith Love. I'm- "

"No I mean they expected to find something in my bag. Something really important. Those weren't muggers. It's all to do with you and your search for forgotten Templars isn't it?"

"Yes it is. I know it is."

Suddenly it *did* make sense. You couldn't fail to put two and two together and come up with – in this case – four. He looked at his watch. "Jo is gonna throttle me... I'll lose my job."

Lilith was in no mood to reassure him. He put his foot down and lost some books from the shelves as the high van waggled on the

60

uneven road. They saw a small helicopter take off and buzz in front of the cab. There was a large black car behind them.

"We're in a conspiracy!" Jack said, but with more excitement than fear. "Classic images: black car, black helicopter. They're all linked! I've got a book about this in the back."

"Sure they are," she said. "They figure that everyone on the planet is separated by only six other people. Six Degrees of Separation, right? That's why all the conspiracies overlap, and it seems as if they're working to some grand plan orchestrated by one big dude. Listen hon, it don't mean doodly-squat."

You could look this up yourself if you're interested. Lilith was too busy going for a particular target to go down that route. She opened up her laptop, turning to it like she would a wise uncle, and having the sort of frisson that Jenny would get when she opened the box with The Head in it.

"Okay... okay... let's Google 'Templar Conspiracies' and see what comes up. Oh, hey hey hey, listen to these first few: *Templar Pope Conspiracy* sounds like a good one, some illustrations about the Templars and their idol Baphomet, and a real humdinger about Templars, the Ark of the Covenant (bullshit!) and the Illuminati; plus one for a book on oak kings, severed heads and our guys. That might be worth checking out."

Lilith's anger and concern was also yielding to excitement. This was the stuff of bestsellers. Best of all she was living it! This was better than having scripted debates with ham actors. And they were clearly being followed by Powers which obviously wanted them alive. Now really they should have been in terror, but in its own way The Head was protecting them both even though they hadn't yet met, and they must have felt something of this invisible grace.

"Are you scared, Jack?" she asked.

He had a good think. "A tiny bit maybe," he mused, looking in the wing mirror to check on the car which seemed to be following them. Mind you, the road was so narrow it could hardly overtake, so he had to allow for a little paranoia. "Truth is, as The Greatest Mobile Library Manager In The History of the World, I'm more concerned about getting this van back to base in time and in one piece."

This was exactly the sort of answer she wanted. Not macho, but not wimpy either. Honest and considered. Mind you, she was so besotted and so horny that any answer just then would have been the perfect one.

"Then I can only say: Home, James!" she said in what she thought was an English accent.

"I can tell you the origin of that," he answered, looking in his wing mirror again.

"Then tell me," she said brightly, leaning over and putting her hand on his thigh. He twitched anxiously and she removed it, charmed by his innocence. "And by the way you never answered my earlier question. The one I asked before those gorillas jumped us."
He didn't want to answer it. He didn't want a blowjob.

"Well," he said, swallowing, "Lord Montagu of Beaulieu had a new chauffeur named James Darling...."

*

Amid all of this there were four lost souls whom everyone forgets: John de Mohun, John de Egle, Robert de Hambledon, and Robert de Sautré. They were as much a part of this as anyone, and as tied up with The Head. And it might sound absurd but everything they did in that fateful year of 1307 was being observed by a group of Japanese brethren hunched around the see-through electric kettle which was now gracing the Holy Casket in which St John's sacred bonce had resided for so long. Somehow, in ways that went beyond physics and was tied up in simple belief and morphic resonance, said kettle (now being spoken of as The Kettle) was proving to be a brilliant tool for remote viewing.

So what did they see? They saw the bearded men in their lonely place, fed up with their lives, desperate for news and yet dreading news, never leaving their swords far from their hands, tetchy with each other and knowing that the Grand Master of the English Templars, William de la More, was due to come soon on his big black horse and check up on them, and probably make all sorts of changes. On top of that, they felt that their solid and holy preceptory with its little eight-sided church inside the walls, had become haunted.

Try to imagine what it was like for them, catching glimpses of strange beings outside their windows, and in dark corners – beings in strange raiments, and with odd hair and gestures – and it was a good job their Rule meant they had to sleep with a light burning all night, otherwise their nerves might have been shot completely. Normal people could talk about such things, but they had to take their two communal meals a day in silence, and were strictly forbidden to argue or even to gossip, so they were in a right state. In their lonely straw beds, dressed only in a nightshirt and breeches, they were not so much feared and fearless Warriors of God but worried lonely men who had glimpses – visions if you like – of a young man beautiful as any girl, and of a young woman with red unbound hair, shamelessly tight clothing with accentuated her breasts in a way that brought sweat to their brows, and a face that was painted in the way that revealed her as a true succubus – a sex demon from Hell.

This was Jack and Lilith Love of course; bits and pieces of them travelling back in time for reasons that only The Head could explain. In fact that moment when Jack had found himself in the courtyard of the preceptory, the grizzled knight ambling past on the old black mare had actually seen him, but quickly looked on ahead in case eye contact should cause him to lose his soul. So what the knight saw was a slim elemental figure merging with the ivy and roses like a faery: nothing he could he could swipe at with his sword.

What those men talked about, the Japanese brethren didn't see, and you couldn't tune the kettle or change channels, just had to accept what was shown. But they muttered with excitement when they saw the four Templars mustering the squires and servants, and covered their walls with what Lilith Love would have defined as 'apotropaic marks' – runes and other things – designed to ward off evil, though they warded off nothing of the sort, and the poor sods had the feeling that the sky was filled with strange eyes watching them, and making strange noises beneath the wind, at a time when their own bleak world was in danger of ending. Which was exactly the case....

*

Jenny was pleased with her new life and still quite happy in her old flat, although you wouldn't recognise it now, she had tidied it so much, and glued the peeling wallpaper back in place with some Uhu, and hoovered the carpet until the bristles perked up like corn. She had to hadn't she, now that she had a lodger, and rather hoped to ensnare a lover before too long. She had a new sofa – well, a new second-hand one – bought with the insurance proceeds of the few killings she had done so far. It was nice and deep and slightly furry, and The Head perched on the cushion next to her, its neck resting on a brand new deep red bath-towel that she had bought from Wilkinson's that morning.

They were watching *Inspector Morse*. The more telly Yahya watched, the more his taste in programmes improved.

"I can tell you who dunnit," said The Head, chewing some gum which, when finished, he had to spit out into the ashtray placed just before him.

"I can always tell," said Jenny rather tartly. "The murderer's always one of the characters with a smaller part, and who is also the best actor. Ssssh... it's dead good this."

John the Baptist smiled. In her own way, even without the aura of Kali, Jenny Djinn could be surprisingly smart. This was sooooooo different to the po-faced and sometimes terrified worship he had had to endure for the past two millennia. He took a deep and satisfied breath and the towel underneath his severed oesophagus rippled. It was like a holiday to him.

"Do you ever get lonely?" she asked when the adverts came on.

The way he closed his eyes for a long blink told its own story. "Well, I was never the only Head. They had a few others. Really weird bastards. They brought along St Euphemia after about 300 years, and some daft bat named Cynthia who had been murdered along with 11,000 other virgins at Cologne, about the same time. They were all right, I suppose, but they had a thing about dear cousin Yeshua and because they'd given their lives for him I couldn't bring myself to tell them the truth."

Anyone else in Jenny's position then would have leapt forward and asked him JUST WHAT WAS THE TRUTH!!!??? Some of the greatest mysteries of the Christian Era could have been solved there and then, in a grotty little flat in the old mill-town of Trowbridge. Jenny wasn't interested in the slightest.

"When you fall asleep, the whole room is filled with light. It sort of seeps out of your pores, it's like a baby's night-light."
He gave the labial equivalent of a shrug.

"Why did you come to me?" she asked.

He knew that she wasn't asking a deep question here, but fishing for compliments.

"Because I needed some fun, and some warmth, and to have someone who didn't worship me, or was afraid of me. Also, I needed someone who would appreciate the importance of a good shampoo, and I wasn't going to get that among the French."

"Is that Jack Hobbes gonna fall in love with me then?"

The Head smiled. "When you become Kali, you have the power to make all sorts of things happen."

Now Lilith Love would have pounced on an answer like that and pointed out it was no answer at all, but Jenny being a simple soul was quite happy with that.

"Will we be able to afford that old mill building that Shaz's got her mind set on?"

St John the Baptist gave one of his sleepy smiles, and his last words before his eyes closed and the light poured out of him were: "Oh yes. There is a woman coming soon who will make it all possible…"

*

The woman coming soon who made it all possible was busy showing Shaz and Tasha around the vast and empty mill. The only sound came from their echoing footsteps on the dusty wooden floors, and the gnashing of her teeth at the thought of her husband's perfidy. She was far posher than the posh tarts from Gloucestershire who would later flood down to Trowbridge bringing their venom and at least two copies of their partner's life insurance policies. She was only doing this because the bitch who should have been doing it had been shagging her husband until his eyes rolled in his head like marbles on a plate. His term, by the way. So Felicity Sinclair-Lazarides (one of The Sinclairs), acting in as mature a way as she could, had given the little cow a good slapping and sacked her, and decided to keep out of everyone's way for a while until she could work out what to do. The fact that there was a possible assault charge out against her played no small part in this.

So she was slumming it, really. And she was irritated by these two yokels pretending that they had grandiose schemes for the Old Mill which they could not possibly afford.

"You're not really with us, are you?" asked Tasha when they arrived at the top floor and looked out over the rooftops of Trowbridge.

"What? What?"

"You're miles away. It's a man innit?"

Shaz was dashing from window to window, getting the whole vista of their little town, and it could have been Los Angeles down there she was so excited. "In-kuh-redible. In-kuh-redible..."

"Are you psychic or something?" said Felicity rather sourly, although she was the last person to sneer at psychism.

"No, I've just been where you are."

Felicity Sinclair-Lazarides, in her puce Jaeger outfit and Jimmy Choo shoes and the subtle tribal-marks (hidden by make-up) done at the Bath Clinic to make herself look younger, looked hard at these women kitted out entirely by Be-Wise and Boots and stopped sneering.

"We can 'elp," Shaz said.

"Really missus, we really can help," Tasha added.

From their faces, they could too. Their sincerity oozed out of them like the like a different sort of light this time. They were Trowbridge gangsters, she thought – or gangsters' molls, rather. With hearts of gold, of course. And a sympathy for downtrodden women of all classes.

Felicity put her Balenciaga bag firmly on her shoulder as a kind of statement and squared up to them both, looking at them for the first time.

"I would like that very much," she said, imagining men of Neanderthal build but with huge cunning doing savage and untraceable things to dear Crispin and his young tart.

"Come an' meet our friend," said Tasha, so they got in the car and went.

*

She parked her Merc on Binyarn Street, her back just touching on the double yellow lines and nudged up against a burnt-out Ford Escort. This was what she expected: the rough and merciless edge, the dark underbelly of Trowbridge society. They went through a battered white door and up a rickety flight of wooden stairs with a loose and thin red stair-carpet hanging onto the middle, one step ahead of the smell of curries from a shop nearby, and crowded onto a small landing while Shaz, the be-ringed one, knocked three times on the door, then three times again.

There was no answer. "Don't worry, takes a while," said Tasha, and Felicity noted how strangely excited they both were, shifting the weight on their feet, their faces almost glowing with excitement. She, who felt she knew something about women, reckoned they were sharing the same man: a powerful, brutal, but often oddly gentle man who knew how to treat women of their class.

Of course, it took a while for Jenny to open the door because she was putting the sleeping Yahya back into his box, and into a locked cupboard.

*

To say she was flummoxed when she was admitted to this poky little flat was a slight understatement, although Felicity was to hugely overstate her degree of flummoxment to the later biographers. Instead of a simian male covered in tattoos and heavy silver chains, sharpening his knives, there was small and trim woman of about her own age, who at first glance seemed about as ordinary as anyone could get. The telly was blaring in the background, showing the old film *Highlander*.

"Hello. I'm Jenny Djinn," Jenny said, as if it were a title that everyone should recognise. With a flick of the remote control the telly was muted, but not switched off.

"She needs some 'elp," Shaz said.

"Her hubbie. The usual thing," Tasha said.

Felicity was – as she half-jokingly expressed it much later – 'sore afraid'. Who *were* these three lunatic women?

"Here," said Tasha, "there's this contract for you to sign first and then our Jen here will get it sorted for you."

"Contract? Contract!?" Felicity snorted. She snatched it from Tasha and read through it. She had a first class degree in law and although she was outwardly snorting as she read there was a tiny portion of her mind which was telling her that, actually, it was rather good. Although it gave no clues as to how the killing would be accomplished, and indeed never even mentioned the word.

"Ridiculous!" she sneered, and flung it onto the table.

"Listen," said Tasha, "if you don't agree to the terms and sign this then we can't– "

"Yes we can," said Jenny Djinn. "For this woman we will. I will."

Jenny didn't have a voice in her head this time. Perhaps the Head had awakened her own dormant intuition, but Jenny just knew that Felicity was an important visitor. And by important, she didn't mean anything to do with class. The other two, far more experienced in the outer world, actually were less comfortable with Felicity than Jenny was. They had almost no contact with people from those upper stratas of British society, whereas Jenny Djinn knew these levels, and these intimately, coz of her passion for the telly.

"I... don't understand. Will you three tell me what it is, exactly, that you are talking about? I'm a busy woman. Lord Bath wants to do lunch."

Tasha looked at Shaz; Shaz looked at Tasha. Tasha and Shaz looked at Jenny Djinn – who sort of beamed at them all.

"I'm Kali, the Death Goddess."

There was a moment's silence and then an ass-like braying from Felicity of the sort that had once got her into so much trouble at Roedean.

"Oh really. Gollygosh it has been interesting. I must say but I must be going..."

Shaz barred the door. "She is an' all."

"Really, she is" said Tasha, rather more kindly. "She can prove it."

"She can prove that she can, without leaving this room, make your husband die ab-ser-lutely painlessly."

Felicity blinked and gave a weak sneer. Weak because it seemed to her that Jenny was radiating light, and there was a strange air of what she later would come to describe as 'ancient sanctity'.

"The deal is this..." said Shaz, going into professional mode, "You'll
get a huge wad from your husband's insurance and the like, right?"

"Huge."

"Just give us 10%."

Another bray from Felicity. It sounded more like a chainsaw this time, the ass having died with astonishment.

"What do you think?" asked Tasha. "In principle anyway."

Felicity sought time by putting on her Smart Lawyer face and scanning through the no-death no-pay contract. At the same time her mind was really scanning through all the shitty things her Greek husband done and failed to do, all the betrayals and insults, and the sheer falsity of their original courtship in which (she saw it now) he had wanted nothing more than the Holy Grail of connection with a proper bloodline such as hers. The fact that she had wanted his wealth was, she felt, hardly relevant.

"In principle?" Felicity said, and she could hardly look at this strange Jenny Djinn because she seemed to shine, with a light that went right through Felicity's expensive clothes and made her feel naked, and very ordinary. "In principle I would give you exactly that, and probably a lot more besides."

Shaz got a pen out of her bag.

"No," said Jenny Djinn. "This one doesn't need a contract."

You can see what was happening can't you? Felicity was about to have what she would later trumpet to any media outlet as her Revelation. The two pals were about to object, but there really was an increasing difference about their friend: this Jenny Djinn bore no resemblance whatsoever to little mousy Jenny Grey – Jenny Grey who had died as painlessly and quickly as all the 'Service Users', as she came to call them, finding that a much better word than 'victim'.

"Look gels... explain to me. Something is going on here. I need to know what. I won't cause you any trouble."

She added that last because they could hear her car alarm going off, as someone broke in and trashed it, though at that moment she really didn't care.

"This is the Time of the Gathering," said Jenny Djinn, echoing the words Sean Connery had just uttered in *Highlander*.

The other three didn't know that however, and the only chroniclers who later ventured to make the connection were generally derided. They never really grasped how empty Jenny Grey had been before she became Jenny Djinn, avatar of Kali.

"So... how do you do it?"

"Have you got a photograph of him?"

"No. No, but...." Felicity rummaged in her bag and brought out a wafer-thin mobile phone. "I've got the bastard on here, a video clip, with him and that cow... Here... I took this yesterday, through a crack in the curtains. I was going to let her husband see it, cause

69

misery and havoc, send it to the tabloids, then use it in the divorce petition."

The other three women huddled around the little screen, Tasha as much interested in the kit as in what was being shown. What they saw was a shaky picture of a surprisingly portly Ari Lazarides humping someone on a desktop, a glimpse of stockings and suspenders, and small items falling to the floor.

"Show me again," said Jenny, and the other two stepped aside and looked on expectantly as Felicity did exactly that. "Poor, poor people," Jenny said, and compassion positively oozed out of her.

"What sad lives. Are there children involved. No? Well, I can send them both home if you like."

"Send them home?" Felicity asked, knowing full well what she meant, but just making sure.

"I can end their lives here, and send their souls to a happier place, their true home. Some call it heaven. It's where we all belong. Somewhere up in the stars. Who wants to live forever?" Jenny added, quoting *Highlander* again, giving the words that Shaz would later have emblazoned on the t-shirts.

Felicity Sinclair-Lazarides, who was now about to become just Felicity Sinclair, took the deepest breath of her life. The scent of Amouage floated from her, as did the far more priceless and sometime unobtainable scent of hope.

Jenny Djinn was now becoming Kali on internal levels; she stared lovingly at the images. The light rippled around her, and for a moment the other woman – who did know a bit about mythology – almost thought she saw the extra arms, waving and weaving light, comforting and crushing. "There," Jenny said. "It is done. Now would you like a nice cuppa? Have to boil the water in a pan I'm afraid. Keep meaning to buy myself a new electric kettle. I lost the one I had..." She giggled then, but no-one had any reason to understand why, and so didn't notice.

In some ways, this was the Time of the Gathering, as the putting to death of Ari Lazarides marked the expansion of Jenny/Kali's powers and the effective start of her ministry, when her disciples – all women – were drawn around her.

"Nice cuppa tea," said Jenny blithely as they sat in silence and sipped, and waited. The smell of curry from the take-away floated into the flat as usual. They could hear distant sitars and reed pipes.

Felicity's phone rang. No-one looked surprised. Not even her by this time.

"Yes? Oh. Yes. Yes, yes. Oh no. No, not at all. Really, no."

You can piece together the sort of things she was replying to. She pressed the red button that stopped the call, folded the little device up into its neat little black oblong and looked at the holy trinity as if she was a supplicant – which in a way she was.

"You can have the Mill," Felicity said. "I mean have it. My only condition is that I want to be involved in whatever is going on here..."

"You already are," said Jenny Djinn, smiling like a seraph, holding open arms (the two visible ones) toward her.

"Dunno about you lot," said Shaz, sniffing the air, but I could murder a vindaloo."

"Hmm, me too," Jenny said. "This always leaves me feeling so hungry."

And what Jenny wanted now, Jenny got, and Mrs Loganathan from the nearby curry house soon turned up with their order, and they sat around eating it in silence – an act which became part of her ritual, compared by some to an Unholy Communion.

"This is good," said Felicity quietly, and they all nodded, for different reasons.

And so it began.

*

Well it might all have been going tickety-boo for Jenny Djinn, but Lilith Love felt her life was going haywire. Here she was, riding in the Library Van from Marlborough to Trowbridge, with all her worldly goods in the back, having been ejected from the Green Man hotel without apology or explanation, found that her credit cards were not recognised when she tried to check into another place further down the street, and that her laptop was unable to connect to the internet. When she tried to contact her agent on her state-of-the-art phone she was unable to get through, and she just knew that was Enemy Action.

Good job she had asked Jack to wait, which he did somewhat anxiously, one eye on his watch and the other on his job, the engine of the Library Van running.

"It's MI5," he said as they drove off, offering her temporary sanctuary in his place.

"It sure is," she agreed, and of course it was. "And did you notice a strange thing… they all smelled of frankincense."

Well if truth be told, they were not so much MI5, but an even more secret organisation whose senior members could call in favours from certain figures within MI5, MI6, the CIA and just about any other security agency in the civilised world.

"They're just thugs," she went on, her mind racing. "Like the Templars, really. You know that the Templars were illiterate?"

"I did, yes."

That pleased her: despite all her troubles, she just felt so good with this guy. Couldn't wait to jump him. Which she would do tonight, okay! "The Order discouraged learning. Bet those guys who leaped on us back there never read a book in their lives."

The hands-free phone rang.

"Sssh," he said to Lilith. "It's my boss. Hi Jo!"

"Jack, darling…. I don't mean to sound mother hen-ish but where the fuck are you? Have the enchanted landscapes of the Downs swallowed you up at last? Or have you just disappeared up your own arse?"

"Just leaving Marlborough, my beloved leader, and coming back to Trowbridge now. It's been hell, really… Had trouble with the wheelchair ramp at the back, the automatic doors jamming, and the engine misfiring and cutting out completely. I got it going but it sounds really rough. Listen…." He revved the engine and clashed the gears.

There was a silence.

"Bollocks," she said. "You'll have to lock up. I'm not waiting for you. I've got a flower show to run and mouths to feed. We'll talk tomorrow. Bye…"

Lilith looked at him with approval. He was so strong, so clever.

"Sorry 'bout that, Lilith," he said, slightly unnerved by her shining face. "My motto is: 'A little inaccuracy can save tons of explanation.' And the black car is still following us by the way."

Yeah, it was pretty scary, all that stuff that had happened since coming here, and she had no clear idea what to do next, but she fingered her little talisman of Sekhmet, glanced at the man driving, and – typically for a Death Goddess – felt more alive than she had done in years.

"Come on Van," Jack said. "Let's go home…"

*

Meanwhile, back at the Grand Lodge of Inner Albion (which was far grander and far more discreet than the infinitely younger Grand Lodge of the English Freemasons), those strange things were happening with the kettle and the Japanese contingent, though the news took a little while to filter through to the seniors in the Order. As usual it was the lower initiates, the Servers, who noticed that the Japanese contingent were unduly obsessed with said device. More than that they were sleepless and red-eyed from their observations, although they were making no attempt to share. Being a kind enough soul, the Grand Master had indulged their interest at first. Found it quite amusing. They didn't get to see the Sacred Head of St John the Baptist, but they had fallen in love with an electric kettle instead! What did they know, eh? Their Order had none of the mature wisdom, none of the spiritual sophistication of his. It was Spoffo who broke the news, by-passing Nyron Hughes in the process.

"They're using it for Remote Viewing, sir."

"What?!"

"They are using it to see… well, I'm not quite sure, sir. They won't tell me. I'm not sure if they are using it to see distant places and events in the present, or like a crystal ball, to see the past and possibly the future."

"We're talking about that bloody kettle, right?"

"The same. Argos. Special offer."

"Right… I'll grill the little bastards and find out what's going on."

"But there's more sir…"

"Oh… go on."

"One of them filled the kettle with water and put it back in the Casket. I saw them do it."

"So?"

"They could get it to boil, just by pressing the button, even though it wasn't connected to anything. And – I'm sure – it also fills itself."

"Bloody Hell…"

73

"I tried to warn Hughes that was what they were after, but he wouldn't listen. They were never interested in amity and brotherhood, sir, as I'm sure you guessed all along. It's Zero Point Energy they want."

The Grand Master looked piercingly at Spoffo. The young man squirmed a little and ran his fingers through his heavily gelled and spiky black hair. Had Jack or Lilith been in his position they might have offered a good book or website to explain more, but in reality that would have been wasted on the older man.

"You toe-rag" the Grand Master said with disgust, striding off to see the Japanese contingent. "And get that shite out of your hair!"

*

Lilith, without thinking it through, had half-imagined that Jack Hobbes would live in a cute little English house with mullioned windows, a typical little garden filled with apple trees, and a stream running along the back. In fact, before she had come over she had typed 'traditional english houses' into Google image search, and the first one that came up, out of 1,530,000 other such, had pretty much imprinted itself upon her brain as the sort all Brits lived in. Remember that for all her wealth and – in her eyes – sophistication – she had never been abroad before. She was as naïve as Jack was virginal. And in some ways her whole perception of the world outside of America was completely formed by what she had seen on the movies, or on television, or via Google, so she really wasn't that different to Jenny Djinn, was she? Maybe none of us are?

When she saw the reality of Jack's house, however, she had to do some rapid adjustments to those images she had formed on her mental screen. The house was squeezed into a terrace off an area he called Newtown – which was anything but. It was small and grey, right next to the main road, hunched between the others like an old man in a crowd. Out front was a tiny 'garden' filled with rubbish. The door opened immediately into a small sitting room dominated by a large fish tank, which gave way into a ropy old kitchen, beyond which – she could just see – was another garden not much bigger than a pocket handkerchief. This was Jack Hobbes' home?! She marvelled in near-disgust. It was clean – immaculately clean – but so small and drab. Once she got this situation sorted out and he was back Stateside, she would show him what real architecture was!

But that wasn't the real problem. In fact, the drabness made him seem even more golden when he stood there in the middle of it. And when she looked out at the traffic thundering past, the windows shaking from the noise, he said: "John Betjeman, the former poet laureate, said that when you're disturbed by noise like that you should pretend it's the noise of the sea..." When he said that, her heart just surged for him the more. That was her kinda guy, sure it was! No, the real problem was something completely unexpected:

He had a mother.

Now that stunned her. She never imagined a guy of his qualities would still be living with his Mom. Well, not so much a homely, cuddly little Mom but more a blue-eyed, down-market version of Madame Blavatsky, minus the cigars. Lilith, it must be said, had never heard of Madame Blavatsky. She only knew the name now because that's how Jack introduced her.

"Lilith, this is my mum. Isn't she like Madame Blavatsky? I've got an excellent book about her by John Symonds – about Blavatsky that is, not Mum. Although she could tell a story about herself too, if truth be told. Mum, this is Lilith. She needs a bit of help. I'll explain later...."

He shot off up the narrow wooden staircase leaving the two women staring at each other. Lilith wasn't good in such situations.

She had a thing against parents, having tried very hard to wipe her own out of her psyche many years before.

The mother said nothing. The fish tank made a sort of gurgling noise. Jack came clattering back down.

"You can have my room. You can use my old steam-driven computer in there too."

"Where will you sleep?"

"I've got a fold-down bed I can use in Mum's room. She doesn't mind, do you?"

The mother did the sort of thing with her face that Yahya did when he couldn't shrug, and went out into the garden with washing.

"Don't mind her," said Jack. "Mum's a bit quiet at times. Has been since Dad died. She's just a bit shy. She likes you really."

Lilith was stunned. This was not what her juices wanted. Not what her mind expected. Not for the first time since she had arrived in England, she felt that she was losing all control.

75

"Couldn't you… I mean Jack, don't you wanna…?"

"Oh don't worry, I'll shower later. Get changed out of this uniform then too. Here, let me carry your things up, and then we'll decide what we have to do." He looked out through the net curtains. "And that black car is still there. Exciting, eh?"

She looked out. "It's not the same one. Really, it isn't. We mustn't let paranoia grip us." She said that with some authority, having written a *succes d'estime* called *Self-Healing Through Paranoia – They Really Are Talking About You. Yes You!*

The mother returned, sans washing, and settled down in front of the fish tank, watching the rise and fall of the little aerating submarine and the tiny blue creatures flitting back and forth through the wrecked galleons. Mrs Hobbes made no attempt at conversation, and nor did Lilith offer any after the first minute or so.

Jack seemed unconcerned as he made them a salad in the kitchen, chattering enough for all three.

"Jack…" Lilith said, as she went into the kitchen to offer help, and to try to snatch a moment's privacy. "You and me… tonight…"

"Don't worry Lilith," he soothed. "This house is secure. No-one will get in. Trust me. Mum… what sort of salad dressing would you like?"

The thing is, Lilith was no slouch when it came to reading people – or American people at any rate. She knew right off that Jack was not as stupid as he was pretending. And of course he knew exactly what she wanted, but he just didn't want it himself. A little idiocy can save tons of confrontation might well have been another of his mottoes. He had a book about that too, and would often read it into the night, or by closing his eyes and jabbing his finger into it, using the first motto he pointed at as a kind of Zen-like answer to his current problem.

The evening passed awkwardly. They went up to his room, the door ostentatiously left open. It was packed with books, literally floor to ceiling, all arranged according to Jack's own Dewey-Decimal System as used by the library service. At least she loved that aspect of the situation. Jack's small room with the single window was packed with more books than Lilith had in her entire 9 bedroom house.

Then Lilith and Jack spent some time on his old PC, with the big old monitor and a ropey old version of Windows 98 (which she thought of as pure undiluted evil) trying to contact the World Beyond. Her own laptop still wouldn't connect to the internet, and neither would her phone. She tried Jack's landline to reach the States but without success.

"When they took your laptop going through Customs, they would certainly have downloaded the entire contents and bugged it."

Exactly right, Jack. He had certainly read all his spy books! More, the lid of the laptop now had a minuscule bubble, a tiny little hemisphere no bigger than a piece of snot, which was actually a gem of British nanotechnology, being a camera with 360º of viewing, full colour, transmitting everything back to Hughes's team who could see and hear everything that went on around...

*

"Geddem off," said Spoffo, whose watch it was, observing everything from the back of a large van some miles away. "Go on Lilith darling, get your puppies out... That's it – oh yes! Lots of silicone there. Bit of nip and tuck too. Grrrrrrr...... Now, come on bitch, lower those panties. What are you: Brazilian, landing strip, or Earth Mama Muff? Come on darling, come on... YES!! Ta da!! A clear landing strip. I knew it!!"

You can tut if you like. In fact you might like to marvel how someone can be a functioning member of a most ancient Order that is directly linked with supernal Mysteries and the Innermost Functioning of whole nations, and still be a complete arsehole. Most of them are, you know, though it shouldn't need the sacred and severed head of St John the Baptist to help understand that.

The back door of the van opened. A waft of cold night air and Nyron Hughes came inside, dressed all in black like a spoof Secret Agent. Deference descended, and decorum.

"The subject has just left the room, sir. Naked. I assume she's going to–"

"Don't assume. Just watch. Just record."

"Yes sir."

That was telling him.

"What have you found out?"

"Well sir, nothing very much at all. She's made some clear passes and obviously wants to share his bed tonight, but he's avoided the situation – and very cleverly if you ask me. I'll play the recordings for you later. Oh and I'm absolutely certain that Mrs Maisie Hobbes seems to have Downs Syndrome, which Lilith doesn't seem to have picked up on at all, judging from her conversations with Jack, sir."

"Downs Syndrome!"

"Yes sir. I'll pull her medical records later to make sure, sir."

"Downs Syndrome... So he's the son of a widow and the son of an idiot at the same time."

"Seems so sir! Is being the son of a widow important, sir?"

"Stop calling me 'sir' like that."

"Yes sir, sir."

"It's very important. Significant. You've read your Dictionary haven't you?"

"No sir. No time."

Hughes sighed. The youth of today, eh? Of course had the connection been two way Lilith would have Googled this mystery at once, and looked the term up in the on-line Masonic Dictionary and seen that in the eyes of Hughes' older-than-the-freemasons Order, being the son of a widow made Jack Hobbes rather special.

"Just watch, Spoffo, just watch," he said, unwittingly adopting Porteous' tone.

So the two of them peered and peered, and studied Lilith's arse as she listened at her bedroom door, and slowly, slowly opened it, and stepped through.

And what was going on in Jack's house just then, when a magnificently naked Lilith stepped through the door and onto the small landing which separated the two bedrooms?

Nothing. Nothing at all. The other door remained closed. She could hear snoring from the other side. She tried whispering Jack's name but there no response. She felt so stupid, so powerless.

I'm a jerk. Okay, she thought sadly, and with no small exasperation. She returned to her room, giving a full frontal that was being recorded and would be replayed time and again by unknown men who would put her in their own virtual reality masturbatory fantasies for some time to come.

CHAPTER 5

Jack was in his library van, and all was not too well with his world. He was parked up outside the Shangri-La Rest Home but there were no takers as yet, and truth be told he didn't want any. He had a lot to worry about: the bollocking he was due to get from his boss in the afternoon; the unwelcome and uneasy presence in his home of the American Woman (for that's how he thought of her) who was at the library accessing the internet from that untapped source; the perennial problems with The Mother (ditto); and most of all the alarming sense that he was being watched at every step by Strange Powers, who were somehow tied up with his innocent visit to Temple Rockley.

"Help me out here lads," he said to himself, invoking his own internal and very fuzzy Powers.

An ambulance came screeching around the corner and its driver indicated that he needed to access the large semi opposite. Jack, who would have been blocking the road, pulled back a few metres to let them in, his tall van scraping into the overhanging branches of the trees. Leaves fell: there was a book in the back which would identify them, when he got a chance. He watched idly. Anything to take his mind off his present concerns. After ten minutes, the paramedics emerged carrying what was surely a dead body on the stretcher. He wound the window down to listen, intrigued. Not only was Jack a virgin, he had also never seen death before.

"We gotta make a fuss about this," said the male paramedic.

"That's eight in – what – seven days?" said his female partner.

"Every one with a bloody smile on his face."

"When I go, I wanna go like that."

"We gotta make a fuss. This isn't right. There's just gotta be some new bug we don't know about."

"Hey you had a smile on your face last night."

The man smiled, reached around to pinch her arse. "Yeah I did, didn't I?"

The ambulance drove off and Jack was left to his thoughts, parked on a tree-lined avenue with not a soul in sight. Actually that wasn't quite true, because at the end of the road was another of the black vehicles that were clearly following him everywhere. Except this one came closer. And closer. Closer still, and nudging so close that if he had had the nerve he could have stared into the whites of the occupants' eyes. If their eyes had whites, that is. If they even had eyes. With a sudden blast of fear at the thought that he might be about to meet a true non-human on the streets of Trowbridge, he reached for the little button which would close the automatic doors, and almost cried out when he felt the van rock as someone climbed aboard.

"Hello Jack Hobbes," said Jenny Djinn, and some (though not all) future historians would argue that Jack was right: by this time Jenny really wasn't human any more.

He was startled, and then relieved, and then bewildered, when three other women came on board who were of course her disciples, though he was not to know that yet.

"He's the one?" asked Shaz simply enough, though to Felicity, who was soaking up absolutely everything, it sounded like *Is he The One?*, so she knew right off this was someone special.

"I'm moving," Jenny said, very proud. "The old mill building next to Tesco's."

"What – that massive one?"

"It's gi-bloody-gantic," said Shaz, browsing through the Romances.

He should have asked loads of questions but this lot looked so weird, acted so weird, that he was having a weirdness overload.

The hands-free phone rang, and saved him. He could see from the display it was his boss, Jo, summoning him to the meeting.

"Sorry ladies, you'll have to leave. I've got to go to HQ and get my bollocks slapped."

"You in trouble?" Jenny asked, with an equally weird mixture of concern and hope. "I could help you."

The phone continued ringing. *How could YOU help me?* he thought, remembering the old insipid Jenny Grey. The other three women, who were still only too human, read his face easily enough.

"Oh she could help you," Tasha said.

"Really 'elp you," put in Shaz.

"Honestly darling... she really could." Felicity nodded.

He gave a dazzling and utterly false smile. "I have to go, really. Good luck with your move, Jenny."

They went outside and stood on the pavement, Jack framed in the rear doors, looking anxious. He pressed the button. The doors gave a pneumatic gasp and closed.

"You shagged 'im yet?" asked Shaz of Jenny, as they watched the van drive off.

"Pretty boy isn't he?" mused Tasha.

"Sublime..." said Felicity, who in her previous pre-Kali life would have been happy to fish for someone like that.

"Dead lovely," sighed Jenny Djinn, with no trace of irony.

*

Lilith was in the library going slowly insane. Although her wafer-thin and enormously tough lap-top was almost useless, she sat on it to keep it safe. The library was buzzing. There was a children's group in the corner being read to by a jolly young woman with a bubbly voice, all of them having so much fun that Lilith wanted to bite their heads off, or at least rip 'em apart. She just wasn't used to being so close to people. It wasn't a healthy or character-building experience for her, as it simply made her feel like a complete alien on a bewildering planet.

Come on, come on, come on... she thought, having booked herself half an hour's free use of the internet, and was waiting with her usual patience – that is to say, almost none at all – for the Polish woman to finish browsing her pathetic little sites. At last, at last, she was able to log on and then immediately tried to contact her agent, PA, and just about anyone over there who might have helped. Thing is, she had spent so long being reclusive, and/or guarding her privacy, that her 'social network' was almost non-existent, and there were few people whose numbers she knew by heart. And the other thing is, she just couldn't get through to anyone. Everything was bounced or blocked, and she just knew it was all due to enemy action.

I'll get a book out of this, she vowed to herself. *A book about REAL Conspiracies, linked somehow with REAL Templars.*

There was someone watching her. The inner cat seemed to sense it. It wasn't paranoia, about which she had written at great length, but a group of Polish youths clustered at the next machine. She knew they were Polish because: a) they had the strange angles on their

81

faces that – as far she was concerned – characterised Poles, and b) Jack had said the town was full of them. One of the gang, a long dark-haired wretch in an old leather jacket, looked around first to make sure no-one else could see him, made an obscene wiggling gesture with his finger which caused the others to erupt into Polish laughter.

Okay, okay, okay... she thought, and Googled: 'english to polish translations' and almost immediately was taken to an on-line translating site which did the trick. She typed in the English words: 'Go fuck yourself you silly little boy', and within a second she got the Polish words, which she said to herself once, under her breath, to get them right, and then declaimed with great vigour and intensity:

"Pierdol siety nierozsadny nieduzo szampan...."

The little group dissolved into laughter. Leather Jacket, grinning, came over and whispered in her ear: "Can I seeing your poosy?" and she knew at once it wasn't her Sekhmet medallion he was after. Still, the guy was handsome enough, bold enough, and she was chewing the carpet with horniness, and she might have had some rough sex in an alleyway with him any other time, but knew she couldn't trust anyone around her. Not anyone. Except Jack. This guy was as likely to be an MI5 agent as a Polack immigrant looking for work in the local sausage factory.

"Go beat your meat," she said, and walked on out without a backward glance.

*

And what was Yahya doing at this time? Yahya – or what was left of him – was being removed from his cardboard box and shown the nice new room that Jenny, under extreme secrecy, had organised for him in the Old Mill. The walls were pristine white, the ceiling was blue and covered in stars. There was a thick sward of expensive dark green carpet, on which Jenny was sitting cross-legged, with Yahya in her lap, covering his eyes with her hands, delighted by the way his long lashes fluttered against her palms. She lifted her hands with a *Ta-da!* And he blinked and looked. She turned him around to help him see 360.

"Do you like it?" she asked, chuffed by it all, so different to her tatty old flat, so pure and clean.

"No," said The Head.

"Oh..." Jenny said, crestfallen. But not too crestfallen, because she was used to being knocked back by men.

"I've had 2,000 years of bloody temples. I want a nice cozy place, all warm and soft, like your old flat."

Jenny Djinn looked at him and stroked his hair. You can't imagine Jacques de Molay, the last Grand Master of the Templars, doing anything like can you? Yahya's eyes closed in pleasure and he sighed.

"Poor bugger," she said softly.

"I was never that!" he said, eyes flashing open. "Just ask Mary."

"Mary... was that your girlfriend?" Pang of jealousy there, even if said girlfriend had died in Provence 2,000 years ago.

"She was until that bastard cousin of mine muscled in."

Jenny stroked his hair and brow again. It soothed him, like a little baby. He never got much of that when the Templars had him.

"Are you happy Yahya?"

"No. In my circumstances, would you be?"

Jenny's heartfelt answer, right off, was No! She understood and empathised immediately. Which was another way that she differed so profoundly from Lilith, because if Lilith had been asked the same question she would have, as like as not, answered something like *Hell Yeah!!* You can see why: The chance to have All Knowledge, to surf the Universe, to be able to confer great and occult powers, and be worshipped and feared, if rarely loved...

"So what can I get you?" Jenny asked, and she would have got the Head anything, really anything.

"I want that couch back. And the telly. And I'd like to try some of that marijuana I've heard so much about. Oh – and maybe a nice plate of steak and chips that I can sniff the essence from."

"Okay," she said blithely, and after putting him back in the cardboard box, off she went to make it all happen. Although she locked the door of the Special Room after her, there was no need to do more. She had told the other three that if anyone tried to peek inside, or talked about it among themselves or to others, or asked questions, then they would die.

"Okay Jenny" they all said, deferential as anything. When they weren't supervising the builders working rapidly to do out the rest of the building, they had their own heads together working out a new long-term sort of contract. This one, Shaz felt, would be delayed action in that the customers would organise their insurance policies first, to aim for maximum payout, and then Kali would do her stuff as soon as the policies came into effect. Kali Inc, as they thought of themselves, would want an advance first though, which would be refunded in the event that death failed to occur.

Insurance men and women in West Wiltshire had never been so busy. They never dreamed that they would soon be paying out such huge sums, at such great frequency.

In the meantime, Jenny Djinn was heading to the recycling centre to get her old sofa back.

*

At about that time one of the arch-movers in Jenny and Lilith's conspiracy was busy sitting in a small office in the Libraries and Heritage Department of the County Council, regaling Jo with tales of his years on the beat in London. He was, of course, wearing one of his favourite uniforms of all time: that of simple police constable. Jo laughed, she offered more biscuits. She spun slightly from side to side in her office chair. For a moment – a demi-nano-second – retirement didn't seem quite so appealing.

There was a knock on the door. "Come in Jack!" she trilled, rather more shrilly than she might have wanted.

The golden one made a hesitant, partial entrance. He didn't see Nyron Hughes sitting squashed into a corner behind the door.

"Shall I put my bollocks on the desk and just let you slap them?" he offered, not realising that Hughes had to suppress a whimper at the very thought. He came fully into the room now. "Look Jo I'm sorry but.... Oh! Oh I didn't realise you had company. Sorry. Hey look, I haven't done anything arrestable have I?"

Jo laughed. "This is Constable David Pugh. Our Community Liaison Officer."

Pugh/Hughes stood up and offered a hand. Jack took and gave as manly a shake as his much smaller palm could manage. He didn't recognise him at first.

"Nice to meet you," said the policeman, but he was really thinking: *Enchanting. Beautiful. Perfect. Want Want Want.*

Jo stopped smiling. She knew Love when she saw it, and she saw Constable Pugh's face aglow with the stuff.

"Jack darling, we've had a directive from our Beloved Master in County Hall – the Great One himself – that you should take this constable on your rounds for this afternoon at least, to let him see how this part of the department works."

Jack looked at Pugh – or shall we just call him Hughes, to save confusion? Hughes look at Jack. Jo looked at Hughes looking at Jack, and at Jack turning his gaze away from Hughes, and finding exquisite interest in the floor carpet, because he finally twigged where he had seen him before. "I saw you near Temple Bottom recently didn't I?" he said softly, in a way that made Hughes shiver. "You and your friends?"

"Not me, squire."

Jack felt uneasy. Jo sensed it and felt she had burble her way into this, for his sake:

"Is Pegasus ready? – or is it Bucephalus today? That van of yours seems like one of those Transformers my nephew used to love – a different thing every day."

Jack smiled and shrugged, unable to conceal his air of worry. In fact, he wasn't sure if the Library Van wasn't changing into the Wooden Horse of Troy at that moment, but felt himself thankful that disciplinary action which was due from the other day had somehow been deflected.

Jo saw them out. She almost felt sorry for Jack but intrigued also. When she had been summoned to the Director's office (highly unusual in itself) to meet 'Constable Pugh', she noticed the deference and almost fear the former had shown the latter; and when they parted company there had definitely been a 'funny handshake' of the sort her late father had used with his Masonic friends.

As the two men walked out to the yard where the vans were kept Jack couldn't help but observe: "Y'know, considering you're only here to liaise with the library service, and see how I deal with the little old ladies and their Large Print Romances, I'm surprised you're carrying a taser, expanding truncheon, handcuffs and pepper spray."

Hughes laughed. "Oh they always get around to asking me about my truncheon! Anyway, little old ladies can be lethal, believe you me. Is this your van? Who's BookBoy? What's a knobhead?"

Jack stroked the wing of the vehicle and told it they were going out again. He put his ear against the side as if listening to its reply, and nodded, as if he'd got one. Hughes was as charmed as Lilith had been. If Jack had ever wanted to become the filling in a sandwich, then those two would have been up for it.

"Are you really a policeman?" he asked, once they were under way.

"What a strange question!"

"Are you really a policeman?"

"I am what you see," said Hughes, and Jack knew for certain that he wasn't.

"What do you want from me?"

All sorts of words and images flashed through Hughes' mind, all of them homo-erotic and many of them involving buggery and fellatio. Like Yahya, but to an infinitely smaller degree, Hughes could travel in his own head across galaxies of perviness when put near someone like this. Even so, he had a job to do. So he pushed all these tempting images into a box and closed it firmly.

Rain started to fall in big droplets. "Just drive," he said, in a Power Voice.

*

Well at least Hughes got a chance to see the Wild Hunt in action that afternoon. But no, it was not a spectral group of huntsmen galloping across the skies to gather the recent dead, while thunder rolled and lightning flashed: it was the name Jack gave to the group of little old ladies waiting in the doorway of Lanstrope House, rainhoods and umbrellas at the ready, carrying their old books in carrier bags and just desperate to get aboard for their new supply.

"Neither rain nor hail nor dark of night will stop them," marvelled Jack, switching off the engine and lowering the rear so that the ramp could operate. "Nor hip replacements, cataracts, bad legs, and emphysema... I daresay your taser would only have a numbing effect."

"It's not a real taser," Hughes confessed. "Leastways, it's not charged up."

"Just as you're not a real policeman."

Hughes didn't have to reply: at that moment, as the doors opened, the women commanded all attentions, and ooohed when they saw the man in uniform.

"Here, show us yer truncheon sonny..." said one, thus confirming a prophecy. And before you could say Catherine Cookson or Betty Neels, the van was filled with half a dozen jostling women. (It was nearly always women, the men having died off years before.) They wanted things discharged and other things issued or reserved, and amid the babble for a moment, Hughes had a simple vision of another life. This was nothing to with reincarnation, or parallel lives. It was to do with wistfulness: a glimpse of a simpler world in which Mystic Orders and Sacred Lodges and Great White Brotherhoods either had no part, or didn't exist at all, and which revolved around good books and teapots, grandchildren, gossip and jumble sales. If Hughes had an anima at all, his was clearly that of a little old lady.

Why do we always say 'LITTLE old lady,' he mused, watching their banter with Jack, turning sideways to let them past, his body armour raked by a broadside of large bosoms in the process.

They finished. Went to the next stop. More of the same. Hughes was almost jealous. And if Jack couldn't sense that this strange man would have given many things to spend one hour naked in bed with him, he could at least sense that there was no immediate danger.

"Are you going to interrogate me?" Jack asked at the end of the final stop, in the grounds of a large nursing home at the edge of Trowbridge.

Normally Hughes would have played all sorts of verbal games and mind games, but he was in love. Really and truly.

"No," he said simply. "No I'm not."

The fact is, questioning of any sort was extremely difficult. The Severed Head of St John the Baptist was not even supposed to exist any more. Talking about it, except under exceptional circumstances, was forbidden. Even the planned and ultimately disastrous showing of it to the assembled Lodges and Orders, was done after exacting dreadful Oaths of Secrecy from all who attended. How could he ask Jack where it was? – and remember he still didn't know about the existence of Jenny Djinn. As far as he knew, the missing Head had something to do with this Lilith Love who had come over here to track down Real Templars. If Kali was loose within the world again, as the Grand Master feared, then it was surely Lilith Love who was the avatar.

"So you're not going to cuff me and put a hood over my head and subject me to White Sound?"

"Never in a month of Sundays!" Hughes exclaimed, making it sound granny-like, and reassuring. "Anyway, I'd use the Greatest Hits of Boney M if I had to do anything like that."

"So who are you really? And what's going on?"
How could he tell him! The whole thing was ridiculous, even if it did have global and even cosmic import.

"What's going on is that your American friend is having wild sex in Trowbridge Park with a Polish stranger."

Jack was not troubled. Perfidies like this never worried him. Had he been the marrying sort, he would quite happily have seen his wife go off with the entire 2nd Battalion, Parachute Regiment, and not felt the slightest twinge of jealousy or possessiveness.

"What's she done wrong? Why are you harassing her?"
"It's more a question of what she has."
"Which is what?"
"Why were you at the old Templar place?"

Ah! thought Jack, turning at the roundabout to go back down County Way, not realising that he was again within The Head's influence, radiating from its new home in the Old Mill. Ah ha! when it comes to conspiracies, then Templars poke their beards into everyone of them, somehow. He remembered that Virtual Reality preceptory on Lilith's PC, and also the Certain Reality vision he had had at that moment. He might have said something, but he suddenly had another of his wobblies, as his Mother thought of them. It sounds light-hearted, the term wobbly, but to be honest when you're driving a 7½ ton Library Van along a dual carriageway and suddenly find the 14th Century smashing against your windscreen like a rain squall then it's pretty damned serious.

Yet try to see it from the Templars' point of view this time, but let's press the pause button first: this is not past lives we're talking about. Jenny, Jack, Lilith and Hughes were not later reincarnations of that lonely bunch in the wilds of Wiltshire. It's just that sometimes you get things impacting on the ocean of Time, like a huge stone thrown into the water, which sends ripples out and out. Maybe the impact was originally caused by Yahya or maybe it was Yeshua, but these ripples were still expanding, still containing echoes of the impact, and affecting the most unlikely folk through the centuries. So the Templars' ripple was something like this....

*

John de Mohun was sitting in his bare room, at night, with the moonlight poking through his high window like a priest's finger. Somewhere outside he could hear the familiar noises of an owl, several dogs, at least two horses, and the wind in the trees. He was warm enough, the little fire in his room was still aglow and throwing off a small amount of welcome heat, yet inwardly he could not stop shivering. Energy seemed to be streaming out of his solar plexus, and any decent medium could have told him right off that this was a psychic chill he was experiencing, not a physical one.

He looked at the heavy bolted door of his sparsely furnished room – more of a cell, really – and it seemed to lose its shape, almost melting but not quite dissolving completely, like a heat-haze he might see quavering above the ground. Someone, or rather Something, was behind that door.

Stay in your bed! said the voice in his head quite firmly, but this wasn't the Sacred Head of St John the Baptist talking, but his own common sense, appealing to the little boy in him, which he sometimes wished he still was.

Get up and confront it! said another voice, which was the more adult and austere one coming from his sense of duty, reminding him that he was a Poor Knight of the Temple of Solomon, a supreme fighting man.

Now, John de Mohun didn't mind fighting the odd Saracen or three, or thirty three. After all, when he was in Outremer, he had gained the reputation of never asking how many enemies he was about to face, but only asking where exactly they were – and galloping straight in that direction. But this... this was unholy. The Sacred Signs they had daubed or even chiselled at crucial places within the preceptory had worked well so far: the demons which had assailed them at full of moon seemed to have been kept at bay. Surely then, whatever foul and fell creature lay behind his door must be more powerful than the others.

He mastered his breathing. Always a good thing to do before battle. Deep, slow and steady. He reminded himself of the words St Bernard wrote about the Templars: 'They go not impetuously and headlong into battle, but with care and foresight, peacefully, as the true children of Israel. But as soon as the fight has begun, then they

89

rush without delay on the foes, esteeming them but as sheep; and know no fear, even though they should be few, relying on the aid of the Lord of Sabaoth. Hence one of them has often put a thousand, and two of them ten thousand, to flight...' Breathe, slow and deep. He would face this menace from Hell as he had faced earthly things. Yet as he stealthily, using supreme courage, reached for his broadsword, sat up in his bed and put his bare feet to cold rush-strewn floor, he prayed to God that he might not meet that red-haired succubus they had all seen, and been sorely tempted by. He was not sure he could defeat that creature on his own.

The courage he had shown among the infidel was as nothing to that which he showed now, reaching for the catch, grabbing his sword more firmly, mastering his breathing and flinging the door open with the words: "Fundamenta ejus in montibus sanctis!" which a priest had told him would drive away devilish forces, though he didn't know what it meant, and didn't trust priests anyway, and had murdered at least two of them.

And evil there surely was, before him then: the head and shoulders of the young demon with long blonde hair, and the blue shirt with oblong device containing the demon's face yet again, and the talons raised as if to clutch. He sliced at it with his sword, trying his second incantation; "In nomine patris et fili et spiritus sancti!!!" and by God and all the Saints, the wraith was cleaved in twain, so that the blade curved forward and its tip smashed into the stone floor, sending up sparks, and at once the corridor beyond was again empty of anything but night, soothing night....

*

You can see what happened can't you? That was Jack he saw in the corridor. He saw him from the waist up, and the hands clutching, because that was how he would have seen him through the windscreen of the Library Van, the hands on the wheel, the ID badge and uniform. He didn't see the Library Van because his consciousness could not make sense of the whole vehicle, and so excluded it from the vision.

Of course the passenger in said Van knew nothing of all this. Hughes simply saw Jack jerk back, as if struck, his pale face going even paler before losing consciousness entirely and slumping in the driving seat.

"Bloody Hell!" said Hughes, who was actually quite good in emergencies like this. He undid his own seatbelt in a trice, leapt across and more or less sat on top of Jack, taking over the steering and sweeping his legs aside so he could operate the clutch, brake and accelerator, doing so with such skill that the traffic following probably wouldn't have noticed anything other than a mild waggle in the Van's motion. He pulled into the exit lane which led into Tesco's Superstore, drove into the far corner of the car park and stopped.

Jack was stirring. Colour was coming back, his face changing from a deathly puce into a faint and normal pink. His head was against Hughes' shoulder, sleeping like a lover, and the older man, thinking he'd never seen anyone so beautiful, looked all around to make sure they were not being observed, and he kissed Jack gently, on the crown of his head, and marvelled that he smelled like a baby. Moving back into the passenger seat again he waited until Jack roused himself, eyes opening with confusion, and then fear.

"What just happened?" Jack asked, having no knowledge. "I saw, like... a thin... vertical flash of light coming toward me and then...then... nothing. How did I get here?"

"Are you alright? That's the important thing."

Jack examined himself, blinked, squinted and nodded. "Thumping headache, but nothing more. Did you taser me or something? Have you drugged me?"

Hughes, who was now more in love than he had ever been in a love-filled life, shook his head. "I would never do anything to harm you," said this man who had sanctioned many killings.

And by God and all the Saints, he suddenly knew he meant it.

CHAPTER 6

It was around this was the time that Jenny Djinn began to go global, and it all happened with surprising speed. Felicity was later to style this the Time of the Annunciation, a term which was laughed at by Tasha and Shaz but which to their surprise was taken up by all those people who followed Jenny in later years, but never actually met her in her short lifetime.

Felicity of course, being what was once called Top Toff Totty, or the Trowbridge near-equivalent of such, knew people who knew People, and before long Jenny was invited onto Michael Jenkinson's chat show as *The Woman Who Did Deaths*. She was invited as the makeweight, the minging local yokel and lunatic who would make the audience feel better about themselves. As all historians would later comment, poor old Jenky never knew what hit him, and for the first time ever he got higher viewing figures than his bear-baiting rival, Jerry Springer.

"Should I go?" she asked Yahya as they sat on the old couch together, smoking filter cigarettes and watching *The Return of the King*, the third and final part of the *Lord of the Rings* trilogy. They were at the point where Aragorn bursts into the Great Hall crying "The beacons of Minas Tirith! The beacons are lit! Gondor calls for aid!"

Yahya didn't answer at first. His eyes were shining. He liked these fantasy type films. Perhaps when you always have access to All Knowledge and Ultimate Truth, a little bit of nonsense can be refreshing. In fact Jenny had once joked about getting him on Mastermind coz he could answer every question about every subject, and they had had a right laugh at the thought of his head in the contestants' big leather chair.

"Should I go on the telly?" she persisted, having seen *Return of the King* before.

"Sssh!" he said firmly out the side of his mouth, still smoking, concentrating on the action, at the point where the old king gathers himself, remembers his balls, and says majestically: "And Rohan will answer!" and then when the music soared and riders rode, Yahya spat out the cig, turned his eyes in lieu of turning his head and said simply: "Yes." Which is what she wanted to hear all along.

And so it began.

*

Oh gosh, people have replayed that episode a million times since. Well you can understand that. If Christians could have bought a recording of Jesus turning the water into wine at Cana, or raising Lazarus from the dead, then the queues would have stretched around continents. And no matter how much his cousin Yahya might have ranted in his secret rooms that it never happened like that, not really, not in that way – the bastard! it wouldn't have made any difference to the sales.

It was only a half hour show, late on a Friday night. It used to be a one hour special every Saturday at prime time, but Jenky, as the media called him, was fading fast. All the great celebrities had been done. All the great scandals unleashed. Besides which, the Great British Public preferred to go out and get hammered than sit at home and listen to old boilers struggling for cheap laughs.

There was only two guests before her: the usually sozzled actor Jasper Blound, who never made it to the top rank despite a rich voice which had given him a long career of 'almosts'; and Tippi Wendover ('Titty Tippi' or 'Bendover Wendover', as the tabloids called her) who was famous only for having been roasted by several Premier League footballers, and having nearly won *Celebrity Big Brother*.

Jenny Djinn and Felicity sat in the Green Room listening to what went before. Felicity was a bundle of nerves. Jenny Djinn was almost Buddha-like in her calm, finishing off her drink and laughing at the inane banter of Jenky as the host tried to get some 'sexual chemistry' going.

"I'm not sure what advice to give you," said Felicity, looking at her watch, almost dreading what might happen. Would the viewing public see the Trowbridge Trout? Or would they get a hint of Kali's Avatar? Either way, it could all go terribly wrong. She wasn't worried about herself: she did not want Jenny humiliated, flogged and then crucified.

A sweating man opened the door and beckoned Jenny to follow. She stood up and followed with what once would have been described as a stupid look on her face, but now seen as one of serenity.

Play the recording yourself: look at Jenky's smug and twattish expression as he introduced this simple woman from a small town in Wiltshire with the words:

"And my final guest is a young woman who has no qualifications of any sort, who has never had a job, claims never to have read more than three books in her life, and has until very recently always lived on benefits. Yet here she is now to tell us about her new career as a – believe it or not – Death Goddess! Ladies and Gentleman, a warm hand for Jenny Djinn…"

Then fast forward through more inane banter which followed, Jasper and Tippi apparently trying to score points for bitchiness, and to be honest it was easily done. Until she plugged into Kali and became Kali, then Jenny was still Jenny, not the brightest soul on the block, with no real verbal skills worth mentioning but an impressive level of calm.

"So, Jenny… or should I call you call you Goddess? or My Lady? or Your Holiness? – Hey stop sniggering out there!" Jenky said, barely suppressing sniggers himself. "Tell us something about your mission. We know you can kill people. You tell us you can kill people from any distance, quite legally – but what is your mission? Jasper… control yourself."

The camera focussed on Jenny. A close-up. She looked right into its lens, and in years to come people would swear they saw a change come over her, so that an average looking young woman suddenly became… beautiful.

"Well," she mused, "if my mission could be summed up in one word, then it would be FUN."

"Fun? Fun!?"

"Yeah. Fun. We've had bad press for too long, us Death Goddesses. I've come here to flash me knickers and maybe bring new… ooh, what's the word…. new metaphors for dying." It was The Head in her head that told her that word, and she knew it was a good one, and Felicity in the wings just glowed with pride. You could see Jenny getting into her stride then, and coming closer to Kali every second. "I think it's time the world knew how kind we are, us Death Goddesses, and not be afraid of Death, and have a bit of a laugh…"

Jasper Blound snorted. Whisky came back up through his nostrils and he wiped his nose on his sleeve. Jenky saw a chance to pull the trigger.

"You're not impressed, I gather. What do you make of this then?"

Close-up on the old ham, who was about to become more famous through dying than he ever was as an actor.

"I rather prefer my goddesses to have a bit of intelligence. I don't like to think the cosmos is being ruled by readers of the tabloid press."

Close-up on Jenny, who was not at all miffed. In fact, she looked at the old soak with huge compassion.

"Listen then, Jasper," she asked gently. "Would you like to try Death?"

Now if you're one of her followers, your DVD will probably be almost worn out by playing this moment. Jasper of course challenged her to proceed, to do her worst, to unleash her lightnings, to strike hard with might and main, using Shakespearian tones which had the audience in stitches. And all Jenny Djinn did was look at him with increasing love, with huge empathy, and thousands – maybe hundreds of thousands – of women later said they could see the mortal woman growing, developing a shimmering aura on screen which seemed like arms, arms which reached out and caressed, so that Jasper slumped in his plastic seat and onto the floor with a great and silly grin on his face.

Tippi started screaming.

Jenkinson called for help.

Felicity applauded wildly from the wings.

Two minutes later when the crash team burst onto the scene and failed to revive him, many people were hurt in the stampede to the exits, and the world knew for certain that Kali was among them once more.

"Good show, Jenky eh?" said Jenny Djinn to the ashen-faced compère, punching him gently in the ribs as she walked on out to her greater destiny.

*

Now the other main player in this drama, Lilith Love, had no idea that any of this was going on. To a large extent she had become an unwitting decoy, drawing all the attention of the Security Services away from Jenny Djinn and becoming increasingly maddened by the circumstances. Like those Templars who felt themselves haunted,

95

Lilith knew that there were, well... forces at work against her. They were outside the windows, listening, watching, menacing. Sometimes she felt like a ball in a pin-ball machine, being whacked all over the place, and dependent upon Jack – Marvellous Jack – for food, money, everything but sex. Though she wasn't gonna complain about that. In fact, she liked his strength in that respect. He was obviously testing her. Besides when she got in heat, as she often did, she had her rough Polack to satisfy those needs: up against a tree in the park, doggy fashion behind bushes. That would do for now.

Mind you, though she couldn't say it outright, she could cope with the Security Services – or whatever they were. She couldn't cope with Jack's mother. And the knowledge that Jack's late father had also had Down's Syndrome almost floored her.

Still, it wasn't even worthy of comment or explanation from Jack himself, and she refrained from prying. In fact he didn't seem to find anything unusual about it, and simply loved his overweight, illiterate, inarticulate, clumsy and slow-moving mother as any young man must. Jack was an enigma, and she loved enigmas. In odd ways, this was all wonderful!

So there they were, standing shoulder to shoulder looking out of his bedroom window at the ominous man leaning on the lamppost, so obviously watching the house.

"I agree Jack, it's not paranoia – it's all real. We are being watched and followed. Your phone is tapped. Your computer is being monitored. We are being controlled at every point."

Once, twice, Lilith had gone out to confront the watcher only to have him melt away before she arrived.

Jack had told her about 'Constable Pugh', and it was obvious to her that it was the same man who had ordered the rectal examination at Heathrow Airport. Pooling together their knowledge and actual experience they could link the Templars with the spooks from – they assumed – MI5, the passive co-operation at least of the local police, probably some Freemasons, and god knows who else in the Library Service.

"Let's Google 'conspiracy theories,'" she said, opening her laptop, brushing her left tit against his arm so that her nipples got hard, and she ached for the slightest erotic response from him. Nothing. He didn't seem to notice. She typed in those words and in 0.08 seconds got 410,000 hits. The first website which came up linked everything from Abraham Lincoln, through Marilyn Monroe, Pan Am Flight 103, The New World Order, Roswell and the Whitehouse Putsch.

"That's not much use to us."

"Try 'trowbridge and templars'" Jack suggested, and although she sort of snorted, they nevertheless got 4,150 hits, mainly listing the electrical and plumbing businesses at Templar Way, Swindon.

"Hold on, hold on...! What about that one?" he said, pointing to a site further down the page. She clicked on the link. It brought up a book on Amazon called *A Catalogue of Notable Middle Templars – with Brief Biographical Notes* by John Hutchinson, and showed an image of the page which referred in block capitals to: SEYMOUR, FRANCIS, first BARON SEYMOUR of TROWBRIDGE. About 1590—1664. Admitted 31 January, 1625-6.

Despite her horniness, despite her frustration with sharing a small room with Jack's idiot mom, she got excited. She was on the track of REAL Templars again. "Baron Seymour of Trowbridge, huh? Well let's see if this guy or his descendants are behind all this shit, huh?" She cracked her fingers and waved them above the laptop, about to show Jack how to Google as no gal had ever Googled before, and get them both out of this mess.

Poor, poor Lilith. Someone needed to save her from her Googling and pull her out of the conspiratorial maze that she and Jack were in danger of entering. A possible 'someone' with the knowledge of how to do it was Nyron Hughes, who was in a room not far from there observing everything she Googled, hearing everything she said, and viewing almost everything she did through one of the best and most minute spy-cameras ever made. As soon as she started to go down the turgid dead-end of Templar conspiracies, he became almost certain she knew nothing of the real thing, or of the missing Sacred Head.

He was just about to contact the Grand Master and tell him this when he got a call on his dedicated mobile from that very person.

"Hughes..." said the voice, leaving a long and angry gap after that first word. "Have you any idea what's going on. No don't interrupt! I mean, can you begin to guess the direction in which you should be looking? No? then you haven't watched the latest episode of *Jenky and Co*?"

"*Jenky and Co*!? I haven't watched that for donkey's years."

"Well let me give you a quick summary Hughes, and then you might see how... shall we say, exasperated, I am."

And he did: he told of the young woman from Trowbridge who believed she was Kali. The demonstration of her powers before 1.5 million viewers (which would rocket to 10 million during the repeat). Plus the Grand Master told Hughes that by putting two and two together, and making a couple of simple phone calls, he had found that the mortality rate for Trowbridge in the days leading up to that programme had gone ballistic.

"Oh fuck..." said Hughes, not sure yet whether he was worried by the Grand Master's ire, or the fact that Kali was loose within the world, and that he might be partly responsible.

"Stop fannying about with that American woman and the toy-boy. Forget them. Get the D Notices out. Spread the bird flu or swine flu or dog flu story. Track down that woman Jenny Gin – as in the drink – and find that Head. And don't scare it away this time."

He didn't say it, but from the older man's grave tone there was no mistaking the 'or else' at the end of the sentence.

"Bugger me," said Hughes, though for once that was the last thing he wanted.

*

It might be imagined in all this hurly-burly that the REAL Templars on the other side of the Time Divide were secondary to all this. The fact is, we could as well tell the story from their point of view as ours.

You don't need the Virtual Reality of Lilith's laptop: just use your imagination to see them around their Great Hall, the high windows open to the fresh air and sun, the simple tapestries (which would be worth fortunes today) rippling under the breezes and making the subjects of Mary Magdalen and John the Baptist shimmer with a strange sort of life. We can imagine the Templar brothers at the long wooden table, tucking into a healthy mid-day meal after a night of worries and a morning of weaponry. Their leader, de Mohun, wore the white mantle we associate with Templars. His two Sergeants, de Egle and de Hambledon, not being of noble birth, wore brown. The youngest, and something of a cuckoo in the nest, de Sautré, wore a new black mantle and his title was that of Draper.

You might think that a girly sort of role for a mighty Templar but in fact it was very highly regarded. As a chronicler wrote: "The Draper or the one who is in his place should studiously reflect and take care to have the reward of God in all the above-mentioned things, so that the eyes of the envious and evil-tongued cannot observe that the robes are too long or too short; but he should distribute them so that they fit those who must wear them, according to the size of each one." In other words, what with that power and his high-born relatives, and him only waiting to be accepted into the innermost heart of the Order by the English Grand Master himself, de Sautré was a right pain in the arse at times.

And if these men seemed worried, you have to believe that in that year when the whole Order was about to be outlawed, they had lots to worry about – quite apart from 21st Century visitations.

They were anxious. Kept looking over their shoulders at shadows. They kicked the dogs which lurked at their feet and under the table, gorging on scraps. They were cross toward the servants and tetchy with the stable-hands. Of course, they didn't have the global communication network available to Jack, Lilith and Jenny, but they were next to the Ridgeway, and the travellers along that were only too keen to bring gossip with as much frequency as Lilith would get emails and spam.

Meals were supposed to be in silence, but de Mohun relaxed the rule, and it was Robert de Sautré who sought to rally them by reading out – again – a copy of the famous missive by the Abbot of Clairvaux which extolled the Templar virtues. As the only one who could read, young Robert did so with solemn purpose, clearing his throat while the others respectfully bowed their heads to listen, thinking the 14th Century equivalent of what a posh twat he was.

"'They' – that is us, the Templars – 'live cheerfully and temperately together, without wives and children, and, that nothing may be wanting for evangelical perfection, without property, in one house, endeavouring to preserve the unity of the spirit in the bond of peace, so that one heart and one soul would appear to dwell in them all. They never sit idle, or go about gaping after news. When they are resting from warfare against the infidel, a thing which rarely occurs, not to eat the bread of idleness, they employ themselves in repairing their clothes and arms, or do something which the command of the Master or the common need enjoins.' Those are the words of St

Bernard himself. In these fell times, we need to remind ourselves of what we are."

"That's nice," said the brooding de Mohun. He turned and clapped once, like Jenny pointing her remote control, and the old man in the corner struck up a gentle tune on the lute.

The other two nodded – point taken – and stroked those long Templar beards which made them look like modern day Islamic fundamentalists. Young Robert would have done that too, but he had barely started shaving yet.

"I am pleased you reminded us, brother," said de Egle, feeling rather uneasy, as if St Bernard had seen right into their preceptory and was speaking to them personally. "And I will labour to achieve this. It is true we must not sit idly nor wait gaping for news. But the fact is there are no infidels around here to amuse ourselves upon. There is little contact with the rest of the Order, and our coffers are nigh empty since the plague."

Well that wasn't true. He'd only said it for the sake of Robert de Sautré, whom the others didn't trust. In fact, the coffers were heaving, as the three seniors had been on the fiddle for years, though they'd not yet spent any of it.

"I think we need relics," mused de Hambledon. "With relics, we can do great things." De Hambledon, whose compulsory beard had grown from his chin in pure ginger, contrasting ludicrously with the thinning blonde on his head, had chimed in so quickly that it was obvious the pair of them had been discussing it. "Aye, and if we have relics" he continued, "we can pay some locals to pretend to be crippled, and then get cured on touching them. Word would spread like lightning. Pilgrims would come by the cart-load."

Young de Sautré frowned. He felt the seniors were winding him up – which they were. You must understand that he was not quite a full Templar yet, and was awaiting his uncle, the Grand Master William de la More, to appear any day now and initiate him personally with all due ceremony. Had he been a bit more worldly, a bit less pompous, de Sautré might have guessed that the others really really didn't like him, thought him a bit of a prick, but had to tolerate him because of his connections.

Their leader, John de Mohun, was also the biggest and the most battle scarred. He was the Casal, the Commander of knights, houses and farms. The others all feared and hero-worshipped him in their own ways, which gave him a marked presence. He never had to say much. Privately, he missed his killing days, like a retired SAS soldier who had once been a fighting cock but now felt like a feather duster. After the fall of Acre, and certain rather shocking deeds of his own, he was finding it hard to adjust to this bleak, sheep-infested posting, and fuming about certain aspects of the Order to which he had sworn eternal allegiance.

"There is another possibility," said de Egle, and if de Mohun had looked up he would have seen the glint in his eyes and those of de Hambledon. There was a long pause. "Women," de Egle said at last, and de Sautré not only frowned again but twitched and squirmed at the same time. "It is said that the Order has Templar nuns at Muhlen and Barbera. In separate convents of course. And we could also appeal for donations. I know there is money in wool – large sums – but come on, brothers... women or sheep? Sheep or women? What are we?"

"Or we could just buy some peasant lasses and keep them in the east wing," said de Hambledon so forlornly that this had clearly been a recurrent pervy fantasy of his.

Even if you could see back in time to that room, you wouldn't have needed to be an expert in body language and non-verbal communication to see that two of the Templars at least were gagging for it. Nevertheless, although the Casal signified he was considering the idea by a slight sideways tilt of his large head, he simply carried on eating, very quietly, very fastidiously, and with enormous inward concentration.

The fact is, he was working on a Plan. It might cost him his life, but when you've seen your own friends slaughtered and then waded hip deep in Saracen bodies after taking revenge, such things had little fear for him. Besides, he needed to hurt the Order as it had hurt him, though he could never have confessed this to anyone.

He clapped again. The lutenist stopped playing and sat with bowed head, like a telly on stand-by. The man had had his tongue ripped out in a remote corner of Outremer and was about to flayed when de Mohun had arrived. Not only was he mute, he was utterly loyal to his Master, and still had the head of the infidel who had deprived him of his tongue, though of course this head had no magical powers, but simply rotted next to his bed.

"Brother de Sautré…" de Mohun said at length. "You have some important relatives, and one of them high indeed within the Order."

All eyes were upon the youngest man. He blushed, and nodded.

"Then I want you to do certain things for me…"

"Anything sire," said the boy-man a little too hastily.

*

Now most people in England, when they upset the Establishment, have their local vicars snipe at them in the local press, but in a very short space of time, Jenny Djinn was blasted by the Archbishop of Canterbury, the Prime Minister of India, the new Pope (who vaguely accused her of killing the old one), the Home Secretary, the Crown Prosecution Service and the Lord Chancellor, the directors of international insurance companies and numerous Trades Union bosses, not to mention the Lord God of Hosts, who wrote thundering letters from an address in Oldham. The Dalai Lama sent his good wishes.

What a dilemma for the authorities! If they acknowledged that she did have the powers of a Death Goddess, they would thus affirm that she was Kali. Absurd! When the police visited they saw what she did with two photographs, and actually provided her with a cast-iron alibi when the news of the relevant death came through. She hadn't left the room, and two police constables had been present at that time. Despite their best efforts they were unable to find any accomplices who may have committed the killing, and in fact the coroner in every instance recorded a verdict of Death by Natural Causes – with a very big smile on each corpse's face. So they couldn't go to court because a successful conviction would depend upon them accepting that she was, in fact, Kali.

In fact, the police left her alone very quickly, feeling out their depth, and telling the CEOs of the insurance companies that the ball was in their court. However, history would record that two Trowbridge policewomen were among Jenny Djinn's first disciples.

With increasing speed, her fan mail and requests for Death came in sackloads, which were filtered through by what some wag termed her High Priestesses: Tasha, Shaz and Felicity. At first they conscientiously read every one, but as the volume of mail grew they just dipped a hand in and took out letters at random. Despite suggestions, Jenny refused to have a website, and rejected the idea of an email address. "If they can't be bothered to write a good old fashioned letter, then they don't deserve my service," she said firmly, which seemed reasonable enough. Her only stipulation was that she didn't do children. She didn't do anyone with children under the age of 18. And she needed two recent photographs. That was all.

The volume of letters addressed *Jenny Djinn, Death Goddess, Trowbridge*, was astonishing. So very many people needed the medicine of Death, and if any were terminally ill then she would do it free of charge. It didn't seem to take any vital force from her: far from it, she got a mild high.

And amid all that mountain of mail she would get, once a week, a letter in a brown envelope addressed to Jenny Grey at her old flat, the only mail she had ever got in that previous life of hers, these being hospital appointments to see Dr McHaffee at his clinic in Bath. She smiled when she saw them, and shredded them personally. She was not ill any more. The Head had cured her. Being a Death Goddess was the healthiest time of her life.

It was not only mail which deluged them at the Old Mill... there was a trickle of people – largely women – that became a stream, a river, and then a broad tidal wave that had the power to sweep everything and everyone aside, like the Severn Bore. There were a few men, too, but by and large (with a few exceptions) they were pervy individuals who just wanted to get in amongst the totty, and were easily weeded out. It all happened so fast, but fortunately Tasha and Shaz seemed to know exactly what do: carefully selected guards on the massive security doors. CCTV cameras to keep an eye on potential intruders and the massed ranks of the press. Strict personal vetting procedures before anyone was allowed into the Old Mill, except for dear old Mrs Loganathan and the others at the Indian take-away, whose curries had unwittingly become part of this new temple's ritual.

Those allowed to meet Jenny did so on the fourth floor after being told how to act, what perfumes or aftershave to wear, and how to behave. The whole inaccessible-guru thing in fact. But no-one – not even a 'High Priestess' – was allowed onto the fifth floor where, unbeknownst to them, The Head lived quite happily watching BBC, for the most part. It/He loved cooking programmes in particular, though a good Western would get the vote every time.

It was inevitable that one man, who had no interest in Death but who had once been very influential in the life of Jenny Grey, should eventually make his appearance.

The four women were having a kind of business meeting at the time. Jenny had just given release to a young but big property developer of unpleasant habits whose wife was particularly grateful. Jenny just sat there at the long table quite happily reading the telly supplement to see what films might be on for her and Yahya, while Shaz outlined her business plans for Kali Inc. Photos of future 'service users' were spread out like tarot cards, for Jenny to look at when she was ready.

"Y'see, the way I figure it, we gotta go global. We've already got two properties in Knightsbridge thanks to the Widow Goldberg, and a prime one in Paris thanks to that very grateful Widower Monaghan. Plus we got this lovely building here thanks to Felicity. And while it's temptin' to go eastward and seek more customers in France, say, you gotta compare this to the general weakness of the Euro at present as opposed to the strength of the dollar."

Felicity blinked. She had to remind herself that beneath the thicko accent, and that despite the complete lack of qualifications, Shaz was a very shrewd woman indeed.

"Absolutely," said Tasha. "So what we mean is..."

"What you mean is," interrupted Felicity, "is 'Go west young man!' You mean America don't you? And all the sad people there who need Kali more than anyone."

Jenny had risen from the table and walked around the room, licking the curry from her fingers and then drying them with a napkin. She looked out of the arched windows toward the park, and the footbridge across the dual carriageway where her mission had begun.

"What I think we also need," added Tasha, "is a more marked corporate image. I've ordered a fleet of seven Citroëns, top of the range, bright red, each one with a cute Dancing Kali mascot."

"Plus we also ordered these dead good red uniforms for any of the girls who wants to chauffeur us." Shaz passed around some photos of the outfit.

"They'll look like ninjas," said Felicity, but only Jenny Djinn knew what a ninja was, and that was because of the telly she watched.

"We'll have the *Daily Telegraph* onto us, calling us all Dykes of Death, or something."

"Fuck them," said Shaz, who until recently had never read more than the Star, but was now devouring the *Financial Times*. "Tasha's right though. I mean, I know the t-shirts we're working on now are cute, and that we're giving lots of old ladies in Trowbridge some good work knitting the four-armed Kali sweaters, but we need to go up-market a bit. A lot."

"What do you think, Jenny?" asked Felicity.

Jenny had her forehead against the glass. It was cool and moist. She could feel the vibrations from the rest of the building. Then her heart surged when she saw Jack's library van coming along County Way, and she was reminded that she also had another life, in which love figured prominently. She would go to see him soon, and invite him around. Maybe Yahya would like him?

Usually when she asked such questions in her head, she would hear Yahya's voice giving a firm reply, but this time there was only silence. So she took that as a possible Yes.

The other three came to join her at the window and looked out upon the world that they were changing.

"Here...!" said Shaz, not dropping her aitches so much since Felicity had arrived, and peering into a corner of the park. "Lookit them two! Hey, cumman look!!"

They all clustered around and looked. There in the distance was a woman with long red hair, bent over and holding onto a tree, being shafted from behind by a young man with his trousers around his ankles, both of imagining that no-one else could see. It was Lilith of course, though none of them knew her.

Suddenly they became rude and feisty Trowbridge lasses again and it was like they were back in The Old Malt the night a male strippagram had appeared. It was Jenny who started first, so they all felt able to let rip accordingly.

"They're like cats in heat. Go on, get stuck in!"

"Go for it!"

"Faster, faster!"

"Look at his arse go!"

"Get her tits out! Grab 'em!"

"Slap them buttocks!"

On and on, wilder and wilder. Lilith couldn't hear them of course: the double-glazed security glass and the sound of traffic between stopped any chance of that. But the girls roared their lungs out anyway. They were all horny too, you see. When word had spread locally that they could bring legal death to just about anyone, then potential shags sort of faded away. And Felicity was right: in due course the *Daily Telegraph* (among others) would run articles about Thugs, Assassins and Trowbridge Dykes and let the readers draw their own conclusions.

So it was in the midst of this ruckus that they got a call on what they termed the BatPhone, only to be used for something important. The receptionist, a recent convert who had been freed from an abusive father and thus enriched by Jenny, felt this one merited a response.

"It's from someone called McHaffee. He's waiting outside. Would like to see you."

Tasha and Shaz looked at their leader, trying to read her face.

"Come on, let's go down and inspect the troops," said Tasha, putting her arms around the two others and guiding them toward the door.

"Who's McHaffee?" asked Felicity blithely as they walked down the stairs.

"It's her old doctor. Thought she was done with all that."

"Is she ill?" Felicity persisted.

"Not that sort of doctor" Shaz answered archly, though it was clear she would say nothing more.

*

McHaffee was a man just above middle age, and the sort of blue-eyes which might once have been piercing but now looked quite watery. He was clean-shaven and well groomed, with long greying hair swept back over his collar, an immaculate dark suit and tie, and rather scruffy black shoes.

He came into the large office and looked around the entire room first, and then sort of spiralled his gaze inward to focus on Jenny, who was standing next to the window.

"Hello Jenny. It's been too long, you know that."

Jenny smiled.

"Like my new home? Better than my old flat off Binyarn Street, eh?"

"I admit... it's a very strange place you're in now, Jenny." That was an old habit of his: always adding her name in every sentence, as if to exercise social skills or else remind her of who she was.

"Never expected this did you? Not of me."

He looked at the photos on the desk. Shifted some of them around with his middle finger. Picked up the little red plastic statue of Kali and examined it.

"You're looking very well, actually Jenny. Have the scars healed?"

She pulled her wrists into her sleeves. Like de Mohun, whose scars were caused by battles of a different kind, she didn't like people to dwell on these. "Press the head and its arms waggle."

He pressed the toy Kali's head and the arms did a jig.

"So who are you now, Jenny?"

"I'm Kali. You know I'm Kali."

He gave what was an affectionate smile which some might think meant *Oh Yeah?* but Jenny herself read as saying *Oh... Yes!* McHaffee put the little plastic Kali back on the desk.

"How wonderfully strange you are Jenny. Really. But why Kali? What has an ancient goddess from the Indian sub-continent got to do with a young woman from Trowbridge?"

Jenny blinked. She did that thing beneath her brain which took her up just one notch from mere Jenny Djinn. Not into the full-on Kali mode, you understand, but more into a Jenny-plus.

"Kali is universal. She's like... like the air we breathe. All of us. Everywhere. Not just in India. Anyway, that Jesus... what's a Jew from Palestine got to do with folk from Trowbridge?"

"Touché," he said, his eyes widening. She never used to talk like this.

"If you don't like the name Kali why don't I call myself Carly. C. A. R. L. Y. Would that be more English for you? Carly Djinn. Makes me sound like a pop star, eh?"

Pursing his lips he asked: "Jenny Grey, do you have power of death over me? Would you kill me?"

"Do you want to die?"

She looked at him, and into him. The poor sod seemed so weary that her heart went out to him, though she made sure to keep her four arms folded and the Kali power in check.

"Erm no, actually," he said at last, his eyes brightening as if he had remembered something or someone which was making it all worthwhile.

"Ah Hah! You've got a new girlfriend! You have, haven't you?"

The good doctor smiled. His tone warmed. "You always were uncannily perceptive weren't you? Have you got a boyfriend?"

"Yes I have. His name is Jack Hobbes. He is drop-dead gorgeous!"

"So you have your Shiva. Will you bring the world to an end? That's what Shiva and Kali do, you know."

She toyed with the photos, putting the edges together, making them into a tau cross. "Yeah. Maybe. Maybe I will. Sometimes I think the whole world has had enough, and needs releasing too."

"Jenny, can I ask you who these people are? Why have you got these photos?"

"Customers. They need release. You would call it death, but I know it's release."

"Have they hurt you?"

"Hell no. Never met them."

"How do you release them?"

"By loving them. By sending them on to a better place. That's why they've all got a smile on their faces. I'm doing them a favour, though they don't realise it at the time."

"Do they haunt you afterward?"

"No. No ghosts."

"Do you hear their voices in your head?"

"No, never any voices, never!"

"Jenny, come away with me."

"Never."

"I can help you. It seems like an age since I saw you."

"That's because it was another age. All is different now. This is the Age of Kali. Everybody knows that. This is my time."

They shared glances: he looked away first.

"There is a place in Bath for you, when you're ready. It's called Tigh Aisling, which means House of Dreams. It's run by me for people like yourself."

"What... more Death Goddesses? There's only one, Doctor, there's only one like me."

Her face shone; he couldn't look at her. Troubled, unnerved, he turned and went, and Jenny pranged on the head of the plastic Kali until it broke in two.

*

If Dr McHaffee didn't know what to make of it all, then Felicity did. Felicity, you see, right from the start, was determined to do for Jenny what St Paul did for Jesus: create a whole new religion for her. It was she who created the famed and iconic logo which depicted Kali with her four arms, and which the established Churches took as a direct challenge to their hallowed crucifix. As she was to tell the assembled members of the press in later years: "Jenny Djinn believed that this is the true Age of Kali. She also believed – knew – that Hell is actually here, on earth. This is Hell, all around us. She also believed that flesh was corrupt, and real life began when you returned to the spirit. Indeed she told me once: 'Who knows if life be death, and if death be life,' and she did more than enough to prove this to us all."

Well that was bollocks, as Shaz and Tasha could have told you, had they survived. Jenny never said anything of the sort. She didn't speak like that, even under the full flow of the Kali. Felicity, the daughter of an England cricketer, was just putting her own spin – and a very strong spin it was – on her whole experience. But there ye go, she was determined to write the Eternal Book of Kali and oversee its chapters of revelation.

Mind you, more sober commentators or observers would insist that the moment when the Head spoke and gave Jenny her revelation actually was the true start of the Kali Yuga, in those parts of Wiltshire at least. Yuga, as Mrs Loganathan could have told you, is just a Sanskrit word for Age. Dr McHaffee knew that too. In the heady hippified days of his youth, in-between tokes, they used to say that *Hey man, you never know an Age is ended until, like, the new one is under way.* They had to say that didn't they, when most of them were so smashed that they never knew what day it was, never mind what Yuga.

But sometimes the great revelations really are only glimpsed in hindsight, more usually when you're very old and sitting in a high-backed plastic chair and the incontinence pad under your bum becomes pleasantly warm, and the nursing assistants smile at you

109

like seraphs and hurry on by. It's the sort of revelation which is tempered with the thought: *If only I'd realised then...* Which is usually followed by the admission: *I actually knew, but I never did anything about it...* Had we seized our own moments, as Jenny had done on the bridge near Tesco's, we could all have become deities, divas, rock stars, captains of industry, or at very least managed to catch our partner humping the local moron in good time to forge a major and beneficial divorce settlement. So there is a Kali within all of us, and a Shiva too. Jenny just happened to seize her moment, and take us all with her.

*

Jack stood next to Lilith Love before the cash-point on Fore Street, and watched her put one of her credit cards into the slot. To her delight, her astonishment and her relief, it was recognised and accepted, and after a trembling-fingered request for an on-screen balance, she quickly saw that her money was untouched.

"I was right Jacko Baby," she said, on the verge of whoopin' and hollerin'. "I just knew it. They've gone. I'm telling you they've gone. We've won, Jack, we have won!"

And then she did let rip with a whoop and holler, but this being Trowbridge, no-one thought she was anything other than a binge-drinker on the razzle, so no-one turned a head. Jack, being a modest sort, was a little embarrassed by the display. Yet he was relieved too, though he couldn't have said what they had won, or who they had defeated, or even how.

Lilith was suddenly aware that one helpless phase in her life had finally ended, and that her power was back. It was not quite like the Kali Yuga, even though the days when she and Jack had been spied upon, listened to, and followed had begun to feel like an Age.

She dived into her pocketbook to get her phone. Seconds later she was having a delirious babble with her agent, who had been having kittens at the strange things that had been going on, and the inability to make contact.

"What a story this will make!" she purred down the phone, while turning to give the finger to some leering Polish lads, one of whom had come to know certain parts of her quite well, if hurriedly.

So there was no dramatic thunderclap or lightning flash to announce that her own Age had ended, just that surge of excitement at the cash machine, and later the almost peaceful feeling of release when there were no longer watchers outside the Hobbes' house, or lurking at every corner.

Lilith finished babbling and burbling. Her agent was relieved and delighted and somewhat amazed: she had never heard her famous client so human before. Didn't understand half of what she was saying, so indiscreetly in the middle of Trowbridge's main street, but the fact that she was alive and well and likely to go bringing in that 10% was all that mattered.

"'Bliss it was in that dawn to be alive,'" she quoted. "'But to be.. goddamned fucking rich again... were very Heaven.' Was that your William Blake?"

"I think you'll find it's Wordsworth."

Oh she just LOVED him even more at that simple response. He was just wrapped up in knowledge like a mummy in its bandages. She wouldn't even check it later on Google. She just had to have him now. Right now.

"Jack," she said, almost conspiratorially. "Where is the best hotel in town?"

*

You might imagine that Dr McHaffee had a lot to think about when he left the woman he still thought of as Jenny Grey. But all that went out of his mind as he sat in his car in Roundstone car park, put the keys in the ignition and suddenly found the passenger door opened and a strange man bursting in. It was Hughes of course. No uniform this time, but a great sense of urgency.

"You're in no danger," said Hughes. "Don't be afraid."

The fact is, it happened so quickly, and the man looked so – well, intelligent – that he didn't have time to go into panic mode.

"CID," Hughes continued, flashing a badge. "We need your help."

McHaffee had the sort of guilt surge that innocent people get when they go through Customs. "Has someone complained about me?" he asked, mentally scanning all the difficult patients on his lists, all the mental aberrations, and all the permutations of accusation. It wouldn't be the first time this had happened.

111

"No. We want to ask you about the woman you've just visited. Calls herself Jenny Djinn."

"Has she been saying fantastical things about me? This is what she does, you know. Her real name is–"

"Jenny Grey. We know that." Hughes beckoned out of the window and Spoffo walked over, carrying a thick buff-coloured file.

"That's from my office! How did you get that!? That's mine. That is highly confidential!"

"Not to us. Now I suggest you drive somewhere nice – Southwick Country Park maybe, there's a nice café there – and we'll go through this together." Leaning out of the window, he told the other: "Stay near the Mill and keep watch. Let me know if anyone new appears."

"Aye aye surr!" said Spoffo, with a pirate's burr, and Hughes was sure there was a deliberate hint of a piss-taking mince about his gait as he started to walk off. He might have said something but a nearby car horn sounded loudly and continuously. It was coming from a brand-new silver Mercedes parked almost opposite, where the driver had suddenly slumped against the steering wheel.

"Stay here," said Hughes to McHaffee, and the two other men went over to investigate. It was what they feared. The driver was stone dead.

"Biggest grin I've ever seen," said Spoffo.

McHaffee, being a doctor and filled with oaths about this sort of thing, came over and did the doctorly things needed in these circumstances, but there was no helping the driver of the Merc; rigor mortis was setting in with unusual speed.

"I know this man," he said to Hughes, his brow furrowed and his face troubled.

"A friend?"

"No, but I saw his photograph in Jenny Grey's office."

The faces of the two younger men were as delighted as McHaffee's was dismayed.

"Let's you and me go for that nice cuppa tea somewhere, we'll look through this file and chat, eh? Spoffo, phone an ambulance for this poor old rich git here."

*

112

If Hughes was getting excited by the progress he was making, Lilith was becoming increasingly frustrated and bewildered by her complete lack of progress in seducing Jack. She had taken a taxi to the Manor Grove Hotel on the outskirts of Trowbridge, had another frisson of delight when her credit card was accepted again, booked a large room with double bed and then almost pushed him into the door in her excitement. In her imagination they were always gonna fuck like beasts, but with True Love and Romance squeezed in there too, between the impacts.

As she hungrily peeled his clothes off and then stood before him as she slowly removed hers, he sat on the edge of the bed and seemed more interested in the latest issue of the *Wiltshire Times* with the blaring headline 'Flu Hits Trowbridge'.

"Jack..." she said sadly. "Is there something wrong? Are you too scared? I'm told I can be too pushy, or predatory. We can take this slowly, just hug okay? Or maybe I've read this all wrong, and you're gay? Are you gay?"

"No, I'm not gay," he sighed.

The small fact is, Jack was a little embarrassed. He had never done this sort of thing before, and didn't feel easy being naked. But the greater fact is that he had no libido whatsoever. Not for women, not for men. He wasn't gay, nor was he straight. Nor were there any dark techniques or tastes which might arouse desire of any sort. There aren't too many individuals like that, but they do exist, and he was one of them. He really was an angel-boy wasn't he?

"Listen Jack, last year I was voted Hottest Female Celeb in two men's magazines and three women's. I've been Ass of the Year, Rear of the Year, and won the Terrific Tits award in *Horn* magazine. Thousands of guys get off at the mere thought of sitting where you're sitting now."

"I'm sorry," he said. "It's just... oh, so many things in my head. But you look very nice though. Really, very lovely."

He looked so goddamned... pure... that she stopped bristling and hissing. Her claws went in and her cold heart melted. She had never been with a cherubim before, and that's what he looked like just then with his pale and perfect skin, the halo of tumbling golden hair.

"Look... what say we just get into the sack and talk, huh? Just talk?"

"That would be nice," he said, folding the newspaper neatly and creeping shyly between the cool sheets next to her.

*

It might have been nice for Jack Hobbes, but the Grand Master, Porteous, was pulling his hair out. Literally. From his nose and ears. Standing in the luxurious bathroom of the Grand Lodge. It helped take his attention from the utter chaos that had descended upon his world since The Head had gone walkabout – if anything without legs could go walkabout, that is. "What the hell have you got yourself into, Perry," he said to himself in the mirror, uttering the name that few others knew. "If they knew, if they only knew what I have to go through, what I really have to go through."

As we've seen, it was supposed to have been one of the great moments in the Secret History of the world but had all fallen apart when Hughes had opened the Sacred Casket to reveal that bloody electric kettle. His own ancient and hitherto venerable Order had been made to look stupid before the assembled Magi, not to mention 'They of the Ennead'. These were the nine beings who really ruled the world, and who came to him in his sleep, in dark places, at unexpected times, and made all his body-hairs stand on end, though he had never yet glimpsed them unrobed, or even seen their eyes, or knew where they went when they were not manifesting.

By and large the members of the Eastern Orders, 'They of the Himalayas', as they were known, had shown great patience and even sympathy, and gone back home with no hard words, except for the Japanese who became so obsessed with the kettle that they had stolen it. The Western Orders, however, his own kith and kin, had wiped the floor with him and were taking the piss behind his back even now.

And then there was K'tan Shui, the rather scary being whom everyone believed to be from another planet, although he had been staying in private accommodation out at RAF Colerne for the past year or so, and if you or Lilith had wanted to find more about that arcanum then you might start with: http://www.ufos-aliens.co.uk/cosmicrudloe.html. From his skin colouring, facial angles and black hair, he could pass for a very hefty Mexican: broad shoulders, narrow waist, stout thighs and big biceps, with an

114

apparent regard for the concept of 'face'. That is to say he didn't like being disrespected. Not only was his body shape odd, he habitually wore dark glasses, though young Spoffo swore that he had seen him remove them once, and that the pupils were those of a goat. Electrical equipment went haywire whenever he walked past.

Porteous cleared the bathroom mirror of mist and looked himself in the eyes, his very human eyes. It was a look that had reduced neophytes and probationers to quivering wrecks in the past, but seemed little more than just a grimace now.

It was funny: here he was in touch with Powers, yet he stood there powerless. He had come up through the Rosicrucians, taken all the Masonic initiations of the English and Scottish rites, been a force within the neo-Templar and Martinist Orders and, as a young man working for MI5 and even more secret organisations, had helped fake the Prieuré de Sion for his French brethren – and then gone on to subvert more cranks and cults than you could shake a trowel at. But if you were to ask him what the meaning of life was, then at this moment in time, he knew fuck-all. If it hadn't been for The Head, the glimpse and experience of that marvellous talking object with such antic powers, then he might have given it all up as a rather silly dressing-up pursuit years ago, and taken up landscape gardening instead.

He closed his eyes and opened them. Behind in, in the mirror, stood three of the Ennead, from the kick-ass lower end of the spectrum. They seemed to shimmer as usual, and fixing his gaze on any of them was like looking through that glass darkly that literature goes on about.

We need to talk, said voices in his head.

With sinking heart, he turned and made his way toward the innermost sanctum.

*

They had just finished the one of the dance classes on the middle floor of the Mill. The dozen or so women lolled around exhausted, but very pleased. Some of them quite liked being part of a twosome and making the Four-armed Goddess. There was lots of lesbo-eroticism loose in the building on these occasions. Mind you, it was not so much a mill as a temple by this time. It was every bit as sacred to the newcomers as the marbled innermost sanctum was to Porteous, and those followers who fancied they knew something about Kali had decorated it using the sacred Kali-colours of white and black on the walls, with gasps of peacock feathers and clusters of hematite in the four corners, supposedly representing courage, death, rebirth and change. What with all that and the red costumes of the women, it was the wildest place in Trowbridge – at least, the only rival to The Ship Inn during Happy Hour.

Each dance was started by Felicity, and if they were lucky Jenny Djinn would join in, then everyone dropped what they were doing and before you could say 'Tango Hustle', the room was aflame with rippling women. If she didn't join in, and went up to her room to commune with – as they imagined – Cosmic Forces, Felicity would give the remaining faithful some right philosophical tosh, so much so that Shaz had to go elsewhere and twiddle her nose rings in frustration.

Ha... when Jenny did join in was it simply because she loved old films like *Dirty Dancing*, *Grease* and *Saturday Night Fever*. In any case, dancing was never the forté of Trowbridge Man at the best of times, so this was a rare chance to have a bit of girly fun of the sort she had never had when she was girly. And if Felicity could have seen Jenny Djinn in her holy of holies, watching *The Big Easy* with Yahya on her lap, her hand on either side of his head, or stroking his brow, she might have felt really stupid, or really scared.

So when she wasn't sucking up to her Beloved, as she termed her, Felicity was teaching the newcomers with statements like: "Kali is the uncompromising mother of death. Her name means 'Time'. It can also mean 'Time heals all wounds'. She reminds us that good really can come of bad situations, and is here to dance courage into our lives at our request."

Puke puke puke, went Shaz behind her back, but maybe that wasn't really fair: Felicity's insight into Jenny-as-Kali was a lot closer to the truth than Shaz's memories of Jenny Grey as she became Jenny Djinn.

"Right, come on gels!" cried Felicity, her voice echoing in the huge room. "Shoulders back and chins up. Bow to the east and float to the south. Rise to the West and flutter to the north. Keep those tums in. Squeeze those pelvic floor muscles. Call on Kali for assistance by your own sacred dance. Listen to the sound of the flute. Move the energy around in your personal space as you bravely dance the dance of life and change. Remember that afterward, you must leave Kali an offering of honey and flowers and thank her for dancing with you, and for reordering the chaos in your life. Do this until the situation you want changed in your life has actually changed. Which it will. So dance gels, dance!"

"*Darnce*, my arse," muttered Shaz. "She gets on my tits."

To her concern, Tasha said nothing. In fact Tasha quite liked it all, really. And doing the two-backed beast dance with Felicity had made her breathless for reasons that had nothing to do with exertion. Sure, it had been quite a turn-on, though she had hardly admitted to herself, yet, never mind her best pal.

Mind you, when Jenny came down from the Upper Room, as Felicity named it, and wanted information, one great advantage of being a goddess incarnate was that she didn't need to Google it, didn't need to phone directory enquiries at an exorbitant rate, or wade through the appropriate books in the library. No, all she needed to do was say something like: "I want you to find out where Jack Hobbes lives," and any number of followers would leap up and do all the work for her. She could have asked The Head of course, but felt that she didn't want to make him jealous.

So she came downstairs when the film ended and said exactly that, no more than that, and you'd have had to have been Tasha or Shaz to realise how commanding she was these days, with such a strong voice and great certainty. Possibly this was because her death toll by this time was into the hundreds, so it was like notches on the heavenly gateposts and her own self-esteem rising like mercury. As one of her sweaty red-clad minions sneaked out the back of the Mill to find out, making her way behind the gathered press and the wanna-be disciples and the fundamentalist protesters, Jenny Djinn beckoned Felicity over.

"Now tell me about Shiva..." she demanded of Felicity, because the younger woman had being doing a great deal of research in this area, none of it involving directory enquiries.

Jenny had no idea that Jack was in perpetual danger of being seduced by Lilith Love of course, and the fact is she would not have worried even had she known. Jack was hers. She knew that in her holy bones. Plus she still kept the library ticket he had made, keeping it as precious as any religious relic. Some day soon she would introduce him to Yahya. Some day soon, she and Jack would get married.

"Shiva?" said Felicity delighted, deeply in love in a pure sort of way. "Shiva is known to have untamed passion, which leads him to extremes of behaviour. He wears a cobra necklace which represents his power of destruction and recreation. The snake sheds its skin to make way for new, smooth skin. Kali incites Shiva to dangerous and destructive behaviour that threatens the stability of the universe, and they dance together so wildly the world is threatened. Shiva traditionally calms Kali and... calms... her."

Felicity chickened out there. She should have said that Shiva traditionally calms Kali and defeats her, but felt that wouldn't have pleased her mistress at all.

"Okay!" said the Trowbridge avatar of Black Mother Time, looking forward to Jack's untamed passion. The fact is, goddess or not, watching that horny romantic film with Yahya on her lap reminded her that whatever his other virtues, he lacked a cock, couldn't fuck – except with her mind – and that she herself was suddenly desperate for it.

To get to the point, the panting minion soon came back not only with Jack's home address, which was easily found by asking a friend at the library, but also with a complete list of the Mobile Library's stops and times which can be found in the main library itself or on its website. As most historians now agree, this was the information which hastened us all just that little bit further into the Yuga.

*

Lilith Love was in her room at the Manor Grove Hotel doing what she did best: she was Googling and writing. Writing her journal and research notes in a state of post-coital calm after having dismissed the Polish sex-machine – though not before paying him quite handsomely for his services this time. Having been more than happy to do it for nothing, the young man went on his way in a state of bliss, so glad he had come to this country and met this mad native woman as he imagined she was.

"Goot. Bye," he said at the bedroom door, practicing his very weak English.

"Beat it," she said without looking up. So he did, and his pals waiting outside applauded when they saw his small bundle of tenners, and told him this was so much better than state benefits, and could they have a piece of the action too.

Now make no mistake, Lilith was still as much in love with Jack as ever, though she didn't begin to understand what was going on inside him. Unlike Jenny however, Lilith did have some insight into herself as Sekhmet, though she had not – not as yet – touched upon The Head's powers in that respect, or even knew The Head existed.

So she Googled up Sekhmet's mate and got the name Ptah. There was nothing particularly esoteric about doing this: it was no more than looking up your partner's star sign and seeing if they might be compatible. There had to be some reason for her being with Jack, and some explanation for him being the way he was. So she saw that Ptah was described as a god of creation and rebirth, craftsmen, artisans and artists, designers, builders, architects, masons, and metal workers. He was the master architect of the universe, and the patron of all Freemasons. Later on he represented the three aspects of the universe: creation, stability, and death, and was usually depicted as a man with a punt beard, wrapped up like a mummy, but with his hands free which grip a great staff made up of the symbols for life, stability, and power.

"Aha, Freemasons!" she muttered, feeling that she was onto something. "I knew they were in there somewhere..." Plus that was Jack to a T, wrapped up himself just like Ptah, yet reaching out a hand to offer her life, stability, and even more power than she had known until now. Then she also thought: Pity about his mom, though. Yet she was glad his dad had died: she couldn't have coped with two idiots as in-laws.

You're clutching at straws darling... you could telepath into Lilith's head, but she would never hear you. If anyone was wrapped up in herself it was Lilith Love. Besides, her book was coming along greeeeat! Far from being warned off by the Security Services, it was all priceless material for the story. She was gonna outdo that phoney Whitely Strieber and do for Templars – REAL Templars – what he had done for his equally phony Grey Men.

She phoned Jack on his Library Van. In between stops at the time, he used the hands-free to answer.

"Jack here. Probably the greatest Mobile Library manager in the history of the world. Can I help you?"

"Listen," she said without preamble or introduction, "what more do you know about Templars near Trowbridge? I mean we didn't get anywhere with that Seymour connection, did we?"

Jack paused and reflected. Well he had to because a gurt big convoy of army vehicles including armoured cars and a tank transporter was making its way across town, and he had to pull across to let them all squeeze past. He didn't want to have the side of his lovely Van defaced any more, and didn't want his knuckles rapped by the Lorry Lord Keith, who felt the pain personally when any of his vehicles got scratched. In that small silence, Lilith found something else to love about him. He really is just like Ptah, she thought, though you'd be stretched to see any connections yourself. Then again, you wouldn't be obsessing about Jack as she was.

"Yes, there are some places associated with them. There's Temple Meads train station in Bristol, but I don't think there's anything left to see there except some medieval sandwiches in the buffet. Templecombe, down in Somerset where they found a painting of a bearded head – but that's quite far. The best place near here is Cley Hill, I reckon, which is right next to the hamlet known as Temple. The hill is supposed to be hollow with a golden ram buried inside it. I've got a book on the van about this. And other myths." (This of course was the same little tome that Jenny had borrowed right at the start of our tale, little knowing what significance it might hold.) "Oh, and not too long ago, Cley Hill was reputed to be the most UFO-visited spot in Britain."

"Ah, that's a crock of shit," Lilith muttered, typing as she listened. Mind you if she'd Googled 'cley hill ufo' she would have got about 210 instant hits. On the other hand, if she had done 'cley hill templars' she'd have got about 591. However, she was busy Googling 'templars freemasonry' instead, and got 518,000 hits which would keep her happy for at a little while yet, and give her at least three chapters in the book she was planning. Despite her scorn, if she had actually been in the Library Van with Jack at that moment, she'd have agreed completely that the next visitor he got, down a quiet street in nearby Bradford on Avon, really wasn't human at all; and if he wasn't actually a flying object, he was certainly unidentifiable as anything from this planet...

The van rocked on its suspension as if either one very fat reader or a couple of sprightly slender ones had leapt on through the automatic door at once. The fact that it was only one person, and a person of medium height, though somewhat wider at the shoulder than normal, made it seem as if the individual in question was composed of very dense matter indeed.

That was the first alien give-away. The second was that all the electrical equipment flashed and fizzled and then just expired. The terminal went black. The radio, set permanently on Radio Five Live, cut out. Even the battery-operated clock and Jack's own wrist watch stopped ticking. Third, there was the peculiar and indefinable odour about the being (well, you could hardly call it a man) which, much later, a journalist quoted Jack as saying was the whiff of sulphur, though Jack had said nothing of the sort. Fourth, Jack had just been reading a book on synchronicity by Fiona Fleming, so it was almost inevitable that after mentioning UFOs someone like this should come aboard. And fifth, he was wearing wrap-around shades on a grey day, and the sort of very expensive suit which, in the context of Trowbridge, marked him right off as coming from another planet.

"Can I help you sir?" asked Jack brightly, and you have to give him credit. He really never felt much in the way of fear. Either because he was the boldest man on the planet or because, as his enemies said, he was too damned stupid to know danger when he came near it. "Fiction or non-fiction. Large print or ordinary print. Romances, Adventures, Thrillers, or some healthy Murders."

The being – who was K'tan Shui of course – said nothing, just looked slowly around as if doing the psychic equivalent of sniffing. Jack noticed that his trousers were baggy at the crutch, as if there was nothing there – like when women wear men's trousers. Earth women and Earth men, that is.

"Or if you have some degree of visual impairment, we've got a decent selection of Talking Books in either CD or cassette format."

K'tan Shui said nothing. Mind you, Porteous had never heard him talk either. The fact is the poor sod could have been telepathing away furiously, but no-one was picking him up. Then he – let's be kind and not call him 'it' – then he did what he had often done to get a reaction: he went right up to Jack, face within inches, and took off his shades and opened his eyes wide.

"Hmmm," said Jack, studying the goat-like pupils without flinching. "Now you're not a native-born Wiltshire lad are you?"

Joking apart, our earthling became just a teensy bit agitated at this point. Not afraid in the ordinary sense, but sort of frissoned if there's such a word. Here was something – or someone – highly unusual, possibly dangerous, yet in context of all the bizarre things happening lately, it was almost to be expected.

The alien put both arms out, palms facing each other, and put them at either side of Jack's head, but without touching.

"Aha! You're going for the Vulcan mind-meld are you?"

Again, nothing was said, and in fact nothing was actually felt on Jack's part, other than his hair standing on end as if he had been touching one of those Van de Graaff generators they had played with at school. If anything passed from Jack to the alien, or from the alien to Jack, it was certainly not perceptible on his part.

K'tan Shui replaced his shades, tapped an odd rhythm with his stubby fingers on the counter and gave a huge smile. Still without uttering a word or sound, he leapt off the back of the van which then rocked hugely on its suspension, causing some Talking Books to be flung from their shelves.

Trying to see which way he went, Jack looked out on an empty street. Not a soul in any direction. As he climbed back aboard, knowing that he had a crate of books to be issued for the next stop, he felt a sudden pang of real sadness: K'tan Shui had reminded him of his dad.

There was a noise. The library terminal was booting up again. The van lights came on. The clock and his watch started ticking. At that very moment, the on-board phone rang. It was Jo.

"Jack… where are you this time?"

"I'm at Frobisher Grove, oh Precious One."

"Well you should be at Marlowe Copse. They're waiting for you."

"But I'm not due there yet."

"Jack, sweetheart, you're an hour overdue. It's 3 o'clock. Are you okay? I mean, really. What have you been up to this time?"

Jack was sooooo pleased. This was the *Missing Time* that was often involved in alien encounters. It had seemed like two minutes, but a whole hour had passed! Now if Lilith had been there and been affected the same way, she might have Googled her way to: http://www.pararesearchers.org/index.php?/20080804511/Alien-Contact-Abduction/Missing-Time.html. Or Jack could have beaten her to it by reaching for the book Missing Time, by Budd Hopkins, which he'd only recent taken on board the van. But he was dealing with his beloved boss Jo and so needed another strategy. Actually, he was about to be elastic with the truth but then thought he'd simply tell her exactly what happened.

"Actually my Beloved Leader, Chugger of Thunder and She Who Must Be Obeyed... I've just had an alien being on board. I'm telling you the truth. He had vertical pupils."

There was a silence at the other end. Jo, whose time to retirement was imminent, lived in the daily state of bliss that Buddha must have felt when he was verging on Nirvana.

"I thought I was the only carbon-based life-form in this area. Bah! Did you remember to mark him in your People Counting file as a new visitor on your van?"

"No, but I will. He was very heavy."

"Then count him as two. Did you enroll him in the library system, give him a nice new card, and record him as a New Reader in your file?"

"I think there might have been trouble doing that Jo. There wee lots of details I couldn't have filled in. I'm not sure what the post-code is for the Horse Nebula."

"That would be BA14 8BS – same as for the Libraries and Heritage Service. Quite a few humanoids there, I've found."

"Then what about his ethnic group? I mean, it lists White British, Afro-Caribbean, Asian and the rest, but there's nothing for trans-galactics."

"What a simple boy you are. Obviously you should use 'Any Other Mixed Background'."

"Language then?"

"Hmmm... tricky one that. Was he – or it – from outside this solar system. Was he from beyond Pluto?"

"Totally."

"Then put him down as Welsh."

"Gosh Batman, I failed you didn't I?"

"You failed the whole Service, grasshopper. You let him get away," said Jo with a voice of infinite sadness. "That could have been a whole new market for the Wiltshire Libraries."

"Sorry Jo... Hey but have you been around town upsetting everybody again? There's tons of Army trucks and tanks all over the place."

"I may have had a few pre-retirement altercations with some silly people in County Hall, and was somewhat tetchy in the electrical section of H. J. Knees, but I don't think the army is down to me this time. I think it's something to do with this bird-flu we keep hearing about. It's all happening around that old mill building near Tesco. So come back the other way. If indeed you can be bothered to come back, now that you've gone interstellar."

"Bye then, Jo. I'm on my way to Marlow Copse now.."

And so, unbeknownst to him, was Jenny Djinn.

And Lilith Love.

And Nyron Hughes.

*

This was the moment when they began to think that Jenny could teleport herself, and also use death-rays. It happened like this.

They were all on the penultimate floor of the Mill watching the army put up huge metal barriers that had once seen service in Northern Ireland. They did this after clearing away all the gathering crowds, sweeping them away like insects under the broom.

"They shutting us in!" cried Shaz with concern.

No, said the voice of Yahya in Jenny's head. *They're protecting us*, he said in a voice of infinite sadness, though she was still too naïve to pick up on that.

"No, they're protecting us," she repeated out loud. "Don't be afraid."

And because she said that, and was so calm herself, none of them were afraid. Though it was possibly a good job for Jenny that they never asked awkward questions, because on her own she couldn't have answered them. They looked up. A Chinook helicopter was hovering low and dangling on cables a massive steel gate that would fit down neatly into the encirclement of walls.

"It's like a prison," said Shaz.

"No," said Felicity, taking her cue from Jenny, "It's like a fortress."
Which it was.

The army engineers worked with enormous speed and before you could say *ablanathanalba* the mill was neatly surrounded on all sides by a daunting steel barrier some 15 feet high.

"Makes me feel proud to be British," said Jenny quite seriously, but some of the girls thought she was being ironic and chuckled accordingly. That was another bonus to being powerful: everyone laughed at your jokes, no matter how weak they were. No-one had ever laughed at Jenny's jokes before. Now, she was a hoot.

"But what's going on in the woods over there?" asked Tasha, who always stood very close to Felicity these days. There was clearly some feverish activity involving camouflage nets and officers and large pieces of equipment.

"Probably their command centre," said Felicity with authority, as if she'd been encircled by steel walls on a regular basis.

Shaz, who stopped herself from sneering, then had a brilliant idea! "Jenny, why doncher do that thing with the trees, like you did next to the bandstand that time, remember?"

Do it, said The Head in Jenny's head.

"Okay!" she said brightly and the rest of the women – the Apostles as they thought of themselves – had a chance to see their leader in action. Not that there was much to see, just Jenny with a smile on her face looking across at the trees and becoming Kali, loving them, adoring them for their style and shape and shade, and giving them the chance to go home...

*

It wasn't only the women around who watched her closely: Jenny was standing before the large window in plain view, studied closely through half a dozen pairs of binoculars from the edges of the trees.

"Is that a shimmer?" asked a lieutenant colonel.

"No I think she's just shaking her tits, sir" said a helpful major.

"Let's see those supernumerary arms, darling," muttered a green hat from the Intelligence Corps.

But they stopped looking then because, one by one and with enormous speed, the trees around started dying. The leaves fell first, shrivelling as if in flames. The trunks darkened and cracked. Branches started to break and plunge to the ground.

"She's got a Death Ray!" said the green hat, who had been reading too many classified documents. And with those words they all fled from the woods, fled for their lives, though truth was they were in no danger at all except from falling timber.

The next time they looked across at the mill through their binoculars, Jenny was missing, though all the rest of the women were still there, some of them waving.

Jenny, meanwhile, was walking quite happily behind the colonel and his men, toward Jack's next stop. The colonel noticed her, and did a double-take.

"How the bloody hell did she get there!" he snarled, though he was under strict instructions not to make any contact with her under any circumstances.

"Perhaps she teleported," said the Intelligence officer a little too loudly, so that some of the ordinary engineers heard and spread the news among their mates like wildfire.

The fact is, he wasn't a very intelligent Intelligence officer or he'd have known of the existence of an old service tunnel from the basement of the mill to a small corrugated iron hut well beyond the wall of this instant compound. Hughes and his lot knew, but their brief was to observe, to wait, and above all not to act until they could be absolutely sure they had The Head back in safe-keeping. That was all they wanted. They were quite happy – more than quite happy – to see Jenny go walkabout like this.

A few people recognised her. None of them really had the nerve to approach. Would you approach a Death Goddess if you saw her walking along the street? Plus the few who started to follow her were discreetly shooed off by Hughes and his gang. Hughes of course, to blend in with the military types that were swarming in this area of Trowbridge, was wearing the appropriate kit. It didn't make him blend in at all, to be honest, but that didn't matter too much: the braid was irresistible.

"Excuse me. Sir," Spoffo said when they paused at a junction to let Jenny get further ahead, "Can I ask why you're wearing the uniform of the First Sea Lord? There's no sea and no sailors within 50 miles."

"Operational necessity, lad. Just scoot over to the other side of the street and watch where she goes. Now!"

Just then, when they turned the corner and saw that their target was headed toward the Library Van, Hughes almost gave a whoop of delight. He just knew Jack was involved after all!

"You're all a-quiver. Sir," said Spoffo softly.

"Piss off," said Hughes, who was almost brushed aside by the woman whose rectal examination he had approved and supervised at Heathrow Airport but who, in her urgency to reach Jack's van, paid no heed to anything or anyone in her path.

"Lovely arse. Sir," said Spoffo, who had observed it on camera many times.

Hughes nodded, thinking of Jack.

Spoffo gave a big grin and melted into the scenery....

CHAPTER 7

De Mohun was a very happy man at that same moment, which was some 700 years before, if you look at it in linear terms. He had spent long hours in his cell, carving. It was a skill he had perfected in various lonely outposts in Outremer, waiting for the next attack by Saracens, trying to focus his mind. Here at Temple Rockley, he had even carved on the door of the chapel the Templar seal of two knights on one horse, which has excited all sorts of interpretation since, involving: poverty and dedication, union of higher and lower selves, heaven and earth, good and evil, or plain and simple buggery getting you where you want to go in life – such as you might find in the showers at Eton. So now he carved and carved and happily carved, and no-one had seen him so content for a long time.

The others thought he was praying, or doing some private penance. The simple fact was that he was carving a head. Life sized. Shaped rather like his own. When it was finished he planned to use real hair to make it as life-like as possible. He carved with great skill and economy, hardly making a noise, using the trusty knife which had taken many lives – not all of them infidels – and various other tools. At the end of the day he would burn the waste on his little fire, looking at the flames and the fire-caves among the logs, as if trying to remote-view in his own way.

You see, there was one secret that would not have surprised Lilith Love in the least, and shown her to be more aware of REAL Templars than the englamoured reading public might have been happy to accept: John de Mohun was a nutter.

There were all sorts of secret rituals within the Order of the Poor Knights of the Temple of Solomon. Rituals involving Sacred Heads (lots of them) and Sacred Whores, imparting Secret Knowledge of the true world. Jack himself had already provided Lilith with a key book which quoted Etienne de Troyes, and which pissed her off somewhat because she couldn't find the same reference via Google. The quote read as follows:

...and at the prime of night they brought a head, a priest carrying it, preceded by two brothers with two large wax candles upon a silver candelabra, and he (the priest) put it upon the altar upon two cushions on a certain tapestry of silk, and the head was, as it

seemed to him, flesh from the crown to the shape of the neck with the hairs of a dog without any gold or silver covering, indeed a face of flesh, and it seemed to him very bluish in colour and stained, with a beard having a mixture of white and black hairs similar to the beards of some Templars. And the Visitor (Hugues de Piraud) stood up, saying to all, 'We must proceed, adore it and make homage to it, which helps us and does not abandon us', and then all went with great reverence and made homage to it and adored that head.

Fact: our Templar had actually known Etienne de Troyes, who had made a token appearance at Acre and waved his sword a couple of times, kacked his pants, then went back to mummy and further advancement in the Order. De Mohun had heard about this ceremony from a number of his better-heeled peers, but the fact is no-one above had ever asked him to join the party. Then when folk below him like the loyal de Egle and de Hambledon assumed he was privy to these dread and awe-ful Mysteries and asked awkward questions, he had to narrow his eyes and look enigmatic. They would be dead impressed because he looked so wise, when really he just wanted to kill somebody.

Quite simply the Grand Master, Grand Prior and Prior didn't ask him to join in because the man was unstable. Look... glimpsing the severed head of John the Baptist would be enough to send a normal person questioning his own sanity. So imagine the effect it would have had upon de Mohun! Had he lived today, he'd have been branded a psychopath, too dangerous even for the armed forces; and if he hadn't been sectioned at a high-security mental hospital like Rampton or somewhere similar, he'd have become one of those freaky Survivalists, living alone in the woods and eating wild dogs and lone travellers, waiting for the End Time while getting heavily into self-abuse. That's the sort of Templar he was.

He sat on the floor of his cell next to the fire, leaning back against the wall, legs stretched out among the shavings, the wooden head in his lap, the last rays of sunlight coming in through the high window while he chiselled, gouged and carved out the nostrils, making them deep enough to take actual nasal hairs. He was prouder of this artefact than almost anything in his life for many years. He thought it was brilliant, and actually it was, it would have got into any art gallery today and women like Lilith Love would spend large sums of money for it. He carved with all of his concentration and all of his skill, feeling that somehow the eyes of the world were upon him – which in some ways they were: 700 years away, at that exact moment, the Japanese were still remote viewing him through the glass of the (by now Sacred) kettle. Though it was lucky he didn't know that or it might have flipped him completely, coz the last thing you want is a mad Templar on the loose with a sharp knife in his hand.

Poor de Mohun... After those unpleasant events before the final siege of Acre in which he had slaughtered a whole community of non-combatant infidels while suffering from what we would now call Post-Traumatic Stress Disorder, he clearly needed help. He needed the love of a good woman, or at very least just a bit of understanding and acceptance from the innermost Order. All he did get from them was a succession of priests. The Order sent you to see priests as nowadays a doctor might send you to see a psychotherapist. Everyone of them had been afraid of him. Everyone had been despised by him. "Priests?" he had once exclaimed, roaring. "Priests throw us into massacres. They give us a bread and cheese then send us into the fray where we are pierced by barbs. They cut up the bodies of martyrs and sell the bits for profit." Which was all true enough, as the world now knows, but it wasn't the sort of thing you said out loud in those days unless you were 6'4" and were one of the finest fighting men of the day. Which de Mohun was.

But now at least as he gouged and carved, and made exquisite nasal passages and was about to start on the ear canals, he took huge comfort in the fact that he had a Plan and one which made him whole again, and would heal his own very troubled head. He just needed a lot of hair and a bit of information from de Sautré.

De Mohun stood up and gathered the wood shavings into a neat pile then threw them onto the fire, feeling that with this waste he was getting rid of at least some of the bad memories which haunted him on a daily basis – haunted him far more than the recent ghosts they had all seen and fought with. The flames damped momentarily and then surged. As he looked at the bald wooden head which was propped in the corner, the flickering light made it seem as if the eyelids were moving in deep and dreaming sleep.

"I have a plan," he whispered to the wall, and curled up on his bed like a little boy.

*

The next morning was a cracking one: pure blue skies, a gentle breeze, a sun that would warm the cockles of an Inquisitor's heart. De Mohun was out there before anyone, shirt off and exercising with his broadsword against one of the four man-size wooden crucifixes that were fixed in the yard. Despite what it may have looked like to passers-by, this was not for any sacrilegious reason to do with Templar anti-Christian heresies, but merely because they represented the human figure and were easy to make, and easy to chop at, and oh so easy to pretend they were real foes.

Chop, slice, slash. Chop slash slice. Thrust, chop, slice. His muscles were corded from the effort, his skin lathered with sweat. In the morning light, he seemed to glisten. Some of the servants loved to watch him when he did this, peeking carefully so as not to be seen and thrashed. He really was being watched just as much as Lilith and Jack had been, though from many different levels.

Young de Sautré was out there next, running almost frantically from his own quarters, seemingly desperate to emulate and creep up to his hero, never twigging that de Mohun's position there on that remote spot atop the Marlborough Downs was a punishment and not a promotion.

"Master," he said, bowing briefly before attacking his own crucifix with young verve and vigour; no-one observing from the 21st Century would have missed the homoerotic overtones of his attitude.

"Don't call me Master. Did you sleep well?"

"I did sire."

"Demons?"

"Not last night sire."

"Don't call me sire."

"Yes si…. Yes."

"Did you write and send that letter?"

"I did. Boy Kent went on my own horse. He will be there tomorrow, God willing."

"God willing!" barked de Mohun, who had his own stories behind that phrase. "Now hit the thing! Don't tickle it!! That's a boss-eyed Arab with chancres on his lips attacking your sister and mother, and hoping to have your arse on a platter. Keep your elbow up. Put your weight behind it. Now slash!"

De Sautré slashed. He slashed so hard that his blade took the top piece clean off, and his impetus made him topple to one side, landing in the dust at the Master's feet.

"That'll do for a start," said de Mohun, though whether he meant the sword blow or the sent letter was debatable. He had noticed a young serving girl with long dark hair, which was exactly what he wanted. "Keep at that until you can no longer lift the sword," he ordered, and off he went to get some scissors.

*

Back in Trowbridge, it was something of an historic moment when Jenny, followed by Nyron Hughes, followed by Lilith Love, converged on the Library Van like priestesses and priest toward their Holy of Holies. The sequence went like this:

Jenny Djinn climbed on board first, pausing only at the door to look in her pocket and get out her library card in which she had inordinate pride, and which Felicity was later to turn into a Holy Relic.

Hughes had followed her closely, but lurked to one side of the van's doorway, out of sight but within hearing. Mind you, it was difficult to lurk with effect when he was wearing the dress uniform of an Admiral of the Fleet, so it was hardly surprising that while he was trying to peer in through the darkened rear window, Lilith Love sneaked up on him from behind.

She knew him at once. It was her business to be aware of people, and she had had sailors on her show before: Admiral Yamamoto, John Paul Jones, and Admiral Nelson with Lady Hamilton in tow. All actors, sure, but she worked with essences and could see right through the costumes, and so she recognised Hughes immediately.

"Oh. My. God," she said. "Well if it ain't Mr... what shall I call you? Everyman? You put me in cuffs! You here to shine a light up my ass again?"

He tried to shush her but she wouldn't have it. She was in a right mood and didn't care who heard. In fact everyone on board the van heard, and that included: Jack, Jenny Djinn, Mrs Prothero, Mr Floy, Mrs Spirt, Miss Cheyne-Flixon, Dotty, and Ms Roniard in her wheelchair. The collective age of this lot was 412 years, given that Jack's remit was to provide services for the elderly. A selection of heads poked around the door to see what was going on.

"Come on board!" said Dotty, who stubbornly refused to be called anything else. "We've got this mad woman from the telly. She's a scream. She's gonna get shot of my old man. Well if she doesn't, I'll take an axe to him meself!"

Jenny Djinn beamed at him. "God, it's like that German film. The one where they're all in the submarine. What's called again?"

"*Das Boot*," said Jack and she beamed even more, and knew beyond doubt that they were so well matched. "Oh my clever Jack, my little Shiva…" Jenny sighed, and a few faces were pulled at that but no-one said anything.

As for Hughes, he was completely compromised. It was pointless trying to run. He and Lilith squeezed aboard the van, edging past the wheelchair. Lilith hadn't a clue who this woman was putting out for her Jack because she hadn't been watching the telly, or trawling Google News.

"Did you shine a light up her arse?" asked Mr Floy, who had been on Convoy PQ17 during the Second World War and lived to tell the tale many times since.

"He sure did!" boomed Lilith, still furious but enjoying herself also. "I reckon he was trying to find the Holy Grail."

"What's up his arse I wonder?" asked Mrs Prothero, looking him up and looking him down.

"His head!" said Lilith promptly, and they all laughed, though there was a flicker of uneasiness from both Jenny Djinn and Nyron Hughes himself.

"Ooh, I do like your uniform Captain. Nice eyelashes too," said Miss Cheyne-Flixon, running a finger up his arm. "I met my first husband at the submarine pens in Portsmouth."

"I met mine at the pig pens near Bradford Leigh," came Mrs Spirt.

Only Ms Roniard in the wheelchair was quiet, though she smiled at everyone almost insanely.

Hughes, meanwhile, stood there feeling like a complete twat, wondering what to do next and still gasping at the sheer beauty of Jack Hobbes.

Surprisingly enough, it was Jenny who took command of this situation. She'd had enough practice at the art of command since moving into the mill and gathering her followers around her. She was also increasingly confident of her powers. "What's wrong with your legs?" she asked Ms Roniard.

The woman was glad not to be ignored, glad that someone – at last – wasn't pretending there was nothing wrong, and that the wheelchair didn't exist. "Oh... I'm just dead from the waist down, me. Strong arms, like. Have to be to move this soddin' chair. But useless down there. Dead."

Jenny Djinn looked long and hard. She was waiting for a voice in her head from The Head, but none came, and to her own surprise she knew that she didn't need it this time. "I deal with dead things."

Years later Felicity (who wasn't there), would describe this moment as akin to the world holding its breath, waiting for something to begin or something to end. What happened next, you see, was astonishing.

"I can make anything die," said Jenny Djinn, who was even now reaching inside her head to become Kali, and it seemed to the rest of them that Jack had switched on extra lights within the van because the interior now glowed. Coming from anyone else, that might have sounded sinister, chilling, but remember that Kali is also a love goddess when looked at cosmically. They all felt warm and safe, especially Ms Roniard. "I can even make death die..."

And she did that thing with the dead legs that she normally did with living flesh and – bloody hell fires! – you could see the withered flesh beneath the skirt filling out, you could almost hear it, like milk on Rice Krispies, and everyone gasped, and Ms Roniard's face had tears trickling down, and then she stood up – Hughes trying to help her at first but getting shoved away – and she pushed the chair back and teetered. She teetered and swayed, but she stood there, getting stronger and stronger and the inside of the van brighter and brighter so that even Spoffo, who was waiting and sneering outside, poked his head in and gawped.

Ms Roniard pulled at the catches which made the thing fold up, lifted her chair off the ground and walked, then with her strong arms, threw it out the back door. Turning around to Jenny Djinn she bowed, and the rest of them did too, even Lilith Love. Well what else could they have done? You don't see miracles on the streets of Trowbridge too often, and this was a miracle, no doubt about it.

"Now," said Jenny Djinn, who was coming down from being Kali, "I'd like this sailor to stay, and this Yank, and my Jack of course. The rest of you go, and go well."

They did, they did go well. Very well. They couldn't wait to spread the word. And although Ms Roniard was a teensy bit wobbly and had to helped by Spoffo, she didn't need the powered wheelchair lift this time, or ever would again.

The remaining three, the chosen ones, looked at this strange being with astonishment, wondering what awesome message, what revelation or miracle, she was about to share with them.

"You know what?" she asked. "I'm going to invite you all around for Sunday tea…"

*

Porteous was in a bad way. He stood robed and barefoot on the black and white tiled floor, under the ceiling of stars, within the walls of eyes, utterly and completely alone in Grand Lodge. In the past he had felt so powerful in this sacred place, controlling the rites, intoning the Words of Power, invoking the Nine. Now he just felt that everything was slipping away. It was only when they had lost the bloody kettle that they realised its value. And above all, he had lost The Head, and was now losing his own head.

You shouldn't feel sorry for him though. If there was one perception that Lilith Love would have shared with de Mohun it was this: When you eventually get access to the innermost circle of any mystic order, and meet those who communicate directly with those Beings who many suppose rule this world, then you'll find that the Masters, Grand Masters and Supreme Grand Holy Masters are just as much tosspots as the rest of us, with as many quirks, as many fears and as many weaknesses; plus the same might be said about the bulk of the innerworld Beings too. They might be angels (or demons!) with powerful and persuasive language, but they're not necessarily smart.

"Fact," as Lilith Love would say. "They might be mighty Adepts but they can also be jerks too. Think of them as jerks first. Deal with it, okay!"

He hadn't got to that point yet, though. He knew that whatever else, The Head was something weird and real and uncannily holy, and had been kept by his Order for an exceedingly long time. He didn't want to go down in the archives as The Grand Master Who Lost It.

There was a side of him which just wanted to go back to his cozy house in Surrey, mow the lawns, play a little golf, and watch the clouds drift over a clear sky. Yet here he was, in some danger of bringing civilisation to an end.

"Bugger, bugger, bugger," he said, in that holiest of lodges.

*

Lilith Love was also alone, in her olde room in the olde hotel, but working furiously. She did this when she was angry or distressed. She would do her thousand words a day, everyday, as a sort of discipline to keep her mind off more human things. Had she allowed herself to peek into the deepest recess, she would have admitted that she was fuming about that Jenny Djinn woman. She was fuming because she knew she was a shyster, knew now that she was in love with Jack too, even calling him Shiva, can you believe, before going on to do that ridiculous trick with Ms Whatever.

Now you might say that Lilith had just seen a Miracle On The Library Van, and that must have altered her attitude. Well... yes and no. Remember that in her TV shows, she had made people rise from the dead so she could analyse them. She had dissed Gandhi, Churchill, the Duke of Windsor and turned Mrs Simpson inside out. Actors all, sure, but how did anyone know that Ms Roniard wasn't of that ilk? That was her take on it all. So Lilith was not too impressed by the miracle; this Jenny Djinn woman just another act, and Ms Roniard just a shill.

What was Lilith working at? Well, she was Googling 'Shiva'. Typing in that single word she got 9,150,000 responses in 0.16 seconds. Of course she was dipping in to find the definition or explanation which most suited her. The first one she looked at said: 'Shiva is responsible for change both in the form of death and destruction and in the positive sense of the shedding of old habits. In Satyam, Shivam, Sundaram or Truth, Goodness and Beauty, Shiva also represents the most essential goodness.' This one really annoyed her, mainly because she felt it rather too close to how she saw Jack herself. She also noted from the same source that: 'Shiva is conceived in his unborn, invisible form as the Lingam. It is always accompanied by the Yoni, which is the female principle, surrounding the base of the Lingam. The Lingam represents the male creative energy of Shiva.' In other words Jack was a big prick. No, she didn't go along with that website at all! Another one noted: 'He is the destroyer and the restorer, the great ascetic and the symbol of sensuality, the benevolent herdsman of souls and the wrathful avenger.'

"Hedging their bets or what!" she growled. "He is Ptah, the creator. No more, no less," she hissed, rubbing her Sekhmet talisman.

"Whadda these guys know!"

Well you know that this was all displaced. You don't need a degree in psychology to guess that she was deeply disturbed by this sudden appearance of this utterly bizarre Jenny Djinn woman who was promising to be a bigger cult that she, Lilith Love, could ever be. Lilith got the US ratings, sure, but Jenny Djinn seemed to getting the worship, and looked as if she was gonna go global!

"Kali? For Chrissake..."

She looked at her watch, took a deep breath, closed down Google and carried on her piece about the REAL Templars. Blocking out all thoughts of what had happened in the Library Van, she looked at her print-out of the famous charges that had been levelled against the Templars at their trials.

Amongst the charges were the following:

1. That on the admission of a new member of the order, after having taken the oath of obedience, he was obliged to deny Christ, and to spit, and sometimes also to trample, upon the cross;
2. That they then received the kiss of the Templar, who officiated as receiver, on the mouth, and afterwards were obliged to kiss him *in ano*, on the navel, and sometimes on the generative member;
3. That, in despite of the Saviour, they sometimes worshipped a cat, which appeared amongst them in their secret conclave;
4. That they practised unnatural vice together;

5. That they had idols in their different provinces; in the form of a head, having sometimes three faces, sometimes two, or only one, and sometimes a bare skull, which they called their saviour, and believed its influence to be exerted in making them rich, and in making flowers grow and the earth germinate; and

6. That they always wore about their bodies a cord which had been rubbed against the head, and which served for their protection.

There were more, but she looked at her own first words on the subject that went: 'At his trial Jacques de Molay denied the famous charge of buggery but admitted that of heresy. Why? Conviction for heresy would bring on the most awful torture. Conviction for buggery would bring a slap on the wrist and a few Hail Marys. Why did he say this?' But really, Lilith's thoughts below the words went like this:

Why did that dark-haired bitch invite three specific people for tea? What was that naval guy up to? What kinda cult was this place in the tacky building? What was the chance of getting this weird flu, about which the naval guy seemed supremely indifferent? And where was Jack at this very moment?

"Fuck fuck fuck," she said, looking up from her laptop and sighing deeply.

There was a soft knock at the door. Her face brightened. She undid the top few buttons of her blouse as her nipples hardened.

"Come in…" she purred, and the Polish guy (she still didn't know his name) put his tousled and increasingly attractive young head around the old oak door.

"I come for mine poosy," he said wickedly, and she didn't know if he was being anatomical or using a term of endearment. She looked in her pocketbook to see if she had enough cash. She had.

"Sure, sure, and bring your pals too!" she added, seeing the other four come in after him, nervously, excitedly, even worriedly. She pressed the little button which switched off her laptop, then pressed some more subtle buttons inside herself which turned her own lap on. And if that freaky bitch Jenny Djinn had invited her to tea on Sunday, she was gonna offer these guys a sandwich right now…

*

138

Where was Jack at that moment? Well it was Saturday, and he was at home with his mum watching her favourite programme, the live final of *The X Factor*. He was on the couch on the left side of his mum, and Jenny Djinn was sitting on her right, and his dear old mum was soooo happy to be in the middle of them both.

Jack hadn't expected Jenny Djinn to turn up at his door. But seeing as she was there with a six-pack of lager, and a ham and mushroom pizza (with extra ham), hot from the nearby Pasquale's take-away, he couldn't rightly turn her away. "Come on in," he said, and Jenny just knew that what he really said was: *I'm really glad you came.*

Now if you were a snob you might it hard to accept what happened next. No no no, Jenny didn't try to cure Maisie of her learning disabilities, no way would she have even tried! What happened was that the two women got on like a house on fire. Mrs Hobbes said right away: "Call me Maisie," and far from being the mute presence that Lilith Love experienced, Maisie turned out to be a real little chatterbox, only slurring some of her words because of her thick tongue, and being as much of a telly addict as Jenny.

And Jack's reaction? Jack was charmed. So Jenny had taken the right approach: to seduce a man like him, get to work on his mum first.

Their conversation was banal, but stuff-of-life. You don't need to know all the details. Their warmth was very real, and that felt so good. The crucial moment, historically, was that Jenny brought havoc to the telly programme by 'releasing' one of the contestants in much the same way as she had done to Jasper Blound on Jenky's chat show.

The theme of that night's programme was Music from the Movies, and there were only two contestants left: Lorelei Mayne and Grant Abon. The former was a willowy blonde from Cardiff, the latter a chunky little ex-postman from the Isle of Wight. They both had perfect teeth for the final. Popular opinion and betting had it that Grant with his spiky gelled hair was going to walk it, and probably would if little Maisie Hobbes hadn't taken against him.

Dear sweet Lorelei Mayne sang excerpts from *The Sound of Music* and *Titanic* and Maisie was up and dancing, surprisingly light on her feet for such a chubby little thing, and before you could blink Jenny joined her, the two of them waving and swaying and smoothing around the little sitting room and it was a real laugh for everyone there.

Then punky Grant started with a mix of songs from *West Side Story* and finished with *Grease*, and oh he was good, you know what I mean! And the audience were on their feet and you could tell that Jenny liked him too but for some reason Maisie didn't, refusing to dance, sitting down with arms folded and her jaw set at a firmly disapproving angle.

"Don't you like him?" asked Jenny, rocking along to his rhythms.

"No, hate him."

In the presence of Kali's avatar, that was almost like the judge in the high court putting the black hanky thingy on his wig and sentencing someone to be hanged by the neck until dead.

"Why?" she asked.

Maisie just folded her arms even more firmly, her jaw rigid with distaste. No-one ever knew why she disliked poor doomed Grant. Probably he reminded her of someone who had called her a mongol, or a moron, or an idiot, as people tended to do in her youth before the gentler and nicer terminology for Downs Syndrome came into being, and at least some members of society got a bit more tolerant. Or it could have been that she loved Lorelei so very much that any competition was just The Enemy in her eyes, under those epicanthic folds.

"I can do something about that," said Jenny.

"Can you?" asked Maisie.

"Easy-peasy," Jenny countered, reaching under her brain for the Kali-switch. The fact that she already liked the hapless Grant made it so much easier to do this. His face was in close up on the screen. He looked so cute and cuddly, a wickedly attractive little boy. She'd have loved a son like that. She loved him, she really did.

Now Jack at that moment was out of the room making tea, though it's hard to say if he would have stepped in and stopped her. Jack was neither fish nor fowl, remember. He had seen Kali's priestess heal, but not yet kill. With his curiosity, and with his weirdly unemotional outlook on life, he would probably see what followed as no more than an interesting experiment in synchronicity. In the event, he was in the kitchen when the lights all flickered, the kettle momentarily stopped boiling, and he heard Grant Abon's soaring voice stop in mid-soar, heard him cough and go silent.

"Biscuits anyone?" he said tritely, coming back into the room with a tray. "I've got some nice digestive or rich tea."

"Look..." said Maisie, pointing with her stubby finger to the screen.

The boy Grant was slumped to the floor, held up by some hunky dancers. There was dead silence in the audience, and then people started screaming again, but for different reasons this time.

"What's he smiling at?" asked Jack. "Has he won?"

"No," said Jenny with absolute shining love. "He's gone home..."

*

Shortly after that, without preamble, Jenny took Jack by the hand and guided him to his bedroom. Maisie gave a huge grin and a big nod of approval. Shutting the door behind them, and locking it, Jenny proceeded to take all of Jack's clothes off and then all of hers. It wasn't like the power-strip of Lilith Love: it was more matter-of-fact, brother and sister-ish. Jenny chuckled throughout, and when they were both naked she pulled him between the sheets and cuddled.

What did Jack make of all this, eh? Lucky young sod!! In a matter of days he had been undressed by two extremely attractive women, been made to feel a variety of luscious female body parts and had his own stroked, caressed and licked. He only disappointed one of the women though. Jack's cuddling of Lilith was compulsory. In contrast, his cuddling of Jenny was pliant and warm. Maybe it was to do with her being a member of the library while Lilith could never be. Yet he still didn't get a stiffy.

"It's dead," said Jenny chuckling, flapping at it, marvelling at his beautiful body. "I can do for this what I did for that woman in the wheelchair."

"Just cuddle me," Jack said, and you know what? Jenny LOVED that. She had been shagged by many men, but had never once made love. Most of them had beer-bellies and stank of beer and cigarettes and unwashed clothes. A few kept their hats on. In each case it was over in seconds. No-one had ever, ever just cuddled her.

Even Death Goddesses need cuddles.

It pushed this one over the edge.

*

But there are two things thing that any historian of this period should understand right from the start:

First, Maisie might not have had much brain, according to 'normal' standards, but where her son was concerned, she had the heart of a lion, and would have run through brick walls for him.

Second, Jack doted on his Mum and thought her just perfect!

CHAPTER 8

The moon was full and the wind was blasting against the outer walls, making its way through gaps and cracks to set the candles of the inner rooms a-fluttering. The four Templars sat around the long oak table in varying states of composure. This was another night when the place felt particularly haunted, and it was a good job de Mohun showed no obvious signs of fear, or else they'd have all hidden under their beds until daylight. They all felt it, this haunting, even the dogs who slouched and hid and looked behind them into the shadows. Evil spirits? Or the souls of those whom the three older men had killed, come back for vengeance?

Actually, it could have been both of those, but as you've already seen, the more likely explanation was that it was Lilith Love's fault this time, rather than remote-viewing Japanese exhausted from their sexual alchemies in the foreign realm of 21st Century England. Lilith, you see, was working on her Virtual Reality Preceptory, and somehow (it was probably The Head's fault) that created a kind of sympathy which reached across Time and between the worlds, and impinged upon our four REAL Templars.

The programme she used on her laptop enabled her to add furniture, change rooms and colours and textures. So when she added decorated shields to be hung on the virtual walls, our men in the 14th Century had glimpses of them: brief shimmering images of light where Lilith was placing them. They rubbed their eyes, the images went. Had there been opticians in that era they would have gone to see one. They didn't talk openly about these things – Templars didn't – but they took comfort that the others were equally affected.

And maybe Lilith's libido transmitted itself across time too, because de Hambledon for one was almost chewing the real tapestries that hung around the place. In fact, demons or not, he was anxious for them all to disperse so he could take up some business with the now short-haired serving lass with the disturbingly boy-like form.

De Egle was wondering if he could forsake his vows of Poverty, Chastity and Obedience, and just disappear somewhere warm and normal, and not haunted, and settle down with a couple of nice compliant large-bosomed 'donats' of the sort he had suggested so often before.

And you probably shouldn't know what was going through the dark recesses of de Mohun's mind. The previous night he had crept out onto the Ridgeway when everyone else slept. He had grabbed a hapless traveller – a pilgrim en route to Glastonbury – blindfolded him and forced him to kneel with a noose around his neck in a travesty of his own initiation into the Order many years before. Then when the wretch had said *Please please please*, *Oh god Oh god Oh god*, he rammed his curved knife up under the back of the skull into the poor sod's brain while saying with utter sincerity "Pax Vobiscum..."

He had to do something to keep his skills honed and his appetite for life whetted. Since the fall of Acre and a brief expedition a few years after that, and the ending of the Order's military glories, life had been dreadful for him.

And meanwhile, young de Sautré, bless him, was reading more words of wisdom from St Bernard, the Abbot of Clairvaux, still hooked on the romance of the Knights Templar, still unable to see through them, and still – as far as they could see – believing that the man at the head of the table was greatest living human being on the entire flat planet. He just couldn't wait for his uncle, who just happened to be the Grand Master in England, to come and meet him next Sunday.

"'They go and come,' de Sautré read from the immortal words of the Abbot, "'at a sign from their Master; they wear the clothing which he gives them, and ask neither food nor clothing from any one else; they live cheerfully and temperately together, without wives and children, and, that nothing may be wanting for evangelical perfection, without property, in one house, endeavouring to preserve the unity of the spirit in the bond of peace, so that one heart and one soul would appear to dwell in them all. They never sit idle, or go about gaping after news. When they are resting from warfare against the infidels, a thing which rarely occurs, not to eat the bread of idleness, they employ themselves in repairing their clothes and arms, or do something which the command of the Master or the common need enjoins.' There we have it," he said smugly, not realising what he sounded like.

In fact you can get inside the heads of de Egle and de Hambledon quite easily and hear them say the 14th Century equivalents of:

What a prick! What an arselicker!!
Makes us sound like those big poofy Knights Hospitaller.
For fuck's sake shut up shut up shut UP!
Bollocks. It's all bollocks!

Meanwhile, de Mohun constantly tensed his muscles, one by one, in sequence around his body. "Fundamenta ejus in montibus sanctis," he whispered quite loudly. Suddenly...

The tension went. Whatever current was flowing through the room and making them shiver inside from a cold that was not earthly, suddenly stopped. They all felt it. They all smiled – even de Mohun. It was as if his words of power, delivered with grim attitude, had defeated the forces of evil. Maybe the words did have some effect, focussing his considerable force of personality through them. Or maybe it was simply a coincidence that the Japanese adepts, drained by their inner work, decided to go to bed; while at the same moment Lilith Love shut the lid of her laptop and powered down for the night.

The men all took deep breaths. The room suddenly felt warm again. They ate a little, in silence. The dogs perked up. Outside, the wind grew stronger and made the candles gutter even more. The youngest Templar angled the letter so he could read just one more paragraph, so excited by now that if you'd had any gaydar with some degree of homophobia, then even you would want to slap him:

"Listen to this next bit. This is very seemly: 'No unseemly word or light mocking, no murmur or immoderate laughter, is let to pass unreproved, if any one should allow himself to indulge in such. They avoid games of chess and tables; they are adverse to the chase, and equally so to hawking, in which others so much delight. They hate all jugglers and mountebanks, all wanton songs and plays, as vanities and follies of this world.' Surely, we must be the noblest Order in the world!"

Fuck off, thought de Egle.

De Mohun clapped twice. The lute player in the corner burst into life and strummed a tune about a young woman walking amid daisies and lamenting her Lord, which was one of the greatest hits of 1307.

Shite, thought de Hambledon, who hated that whining song, and didn't like anything that couldn't be whistled. Then he started mentally planning his fuck for later, and how he would do it, and where, and what he might get her to do for him, and to him. Also, because he was a romantic sort as far as Templars go, he decided he might ask her for her name, once he had had no more use for the gag.

Their Master clapped again to switch off the music. He yawned and was about to extinguish his own candle when there was a distant hammering at the gates. His eyes lit up. He was hoping for something very specific. The other three reached for their swords, which were never far from their hands no matter what the occasion, but de Mohun was up and out as if it were Saracens at the gate, and him ready to take them on empty-handed. The other three were quick to follow.

The gate-keepers were there already. They'd have had their heads bashed in if they hadn't been. The preceptory might have been situated in a calm and quiet area of Wiltshire, just off the main road that was usually well-lit by moon and stars, but they had to act as if they were an outpost in Outremer, with the blackest savages outside. Which wasn't a bad idea, considering how unpopular the Order had become of late.

"Open!" shouted de Mohun, striding toward the gates, lights coming on everywhere, people hurrying out.

There was nothing much to see, to tell the truth. Just the Boy Kent returned on de Sautré's half-dead horse who had clearly been at it non-stop, the torchlights around turning him and the horse and all their sweat into a pale gold.

"You have something?" said the Templar.

The young man nodded, knackered, reached into a saddle bag and drew out a rolled up piece of paper bearing a wax seal. He didn't have the strength to speak, but there was nothing he needed to say.

With a nod, de Mohun gestured to de Sautré to take the letter.

"Is there light enough to read it by?"

The young man broke the seal, unrolled it and angled it to get the moon's light straight on. De Mohun used his broad body as a wind-break for him. "It says…"

Show off, thought de Hambledon.

Prick, thought de Egle.

"It says that Engayne, and Grandcombe will leave the commandery in Templecombe on Tuesday to be here on the Sabbath, and will be very proud to meet the Grand Master – who I am humbled to say is mine own uncle, as you all know. He – Master

Engayne – also adds: 'Tell my old friend de Mohun that I am exceedingly keen to attend to that other matter, of which we may not speak aloud.'"

What other matter? thought de Hambledon.

What other matter? thought de Egle.

What other matter? thought de Sautré, turning the paper to see if there was anything on the other side which might explain.

That was the great thing about the Templars – and any other organisation of that sort, ancient or modern: there is power in secrecy. The simplest item can become numinous if you control the secrecy surrounding it.

De Mohun beamed. Or maybe the moon and the torchlight just caught him squarer in the face just then. His little Plan was working. "The Sabbath then. We have time. Come you two..." he said to his sergeants. "There are things I want from you. And you, de Sautré, can go to bed and keep your hands above the covers like good Templars must."

He slammed the great gate in the face of the exhausted messenger-boy and never gave him another thought. De Hambledon and de Egle grinned with delight: this was just like the old days! They twirled their swords above their heads as they followed their hero into his private rooms.

*

Look, the blessed Plan was simple. If he had been a soldier today he would live by the old acronym KISS – Keep It Simple, Stupid. Lord knows, de Mohun was no tactician. Nor was he the brightest of souls. In his warrior heyday, a succession of leaders had used him like those remote-control robots we see today used for detonating car bombs: Right a bit, left a bit more, forward... now charge! Superb individual fighting man he might have been, but in modern terms you might describe him as a couple of wafers short of a communion. The Plan was this...

De Mohun planned to kill the Grand Master. He wanted to destroy the Order in England at least – not by cowardly acts of blabbing to the   priests and thus the Pope, and not for 30, or even 300, pieces of silver. He wanted to slice William de la More because he had had enough of the Poor Knights of the Temple of Solomon.

They were not poor, they no longer functioned as knights, and what the fuck Solomon had to do with it all was beyond him.

As for Master Engayne... He wanted to slice him because Martin Engayne had shown great cowardice leading up to the siege of Acre, and been instrumental in getting de Mohun sent to Temple Rockley, to keep him out of the way. De Mohun didn't dwell too much on the details: he did the personal, medieval equivalent of slamming shut the lid of his own laptop in that respect.

So those were his motives.

In the letter de Sautré had written for him he had simply said: *The Grand Master is coming. He is bringing a certain thing about which we cannot speak. Bring that blessed item of yours. The Grand Master would like to see it.* It was a bit more flowery than that, but you get the gist.

Everything in that letter was true. Templars, after all, had sworn to be always honest. When de Mohun referred to the 'certain thing about which we cannot speak', he personally was referring to de la More's prick. When he referred to that 'certain item' of Engayne's, he meant the Sacred Head. And of course the Grand Master would 'like to see it'. Everyone would. But once Engayne assumed that the Grand Master had made a specific request, he would be over here at Temple Rockley with his tongue hanging out, ready to lick arse and get further advancement.

Actually, as Lilith could have told him via Google, or Jack via his lovely real books, the secrecy worked against de Mohun here. The Templars of Templecombe were not in possession of a Sacred Head at all, only a painting of one which looked a bit like Cat Stevens. Who knows where Yahya's head was at that time. Probably in Paris. There were all sorts places claiming him and you've got to do what Lilith did and type 'Beheading of St. John the Baptist' into Google and be led straight to Wikipedia. Here are just some of the Sacred Locations that de Mohun would never have known about except through gossip and hearsay, yet with which Lilith Love was already very familiar:

- San Silvestro in Capite in Rome
- Amiens Cathedral, France, brought home by Wallon de Sarton from the Fourth Crusade in Constantinople.
- Halifax, West Yorkshire, England, where it is said to be buried.

- Turkish Antioch.
- The Umayyad Mosque in Damascus.

Istanbul was said to possess Yahya's arm and a piece of his skull in the Topkapi Palace, as does the Coptic Orthodox Monastery of Saint Macarius the Great in Scetes, Egypt. While Yahya's right hand, with which he baptised his apparently irritating cousin ('the hand that touched God'), is said to be in the possession of the Serbian Orthodox monastery of Cetinje, and also at the Romanian skete of the Forerunner on Mount Athos.

In any case the Order had in their possession many heads which made no pretence at being anything to do with The Baptist. Lilith had already dealt at length with the comments of Jean de Turn, treasurer of the Paris Temple who had spoken of a painted head in the form of a picture, which he had adored at one of these chapters. And she devoted the large part of a chapter to Stephen of Troyes' description of one of the Templars' Paris ceremonies, of a sacred object being 'brought in by the priest in a procession of the brethren with lights; it was laid on the altar; it was a human head without any silver or gold, very pale and discoloured, with a grizzled beard like a Templar's.'

As her mind inhabited that Virtual Reality preceptory and used it as a focus for her research, Lilith already knew far more about the Mysteries of the Sacred Head than the REAL Templar de Mohun ever would – and this was some time before she actually met Yahya and became a Death Goddess in her own right. She was also planning to cut and paste the Templecombe image and set it up in her Virtual Reality Preceptory as it took on more and more detail, and you can imagine the effect that this would have upon the 14th Century occupants of the real thing, if they ever glimpsed that. It might have turned them to religion!

Yet even that wasn't the REAL treasure of Templecombe. It was more a case that the Templars there, bumbling along in much the same way that ours were doing in Temple Rockley, had taken charge of several rather priceless manuscripts which had been sent over from France against the day it all went very, very wrong – which any fool could see was imminent. These manuscripts would be priceless today: then, they were just explosive – if you could read, and if you knew Hebrew and Aramaic tongues, and if you wanted your

149

Christianity turned upside down and inside-out by those details which have become almost standard now, about Virgin Births, Resurrections, Marriages, and the real nature of The Magdalen and her first lover Yahya, which would make your mortal head spin.

Our grizzled Master of Temple Rockley knew nothing of this. All he was concerned about was that if either Engayne or William de la More were gagging to see a REAL Sacred Head before he had a bit of fun with them, then he, John de Mohun, had just the item to show them...

*

This was a lively day back in Trowbridge. If you approached the Old Mill through any of the streets you would see various people wearing those masks they all use in Tokyo to keep out the smog, although these were specially designed to protect against The Flu. That is to say, they did absolutely bugger all, coz there wasn't any Bird, Dog or Swine Flu, and a lot of the people there knew it. Really, The Big Flu Scare was still being made to run in the media, but it was very difficult to hide the fact that something Very Odd was going on in that small town at that moment. The mill was surrounded foreign journalists, camera crews and paparazzi, and all the D Notices in Britain couldn't have kept that lot out. MPs were turning up in their droves. The Freemasons were out in force, as was every cultist and occultist who had ever hoped for a bit of gratuitous grace and exciting weekends. The air was full of black helicopters trying to get exclusive shots of the activities inside – or at least they were until Porteous did his Grand Master thing and contacted people who contacted people who got rid of those irritants at least.

The Head had been right as ever: the high artificial walls that the army had erected were acting as protection rather than containment, for the crowds were milling and massing so much that dual carriageway past Tesco's had to be closed, and not all of them were there to worship. There were fundamentalists from every religion, of course – you'd expect that. Glowering Christians of every denomination waving their crosses and placards; New Age pagan types with their ankhs and drums; hard-core Kali worshippers from India coming to either complain or voice their support; local converts of Jenny Djinn just aching to see her or touch the hem of her dress... Then there were also reps from all the major insurance companies in the Western world who wanted to know why their policies were taking such a pounding. In fact some of them had stopped issuing any policies for the foreseeable future, until this whole bizarre thing was sorted. While scattered discreetly among all that lot were agents from just about every security service checking to see if any of this might impinge upon the safety of their own particular realms.

This, then, was the day when Nyron Hughes, Jack Hobbes and Lilith Love were invited into what used to be the old mill building, but was now globally becoming known as The Sanctuary. It was an important moment in the story of course, but you have to realise that all these vignettes were just fragments of the whole thing. All sorts of other things were going on continuously, all over the world by this time. For example:

Lilith was writing furiously when she wasn't engaged in all the bits and pieces of life surrounding Jack and her love for same.

Jenny Djinn, aka Kali Ma, was developing her powers to such an extent that she could 'release' whole sackfuls of requests almost without studying individual photos, as she used to.

That came to really annoy Shaz, because she never had time to sort out the contracts and – potentially – she saw them losing money hand over fist. Mind you she found her own compensation in shagging some of the soldiers who had been set as guards.

Tasha meanwhile had – completely unexpectedly – discovered True Love and deep sexual gratification in the arms and quim of Felicity.

Felicity meanwhile, when she wasn't teaching Sacred Dance and helping with the T-shirts and four-armed sweaters, was busy writing what she hoped would be a Newer Testament, and felt like a little angel because of it.

To an extent, the only two in The Sanctuary not 'at it' were Yahya and Jenny herself, but she had been fortified by the cuddle she had had from Jack, and the anticipation of more. Yahya, meanwhile... well, no one could ever get to the bottom of his needs. Not that he had a bottom anywhere on this plane.

In fact the rest of them in the building were all having sex in one form or another. It must have been the daily proximity of Death that made them all so horny.

So Nyron, Jack and Lilith Love were admitted through the gates by Spoffo. Hughes was not surprised. This was basic policy: when you have an enemy you can't fight, then involve yourself with them. Spoffo was now in charge of security. The Order was quite certain they knew where the all-important sacred Head was, but they also knew that any attempt to snatch it, or take it by force would never work. Softly-softly-catchee Yahya was the tactic.

"No fancy dress today? Sir?" said the young man as he clanged the huge gate shut behind Hughes, Lilith and Jack.

"Piss off. Sonny." This from Hughes, who had often suspected that Spoffo was working for MI5, and so had his own agenda within the Order.

"Are you in yet?" asked the voice in his head, which was the Grand Master, Perry Porteous, through the tiniest of ear-pieces.

"I'm in!" Hughes whispered.

"Exciting ain't it!" exclaimed Lilith, who had excellent hearing.

It was Shaz who showed them around, fresh from a brief and vertical encounter with a corporal on the morning shift. They started on the ground floor among the newcomers and worked upward. Felicity had had the style and insight to have the whole edifice internally restructured to contain almost a hundred small but cozy 'cells' that the followers could sleep in, a large kitchen and refectory, toilets and showers, laundry, lecture rooms, a floor for 'sacred dance', exercise rooms, and the all-important outer temple. The visitors being genuinely charmed and fascinated by everything – especially Lilith Love who saw the whole world in terms of possible material for her books. When she caught a glimpse of Ms Roniard walking stiffly from one mailbag to another, sifting through the letters for new customers, she just beamed.

"See! I knew she was just a shill. I am never wrong."

Hughes, who knew everything about Ms Roniard from her Passport number down through to the date of her next appointment to sort out her haemorrhoids, including all of her medical history on the way, wasn't so sure.

Jack just beamed. He couldn't wait to tell his boss Jo tomorrow, and twit her about new readers that he'd failed to get. To him, all new experience was good experience. This was not just a converted mill: this was the Grail Castle, Hogwarts, Camelot and Shambhala rolled into one. "Hello!" Jack said to everyone and everything, and they were all pretty much charmed.

And so the hapless pilgrims worked their upward, ever upward. There were no lifts, just winding stairs. The higher they got, the further they could see across the chaos outside. The people massed against the walls like a huge pulsating scab, the noise of drummers drumming, vicars chanting, insurance reps a-weeping, frustrated wives a-wailing....

"This is great," panted Jack Hobbes, pointing at the disappearing black helicopters. "This is all the conspiracy symbols together, here in my backyard! Men in Black, black cars, black helicopters, aliens... We just need giant Lizards and the Duke of Edinburgh." He panted because he was slightly out of breath from the climb. Hughes, whose job required him to be a great natural athlete, and Lilith, who had great natural sexual athletics with half of Eastern Europe to keep herself fit, were untroubled.

They came to the penultimate floor. The original disciples were still there and Felicity was lecturing them, with Tasha looking on almost reverently. Shaz made no attempt to hide her scorn as they stopped to listen.

"Now, since Our Lady has inaugurated the Kali Yuga, it is important to have her element of iron on Her altar. I used Hematite, personally, as well as this rather charming iron figure of Her. Flowers on our little altar offer a nice balance, and I always prefer orchids. The delicacy of an orchid along with its natural grace is deeply symbolic for Kali's altar. The orchid reminds us of ourselves, inside."

You didn't need to be a telepath to hear Shaz think: *Who the fuck does she think she is? What does she sound like, eh?*

The women listened, enrapt. Felicity went on:

"I have also placed a peacock feather and a small mirror on Kali's altar. You must dedicate your own altars to Kali by lighting some incense and candles and sitting quietly in contemplation for a moment. State your intent. It can be about facing your fears, learning more about our cycles, mourning a death or celebrating new birth. Meditate on how Kali's altar can best serve you. When lighting the candles to Her, realise that you are symbolising your own inner light."

Crap, thought Shaz, and Hughes and Lilith were inclined to agree. Jack just took it all in, as ever.

Now you mustn't imagine that Felicity had had any particular cosmic insights of her own. She made the mistake then of going a revelation too far with the next piece, not realising that Lilith with her laptop was Googling crucial sentences.

"As a Mother, Kali was called Treasure-House of Compassion, Giver of Life to the World, the Life of all lives. Despite the popular western belief that she is just a Goddess of destruction, she is the fount of every kind of love, which flows into the world through women, her agents on earth. Thus, it is said of a male worshipper of Kali, 'bows down at the feet of women,' regarding them as his rightful teachers."

Lilith Love looked up from her screen and told them, *sotto voce*:

"You guys should try looking up themystica.com. Kali Ma. It's all in there, word for blessed word."

Felicity heard the comment and looked somewhat embarrassed.

Tasha looked angry on her behalf, and wondered who this loud-mouthed tart was. Shaz warmed to Lilith immediately.

So really it only needed Jenny Djinn to make a grand entrance for the scenario to be complete. The atmosphere in that room was certainly charged. It might have been the sexual tensions that were flowing through everyone, it might have been the knowledge that somehow these ordinary people from an ordinary town in Wiltshire were involved in events that had a global and perhaps cosmic significance, or it might have been the fact that The Head upstairs was awake and surfing the aethers, and making everyone there sense him. Whatever the reason they stood before the solid oak door that led to the Upper Room, as Felicity called it, and felt like naughty schoolchildren outside the headmaster's office.

Naturally, Jack then had one of his wobblies. Who knows what caused this vision but vision it was, and it might have been prescience rather than a remote viewing of the far past....

He suddenly found himself in what seemed to be a lodge, a large eight-sided room lit by candles. The flooring was polished wood, walls were bland and old stone; there were no symbols or decorations of any kind. The era was indeterminate. It could have been the remote past: it was actually an intimation of the future. There in the middle was a flickering figure of a naked woman with a

154

cat's head. This, he knew, was Lilith. He didn't recognise her inner feline nature as shown by the animal head: he recognised the tits and crack. He also had a sense that there were others around him – men in white mantles with red crosses – but they were flickering too, as if they were not ready for this place, this time....

"Jack... Jack....!" came the voices of Lilith and Hughes, both of them physically supporting him. Felicity looked on horrified, worried that Kali was at work here, though nothing could be further from the truth.

Simply, The Head's power was touching on Jack's psyche again. It was doing funny things with Time, as Yahya was wont to do, tossing together bits from the past, bits from the future, and mixing it all up in the present like a Caesar Salad. That was an intimation of Lilith as Sekhmet that he glimpsed. The men with the red crosses were our Templars from the 14th Century, haunted by glimpses of the cat-headed woman across time. That's one of the things they confessed to at the Inquisition: worshipping a cat. However you'd confess to anything under the tortures they would be put to. It was partly right. The door to the Upper Room opened. Jenny Djinn appeared in what Felicity described later as a blaze of light, but which was only the 150 watt bulb that was used for the final stairwell.

"My Jack!" she said with some concern, hurrying over and pushing Hughes aside.

"What's going on?" asked an urgent voice in Hughes' head.

Fuck off, he thought, because he was still besotted by this beautiful young man, and wanted no harm to come to him, ever.

"I have paramedic training," said Hughes, regaining his composure. It was true, actually. He had been superbly trained in a variety of skills, not all of them lethal or subversive. So he took Jack and lowered him gently to the floor, putting him in the recovery position, curled up almost on one side, his long blonde hair flowing over one side of his face and brushing the floor. "His pulse is... steady. His breathing is... regular. He will be alright, I'm sure."

"Bless you..." said Jenny Djinn with the full power of a woman in love, and it powered over Hughes like a warm breeze, and Felicity told herself that she had to trust this man above all men.

Jack's eyes opened. He licked his lips and gasped a couple of times. His mum would have described this to him as just another

155

wobbly, so he wasn't too troubled. He looked around all the faces and grinned, and it was like sun rising.

"I've been told to invite you all to come upstairs," said Jenny Djinn to the three guests. "Not you!" she added to Felicity, when she saw her eyes start to pop with excitement. "Just these three."

Felicity nodded and almost curtsied. She really was a very good disciple.

*

The two women who would almost destroy the world went up the stairs together, Lilith Love just a step behind Jenny Djinn. Then came Jack, and then came Nyron Hughes, following behind Jack and trying not to whimper with delight.

Porteous' voice came into Hughes head: "The camera. Get the angle right. I don't want to see that boy's arse. You know what I want to see!"

It was a Damascus Moment for Hughes, that. Or a Trowbridge one. There must have been some deep inner symbolism for him personally, ascending a wooden staircase at the behest of some modern goddess, while staring at the rear of the most perfect human being he had ever seen... yes, he knew what Porteous wanted to see. So he took his right thumb and put it under the tiny camera in his lapel, and his right index finger on the lens, and squeezed until he felt it break.

"Hughes! Hughes we've lost the picture. Can you understand how anxious I am Hughes, can you? Hughes?"

With his left index finger, he dipped into his ear and removed the device as if it were wax, and crushed it also.

I'm free, said a voice in his head, but it was his own voice for once. There was a series of doors, a series of rooms, one inside the other. Nothing particularly esoteric about any of them, mostly empty, with only a few old telly magazines scattered on the floors that Felicity would later preserve. Yet there was an atmosphere about the place, they could all feel it, a sense of warm and thrumming power, and Hughes of course knew exactly what was causing that. The Head was awake. He had been on the fringes of this phenomenon before.

156

"Leave that thing," said Jenny Djinn to Lilith Love, indicating her laptop, and to her own astonishment the American put the device down on the floor without a murmur.

The last door. A very unexceptional door. The sort of door you'd find leading into your own sitting room. In fact they could hear *Songs of Praise* just starting beyond it and Jenny saying: "Oh shit... he hates that programme! One moment please..." before going in and closing the door after her.

The trio huddled, each one listening intently to what might be happening within, their eyes gleaming; they were like children on their last waking moments before Xmas. The door opened slowly.

"Come in," said Jenny Djinn softly, and they didn't need to be told, they all kept very quiet, stayed very gentle, and found themselves in the special room that Jenny had prepared for Yahya, with a couch in central position and the old telly with remote control perched on top, now switched off, blipped into silence. They came upon the couch from behind, and didn't see Yahya at first. Jenny beamed at them. It was so good to be allowed to share this Mystery with someone else at last – especially her Jack. She angled herself so she could see their faces when they saw his face.

It should have been a screaming moment, but there was something about Yahya's power, or presence, which made it all very safe, and almost natural. So they came around the side of the couch and saw him there, and stayed very very silent as he smiled at them all, and if he couldn't turn his head to scan them, he moved his eyes from side to side and widened them as a substitute for nodding, which is never very wise when you've got no shoulders.

"Jesus fucking wept..." said Lilith Love.

"Nope! Not him honey!" sighed Yahya.

"You've... you've got an American accent," she said wonderingly.

"I speak every language. I speak the sounds in your head," he said to Lilith as he had once said to Jenny and so many more before her.

"Bloody hell..." said Jack with delight, though he did wonder if Jo would want him to get even this one enrolled as a new reader.

"Hello again," said Nyron Hughes, who had heard of this but never been allowed to witness it before.

"Good to see you, boyo."

"Jesus fucking wept..." said Lilith again, and The Head's eyes rolled.

"This isn't Jesus, it's Yahya,' Jenny said. "That's his real name. That's what his mum called him."

"This is St John the Baptist," explained Hughes, who felt a surge of pure bliss that he could talk openly about this at last.

"Sit down," said The Head, and they all did so. If he'd had a body you could say they sat at his feet, but in this case they sat down a yard or so beyond his Adam's Apple, Jack being squeezed neatly between Hughes and Lilith, with Jenny Djinn behind them, queen of the world – or queen of her world at least.

Really, you'd have chuckled to see how drawn in they all were, and there just didn't seem to be anything bizarre about the situation. Hughes was already familiar with The Head of course, though he had never heard him talk before. Lilith was by this time Googled up to the hilt with knowledge of the Templars and their Sacred Heads, so this was no surprise to her intellectually. And Jack was just taking it all in his stride, as he always did: he knew about conspiracies: he was beginning to see how they were all linked. And this was all so much better than doing a Stock Rotation in the Wiltshire Library Service, though it would have pained his boss to hear him say that.

"Okay, work with me now you guys. There are things that need to be done," said The Head, and if they didn't all inch forward physically, they did so figuratively. None of them knew what was coming, not even Jenny.

"You," he said to Hughes, "stay here. This is your new role. You will look after my friend Jenny. Forget old Porteous and the Grand Lodge and all that. This is the New Order. You are the new Grand Master."

Ooooooooh, they all thought, and Hughes' own head grew and he felt exceedingly glad.

"You," he said to Lilith Love, "will buy that hotel and stay there. Yes buy it. They will sell. Take the Shaz woman with you. She will do the finances, and teach the Polish boys some English."

Lilith blushed. Being spied upon by MI5 was one thing, knowing that others were watching her from other levels, was a bit embarrassing.

"Me? What about me?" asked Jack, so little-boyish the others all grinned and wanted to cuddle him – and more, actually.

"You will go with this Lilith. You will take me with you."

"NOOOOO!" cried out Jenny, and even she wasn't sure if she was crying out at the thought of losing her Head, or Jack.

"YEEEEESSSSS!" roared back The Head and by god it was a roar and a half. People downstairs thought it was a jet flying too close. The people in the Upper Room were all thrown back, not figuratively this time but physically.

Lilith steadied herself and smirked. She looked like the cat with the cream.

"What will happen to me?" Jenny asked in a still small voice.

The Head thought. You could almost see his spirit rushing back and forward through the Possibilities.

"Okay... Change of plan. Jack stays here with you for the time being. But you needn't worry because you'll still have your powers. You will still continue. Just be yourself. I was only ever going to be with you for a short time. Besides, I will always be in your head, until the end of Time. You won't lose me."

She smiled. Well, she had no option. She'd keep Jack, and keep her powers, the Kali Within. Even so, as if to make her feel loved, Yahya sent across a burst of pure warmth to compensate for the rest of it. A thought came to her:

"It's like the film *ET* innit? The moment when ET touches Eliot on the forehead, and says: 'I'll be right here...' which is where I always cry." Once she'd made that connection, drawn that parallel, her universe was in place again.

"Yeah. Sure," said Yahya, his accent becoming more and more American. He'd enjoyed that film too, except he would now call it a movie.

"Okay Jenny Djinn. It's been great. It was fun. Now goodbye..."

Well there wasn't a lot any of them could say. Not easy to argue with the severed and sacred head of St John the Baptist. Jenny looked away as Lilith carefully, without qualm or fear or queaziness, picked up Yahya by the ears and put him into the box that had once held the kettle.

"Shall I close the lid? You gonna be okay?"

"You look just like Mary Magdalene," said the voice from within the box. "Grrrrrrrrr....."

*

159

If there was a massive crowd outside the mill in Trowbridge, there was a lesser gathering of folk outside the preceptory in 14th Century Rockley, their dark shapes emerging with the dawn. Mind you, considering the small population then, it was proportionately huge. They just stood there, quietly, many of them with hands clasped as if in prayer. Not a word, not a sound. Like crows. They looked as if they'd been there most of the night before. Almost all of them women.

The Templars, who were already up and dressed and ready for The Plan, looked at them with curiosity.

"So many old people out there," said de Egle. "What do they want?"

You would probably laugh if you saw them yourself, and heard that comment. The bulk of them were probably in their mid-30s, though there were some much younger. If in the 21st Century we use terms like: 50 is the new 40! Then in the early years of the 14th Century we would have to say conversely: 30 is today's 60!

"I'll go and talk to them," said de Sautré.

"No!" said de Mohun, who knew exactly why they were there. Recently a man had been killed on the Ridgeway. Then another had been found dead – cause unknown. They didn't use the words 'serial killer' but rather thought in terms of a great evil being loosed upon their world. So they had sought de Mohun's protection because that was his job – to protect pilgrims and travellers. He had listened carefully and vowed to catch the beast who had been doing all these things, turning the once peaceful Ridgeway into a road to hell. Two more men died despite this. It was evil that was stalking the Ridgeway perhaps, but also madness. It took them some while before they realised the source of both was de Mohun himself, and some time more before they dared confront him.

"They're all women!" said de Sautré, ever the innocent.

Well of course they were all women: many of their local menfolk had been murdered. Those who remained would stand no chance against a Templar. It would have been like sending a soldier with a bayonet up against a Challenger tank. But they had figured that a Templar would not strike a woman. So the women made their remaining menfolk stay at home: this was their fight now.

"No distractions. Ignore them. Don't even speak to them in passing," de Mohun said, turning to de Sautré. "You will ride south

160

now and meet your uncle, escort him safely here. Take my horse. Ride hard."

That was like saying: *Here's the keys to my Ferrari, sonny. Give it some welly on the motorway.* The little creep was up and out and off before you could cry 'Beau Seant!' which the Templars often shouted when they rode into battle, a charge to 'Be Noble' or 'Be Glorious'.

The three older Templars watched de Sautré ride off, then looked at each other and laughed.

"Are you ready for this?" asked de Mohun, who trusted his two colleagues with his life.

"Yes. Yes we are."

"We will become outlaws, you both know that."

"But now we're merely bankers. I hate being a banker. Does anyone love bankers these days?" de Egle said.

"Bankers and tenders and counters of sheep. I hate sheep. Being an outlaw sounds healthy," de Hambledon added.

Whatever spiritual things might have gone on at the highest and innermost levels of the Order, these lot were just thugs at heart.

"Then go now, and go well," de Mohun said. "Do what it is you have to do."

The two men looked pleased. They couldn't wait to get stuck in. Soon, west and south of Rockley, they would know again what they had known for so long in the Sancte Terre, the Holy Land: fighting, devilry, death. And maybe a bit of rumpy-pumpy among the peasantry.

"What about those women out there?" asked de Hambledon.

De Mohun glowered, rolled up his sleeves. "I'll soon sort them out..." he growled, and for those aged warriors who had spent most of their short lives fighting, it was just like old times.

*

This was almost where we came in: the moment when Jenny Grey stopped off at Cley Hill for a pee, had a vision of men from another age, lost her electric kettle and then took possession of The Head without realising. Try and see it from de Hambledon and de Egle's viewpoint, as things glimpsed out of the corner of the eye...

In those days when you lived in bleak and remote places, with far less to disturb or occupy your senses, there was probably a far higher level of innate psychism than we have now. Goodness knows they had felt haunted enough in the preceptory, but now at the foot of this ancient glowering mound of Cley Hill, they were equally assailed. They were not ghosts, so much as Time Slips caused by The Head, though perhaps there is little difference in the long run.

The Templars saw the Green Man straight away. In the 21st Century this Indian assassin might have blended perfectly with the landscape thanks to his camouflage, but back there in the 14th they saw a shimmering translucent outline, lurking, clearly not interested in them at all. In fact he shimmered and glowed and faded and pulsed in much the same way that The Nine did in the meetings of Grand Lodge, so you can draw your own conclusions about what *they* were, too.

The cars didn't impinge upon them. That is, their consciousness didn't try to re-shape them into carts or wagons: they just had a sense of something large and invisible and creating a presence in the air around them. Had they had much of a religious bent, they might have thought they were near God, so they wouldn't have been too different to the 21st Century morons who deify their vehicles and shape their lives around them.

But they certainly picked up on Jenny Grey, as she still was then, squatting amid the bushes, legs wide apart like one of those rude carvings in ancient churches, like one of the sheela na gigs that Jack had a book about and which Lilith could have Googled... Jenny didn't appear solid to them, but they certainly knew she was there, and they tried hard not to look.

De Egle and de Hambledon remained hidden, their faces completely covered by masks made from old sacking. If they'd been doing this job today they're the sort who would have used women's tights and had a right laugh about how their ugly faces were changed out of all recognition. They also wore old clothes, green and grey tops and leggings, which blended in with the scenery quite as nicely as the Green Man.

Were they nervous? A bit. But more than that, they were excited. Despite the eldritch nature of the place, it was a glorious day for a good killing, and they could have some fun with the softies from Templecombe who – they felt sure – were certainly into buggery. This was soooooo much better than making loans and collecting debts, and trading bloody sheep. This was man's work at last!

162

They knew that Engayne and Grandcombe's party would have stayed overnight at nearby Temple Farm, one of those Templar places in Wiltshire which have so far eluded the knowledge of the websites, but which was just as much within the Order as any of the bigger properties. In fact, as the library book Jack had issued to Jenny right at the beginning of this tale had explained, Cley Hill was supposed to contain the statue of a Golden Ram, so this little enclave had their own Mysteries too, even if The Severed Head was not one of them.

This is what happened next...

There was no car park then, of course. Just a narrow dusty path around the foot of the hill which wound through the ancient forest that still covered much of medieval England. The Wildwood, still in its glory. Their targets had no idea of the fate awaiting them. No-one would dare attack a Templar convoy, for the reputation of power is power itself, and the Order still had some reputation in these lonely parts. There were only two outriders – young men who had barely started shaving – who had to stoop to avoid the overhanging branches. More seasoned escorts in such a terrain would have walked their horses, but these lads were playing at knights, not knowing that two very seasoned fighters were waiting for them, trip wires across the path, each armed with every variety of cutting and chopping instruments, plus two loaded cross-bows each that were smaller than the normal ones you might associate with William Tell, and specially designed for rapid close-quarter use.

De Egle and de Hambledon – John and Robert to their proud mothers – made sure that the bows were ready, that their discharge would not be impeded by branches, and that their line of flight was clear. As the party approached they saw that the outriders were not wearing armour under those famous white mantles with the red cross-pattes, and this made their own task easier.

The poor lads didn't stand a chance. They were too busy guiding their horses while bending and stooping beneath the canopy to keep an eye open for danger. Unless you were battle-hardened (and these weren't), you wouldn't recognise the twang from the bows. Unless you're close to the bolt's flight path, you wouldn't hear them travelling across the short distance at enormous speed.

They rode a little distance ahead of the wagon. They were arguing as to whether, in a fair fight, Goliath could have taken

Samson, or whether Saladin could have passed muster as a Templar knight, given the hard nature of the training.

When the bolts thudded into their chests, they knew nothing more and cared even less, and fell to the ground like sacks of potatoes. Their horses whinnied, and one of them bolted, being brought down with much noise by the trip wires.

Engayne and Grandcombe, riding in some comfort in the four-wheeled wagon containing their treasure, finally realised that something was afoot. Engayne showed this by calling out 'Beau Seant! Beau Seant!' and reaching for the sword that lay at the bottom of the vehicle, while Grandcombe showed it by blubbering. Following behind the wagon were four esquires, younger even than the riders, and these were hacked down by our Robert. Grandcombe had stopped blubbering but was now making bubbling noises from his lungs, coz he got one of the other bolts into him and was now on his way to Templar heaven. Engayne never managed to reach his sword because de Egle had a very sharp knife to his throat and was thus keeping him very very still.

"Death to your Grand Master, the sodomist! His day is nigh," de Egle spat. "As for you…"

As Engayne told it later he smote the villain with a mighty blow, cut down the other ten ruffians single-handed, but was unable to kill the last one, who rode off with exceeding haste and cowardice once he had felt the mettle of a true Templar Knight.

Which was complete bollocks. De Egle had deliberately let him escape, so that the man from Somerset took up the loose horse wandering beyond the trip wires and galloped off at full speed both to save his neck and warn his precious Grand Master. This was all part of The Plan, and as far as such things go it had worked perfectly so far.

The two Templars from Temple Rockley (who unbeknownst to them were about to become two of the last Templars in England) now swarmed over the wagon and looked with delight upon the great chest that obviously contained treasure. They were high as kites after all that killing. It had done them the world of good. Now all they needed were a few jewels and bit of gold to make their day perfect.

"Paper," said de Egle with disgust, riffling through the documents.

"Shite," said de Hambledon, snatching up more and then throwing them to the wind, hoping there was something valuable underneath. Soon the large box was empty: no sacred head, no 14th Century equivalent of a see-through electric kettle, not even a few spiders... just a pile of utterly priceless documents that could have challenged and even destroyed the Roman Church had they ever been published.

"Right," said de Egle, removing his mask and looking down the trail. "The big poof went that way, so we'd better get moving and head this way if we want to get back before him."

De Hambledon pulled the bolts from the victims, wiped them clean and put them back into the little quiver. He also picked up a few of the manuscript sheets for later, for when he wanted to wipe his arse.

"Good morning's work," he said, and started to whistle.

CHAPTER 9

Lilith Love was in awe. She had been in hate before, in passion, in disgust, fear, loathing, scorn, and admiration, and just about every human emotion that didn't require electro-convulsive therapy. But she'd never known awe. There, in that cardboard box, resting on top of the neatly piled manuscript about REAL Templars, perched before the mirror on the polished dressing table in the olde hotel, was The Sacred Head of John the Baptist. Never in her wildest dreams (and she'd had some pretty wild dreams when experimenting with mescaline) had she ever thought she'd find this.

Gently (which didn't come naturally), carefully (which was a rough skill), she opened the box and saw the head – which of course she now thought of as The Head – and smiled back at it.

"Hi..." she said, shy and little-girly, in a way that no-one had ever seen her before.

"Okay, let's get on with it," said Yahya, very brisk and almost professorial. Naturally, she just loved that. Like many dominant women she fancied that she liked dominant men, but those who also had great minds as well as hard bodies and big cocks, though she had never yet had the full package. She knew that she was never gonna get that with Yahya, of course, but this first command was a good start. Lilith would sacrifice her own mother for Knowledge, and this strange and highly animate object could give her all she could ever want, and more.

"Right. Sure. Now if you'll just lemme boot up my laptop first, I've got a whole slew of questions for you."

"Not yet lady. There are things you gotta do for yourself, first. Put that stupid thing down."

Lilith looked up startled. She put that thing down which had once been her life, but which now really did look, well... stupid... and sat before him.

Yahya was clearly working on a Plan of his own that was every bit as good as de Mohun's. He'd had a bit of a holiday with Jenny Djinn, now he had to get back to work.

"Close your eyes," he said, exactly as he had done to Jenny Grey.

"Let the world come through to you. Me and the Powers will make the links."

"I don't understand"

"Close your eyes. Peace, be still..."

She clutched at her Sekhmet talisman, closed her eyes and relaxed, and she too felt as if she was floating in space, in light, and from outside her room, in the hotel garden, she heard cats fighting and then purring, or it might have been herself doing that, it felt so marvellous, so right. Then she felt as if the very shape of her head was altering, and suddenly had exquisite hearing, so that she could hear the very heart-beats of the cats outside, and such perfect sense of smell that she could almost have navigated her way around with her eyes closed, experiencing the world at olfactory levels. Then, as Jenny had done not too long before, she opened her eyes again. The room was exactly the same at one level but it seemed brighter, somehow, as if she was seeing something behind it, or beyond it. Exactly like Jenny in fact.

It's a pity she couldn't have shared notes with the latter. They'd have twigged at once that he was feeding them a sort of well-worn chat-up line.

She looked down at herself. The same designer clothes, the same exquisite figure. But she felt soooooo different.

"So what am I, Mr Head?" she asked, awestruck.

What he said next was almost word for word what Jenny had heard, though neither of them knew that.

"Well," Yahya mused, "I think you got fixated on certain tactile, olfactory and acoustic items, and so your innermost essence was up and running before I could step in. Which is no bad thing. That's why they kept me in sterile rooms in the past couple of millennia, so people like yourself wouldn't get carried with the unexpected. Which was so goddam boring if you ask me. So I reckon... all things considered, and looking at your spiritual essence rather than your corporeal.. I'd say you were..."

"Who?!"

"The cat-headed goddess Sekhmet. The Death Goddess."

Lilith didn't laugh. She knew it was true, and felt that her Sekhmet talisman had always been guiding her. With her eidetic memory she could see the quotes she had Googled:

Sekhmet & Her Function... Sekhmet's action is always the right, or 'appropriate action'. When She destroys it is an appropriate destruction or vengeance. It is never chaotic or random. It is always what is needed at the time.

And also:

Sekhmet symbolizes the struggle of the positive and negative elements of the universe. By appeasing her, victory of Harmony over Disorder, and Life over Death is assured. As with the powerful, little understood forces of nature, Sekhmet is feared.

"Yep, that's about right," said Yahya, reading her mind. "You're another Death Goddess. Can't have too many of those."

"How do I kill?" she asked, having no qualms about this. "Do I have to lurve them to death like that Jenny Djinn?"

"Nope. You just need to find a reason."

"A reason?"

"Try it."

"Listen John – Yahya – where do I begin!?"

"Start small."

So Lilith Love had a good think. She thought of all the people who certainly deserved to die. Millions of them, throughout history too, even though they were dead already. Start small, insisted a voice within her head, and then her gaze alighted on a spider in the corner of the ceiling. She had never liked spiders. And had certainly been irritated by that one up there. What use was it? Did anyone or anything love it? She'd never seen any baby spiders or wifey-spiders. The Head's presence was in her own head, showing where to find and press that button under her brain which would enable her to become Sekhmet. And if there'd been a mirror near she would probably have seen herself with the head of the lioness: she could certainly hear herself roaring in the ecstasy of power. You can go, she said to the poor arachnid, and it stopped in its tracks, aware of a Force bearing down, curled up and suddenly fell to the carpet where it lay like old snot.

Wow, she thought, in awe of herself this time. What else could she do? What else! She looked at the rubber plant in the corner of the room. She had never liked that plant. It got in the way. It wasn't even pretty, or particularly healthy looking. It needed watering, which she was too busy to do. It blocked the light. *You can go*, she said in her thoughts to the poor rubber plant, and within a second – maybe two – it looked as if a blow torch had gone all over it, the leaves blackening and shrivelling before falling off, until only a pathetic stalk remained, bowing toward the new Death Goddess like a question mark, as if in obeisance.

Lilith-as-Sekhmet breathed heavily. She felt herself returning to her more mortal form, and walked toward the remains of the plant to touch it, and felt it crumble to dust.

Remember plant, thou art dust, she thought.

And unto dust thou shalt return, finished Yahya in her head.

She looked at him. Worlds of possibility opened up in her already extraordinary life. This was amazing, this was extraordinary. She was panting, a cat in heat.

"Thank you," she said to Yahya, bowing in respect as she had never done to anyone before.

Yahya grinned. It wasn't an innocent grin.

"And now I want you to take all your clothes off," he said, licking his lips…

*

You can use your own faculty for Remote Viewing now to summon up pictures from the upstairs café in Tesco's, which had been turned into the Command Centre of all those organisations responsible for the Safety of the Realm. Not all of which were what they seemed, and each one riddled with… secret agents.

"You, two coffees," said Porteous to the cute young girl in the army uniform who, despite her Wiltshire accent, was actually from a small town in Byelorussia and working for the FSB, which, as Hughes had tried to explain, was once known as the KGB.

"Excuse me miss… I'd prefer tea please, if you don't mind," Dr McHaffee interjected. "Milk with two sugars. And perhaps a few biscuits? Digestive. Thank you very much."

It's a pity that neither Lilith or Jenny could have put poor old Porteous out of his misery there and then. But they didn't know he existed, and he himself had begun to feel he didn't exist any more. Can you imagine his agony when Hughes destroyed the mike and cam? Can you picture his frustration? He was going out of his mind with worry. Not only did he have some of the Nine reproaching him, but even worse – even colder and more ruthless – he had the French agitating as only the French can. He had to watch his back. Things were so much simpler in The Mother Lodge. Here on the raw streets of pissy little Trowbridge, worlds were in danger of ending – his own in particular.

"You have access to the woman calling herself Jenny Djinn," Porteous said to the urbane and admirably unruffled person of Dr McHaffee.

"She is a patient. And those are clearly her files – my files – which you have. I suppose I should call the police, but you probably are the police."

"Believe me doctor, you don't want to know what I am. Sometimes I don't want to know it myself."

"What do you want from me?"

"Help." It was hard for Porteous to say that, in any context.

"By that I presume you want me to Section her, so you can burst in and carry her off completely legally?"

"I thought of that. But we can do that ourselves."

"Assassin's bullet?" chided McHaffee, wide-eyed and rather scornful.

"No. Wouldn't work. You wouldn't believe how that wouldn't work. I need someone who can get near her. I saw you get near her."

"I can get near her," McHaffee reassured him.

Porteous' face lit up. This was the best news he'd had all day. This man would be perfect for the Order! Then he saw McHaffee's own expression, and it wasn't cowed, wasn't edgy as so many people were in his presence. "You have a price. I can tell by the way you're smiling and leaning."

McHaffee smiled and leaned some more: Porteous would be an excellent psychiatrist! he thought.

"My price is either very low or impossibly high, depending upon your own set of values. I simply want to know what is going on. I just want the truth. I'd be able to tell if you were lying, so don't even try. Tell me what is going on – exactly what is going on – with my Jenny Grey."

Porteous stared beyond McHaffee's head, through the walls of Tesco, into the stratosphere and beyond even that, into the cold depths of interstellar space, from which all emerged, including The

Nine and the irritating K'tan Shui. He gave the sigh of a man who has nothing to lose.

"I am the Grand Master of an ancient international Order which can trace its origins back through the Freemasons (although we're not Freemasons), back beyond the Templars (and we're not Templars, either), through the Essenes and Egyptian Theraputae (and, it perhaps goes without saying, we're not them, either), back to the courts of the mighty pharaohs and beyond them to those genius engineers who built Newgrange and Stonehenge, and beyond even that to the heyday of Atlantis. I have direct links with the heads of governments across the world and can summon up armies. I am sometimes in direct telepathic contact with the discarnate beings known as The Nine who are the true rulers of this world, and mediate their commands for the rest of us. All that stuff around the mill? I did that. Why? Because in there is the severed head of St John the Baptist, which talks, and can give access to All Knowledge, and powers that you could never believe. There..."

"Extraordinary," said McHaffee, giving a polite smile to the girl who brought the tea and coffee, and who was recording everything for people sealed in a casket-like secure room a thousand miles away.

"Not only that, but the Japanese have learned the secrets of anti-gravity from the electric kettle that one of my acolytes confused with the True Head."

"Electric kettle?"

"See-through. From Argos. But it soaked up something of The Head's powers. The Japs learned about Zero Point energy and anti-gravity from it. We're doomed."

"Doomed?"

"Imagine... no need for oil, no need for the Middle East. They will descend into chaos. No need for petrol stations, no need for cranes or heavy lifting equipment, or petrol-powered cars or jet aeroplanes. Mass unemployment, anarchy."

"All because of a kettle?"

Porteous snorted. The man was probably an idiot, after all. Or was preparing to Section him, not Jenny whatever-her-name-was.

"Kettle... it was more than that. It was the famed Cauldron of Plenty. There are books about it, but you don't believe me do you? Come... come to the window with me. I can call up helicopters, tanks, riot police. What would you like? A helicopter? No problem. I'll make it hover over the mill and waggle."

With the weary air of man who has almost had enough, he flipped out his phone, pressed a few buttons. Nothing happened. Porteous looked at the display, his brow furrowed. "Maybe I can't get a signal from here. Let's move down here."

He tried again. Nothing. And again. And again.

"Perhaps you've run out of credit?" McHaffee suggested with a kindly air.

Porteous was shaking. He knew what this meant.

"You seem troubled," McHaffee said, in best caring doctor mode. "Who are you looking around for?"

Porteous was looking around for the shadow of the guillotine: he knew the French had probably already taken over, that he had displeased The Nine, and that the Gates of Hell and an early retirement on a Civil Service pension were beckoning.

"Listen," he said, grabbing McHaffee's lapels, "come with me. It's not safe here. We must–"

He stopped short because Spoffo had appeared as if from nowhere with some beefy minders, and the plasticuffs were on his former boss before you could cry *M'aidez!* Actually he couldn't have cried anything because a bit of tape was put over his mouth at the same time. McHaffee frowned, slightly, but having used the chemical cosh in his own clinical practice many times in the good old days, he wasn't going to argue.

"What do you think, doctor?" Spoffo asked.

"You're right. Barking mad, to use your phrase. A classic paranoid schizophrenic, as you said – though it's not a term I'd use these days. Too much dopamine flowing through his system. Still, never mind. I'll sign any order you need to get him off the streets. Just give me back that file."

Spoffo gave the deep sigh of a man who now had everything to gain. That poofter Hughes had gone over to the other side. It felt so good to be the new Grand Master, the youngest in its secret history. He was certain he could cope with the French.

"Listen doc, just one quick question: is it possible for a man and woman with Downs Syndrome to have sex and create a baby which is perfectly normal?"

McHaffee frowned and looked inward. "Yes. Yes it is. I knew of a young couple with Downs who had a perfectly normal baby boy. Because they couldn't really cope, the boy was brought up in care, and then when he was a young adult came back to look after his mother after she became widowed. Why?"

"No reason. Thanks for your help. Allons..." he said smugly as they marched poor Porteous away. "Now we can really get stuck in..."

*

Listen, if you have the slightest degree of sensitivity, you really don't want to know too much about what Lilith and Yahya got up to in those first couple of days. It would make your own head spin round like in *The Exorcist* and your stomach heave and force you to say something like *Uugggggggggh!!!* On the other hand, if you're a coarse but imaginative soul you can put two and two together and work out that Lilith – who had lived entirely in her head for most of her life – was having the most unusual but satisfying sex she had ever known with a man who had lived as a head for 2,000 years.

The sun was setting beyond Trowle Common. The sky was every shade of red, islanded with thin ochre clouds, and it seemed to Lilith that she was looking out over a tantalising and parallel landscape that could surely be explored. Especially now that she had Yahya. They sat on a bench on her verandah, enclosed by the high walled garden, Yahya's head on her lap and looking outward. No-one, on pain of Lilith Love's considerable fury, was allowed near. The Polish Contingent, as she thought of them, acted as discreet and highly-paid guards. As a bonus, each of them had had Shaz upside down and inside out, and (discreetly) proclaimed her a far warmer and better ride than their scary employer. To them, sex with Lilith sometimes felt like putting your head into a lion's mouth.

"Why don't you like Jesus? – I mean Yeshua."

Yahya spat, though where he got the phlegm from, she couldn't have said. The air around them darkened at the very mention of the name.

"It should have been me. The Messiah. 'I could ha been a contender,'" he growled, taking off Marlon Brando's famous line from *On The Waterfront* that he had watched with Jenny only the previous week. "Plus he stole my girl. Mary. We had a whole new religion already. Then cousin Yeshua appeared, smug and superior as anything, flaunting his DNA. Hell I'm descended from the House of David too! Mary, well she… aaah."

"How did he get his power – Yeshua, I mean?"

"Through me, how else. Look him up in the Talmud and you'll the see the guy was a magician. They all saw right through him. Standard practice to get a severed head and make the soul work for you. The better the head, the better the sorcery. All kindsa guys have done this before and since."

Lilith couldn't wait to Google all this later, so she had it down in print from other sources. Try it yourself: just tap 'Talmud Jesus Magician' into the search box, press OK, and in 0.2 seconds you'll get 18,500 references, though none of them from Source as manifested next to Lilith.

"But did he…"

"No more!" said Yahya, his mood changing at the memory of the good old days. The wind in the walled garden swirled, and spiralled up leaves like a mini-twister. The sky darkened more and the temperature plummeted. Yahya grimaced and his eyes rolled. This was dangerous ground. Lilith decided to back off.

"Okay, okay, so what you got planned for me, huh?"

The Head took a deep breath. She felt it go through his nostrils, down his windpipe and out between her thighs. He took another and the sky lightened, the whirlwind of leaves collapsed upon themselves, it became warm again.

"I just want you to be yourself," he said, and not many men had ever said that to her. He was like a god to her.

"We can start a new religion, honey," she said. "Me and you."

"I used to like honey," he mused, his eyes going dreamy with remembrance. "Honey and locusts. Mmmmmm…"

"You shouldha said! I can get you that. I'd get anything for you."

He smiled. It was an angel's smile. "Thanks. Thank you, Lilith Love. In the meantime I want you to practice a little more killing."

Okay, she smiled, stroking his hair, happy as a little girl – happier than she had ever been even when she'd been a little girl. She didn't know – how could she have known? – that Yahya's own motives were not much different to that of de Mohun's: destroy everything and everyone who had ever entrapped him, or used, or insulted him.

"I don't know too many folk here in England, but I know a whole bunch back in the States who deserve to go. Can I do it from here?"

"Distance is no obstacle. Nor is Time."

"Can I start with the President?"

"Start small," he reminded.

She thought. She thought hard. She roamed the Time and Space of her own life. "There was a little fat guy in my home town who owned the White Castle burger bar, who once got fresh with me, and I was only 15. His name was Mr Papadopoulos. He smelled of grease and cigarettes and had sweat stains you could wash your underwear in. Would he do?"

"Perfect. Now think of a reason for him to die."

"Would two hundred reasons do? Maybe he's already dead."

Yahya's eyes glazed over slightly, as if looking at a remote viewing screen inside his head. "No, he's still there, living two blocks away, but retired. I think he's still got the same shirt on."

Lilith beamed. This was gonna be fun, and worthy. As she thought of reason after reason, her head seemed to glow and radiate flames of energy, so anyone psychic would have seen her become the lion-headed goddess Sekhmet, and felt the danger, the sheer power. Somehow, she just knew that the old creep had died, with a puzzled look on his stupid fat face.

As for Yahya, he just sat there on Lilith's lap – as far as a severed head could actually 'sit' anywhere – and closed his eyes in bliss as she did a bit of Indian Head Massage while bringing Mr Papadopoulos' life to a very rapid and unlamented end...

*

When Lilith was serving her unseen and as-yet-secret apprenticeship in the Manor Grove, all hell was breaking out around The Sanctuary that held Jenny Djinn and her devotees. There were heavily armed troops in the compound now, and armoured cars. An exclusion zone had been declared for the air-space around it. Any press helicopter attempting to approach it would have been shot down. Even so, the D Notices slapped on the media by the Security Services were ineffective: this was too big. The crowds were even bigger, more turbulent, and completely international. Everyone, at some level, wanted a piece of Kali for many differing reasons, not all of them wholesome. Senior figures from the Inland Revenue were tucked away within the mob, wondering if anyone in that big old besieged building had filled in a single tax return for that year. This was all incredibly exciting for the town as a whole! The shops, pubs and crack-dens emptied. Children played hooky despite their parents' dire warnings. No-one went to the library anymore – a fact which would have dismayed Jack had he known. The T-shirts and sweaters that the disciples were making sold a storm as they were passed over the walls and cash thrown back in return, no receipts. It was as if the Second Coming had begun here in West Wiltshire, which is what a lot of folk earnestly came to believe, while others firmly rejected the very idea and turned walking sticks into offensive weapons.

Jenny, Jack and Nyron Hughes stood on the top floor looking out over the crowds, scanning them with binoculars and picking out familiar faces. Jenny continued to wear her invariable 'civilian' clothes: simple outfits in pale solid colours which showed off her slim figure and something of her shapely legs. The two men were togged up in the red jump-suit outfits that Felicity had made de rigeur, as she termed it. Hughes, who was fussy about the uniforms he personally would wear, felt rather swish in this kit, while to his eyes it made his Jack look…. edible. He stood hard up against the wall, angled slightly to hide his stiffy.

"That's Madonna!" said Jenny with excitement, pointing into the masses. The two men looked slightly embarrassed but she explained: "No, not the religious one, I mean the singer. She used to have a big house down the road." Which was true enough at that time, Ashcombe Park, and it might well have been her though neither Jack nor Hughes could pick out her face amid the heaving swell of the curious and the fanatical. "If that's not her then I'm a virgin. And look look! Near the tree that I blasted… That's Sting. The midget with him might – just might – be Tom Cruise. Or is it one of the Krankies?"

"Look!" came the next excited observation. "Dame Edna Everage!!"

Actually, it was the Bishop of Bath and Wells come to see what the fuss was about, but no-one could have been completely sure at that distance, even with binoculars. The fact is, neither of the two men could be sure that Jenny was wrong, so they started to play her game, acting as if, so before long they'd picked out Anthony Head, the man from *Buffy the Vampire Slayer*, half of the cast of *Casualty*, Timothy West and Prunella Scales, just about everyone who had ever acted in *Dr Who* and at least two definite sightings of girls from *Eastenders*. Though as Hughes chipped in with Elton John, Julian Clary and Boy George, he was rather shrivelled when Jenny turned to him with gentle exasperation and said: "Now you're being silly..."

There was a knock at the door. Felicity came in with a silver tea service on a silver tray, and you could tell she was jealous of the men, and their being allowed so close to her Kali Ma.

"There you are Mother," she said, bowing slightly, careful not to spill anything on the tray. "And Tasha has brought up a huge selection of the most recent pleas... there's another twenty sacks downstairs. Your daughters are working on them now."

Jenny smiled. Mother. Daughter. Such bollocks! She who had never had children, nor ever would, was now mother to a multitude. She looked into the sort of big white sack which once had held laundry in the local hospital and plunged her hands among the letters, swirling her palms into the depths, smiling benignly, almost as if she were stirring her love into them. Again, the light, the sense of rippling arms, the power and the love. Everyone present looked on with wonder. For a Death Goddess, she inspired a feeling of absolute safety.

"There," she said. "They've all gone Home." She always said that last word with the slightest emphasis on the H, and made it sound very wistful.

"All of them?" asked Jack, and his own two admirers delighted in his clever question, he really was so very very clever! He picked up one which had fallen to the floor and peered into the brown envelope. It had the obligatory two photographs stapled onto the written plea. They showed a young man he had gone to school with, who had delighted in calling him a poof, written by a girl who had once cut up his library card. Jack felt no antagonism. He was not so much a master of forgiveness, but of emotional indifference. Besides, he was just so interested by the whole thing.

"How many have you released now?" asked Nyron Hughes, readjusting the elastic of his trousers, trying to redirect the flow of blood into some other area.

Jenny shrugged. Felicity answered for her: "Thousands. Her loving is growing daily, and with it her power." She spoke softly, as people who feel they are 'spiritual' often do. It was true enough what she said though. "We've also started using her photograph. People have reported great success just by placing this under the pillow of the person they want to release." She showed them the computer-enhanced photo which showed Jenny before a black but starry background, the light oozing from her, and you could see the Kali, arms an' all.

"What now?" asked Hughes, who found this all so different to the hairy-arsed male adeptii of his previous Secret World. "What should I do?"

Jenny looked out at the crowds again. She felt hungry, as she usually did after such a Sending. "I think you should phone Mrs Loganathan and order us a nice vindaloo..."

*

It was about this time that Mrs Hobbes received her first visitation. Since Tesco' s had been made out of bounds, she' d had to use up the last of the stuff in her freezer, so there she was doing a couple of chicken fajita wraps in the microwave and waiting for the ding! when she suddenly sensed a presence behind her. The tube of the ceiling light flashed on and off and then decided to stay on, flickering, almost grey in tone. The microwave just packed in completely. She turned slowly, very afraid, and was somewhat bewildered to see a strangely chunky man in the doorway, wearing full evening suit with bow-tie, and he might have looked rather nice if it hadn't for the mirrored glasses. She took a deep breath and released it. He clearly meant no harm, and at least it wasn't one of her social worker team.

"You didn't knock," she said, which considering this was the first time she had ever spoken to an alien being from another galaxy, took quite a lot of nerve.

K'tan Shui cocked his head to one side, drummed his fingers on the kitchen table and smiled.

"Go out again and knock," Maisie insisted. And to the astonishment of all those agencies who were covertly observing every moment of K'tan Shui's time on Earth, he did exactly that.

Now what you must know about K'tan Shui, and which only a couple of humans suspected, is that he had the same degree of learning disability as Mrs Hobbes, and that alien races also have their equivalents of Downs Syndrome. Not all of the alien races – few of them in fact – are super-advanced. Intelligence is not proportionate to distance from Earth or size of space ship. No-one ever knew the full story of K'tan Shui, or found out why his strange 'ship' should have crashed into the side of Cley Hill after leaving a wonderful crop circle at the side of it. Despite the best boffins in Britain making their best attempts to communicate, they didn't quite realise that he himself had not the slightest idea of how his space craft worked, or why he had landed where he did. If we can speculate at all, he was probably not so much a messenger from an advanced and distant galaxy, so much as an unwanted idiot child, dumped on the Wiltshire Social Services for them to deal with.

"Come in!" said Maisie brightly, for it wasn't often that she got visitors who weren't carrying Care Plans.

K'tan Shui came in, this time clutching a rose that he plucked from the bush outside her door. There was no stem, just the head, some petals falling over the floor, but the gesture was a winning one. He gently threw the rest of the petals toward her, like confetti, then bowed and drummed his stubby fingers together. How could she not be charmed! He took his glasses off and she looked into the vertical pupils, and said those Words of Power that have helped make Britain Great...

"Come and have a nice cuppa tea..."

The light above steadied, and the microwave dinged.

*

Jack was in the inner sanctum, sitting on the couch next to Jenny Djinn, totally fascinated by everything. The little telly was still on – Jenny kept it going all the time – but by now it was connected to satellite and picking up channels from all over the world.

"Here," she said, offering the remote control to him as if it were Excalibur. "Choose whatever you want."

She meant a good film, preferably one of the golden oldies like *The Quiet Man* with John Wayne going back to Ireland and beating the shit out of Victor McClaglen. But he was interested in the foreign

179

news. The British channels were still plonking dutifully on about The Flu, showing people with masks and dead creatures all over the place, and advising people not to travel to or from Trowbridge. But the rest of the world was clearly aware of, and obsessed by, the earthquake of events happening just outside, of which Jack was at the very epicentre. The French channels in particular couldn't get enough it, and there was The Sanctuary on TV5, and rapid interviews with anyone who had a connection with events, however tenuous. He hoped his mum was watching.

"Amazing..." he gasped, and it was! "Look you have to tell me about The Head. Where did it – he – come from? How many other powers can he give? Do you miss him?"

That's just a summary actually. He had dozens of questions. Jack was a blank book aching to be filled. In some ways he was like Lilith in that he craved Knowledge with a big K more than just about anything.

"Yahya has gone," Jenny said firmly, turned on the couch so she could look him full on. His hair was angel-golden, his eyes the purest blue. "And he's given me you! Remember those cuddles, hey hey?" Nudge nudge. No need to wink.

"Yeah, that was nice, but... but..." She leaned over and kissed him full on the lips, but they were dead lips, as dead as his dick had been. He wanted gnosis, not naughtiness. "Oh please tell me everything. Please?" he said, pulling away gently.

Jenny Djinn sighed. He was a right tease this fella of hers! So she sat back and told him everything from that moment in the car park at the foot of Cley Hill, up until the present, but the sad fact is that she didn't have that much to tell. She was like K'tan Shui in some ways: no learning disability – certainly not – just a complete lack of interest in the whys and wherefroms. While Lilith Love at that very moment was attempting the impossible task of draining The Head of everything it knew, Jenny had never bothered to ask it much at all.

"Where's the original kettle gone?"

She didn't know, or even know that Nyron Hughes could have told her.

"Can he teleport far?"

She didn't know. Hughes could also have told her that, according to his experience with the Order, The Head had a range of a couple metres, but was exhausted afterward. That's why they were able to keep him one place.

"Look Jack," said Jenny, slightly distressed that she couldn't answer his questions, not wanting to feel stupid again like Jenny Grey. "Look, just come and watch a film with me, like Yahya did.

"Do you miss him?"

"I've got you," she answered, giving him a huge and disturbing smile, wrapping him in all sorts of emotions which might have felt like many arms.

"Are you really Kali?"

"Yes. Yes I am."

"Will you destroy the world?"

She gave him another beaming smile. Jenny Djinn might have had no real education but she had learnt the first lesson of the guru: if you don't know an answer, be enigmatic, say nothing, let the pupil fill in the silence. She opened the telly magazine and scanned the offerings. "Ooh look, *3.10 to Yuma* is on in five minutes. That's dead good. Then we can go to bed and have another cuddle."

Jack frowned, though she never saw it. Jenny might have been the avatar of the goddess but she didn't know doodly-squat about basic human things.

"And later," she offered, "if there's anyone you might want released, I'll do it for you specially. I'd do anything for you."

"Just promise me one thing, Jenny..."

"Anything."

"That you'll never, ever, 'release' my Mum."

She smiled. "I promise. Kali Ma promises."

And that was good enough for Jack.

*

Lilith Love got the hang of becoming Sekhmet with no trouble at all. Unlike Jenny she had no qualms about women or children, and she didn't mess around with terms like 'release' or sending them 'Home'. She liked the killing, plain and simple. Although she never saw the victims, she knew in her bones that they were gone, and felt wonderfully full, gorged in fact, and often went to a mirror to check whether it really was just lipstick that she still wore or pure blood.

In truth, if you had to become the victim of a Death Goddess, then you'd probably prefer Kali.

Because all Lilith's first victims keeled over back in the States, no-one so far had made the connection with events in Trowbridge. Even in the States, with their high murder rates and the like, it took a while before anyone over there realised that something was remiss. Once again it happened because Lilith's phone call to her agent, Gloria, was picked up by a young American woman working for the National Security Agency this time. It was her job to hear things in her head, just as it was for her counterpart at GCHQ. If you want to find out how the NSA differs from GCHQ then you might want to 'do a Lilith' and Google the former, which will take you straight to www.nsa.gov and if you click below the fierce image of the eagle, you will see in the very first paragraph:

The National Security Agency collects, processes and disseminates foreign Signals Intelligence (SIGINT). The old adage that 'knowledge is power' has perhaps never been truer than when applied to today's threats against our nation and the role SIGINT plays in overcoming them.... SIGINT plays a vital role in our national security by employing the right people and using the latest technology to provide America's leaders with the critical information they need to save lives, defend democracy, and promote American values.

Any excuse for a good bit of spying, eh? More voices in the head. So what happened was that when Gloria asked her *what was going on over there*, and *was she infected by this weird Flu in little ole Trowbridge*, and *did she believe it even existed?* Lilith laughed so loud that said agent had to put the phone down for a moment while her hysterics subsided. Then it all poured out: REAL Templars, the severed head of St John the Baptist, Death Goddesses, of which she was one. *Sure. Really.* She, Lilith Love, was now the avatar of Sekhmet, the Lion-headed One. She told Gloria of several people she had killed, explained something about Sekhmet and advised her to do some research on that deity asap, and asked her if she wanted any help to off anyone – anyone at all. And as she poured and roared, and as Gloria sat down in disbelief, people across the Atlantic at Fort Meade, Maryland, listened and pondered, listened again to the recording, pondered some more, then contacted people higher than themselves.

There were lots of hawk-faced men in suits in what they called a Secure Room, marvelling that they'd got that ball-breaker Lilith Love – the Lilith Love – in their sights. Lots of acronyms in their conversation. The jargon was exploding like shrapnel and bouncing off the walls. The essence of what they said was this: The events she talked about in England – the Death Goddess thing? – were confirmed by the British Security Services. The people she named did all die in mysterious ways. But it all boiled down to one question: absurd though the whole thing may seem... Can she harm the president?

No-one was willing to take a chance. And given that the Brits were taking their own native Death Goddess very seriously indeed, they really needed to get someone on Lilith Love's case, without telling anyone.

So historians have argued that that, really, was the moment when it all started to fall apart. Though perhaps we should take into account the crucial moment when Lilith learned how to stop the clock, because it was then that her powers really took off!

*

The clock in question was on the wall in the room she used exclusively for penetrative sex. If we have to define it so explicitly, it is only to avoid the details of what went on between her and Yahya in her Inner Sanctum. The poor clock was nothing special, just a big round thing with a silver casing, white face and black hands that had been bought from H. J. Knees Department Store in town. She came to dislike this clock because of its tick. She hadn't even noticed the tick before until she was bent over at the windowsill, being taken from behind by her Polish lover, with the others waiting their turn.

It was a perfect evening. The air was filled with bird-song. There was a thin crescent moon. Somewhere in the distance she heard the sound of children playing, brought to her on the pure breeze. Her mind was afire with all the knowledge that Yahya had given her before he slept – knowledge which the NSA knew was power, and which was meat and drink to her. It might have been idyllic except that the guy was clearly thrusting in time to the tick, a precise 60 strokes a minute.

Sure, she could have told him to change rhythm. Sure, she could have told one of the others to take the battery outta the damned thing and throw it in the garbage. But for some reason she decided to see if she could kill something that wasn't actually alive.

She could. Sure she could. She didn't even have to go into full Sekhmet mode for such a teeny little thing like a clock. She just visualised the second hand stopping while she said to it in her mind: *Stop!* Above the squelching noises made by the large Polish sausage slamming into her rude bits, she heard it stop. None of the others in the room noticed, of course.

Her mind raced. If she could stop a small piece of machinery, what about something larger? In the distance, coming up Trowle Common, was a big delivery truck heading toward Asda – which got all the trade now that its main rival, Tesco, was out of commission. *Stop!* She thought, sending the word bounding and pouncing toward the vehicle, squeezing with every mental and physical muscle she had. The man within her (and we are talking Pole here, not animus) grunted as he climaxed. And the truck... it stopped. She could see the man climb down out of the cab and look at all the pieces that might have gone wrong. If she didn't actually hear him scratch his head and swear in bewilderment, then she should have done.

"Next!!" she said and, as the English of these guys was pretty good by now (in certain specific areas), Pole Number Two mounted her and started to build up a rhythm. She looked at the silver gleam and contrails of a distant aeroplane and grinned, and knew now that she could take this one, easy peasy.

Conscience? Nah. It wasn't Lilith Love who was about to down an airliner and all in it – it was Sekhmet. Sekhmet did no wrong. Sekhmet just was.

Stop! she willed toward the plane and it did that, it just fell from the sky like a stone, somewhere in Gloucestershire, though they wouldn't learn the details until they caught the news, much later.

"And the next!" she said, verbally this time, to the energies behind her. "Aw, c'mon on you guys, I'm hungry!"

CHAPTER 10

John de Mohun sat beside the table in the refectory and rolled the grip of his battle sword between his palms, point down on the stone floor, the blade half-revolving back and forth and sending scythes of light onto the grey walls. Like Lilith, he also felt hunger, but his surged from his stomach rather than his loins, and came with a great and almost spiritual sense of calm, sweeping over him in waves. It was the feeling he had of a job well done, and he only needed to follow it with a nice meal to celebrate. He used to feel the same after battles, and his men joked that he was like a big kitten then, you could have done anything with him, said anything to him. Not that they actually did, you understand, coz even when he was in this almost cuddly mood, they were still facing a giant killing machine who would rather fight than fuck, as the saying went. You could never imagine that he once had a mother.

He clapped. The minstrel in the corner started up with that rollicking ballad 'Nutting, Nutting, Girls Love Nutting' – which was a 14th Century euphemism for rampant sex, of course – while two nervous young women with very short hair brought him a nice bowl of pork broth, and they didn't complain when he goosed them in passing. It was just his little way. It meant he liked them. "Thank you sir," they said in unison, but hurried off.

Ha....! If he had tried that with Jenny Grey 700 years later, she would have given a rueful smile and let him go on for a shag, and rather hoped he would hang around afterward. If he had done the same with Lilith, then depending on whether she was in heat or not, she might have chewed him out, or given him a straight punch in the throat, or else mounted him there and then.

As he waited for the broth to cool, blowing it slightly and adding salt, he ran the whet-stone along the edges of his great sword for one final time, to the rhythm of the song. The hauntings which had affected them all had stopped. The probable reason for that was because Jenny Djinn, Jack, Lilith, the Japanese and all the rest of them, were now so pre-occupied with their own situations that dapping across Time to view a few smelly Templars wasn't really feasible. The preceptory was calm. The protesters from the other day were not likely to protest again. And the Grand Master was on his way, like Santa Claus – although of course that fat red bastard hadn't been invented yet.

Oh, he felt so good! The reason he felt this way was because everything was ready. Soon, William de la More and the two arseholes from Templecombe would be sent the way of all flesh, and this age – this world of his – would be at an end. No going back now. He always liked this sort of inevitability, when there was no need to make any more choices, and everything had to happen as it was meant to happen. He had been trapped in this shit-hole for too long. The Order meant nothing to him now, and hadn't for many years. Not that he intended betrayal: no, he just wanted to destroy it.

De Sautré was out of sight and hearing, attending to the deeply shocked and exhausted Master Engayne. The latter was a hero. At least in his own estimation. Not easy to gallop 40 miles when you've got piles like dreadlocks. Not after having fought off two dozen outlaws, and witnessed your best friend murdered by another six at least.

"Tut tut," said de Egle, who had greeted Engayne at the gates of the preceptory in full and immaculate Templar gear, showing no signs of the gallop he himself had just made.

"You would have smote them right hard," said de Hambledon joining in, who had the casual air of a man just come back from a nice stroll rather than that manic ride across hill and vale. "With might and main, and calling on St John, no doubt!"

"Aye," said Engayne frowning, remembering the battle, more fierce in the remembrance than he had been in the fighting itself.

"The Grand Master will hear all about it on the morrow," said de Mohun, and had to resist a sneer when he saw the man's face light up at the very thought. "Now let his young nephew here take you inside and give you refreshment. Then later we will be honoured to hear your whole story."

Honoured...? Bah! At this point the other three wanted to throw up. De Mohun might have been a psychopath, and the other two complete idiots for being willing to follow him through the very Gates of Hell, but at least they had a basic sort of integrity. No arse-licking for them.

De Mohun clapped his hands twice and the minstrel stopped in mid-flow, just as he was about to sing the hook line about the two white birds inside the girl's top. De Mohun gave a dismissive wave and the minstrel left the room to go and find a couple of white birds for himself.

De Mohun went to the door and each window to make sure that no-one was lurking.

"John, Robert," the very imperfect and ungentle knight said to his two loyal friends once he knew the three of them were quite alone. They stiffened. Whenever he used their names like that it usually meant he was going to send them out on a mission. They were like Pavlov's dog. They stopped just short of putting out their tongues and panting. "This time tomorrow, everything will end. Everything we once believed in. If we survive, everyone in England will turn against us. Everyone in the order will be hunted down. *Our very souls* might be at risk."

"Then let's go to Scotland," said de Egle. "They are much smaller up there. We could make a good living as murderers."

"Somewhere wild, with no sheep," de Hambledon added.

"The point is… are you with me? I will think none the less if you choose to ride out now and find soft lives with buxom women. You do not have to do this."

The two men looked surprised, almost hurt. They had loyalties that we might find hard to understand, if we have never been in battle.

"Of course," said de Egle.

"Certainly," echoed de Hambledon.

The great figure of de Mohun embraced them both: there were tears in his eyes.

*

On the top floor of the Old Mill, Jenny Djinn was in full flow as Kali Ma, and people in the world beyond were dying in great numbers. For some of them, it was the happiest moment of their lives. For Jenny, the room in which she worked was filled with loving-kindness, like incense, and Jack sat before her taking it all in after being assured that his own beloved Mum was not going to be released in any way, not ever.

Downstairs, meanwhile, Nyron Hughes was in a state of some delight. He was on the floor now known as the Dance Floor, surrounded by a circle of women led by Felicity, and learning how to get in touch with his Inner Death, as she termed it. Of course he knew it was a right load of old tosh, and that Felicity was making up the details of this new religion as she went along, but then again maybe the same had been true of his old Order.

"You are the axis, Nyron. You are the Omphalos. Turn and turn... Dance ye all! Come on gels – Dance ye All!"

Well, he'd been called a lot of things in his time, and had been branded as homosexual, bisexual, heterosexual, metrosexual and downright omnisexual, but he'd never been an omphalos before. When he saw Jack later he'd ask what it meant, and try to get him into bed.

It was soooooo different, being surrounded by all these women, as opposed to the masculine dominance of his former Order. He could get used to this! In fact, the poor sod was almost out of his head with delight, and feeling free. If knowledge was power, he realised then in this little town on the edge of nowhere, that he didn't want power, and had never wanted knowledge. Not really.

They stopped for coffee. Large cushions and larger bean bags were thrown over the polished floor. The women all flocked around him, even though most of them were in openly lesbian relationships now. They felt safe with him – that's what they said. It made him feel very strong, whereas Porteous had just made him feel like shite much of the time.

"This is so good," said Tasha, sitting down next to him. Air was blown from the vent-hole of the bean bag like a fart, and they laughed. They both stank of sweat. It didn't matter. Soon they would all get clean together in the collective showers, and no-one would bat an eye when he joined them. Felicity had a spiritual reason for this which she expounded in a particularly long lecture, but the simple fact was that she enjoyed the perviness that many naked bodies, warm water, and adequate supplies of non-allergenic soap could induce.

"It is," he said softly, "It is indeed." He marvelled that all these women had – though they didn't know it – been empowered by the severed head of St John the Baptist. As far as they were concerned it was all down to Jenny Djinn, their Kali Ma, who had meticulously kept herself away from all these shenanigans going on beneath her feet. The truth is, she wasn't interested in them at all. She had her telly and video, she had her Jack, she had her new career, and Yahya was always within her head.

"We all want to shag you, you know that. Well, most of us."

He beamed. "Thank you very much!"

"I've heard you're – you know.."

"Bit of a whoopsie?"

"Yes, well."

"I can rise to the occasion with women."

"But it's that Jack you want, isn't it? You love him don't you?"

"Is it that obvious?"

"Yes. Your face shines when he comes near. Nothing wrong with that. He's Jenny's fella though. She told us that from the start. I feel the same for Felicity, though. She's gollygosh good, as she likes to say. But I still fancy men!"

They looked down upon the ever-present crowds. Hughes saw Spoffo at the gate, doing his guarding thing. He was so glad not to be connected with that lot any more, and never wanted to see another man in a hooded dress as long as he lived. There were no intrigues here within The Sanctuary; people were essentially nice, when they weren't putting forward names for being Released.

At that moment, Felicity's clarion tones sounded like the Imam's call to prayer, and they all made their eager way to the shower block.

"Stand next to me in there, big boy" said Tasha, though it was clear from the cluster of women around Hughes at this point that she was not the only one with this idea.

*

As for Felicity herself, the St Paula of this new religion, she was happier than she had ever been, and was busy putting up small notices around The Sanctuary announcing details of her next (inspired) lecture, the contents of which she had entirely found by means of the search-engine Yahoo. So she wasn't any different to Lilith Love in that respect, although the latter certainly had more brake horse-power than she did when it came to intellect. The lecture was entitled: 'Thanatology – The Scientific Study of Death and Dying – and Love.' The substance of the text went:

189

Death Education courses, and the hospice movement are all signs of the changing awareness, and – with the help of Our Lady Jenny Djinn – point toward the growing desire to integrate the inevitable. Soror Felicity will talk about the myths of Death: the Chapel Perilous, the Dark Night of the Soul, or Crossing the Abyss. She will describe how ego death has also been considered an important milestone on the seeker's path in some spiritual traditions, and outline the long indigenous ritual use of sacred plants, the ingestion of which sometimes features a figurative death and subsequent rebirth as a shaman or as an adult member of the community. She will encourage everyone to talk about their own visits to the spirit realms, and of communication with their deceased/released ancestors.

Good job Shaz was no longer here. She'd have thought that was all a death-rattle too far. Complete bollocks from a posh tart. She was far happier where she was, being rammed by The Poles, and attending to the minimal needs of the mad yank. And if Lilith had been there she'd have used Google and zoomed right in on the URL in question, and if you're interested in seeing the true origins of the religion you can look it up yourself (if the website has survived after those dreadful End Days, that is).

Mind you, Jenny too might have quibbled just a tad about that poster too, had she bothered to appear instead of spending all her time doing – goddess knows what, as Felicity would say – with 'that Jack.' The pair of them, the Holy Couple, were lost behind those doors which led to the Uppermost Room, and no-one dared disturb them.

So you can understand that Felicity saw everything in terms of predestination, and the blinding light she got from Kali's avatar on the 'Road to Trowbridge Revelation', as she termed it in a small pamphlet which became almost a first Gospel. "Now come on gels!" she cried. "Kecks off and into those showers – you too Nyron. Cleanliness is next to goddessliness."

Hughes laughed. He had a sense that the world was on the edge of complete destruction, but here on the middle floor of an old building in Wiltshire, it all seemed so terribly funny.

*

Actually, if Hughes had had some cold statistics to hand, even his laughter might have died. It might be easy to find life risible when you're the only man among a bunch of frequently naked women, surrounded by tits and bums and well-lathered willingness, but when you've got a spreadsheet that detailed the sheer extent of the dying, and the latest projections showing that it was on a steep upward curve, then even the most callous of souls might have given a little gulp.

Spoffo stood at the gates of The Compound, as he thought of it, and wondered how he was going to get access to The Head now that Hughes had become a renegade. He too had seen the spreadsheets: the fake ones which the government would supply to curious or suspicious parties who invoked the Freedom of Information Act; and also the REAL ones, which had the power to cause global panic and widespread rioting if the information were ever to be made public. In this case, Secrecy was Power. In Britain at least, if the killings continued at the present rate of increase, there would no men left on the island within the next six months. All cunning plans aside, he turned more and more to the idea of a Typhoon fighter-bomber blasting the whole building to smithereens with a small thermo-nuclear missile.

He looked outside the massive steel gate through a peephole that he couldn't help thinking resembled an arsehole, and what a lot of shite he saw out there! The army, under his direction, was allowing a few candidates near the gates just to keep the populace happy. That tart from the telly with the big tits, Tippi Wendover, had approached earlier and almost offered him a shag if only he would let her inside. Then she had been followed by various female pals from the casts of *Coronation Street*, *Eastenders*, and *Fishermen's Wives*. Add to these the various weirdos who introduced themselves as Shiva (many of them with strong Birmingham accents) and who had come offering their services to their beloved Kali, then young Spoffo could be forgiven for thinking he was in Headcase Heaven.

Mind you, considering the stakes, he had had to let that lot through just in case. After all, no-one would have believed Jenny was Kali until recently. Maybe – just maybe – an avatar of Shiva was out there too, and would come and sort out the mess. None of them had been able to prove themselves, however. They were all sent packing. On the other hand, he definitely forbade any of the dozen or so geeks claiming to be incarnations of Krishna, Vishnu, Jesus, Horus the Hawk God, Thoth, Quetzalcoatl, and Errol Flynn.

A voice came into his head through purely electronic means. It spoke perfect English, but with a marked French accent. Those shadowy but eminent figures who had appointed him, and had also dealt so ruthlessly with Porteous, were keen on a solution. They needed to know that he had a Plan. Time was getting short, the world itself was in grave danger, and The Nine were agitating something chronic. They wanted The Head back before it was too late.

"I'll act soon," Spoffo said out loud, knowing they would hear him. "I know exactly what to do," he lied.

*

"Whoopee!" said Lilith as all the passengers and crew of a Jumbo suddenly started to look puzzled, leading to another airliner biting the dust – or rather the cold waters of the North Atlantic.

"Oh bless…" said Jenny softly on the other side of the town as another sackful of fellas, scattered over the entire country, died with chuckles on their cheeks.

It was all really serious by this time. They were both at it – Lilith and Jenny – cutting away increasingly large numbers of the population and putting the morgues, funeral parlours and medical services generally under enormous pressure, not to mention causing unimaginable grief to those left behind. Hospitals in the US and the UK quietly and separately adopted a policy that if they received an emergency call relating to an unexpected death, they should ask the caller if their looked puzzled (US) or happy (UK), and if so, they knew it was not a priority. The military in both nations was drafted in to deal with these cases. Mass graves had to dug in some of the poorer areas.

You saw what a head-banger de Mohun was, and his two loyal pals were not that far behind. But compared to these two women, he was St Francis of Assissi, Dale Winton and Archbishop Desmond Tutu rolled into one. They might have been goddesses, but they were also becoming complete and utter lunatics with every hour that passed.

Lilith was the first to realise she could turn her power up a notch. She saw an airplane taking off live on www.cnn.com/video, showing Mort Slaley, the US Vice President setting off on a peace-brokering mission to Africa, and she just couldn't resist it, she was like a little girl stealing candy. She had a thousand reasons as to why that plane should crash, and why Slaley was a waste of space. So just as the commentator was breaking out of his boredom, the astonished and (largely) horrified world saw the plane suddenly plummet to the ground for no apparent reason and explode in the suburbs to massive loss of life.

TERRORIST OUTRAGE! screamed the media across the world.

"Nope," said Sekhmet, "just lil ole Lilith Love, honies," she half-growled, half-drawled, doing a Southern Belle thing. "Ain't I just the greatest lurve Goddess ever?" she looked at Yahya, but he was sleeping. Typical man.

Kali Ma, on the other hand(s), aka Jenny Djinn, discovered that she could love collectively. There she was on the couch, arm around Jack and not at all aware of how awkward he felt, watching the film *Brassed Off* which starred Ewan McGregor and Pete Postlethwaite, about brass bands up North; and when it had finished she said, fatefully: "Ooh, I just love brass bands. I really love them."

Guess what happened... Yep, her surge of love for brass bands carried her into the Full Kali and before you could say *Oompah*, every card-carrying member of a brass band in the country gave a sigh of delight and went on. Jenny, meanwhile took delivery of another nice curry from that nice Mrs Loganathan, and felt ever so proud of herself.

Now there was no use in criticising Jack during this, because although he was next to her on the couch and became aware of her radiance, and the sense of light whirling around her like arms, he didn't actually know what effect she was having in the world beyond this little room in Trowbridge. There was no mention of it on the news, and it wasn't until some trombonist's long-suffering wife contacted her equally long-suffering pal whose husband played the French Horn (and that was all he played, she moaned) in a rival band, that she and the others realised what had happened. Even so, when this appeared in the newspapers, no-one knew quite what to make of it. The scientific establishment tried to write it off as a kind of airborne virus linked with the spittle that tended to flow when tunes like 'The Dambusters March' were given some welly in public places. The women – the wives – knew better. Within 24 hours of the funerals, they had organised three coach loads of relatively grieving relatives to go down to Trowbridge and see exactly what was happening. And several of them from Yorkshire wondered whether this strange woman claiming to the a goddess could do for the Inland Revenue what she had evidently done for metal musicians everywhere...

*

Jack took his head out from under Jenny's armpit, rubbed his hair and looked at his watch. "I'm worried about Mum," he said, and made to get up even though the film they were currently watching, *The Quiet Man* with John Wayne and Maureen O'Hara, hadn't finished yet. With surprising strength and almost a hint of ire, Jenny pushed him back onto the couch.

"Your mum is alright. She's happy."

"Do you know that? She has 'special needs', you know."

"So have I! Yes your mum is fine. I know that."

She didn't, actually. Yet the truth is, Mrs Hobbes was very alright. She had fallen in love with that alien, K'tan Shui, and he with her. They were making unusual love in every room of the little house, though you don't want to know too much about that. Let's just say that the neighbours were complaining, as their dogs were making strange whimpering noises because of what they sensed next door.

"She needs help sometimes."

"So do I!! Jack, she's very happy and doesn't want you back yet. I wouldn't let her suffer, believe you me. I love your Mum..."

Jack looked at her sharply. "Don't you dare release her. Don't you dare!" Jenny had never heard him speak like that. She quite liked it. "I want you to promise again, but this time on your life, that you will never ever under circumstances 'release' my Mum."

"I promise Jack. On my life. I told you that! Me and Kali both. Never, ever."

There was a buzz near his testicles. It was his mobile phone on vibrate. It was Jo, his boss.

"Hello Jo..."

"Ah... Precious One! So you still exist? You've not been swept by these plagues? You're not issuing and discharging in the great library in the sky?"

"What, Salisbury you mean? No, I'm here in Trowbridge. I'm on the top floor of The Sanctuary. Can't say too much though."

Good job he didn't, coz the Security Services were listening to every word, and Spoffo was right next to Jo herself, looking menacing. Actually he thought he was looking menacing, but to Jo's eyes it was a clear case of Irritable Bowel Syndrome.

"Well pardner, the fact is... if you don't turn up for work on Monday you will probably be sacked. I know the world is falling apart, but the Library and Heritage Service must go on – or so they tell me. It's all arseholes as far as I'm concerned."

Jack could sense she was not alone. Anyone could have.

"How's my beloved van?"

"Trigger, you mean? Or was it Pegasus last time you spoke to it? Oh she's fine! I've made a few slight improvements to it though."

"What – go-faster stripes? Air spoiler? Chunky tires and poundin' sound system?"

"Hm, well, you'll see them when you come back to work – if you ever come back. Just be careful up there, that's all I'm saying."

They said their goodbyes and he switched off his phone. It was almost out of juice anyway. He went over to the window and looked at the huge scab of people surrounding them. The fact is, it had all been incredibly interesting and exciting and so magnificently bizarre, but he was starting to feel trapped, though he was far too nice and polite to mention it outright. Something had to be done. At very least he didn't want to be sacked because – ending of the world or not – he really enjoyed his job and missed his beautiful Library Van.

Jenny came up behind him and surveyed the crowds.

"They've come to me..." she said wonderingly. "They've come to me. Oh bless them!"

"Half of them love you, half want to kill you."

"This is the best moment of my life," she sighed, putting at least two of her arms around him, and sending her light of love and death surging out through the window like a beam, suffusing everyone in sight, and from where Jack stood it was like watching dominoes toppling, the deaths started at the front and swept out over the crowds like a tidal wave, and you could hear the collective gasps, like a great but suppressed orgasm, and within seconds the park was filled with overlapping corpses, smiling their way to their own heavens.

"Jesus…!" he said, for this was the first time he had witnessed the full monty.

"Don't talk about him…" whispered Jenny in a distinctly lower case voice, as if Yahya might have been listening. "Anyway, let's finish watching the film and then we can have some curry."

Jack stayed at the window while she went back to the telly. *The Quiet Man* trundled to its climax, the bit where Sean Thornton – John Wayne – went to get his woman, Mary Kate Danaher – Maureen O'Hara – who was hiding in a railway carriage and just desperate to be found and dragged out, and then hauled several miles across boggy ground for the sake of her Honour. Jenny was secretly rather hoping that Jack would do something equivalent, something really masterful, and make her feel wanted. Even at this late stage she hadn't entirely lost her humanity.

"Here," she offered, holding the remote control out toward him.

He looked out the carnage, and hard at her, and at the back of his mind he heard the priest and the vicar finishing off the movie with the toasts: "To England, where things are always serious but never hopeless. And to Ireland, where things are always hopeless but never serious." Jack knew that he was now in a country where things were both serious and hopeless, and with no apparent chance to escape.

He switched off the video and the news burst on, with a bit about the Japanese having apparently discovered anti-gravity, showing a small woman lifting a Daihatsu van and showing far too much in the way of teeth and gum. *This was going to be liking to discovery of the wheel!* crowed the Japanese presenter to his Western audience, highly excited.

Below Jack, outside, the gates were being opened and those soldiers within the compound who had been out of Kali's line of sight and thus avoiding the Trip Home, cautiously approached the masses of corpses.

This is serious… thought Jack, who had no plan whatsoever.

*

Mind you, Jack's Mum was a bit worried herself. If she had looked out her bedroom window and twisted herself 45°, she could just about see the top of The Sanctuary. Perhaps it was a mother's intuition, or perhaps Jack had managed to telepath her, but she had a sudden pang of worry. Probably everyone in Trowbridge and surrounding villages at that moment had felt... something... ripple through their lives, like a warm and subtle tsunami; it was a marvel they hadn't been released, too.

"Jack," she said to K'tan Shui, who sprawled obscenely on the bed next to her, showing how he could bend his knees both ways. Now the alien's own powers of language might have been a bit deficient but he understood her sudden concern. He was a parent himself, actually, having spawned several dozen chicks in that far distant galaxy of his, so he had the sort of empathy which can give what seems to be telepathic powers.

"Dza... dza... dzak. Dzak!"

"That's right, my Jack. There's his picture," she said, pointing to an A4 sized school photograph on her dresser, and him in the pert uniform of Clarity School where he learned everything there was to learn about being bullied and beaten up, and hearing the yobs slagging off his 'mongol mum and moron dad' in the days before there were proper policies in place. "He's late. I'm worried."

K'tan Shui opened his hand to reveal a small piece of crumpled cellophane which then unfolded itself, then again, and again, until he had a sizeable square that could have held a pot of tea for two, but which instead bore a live picture of Jack looking forlornly out of the window...

Maisie gasped. Not at the technology – if that is what it was – but at how sad her son looked, how worried. K'tan Shui agitated the corner of the sheet and the image zoomed in at first, so she could every pore on that perfect face, and then zoomed out again so she could see exactly where that window was.

"Right," said Jack's mum, reaching for her clothes first and then her handbag. She didn't need to say any more than that. You didn't need to be a mum or an alien to know exactly where she was going next.

*

197

"I need your help," said Spoffo to Nyron Hughes, as they stood just within the gates of The Sanctuary and surveyed the human wreckage beyond.

"Yes you do," said Hughes, smug as hell and probably loony as hell by this time. That's what happens when you get sucked into cults of any kind: it's not so much that you lose your soul, but that you lose perspective. Especially when you get in with a cult leader who happens to be a real live Death Goddess and you get treated like a minor god yourself, when everyone else has always treated you like shite.

"We have to get The Head back."

"Yes you do." Hughes was all smarmy and beaming. Having just showered with 30 naked women played no small part in this. "And I can help you, young Spoffokin, really I can." He put his hand on the other man's shoulder and gave him a look of complete sincerity and earnestness.

"We need to get it without it disappearing again, or else giving that woman so much power that the whole world gets zapped. Our bosses – *my* bosses – tell me this almost happened before, but it was written off as bubonic plague."

"Mais oui. Certainement!" teased Hughes, who knew exactly who those bosses were.

"We've had snipers trained on her from a distance but their guns just froze."

"Absolutement."

"Look fuck off, Hughes, if you're gonna take the piss. There are people dying in huge numbers and that bitch up there is responsible, and if you don't help then so are you."

"I can help you."

"How?"

"I can tell you something that will alter every plan and backup plan you've devised so far. I give you my word that my information will be correct, and that once you know it then you'll be able to leave this place without a second thought."

Spoffo looked his former boss right in the eye. He had had long training in the arts of discerning liars, and even longer training in how to lie without being sussed. To the very best of his knowledge,

Nyron Hughes was being completely sincere, even if he did seem to be spaced out of his head by everything.

"I'm not playing a double game, Spofficle old pal. On my mum's life."

That last was sort of an in-joke. Their organisation had, in the past, exerted extreme pressure on individuals by targeting their entire families.

So Spoffo thought. He thought and thought. Silence. More thoughts. Hughes eyes were shining: his pupils were huge, two lamps.

"So what do you want from me?" Spoffo asked, his heart sinking, for he guessed that it would involve him bending over and thinking of England.

"Just a few moments in which I fulfill my wildest dreams, dear boy. And then I'll tell you all. Come inside, why dontcha?"

As the army outside started loading the corpses onto lorries, chucking them with dull thuds onto the flat bottoms of the trucks, Spoffo allowed himself to be taken by the hand and led up the back stairs, feeling like dead meat himself.

*

If you have to admire anyone in this entire saga, then it's probably Maisie Hobbes. The rest of them were just reacting, responding and dealing with things from purely selfish or profoundly stupid motives. But Mrs Hobbes was... magnificent.

You can do that remote viewing thing you've learnt by now and watch that dumpy little mum, with her charity shop flowery dress and red anorak, her cheap little white socks falling down her thick ankles, and ghastly pink trainers, clutching the handbag which contained nothing much that richer people would consider at all important: battered photos of Jack, a comb and brush with pictures of the Spice Girls on, a blue plastic purse that was bulging with coins. It bulged with coins because she couldn't count properly, despite all the efforts to teach her over many years, and so when she bought things she always gave notes and got the change. But if her true worth was measurable by the love she felt for Jack, and the concern that was raging through her huge heart, then she was the richest woman on the planet, and the bravest, and the angriest.

K'tan Shui followed on just behind, moving in that odd almost serpentine way he had, making those strange glottal noises which earthlings had tried to interpret as speech but which were probably just strange glottal noises without any meaning whatsoever.

They came to the grinning ranks of the dead in Tesco's car park and she didn't pause, never said sorry to them, never felt fear or disgust, just fixed her gaze upon the window she knew Jack was behind and ploughed forward, like something out of the Light Brigade, and thinking of nothing and no-one else but Jack, her lovely Jack, even though corpses' bones made crunching noises under her feet, and dead mens' chests made gasping noises as her weight expelled the air from dead mens' lungs.

Young soldiers tried to stop her. K'tan Shui did something with his finger joints and knuckles that seemed to send electric shocks up and down their arms so that sparks came from their fillings. Suddenly the odd couple found themselves looking down the barrels of a dozen SA80 assault rifles and it might have been The End for them both if a very troubled looking Spoffo hadn't appeared and told them to put their weapons down, so they did, and Mrs Hobbes marched on.

Spoffo had recognised them both, of course. Mrs Hobbes he just scorned. The alien scared him witless. The pair of them were here for a reason but it no longer mattered. "Let them through. Leave the gates open. You three leave those bodies and follow me," he ordered, ever so masterful, and walking ever so awkwardly, for reasons you can guess. Still, a bit of buggery had bought him Knowledge. And if this Knowledge didn't immediately lead to Power, he at least knew that the sacred head was no longer in The Sanctuary, and that he had to start all over again. Hughes was watching him from an upper room, grinning like a boy who had just had his dreams come true. He looked anywhere but there. Walk straight, don't grimace, don't think about your arse, don't think about your arse…

In fact he looked skyward: there was a helicopter swooping low over Trowbridge like a gnat. He knew it at once: a French EC665 attack helicopter which really shouldn't have been in British airspace at all, but then these were the End Times, so what the hell, eh?

"He's on the top floor, Mrs Hobbes," Spoffo said, but she already knew that and was through those gates and heading up the stairs as fast as her little legs could carry her, determined to get things sorted once and for all.

*

"Mum!" said Jack with surprise, when she burst in on them, panting, the climb up the back stairs having been a bit too much for her. "Are you alright? Come and sit down. Take it easy."

She collapsed on the couch, while her new fella – it's doubtful if you could call him a new 'man' – stood behind and rubbed her temples and sort of gobbled deep in his throat.

Jenny Djinn, who was still in her power but who had enough humanity left to recognise someone she liked, grinned. It was like the sun. Even K'tan Shui seemed a bit wary of this shining entity who stood there with her arms outstretched, and every one of them there would have sworn that they could see all four of them. In fact K'tan Shui did what he often did – simply disappeared, without anyone realizing he had gone until later. There was probably no occult power involved here: schoolchildren can do this stuff all the time.

"Jack... you're late for tea," Mrs Hobbes panted, lying through her teeth coz making his tea had been the very last thing on her mind during the previous few hours when she learned astonishing things about alien physiologies – not to mention going into orbit, g-forces, and angles of re-entry.

Jack was still stunned by the sea of death outside. It was all too much to take in. He could cope with irate readers disputing overdue books, took it all in his stride when the library on-line system went down and he had to work in backup, and could laugh in the face of Stock Rotations when other men would quiver, but this...

"Mum," he said, leaving the rest dangling in the air, though what he meant was *Shut Up. Don't Say Anything Stupid* – which, sadly, was what too many people had said to Maisie Hobbes from the moment she could talk. Hey but he was young, he didn't twig that his mum had a Plan too, just as much as the legendary Templar de Mohun, or that scion of the Secret World, Nyron Hughes, and all the rest of them. Hers simply involved getting her son free of this clearly diseased mad cow.

Felicity came to the door and peeked in, almost fearfully. This was the Holy of Holies! She was supposed to be furious that these outsiders, these weirdos, had got close to her beloved Kali Ma. Yet the goddess was clearly happy to see them, and apparently knew them well, and besides she was so keen to see exactly what it was like up here, that her nosiness got the better of her indignation. Yet all she saw of note was a couch, an old telly, and a pile of equally old videos and DVDs of the sort you can pick up from the many charity shops in town.

"Mum…" said a soft loving voice to Maisie but it wasn't Jack's voice it was Jenny's. "Well I feel that you're almost my Mum now, given what's happening between me and Jack."

Mrs Hobbes and Hobbes Junior flashed each other Looks. They were the sort of Looks which are so tangible that they could carry information like the wires on a telephone. In a nano-second Maisie understood that nothing whatsoever had happened between Jenny and Jack, and that the former was only just a teensy bit sane by this time, and that her boy needed rescuing.

"I never knew my own Mum," Jenny continued, which was true enough, "But I'd have loved one like you." Which was true enough also, and you shouldn't knock Jenny for saying it. Now you might sneer or chuckle at Maisie because of her Learning Disabilities, but she doted on her son, adapted her whole life toward making him safe and well, used every portion of her awareness to make sure he was happy, and would have walked through walls of fire to protect him. You can't ask for much more from a mum than that.

"Come and sit down Little Mum," said Kali Ma's vehicle. "Let's have a nice cuppa tea then I'll perform a marriage service for me and Jack. I can do things like that you know. I've married lots of the girls here. I'm like a ship's captain. I'm sure Jack's got a book about it on his lovely van."

He hadn't actually and shook his head to signify this, and also clear it. Jack felt his whole body turning to jelly. Normally things just passed him by without touching him, but this was all so bizarre and embarrassing. He didn't want to look at the others in the room. He found great interest in his feet, which he shuffled on the bare floor.

"Got an idea, me," said Maisie, still breathless and sweating a little from the climb, "why don't me and you have dance. Like last time. Sat' Night Fever here. I got this video too. Love this. Have dance, yeah? Send this lot away, just us family."

Mrs Hobbes was a genius: that word 'family'. It opened all the boxes for Jenny, hit all the buttons. So Jenny Djinn peeped out from Kali Ma and grinned. Oh she had loved that innocent time in Jack's house when they had danced together! "Go..." she said to Tasha and Felicity and – pouting – they went.

Now the mum's Plan was simple as anything, even simpler than the Keep it Simple, Stupid plan that de Mohun had, and Jack twigged at once coz another of those Looks flashed between him and his Mum. All of which just goes to show you don't to be an alien or a severed head to have genuine powers of telepathy – just a bit loving kindness and empathy.

Knackered and fearful though she was, Maisie put on the video and organized where they would stand so that Jack would have a clear exit behind their backs. She put the volume on full blast so that Jenny wouldn't hear his footfall on the floorboards, made her own face radiant and full of fun and laughter, and got Jenny Djinn doing the Tango Hustle while the world died.

Now Jack did have some idea of what an heroic and supremely cunning act he was witnessing. He might have worried about leaving his mum there but he remembered the promise Jenny had made earlier about not 'releasing' her, not in any circumstance, not ever, never. So, knowing only that he had to get out, and get out now, he started to tiptoe backward to the door while Jenny was fully occupied with her mother-in-law's dance moves. He might have just bolted but he managed to control himself and tiptoed nervously but even more cautiously to the door, feeling like Jack at the top of the beanstalk, half expecting to hear a *fee-fi-fo-fum*, but finding his eardrums rattled by the falsetto tones of the Bee Gees singing about *Stayin' Alive* instead, which was exactly what he wanted to do.

*

Lilith Love was dressed only in tawny, one piece body outfit that fitted her like a skin, of the sort that you might wear at the gym, with poppers at the crutch for easy elimination or quick sex. She was leaning on her elbows looking out of the window, toying with her talisman and doing something which sounded wondrously like purring. There were cats everywhere: big cats small cats, tabby cats and wild cats, all rubbing themselves up against the walls, or trying to get in through the windows. If you could almost see the four arms of Jenny Djinn as she became more and more absorbed by the goddess energies of Kali, then even the least psychic person could almost see Lilith as being more lioness now than human, as Sekhmet consumed her. She didn't so much walk as slink. She didn't stroll so much as prowl. Her naturally red hair had naturally frizzed out to give her a distinct mane. Her nails had grown to become distinctly claw-like. She took deep breaths which might once have been part of her yogic health regime but these days were more feline in nature, so that she sniffed the secrets of the world beyond, and knew things that we humans could never know. In short, she could smell Jack from three blocks away, and half-purred, half-growled with anticipation. Maybe The Head had been playing games, putting the *fee-fi-fo-fum* motif into Jack's mind, because Lilith now certainly could smell the blood of an Englishman approaching – her Englishman – owning him in her own mind as much as Jenny just had.

The fact is, she was in heat. She needed to be had. Thrusting her exquisite arse toward the Polish Contingent had been enough to get the required response from them, but Jack was never going to succumb like that. She would have to get him inside her somehow.

"Can I watch?" asked the Head, tongue in cheek – which when you think about it was about the only thing he could do. He was perpetually inside her these days on other levels, just biding his time, and working on his own Plan.

In fact, as young Jack hurried along the eerily empty streets, that true object of her desire was rather troubled to see that the Manor Grove had become just another smaller though more user-friendly version of The Sanctuary, with equally watchful guards and an air about the place that was more threatening than hopeful, and you couldn't imagine anyone basing their holidays there and using it as a means of exploring Trowbridge – twinned with Leer in Germany – Gateway to the West Country.

Jack was expected. A succession of Polish fellas that he had once seen lurking around the pubs in the main street, or emailing home from the free internet connection in the library, led him through room after room, closing the doors carefully behind him each time, as if sealing something or someone in. He couldn't tell if their faces were sallow because of lack of sunlight, or were showing fear. Quite simply, it was because they were shagged out.

"Hi!" said the familiar Shaz brightly. She should have been like the fellas, but in her case all the sex was making her bloom. She had two more nose rings, and three in her eyebrows. "Follow me," she said, kicking aside an old grey mouser with drooping whiskers which acted as if it owned the place; and when they came to what was obviously the penultimate room added with real enthusiasm: "Fan-bloody-tastic to see you!"

So she was happy enough. She had had more rumpy-pumpy in the past few days than most women ever get in their lifetimes, and had sort of fallen in love with Lilith along the way, so that was understandable. This was all light years away from the days in which a visit to Wetherspoon's, or Happy Hour at The Old Malt was seen as a highlight to the week. Now she had her own goddess to get excited about, was at the centre of world events, and so Tasha and that stuck-up cow Felicity could get stuffed. Not that she fancied Lilith, or had sex with her, but she had come to feel excluded from the Jenny Djinn circle and undervalued despite all she had done with those contracts. Now, at least, she had something of her own to trump about.

"She wants to see you," said Shaz, and you could almost hear that 'she' was said with a capital S. Poor cow hadn't a clue about Yahya, or what all this chaos was about, but when you get sucked into something as deeply as she was, then the absurd and the unjust become normal; you grab what you can for yourself from the chaos, and it all ceases to matter after a while.

"Jaaaaaaaaaaaack!" said Lilith in that soft, throaty and definitely feline voice, opening the door to him and waving Shaz away. "I am sooooooo pleased to see you."

She was too. She probably only had about 15% of Lilith Love left within her psyche, but it was enough to remember how much she loved him, and the fun they had had in the brief time together. Love, after all, defines itself not by the long haul, but by the moments.

"Oh Jack, my Jacko, you would not believe the things I have learned from Yahya here. I know what really went down between him and the other guys – you know, Salome, Herod, Mary Magdalene, and The Big Man himself. The scam they worked with the cross, that situation with James and that creep Paul. Then he taught me about the Princes in the Tower, the REAL history of the Templars, the way the Freemasons ended our Revolution, who really did the Ripper murders, the Vatican suppression of some VERY embarrassing scrolls from Qumran, the true assassins of JFK and Pope John-Paul I, and all you could ever hope to know about Area 51..." she paused for breath, her nipples were hard with excitement. If her eyeballs weren't actually rolling in their sockets they gave that impression. "They're all connected Jack, all of them."

Jack smiled one of his radiant smiles even though the atmosphere was dreadful, and could probably have been measured by electrical equipment. The object he had come to see – The Head – was sprawled obscenely in the large armchair. Now it's not easy to sprawl obscenely when you have nothing below the larynx, but something about that open wind-pipe and the shrivelled flesh around it... ugh! It was like catching your granny flashing.

"Hello Jack," said Yahya, though he couldn't be sure whether the words had been uttered or were just in his own head. *This will all be finished soon. All of it,* came a thought from nowhere.

Well of course that sounded menacing, and he was about ask outright what was going on when Lilith put her tongue down Jack's throat and waggled it about, taking his hands and putting them on her bits and tits, but he just let them fall off and stood there limply, speared by that mighty tongue, dangling from her mouth like a piece of raw, dead meat.

"Jack Jack Jacko, you are one helluva tease. I like that, I really do."

"Sorry," he said, though it was clear to anyone that he wasn't at all, but he had to buy time.

"Hey listen, you wanna fool around some?" She said. Jack frowned. "Hey no, lighten up, I mean *really* fool around, not screw around. You wanna see my powers? Okay, okay, let's see what we can find huh?"

She dragged him to the French Windows, opened them and looked out. Good job none of the Polish fellas or Shaz were out there just then coz she would have wasted them without a second thought, like swatting flies. Looking out over the wall across the remains and west Wiltshire and toward east Somerset, there was a veritable wasteland. No trees, no hedgerows, no livestock.

"Gone!" said Lilith in delight. "I did that. Target practice, yeah?"

"Lilith, I..."

"What, you love me? Is that what you wanna say? I can read your mind, sure I can."

"Lilith, I will be the best friend you can ever want, if you will promise – promise with all your heart and mind – that whatever happens, you will not harm my mum."

If lionesses can look surprised, given their differing facial muscles, then she did then. "I promise!" she said, and might have pounced upon how he would define 'best friend' when she saw the helicopter hovering in the middle distance. Her face lit up like a child's might, on seeing a new toy. "Oh, look... see that Jack?"

He'd noticed it before, and thought how evil it looked. He didn't need to access the Library Van's copy of *Helicopters (Military Hardware in Action)* to know that he was being observed by the immensely powerful cameras that all such vehicles carried.

"Jack, Jacko, Jackie – or even Jacques! Do you like toys like that?"

"No. No, I don't. It's just a noisy killing machine that messes up the atmosphere and leaves a huge carbon footprint."

Lilith smiled a lioness smile. "That's a good reason for it to go..."

And to Jack-Jacko-Jacque's astonishment, the helicopter swayed from side to side, then from nose to tit, then spun around as if some invisible giant had whacked its tail, and within seconds it had plummeted to the ground and burst into flames and mushrooming smoke. Anyone who hadn't seen the forgoing might have assumed that a small thermo-nuclear explosion had been triggered on Trowle Common.

"Well done baby," Lilith purred against him.

Jack was shocked. He pushed himself away. "I didn't do that! Did I?"

"Ptah!! she spat. "Sure you did honey. You gave it a reason. It only needed a reason. You're taking on my powers now. We'll make a great team, huh?"

Jack looked at the devastation. He looked at the woman. He looked at the severed head of St John the Baptist.

I've got to stop this, he thought.

Yahya smiled. *Then do it*, he telepathed back, as Lilith took off all her clothes again for one last End of the World assault on Jack's virginity.

CHAPTER 11

So there we are in the Great Hall of the preceptory at Temple Rockley, which was set in a place now known as Temple Bottom, next to the enduring Ridgeway, and it was like the Last Supper in there. For some of them, that's exactly what it was. They sat around the long table, wiping their lips as they finished off their meals. Candlelight glittered in the polished bits and pieces of the armour and weaponry that they'd put politely in the corner by the door, as we might put wet umbrellas. The old black dogs munched at the scraps which had been thrown on the floor, and the minstrel played a quiet tune about sheep and hungry shepherds and hey nonny nonnies in the corner. Servants continued to scurry to and fro in a state of constant fear, and the Templars in their best civvy kit were sitting very nicely, no elbows on the table, long beards held neatly back from the food. More exactly, William de la More sat at the head with a still-quivering, whining and boasting Engayne to his right; his nephew de Sautré to the Grand Master's left, with de Hambledon, de Egle further down, plus two others from the visiting entourage sitting meek as lambs and trying not to look at the scary presence of de Mohun at the opposite end. They'd heard of him as a fighting legend, and an absolute stark raving eye-rolling madman who would bite out your tongue and shove it up your arse if you upset him. That was more or less right.

Mind you, in some ways the young creep de Sautré seemed a bigger idiot than any of them there, totally unaware of their boredom and scorn as he tried to impress his uncle the Grand Master by reading out from that bloody letter by St Bernard about the Templars. If there was ever any justification for the average Templar knight not learning to read and write, it could be found in him. He droned, but excitedly:

"'Thus they are' – that is to say, we Templars – 'in union strange, at the same time gentler than lambs and grimmer than lions, so that one may doubt whether to call them monks or knights. But both names suit them, for theirs is the mildness of the monk and the valour of the knight. What remains to be said but that this is the Lord's doing, and it is wonderful in our eyes? Such are they whom God has chosen out of the bravest in Israel, that, watchful and true, they may guard the holy sepulchre, armed with swords, and well skilled in war.'"

"True, very true," de la More said, but his eyes were blank as he spoke. He farted. No-one turned a head. Farting was almost manners then. The serving girl with the short hair was on hand to waft the stink away and follow it up with the naked flame of a candle. You didn't need extractor fans in those days. Is that a boy or a girl? he thought, looking at the cropped wretch that de Mohun had probably tupped, and deciding to make a visit later on to find out.

They all chatted, all very tired but having to do the polite. If you could hear their conversation you might be a little shocked. They said 'cock' a lot, and commented that cock was their true business in life, and how they prayed to cock every night before sleep; but this was nothing to do with the sodomy for which they became accused, but simply because 'cock' was their slang word for God. They said 'shit' at necessary times, but that wasn't even a swear word and didn't become so for another 500 years. While the word 'cunt', which still has the power to stop some people in their tracks in the 21st Century, wasn't even in the reckoning. In fact, had Jack been commenting, he could have tracked down and shown you the various spellings used by Chaucer in the Library Van's one copy of *The Canterbury Tales* and told you how the area of Kennet in Wiltshire had the same derivation – though he wouldn't have said that word in front of his Mum.

Still, Jack wasn't there, and things were so busy at the other end of the Time Shift that there were no watching spirits, no eyes, only the voices – faint whispers – in de Mohun's head of all the people he had slain in the good old days. He was no different to Lilith in that respect, and might have taken comfort from the fact that the succubus which had once haunted him also had the same affliction.

"Tell me again, Engayne, about the turds who attacked you. Over four score, you said?" asked de Mohun.

At least, at least. God but he had been brave! He might not have fought the heathen in Outremer, but he did right valiant things in deepest Somerset less than two days ago. De Egle and de Hambledon stifled yawns a little bit too obviously.

"Wonderful. You are a lion-heart, sir. Have some more wine. And the rest of you. Sup up lads!"

Even the most ardent teetotaller would sup up when someone like de Mohun offered them the jug. Pretty soon, the visitors were all pissed.

William de la More however, who never touched a drop, firmly declined, pushed his plate away and sat back in the large oaken chair. The Order of the Poor Knights might well have been corrupted and unpopular, its original remit might have become obsolete or untenable, but he was no fool. The three knights of Temple Rockley were clearly scornful of both Engayne and the insufferable prig Robert, his own nephew. If he had learned anything out in the Holy Land, it was the Saracen belief that an enemy's enemy was necessarily your friend. While Engayne and young de Sautré were hardly enemies, he was sufficiently unliking of them to have a certain sympathy for the three old dinosaurs whose time had long since passed.

"The markings on the walls…" de la More commented, referring to those marks which they had used to drive away the demons.

"We have had… visitations," answered de Mohun.

They all understood. The 14th Century was a very haunted one. Even de la More's place had his own symbols, rather as we would put up signs today saying 'Neighbourhood Watch' or 'No Dog Fouling' or 'Keep off the Grass'. No-one thought twice about such things, and sometimes the spirits didn't either. So the Grand Master nodded, tapping his fingers together.

"In truth, I have heard good things about you from the locals, Brother John de Mohun." Eyebrows raised in unison. There were those in the room who could not possibly imagine what good things the locals could find to say. "As we rode through the villages they came and told me. You guard the Ridgeway right well. You smite wrongdoers. And you have given each of them large sums of money, to see them through difficult times."

You could almost hear them sucking their breath through what remained of their medieval teeth. Individual Templars had to give their own wealth to the Order. And seeing as Temple Rockley's role next to the Ridgeway was little more these days than the sort of small bank you might find at airports, then the money must have been taken directly from the Order.

De Mohun smiled. You see, when he told his two underlings a few days before that he would deal with the silent protesters at the gates, you might have thought he was about to splice their heads open. No, he did the most unexpected thing of all: he opened the Templar coffers and gave it all away. They had all stood there for a moment, equally silently, but they were pragmatic souls, and scared shitless too, so they took it and just disappeared.

There was no need for Big John to say anything, and anyway whatever other vice he might have had, he was incapable of that sort of lying. So he just smiled, and looked fiercer and weirder than ever, as he cut up the last of his steak and shovelled it into his mouth, tipping the bones onto the floor and idly watching the dogs snarl over them.

Really, the two men at each end of the table were as formidable as each other. They looked at each other and something passed between them that was almost like the empathy that old and formerly warring soldiers talk about. And de Mohun knew, that at this moment in time, de la More had come to the end of his own road. There were demons of a different kind approaching him, and a sense that his world was about to end anyway, what with all the troubles in France. If he could have retired to the country and race horses and ride his peasants – and vice versa – he would have done. If you want to know more about all that period then just input the words "templar 1307" in the Google search box and you'll get 56,400 explanatory entries in 0.25 seconds, and learn some things about the Order's demise which will make your own lives feel very cozy, and think: Poor buggers... though they were never either.

"Tomorrow," de la More said softly, as if the others on the table didn't exist, "we must talk."

And tomorrow, thought de Mohun, you will be dead.

*

If you're reading this, then of course you survived those End Times and all the chaos that preceded them, and like the Duke of Wellington after Waterloo you would probably comment: "It was a damn close run thing..." Close? It was a bit like a Cup Final in which your favourite team won 5-4 with the last kick of the match in the last second of extra time, after having had half your team sent off for the unsportsmanlike behaviour of dying, with the match constantly interrupted by vicious pitch invasions.

Now that most of us know where it all stemmed from and can see through the official nonsense of Bird Flu, Pandemics, International Terrorists and their assorted Dirty Bombs, we can sit back under the comfort of homes powered by our Japanese-designed Zero Point Energy outlets and marvel that it had all been caused by two silly women – Jenny Djinn and Lilith Love – who fell for a Mobile Librarian in a small Wiltshire town that was named after trolls.

By this time they were both out of control: Kali's dance had become more frantic; Sekhmet was raging through the atmospheres. If you'd been a fly on the wall in either The Sanctuary or the Manor Grove Hotel you'd have noticed the telly blaring out in the former, and the on-line CNN news on the laptop in the latter, talking frantically about the global crisis in oil – which was about to become redundant thanks to ZPE – and creating huge tensions in the Middle East and all oil-producing areas. No-one wanted to buy oil any more. No-one wanted to build heavy equipment such as aeroplanes, ships, tanks, trains, cars and cranes, until they saw how the new energy would pan out. There was mass unemployment and huge stresses. Stocks and shares were plummeting. Nations were gearing up for war. If only they knew that it was all because of the see-through electric kettle from Argos which had soaked up the powers of the Sacred Head...

"Have a cuppa tea," said Maisie Hobbes to Jenny Djinn, both of them oblivious of what was going on outside that room. The latter rang the bell and Felicity appeared, with a face like a slapped arse, and huffed off downstairs to prepare a tray as ordered, fuming that this little Mongol woman who had appeared from nowhere should be so favoured.

The news switched to the crisis in Africa. There were the usual harrowing images of starving children that everyone ignores, and the two women sat on the couch, sweating from their dance work-out, and watched.

"Love little black babies, me," said Mrs Hobbes, still trying to divert the other's attention from Jack's disappearance. "Poor little things. Wish I could help them."

"Do you?" said Jenny, whose eyes were now silver, like Rosemary's Baby. "Do you love them?" So she did that thing right there and then which enabled Kali Ma to manifest and you could be sure there would be no need to send in your donations after that, or do a follow-up documentary for that batch of suffering mites.

On the other hand, at the same time across town, Lilith Love was still aching at her failure to have cosmic sex or even a good earthly grope with her Jack, and was about to displace all her frustration on those Irano-Syrians whose secret Weapons of Mass Destruction were about to be unleashed, as revealed by CNN.

"Those jerks..." she growled, looking at the Foreign Minister and his cohorts who made noises of about the regrettable breakdown of communication with both Tel Aviv and Tehran. "I can think of a thousand reasons..."

And to Jack's horror, she thought of a thousand reasons there and then, and you could almost see them flashing across her leonine brow, and if she didn't expand literally, there was a sense that she towered and roared, and sent all her death-energies eastward, using the screen on the laptop like a gunsight. Well... the rest is history. Still, if the fatalities were huge in terms of all those connected with that crisis, it ended the crisis and averted an almost certain nuclear war.

Jack looked at The Head and you can see that there was a distinct parallel here with the look that William de la More gave John de Mohun down the length of that table at what was effectively the same moment.

You want to destroy the world, thought Jack.

Yahya smiled.

You want to harm my Mum, he thought again.

No way was he having that!

*

Spoffo stood were in what used to be the frozen food department of Tesco's. He looked into the freezers and saw that the packets of fish fingers, chicken, beef, and assorted wraps had all defrosted and were probably poisonous now. The lights on the high ceiling had given out due to unexpected electrical surges.

Kill the woman, said the voices in Spoffo's head. He was young, he had never communed with The Nine before, and here they handing him reins of power he once could only have dreamed about, and without all the processes of initiation, either, so they must think him really special, eh?

Which one? he asked, and the nine radiances sorted of danced up and down as if he had asked a stupid question.

The one now known as Kali Ma.

Poor sod. He was becoming as haunted by The Nine as de Mohun was by his time-demons. The only difference was, he welcomed the haunting. Trouble is, you can't feel too impressed that The Nine, who are said to rule the world, spoke to a mere sprog like Spoffo. In fact, no-one should feel impressed or awed by The Nine at all – whoever or whatever they are – coz even someone not particularly bright like Jenny might have noticed that they have, over many millennia, made an absolute cock-up of everything they got involved in.

Listen... remember how John de Mohun drove off his own spirits by shouting the Latin: *Fundamenta ejus in montibus sanctis!!?* Even though it didn't mean a damned thing, really, it worked. You, or Jenny, or Jack, or Spoffo could have driven the awesome and awe-ful Nine to oblivion calling out something like *The Somme, Auschwitz, Darfur!!* said in the tone of utter reproach and contempt for allowing such nightmares to happen. He might have done it. He might have saved the need for Jack Hobbes to step in. There was still a tiny fragment of Jack-the-Lad humanity in him which made him dither. But then the blood lust came upon him like a wave and he just wanted to kill, and wanted Their approval more than anything else. Hell, he could forget his sore arse and recent humiliation if he could achieve both.

"I'll do it!" he shouted to the greening packs of 100% cod fish fingers. "Thy will be done!!" he cried, his shrill voice echoing back to him from the far side of the superstore.

*

Spoffo had his men ready. Alpha Team was going to storm The Sanctuary and shoot Jenny. Delta Team was taking up its places around The Manor Grove, just observing at the moment but ready to act. He knew that Hughes was upstairs among all the women, and Spoffo felt vaguely virtuous at the thought of killing him too. At least his former boss could now tell his mother that he had come good at last, surrounded by women on his death-bed.

214

Spoffo was excited. The thought of using his gun almost gave him a stiffy. He would have understood what the three rogue Templars at Rockley preceptory felt like.

To his right, across the road, the corpses were being loaded by diggers. His two men were behind him, breathing heavily, not too happy at the thought of killing civilians but determined to Do Their Duty. His hand was sweaty and sticky on the butt of the cute little Sig Sauer P230 handgun, with the low-velocity bullets. His anal sphincter kept squeezing itself tight. The images and sensations of what Hughes had done to him kept rising in his head, but he shut them out, using his orders from Above as a lid upon his shame. Three bullets for the bitch with four arms. The remaining four straight into Hughes's huge and nasty cock.

*

De Mohun led William de la More down the long corridor, using the light of a single candle. He knew that his best mates John and Robert would, when they were out of earshot, be cutting the throats of Engayne and the drunken and un-armoured Grand Master's party who had never had a fight in their pampered lives; then they'd have some personal sport with the odious nephew. He had no mind to join them yet. He had an Order to destroy. Yet like Spoffo, he was almost sexually turned-on by the anticipation, the blood-rush, the coming together of many separate things.

The Grand Master followed, limping slightly from an old wound. He noticed that the hot wax poured down from the candle onto the other man's hand and he never flinched.

"You have been a Templar for longer than some of them have been alive," offered de la More as a kindness, although he was taut as a bow inside.

The other man nodded. He didn't say much, but when he did... he didn't say much.

"In here," he offered, indicating the great door of the chapel which bore the image he had done of the Templar seal – the two knights on one horse. "I carved that," he said, running his hand over the shapes. They stared at it for a moment; the flickering light made the horse almost mobile. They stood for a while and if de Mohun thought the Grand Master might make some nice comments about it, he was dead wrong. So de Mohun gave a sort of awkward flourish (not being a ritualist) and ushered the other man through the creaking door. "Herein is our Mystery. Herein is the beginning and end of all things." Anyone else would have sounded a bit twattish saying that, but it came across pretty strong in those surroundings.

Now press that pause button again and consider: if he'd had any sense, de la More would have turned and ran. The fact is, however, he did have balls – bloody big balls in fact – no matter what his other faults. He'd been a warrior himself, had led from the front, had slaughtered and forgiven and ransomed like the best of them, but also had a special power that that many people never manage to attain, no matter how many sacred objects they accumulate, no matter rich or how influential they become: he had integrity.

More, he actually had a vested interest in the secret that de Mohun had hinted at. In fact, if you'd had time to do enough Googling, or been privileged to have asked The Head, and if the web-sites in question had survived, you could have learned that there were actually four main icons that the Templars held dear. One was kept in London, one was kept in Lincolnshire, another in Yorkshire and a fourth in or near Bristol. These four icons had been brought to England by our William de la More sometime before the French Templars were all arrested, on that dreadful day of Friday 13th October, 1307. William knew that he would only have a few weeks to get the icons to safety before the arrests would start in England, too. No-one knows what these icons actually were, but somewhere within the arcanum a Sacred Head was surely involved. Oh sure, Lilith could have told you the full details, but at this time she was so possessed, so out of her own head, that straight answers were damn nigh impossible.

In a strange sense, though, Lilith was actually in there waiting for them, and neither of them expected her. The two worlds of the 14th and 21st Centuries were so overlapped by these characters and the machinations of Yahya, that it was hard to tell where one ended and the other began.

You see, at that very moment 700 years away when the two Templars entered the chapel, the avatar of Sekhmet was curled up on the bed, fast asleep and dreaming, and giving the sort of gentle snores which sounded like purring. All the while her Virtual Reality

Preceptory was thrumming on the open laptop, and the CGI characters were pulsing away within the scenes.

The thing is, whether it was a cross-over of energies causing by The Head's fell influence, or possibly because we might all be CGI characters on some cosmic computer somewhere, as one of Jack's books speculated, both de Mohun and de la More were startled by the sense of a great cat within the shadows of the chapel – or rather, of a naked woman with the head of a cat. It was weird. Dreadful. The larger than life image shimmered in the angles of the chapel like pale and insubstantial wax, and it was a good job the eyes weren't open or the two men might have flipped. Lilith's echo through the centuries? Although we can never find out for sure, now, remember what she had Googled aeons away: the charge that, "...in despite of the Saviour, they sometimes worshipped a cat, which appeared amongst them in their secret conclave."

So that's the answer to that Mystery, is it? In later years when they were put to the rack and asked what dread thing was seen within their lodges, one of these two answered in all honesty that he had seen a great and unholy cat there, which was true enough, even if it was wrung from him by great and hideous tortures.

The great John de Mohun had been as startled as his companion to see that Thing in there, though both of them mastered themselves really quickly. Actually, that wasn't too hard for them to do that, because when you've been faced (many times) with thousands of screaming Saracens wanting to cut off your genitals and then skin you alive, you can rise above such frissons caused by the harmless undead quite easily.

The image wavered, it faded, it disappeared. Which was possibly linked with the laptop's programmes closing down as batteries ran out.

The two men glowered. Each thought the other responsible for the foul creature they had just seen, people owning ghosts as we might own dogs, though neither would have admitted to having seen it. There might have been words, de Mohun's simple Plan might have been scuppered, but suddenly the last Grand Master of the English Templars saw what he had been brought to see: the ornate box placed neatly on a plinth, with the lid open and the shadowy outline of a human head inside causing his heart to leap, and prompting him to bow toward it.

"I did not believe," he said softly, with a lump in his throat. "But I see it now. I am blessed…"

De Mohun nodded, grinning mightily.

*

Spoffo and his two subordinates climbed the stairs which went around the outside of the building, guns at the ready. It was like being in a movie. They wished that everyone was watching them as they, in their minds' eyes, were watching themselves: Heroes, that's how they felt. Each one was Bruce Willis in *Die Hard.*

They made no attempt at silence or secrecy, and would shoot anyone who approached them, though none did as they were all in one of the dance classes, knitting four-armed sweaters, or rutting like beasts in their cells. Spoffo knew his prey would be on the top floor; he never expected her to fling open the final door at the top of the final staircase and stand there welcoming him. Whether it was the light from outside, behind her, or whether she was in her power, she didn't half shine! She was wearing a long white dress, as if for a wedding, and you could see right through it. And there was Hughes next to her, grinning obscenely, thinking that the knowledge he'd recently had of Spoffo was power, and that he could use it now, and humiliate him again.

"Spofficle! Did you know that rhymes with testicle!! Speaking of which why don't you come on up and let us–"

He never quite finished. That was because Spoffo shot him right in the forehead, giving him the sort of Third Eye you see on yogic icons, and if his facial muscles could have registered surprise before the bullet rattled around in his skull and turned his brain to porridge oats, then they did so now before he crumpled.

Jenny Djinn seemed more curious than troubled at seeing this. Mind you, when you've just finished destroying hundreds of thousands of innocent individuals, the sight of one more corpse was hardly likely to make her shriek.

She raised her arms in a kind of benediction, which – as well as bestowing grace – showed that she hadn't shaved her armpits for some time, although the rest of her was clearly in good feminine nick as the fellas at the bottom of the stairs could see. The three agents from the mysterious Order behind the Orders, took one look at this

218

strange woman, looked at each other to make sure they all agreed this was the right one, raised their weapons and took aim.

Now Jenny came within a fraction of a second of receiving a salvo from her attackers. The thing that saved her was the fact that they were all being strangled. This had never happened to Bruce Willis in any of their movie scripts. They might have been members of a very secret service, and highly trained in all sort of dark arts, but they'd never learned the art of sneaking up on people like the Thuggees had just done, and who stood behind each of them now, using scarves inside which were large coins, crushing the windpipes of each poor sod and giving them unremarkable deaths before throwing their bodies down the stairs, then disappearing through a side door as if they'd never existed.

Then picture the empty stairwell bright with light, with Jenny Djinn at the top, three corpses at the bottom and – to her delight – Mrs Loganathan in her best purple sari stepping over the bodies with another vindaloo that she hadn't even ordered.

"You saved me," said Jenny simply.

Mrs Loganathan gave an ancient salute. "You are Kali's daughter. We have always been watching you."

Press that pause button again and get your head around this: the Thuggee at Cley Hill had been nothing to do with the Sacred Head. His only mission was to protect Jenny. In fact, Jenny had been looked after by devotees she never knew she had, and they had been in place even before The Head came into her life. So did Yahya's powers cause Jenny Grey to become Jenny Djinn, and thence Kali Ma? Or did he simply do a sort of cosmic con trick and merely announce what was going to happen anyway, taking full credit?

No-one will ever know.

Mrs Loganathan walked on up the stairs, her own face shining, out in the open at the last. She was about to join Jenny in the sacred Upper Room and openly commune with her goddess, when a thundering voice came from the bottom of the stairwell:

"Jenny Grey... JE-NNY GREY!!" This from Dr McHaffee, who looked very ruffled indeed.

The Indian lady spun quickly, ready to defend, but the young goddess put her arm on her shoulder and smiled beatifically.

The smile seemed to make him flip. "Jenny, this is all in your head. THIS IS ALL IN YOUR HEAD!!"

Hey, but she knew that didn't she? She knew that better than anyone.

"Hello doctor," Jenny answered, calm as anything, and none of it caused by Prozac. "Yes it is. Actually my head is on the other side of town, and my Jack is there too. Or should I call him Shiva now, Mrs Loganathan?"

The older lady beamed and nodded, nodded and beamed. The good doctor looked as if his own head was going to implode.

"Shall we go and see them? I think we're just about finished here..."

*

It's amazing the effect that a little flickering light can have upon a person's mind. On the other hand, the whole of Hollywood was based upon that very thing, so we shouldn't be too surprised by what a single candle could achieve when its light played upon the carved head in its box. Especially when the atmosphere was filled with a sort of grim intent. The two of them – de Mohun and de la More – were dab hands at radiating moods like great tides. Anyone else present in that room would have felt two great and deep ocean currents colliding, and swirling to create a vortex down, down into the darkness.

William de la More saw the Head, took a deep breath and sort of staggered down to his knees, and because he had one gammy knee-joint caused by an old wound, it wasn't the most elegant of movements.

It blinked, he thought. *I saw it blink!*

Woah....! you say, 700 years away. Is the wooden head that de Mohun made the same one that our Jenny stumbled upon? Did the power of the human mind and human needs, helped along by the cosmic agenda of the mysterious Nine, make it become flesh along the way? The head seemed very alive to de la More. Was it only a trick of candlelight? Were Jenny and Lilith and Jack the victims of some kind of collective hypnosis? There were many heads, remember, as Lilith had Googled historical facts about half a dozen others. Just as you can make the past come alive to serve your needs, the only relevant fact we need to accept here is this:

William de la More, the last Grandmaster of the Templars in England, thought the object before him was an object of rare and holy power, and he never gave a thought to provenance, or even dreamed of poking it with a stick to see what it was made of.

Actually, he might well have done exactly that, but at the moment he bowed his head, John de Mohun gave him such a smack with the flat of his hand that he knocked the other man across the chapel floor. He tended to strike like that, did our John. None of these punches that you see in westerns, which are apt to break the knuckles of the attacker. He favoured giving his victim a good slapping, sometimes with cupped hand to the ear, so bursting the ear-drum. Ye gods but it hurt. Plus it was also humiliating, like you were a mere boy getting punished by teacher, in the bad old, good old days when teachers had power.

"Ooooooh," said de la More unsurprisingly. "Aaaaah!" He was a bit embarrassed that the Holy Head before him saw this, and his being taken by surprise, and him being the Grand Master an' all.

Now this was the moment when our John would wade in, both hands flying, kicking, head-butting, gouging, biting... What he never realised, however, was that dear William was – as they say – hard as fuck. He didn't get to be Grand Master of the Templars for nothing. It wasn't achieved by funny handshakes or bending over in secret places or mere bribery. It was because he was smart, and every bit a fighting man.

So as our John did his wading in bit, he was startled to find the other man shoot up from the floor and punch him in the groin, with all of his weight behind it, helped by the 14th Century equivalent of a knuckle-duster.

"Ooooooh," said de Mohun this time, and you can say what you like about this sort of thing, but it stopped the voices in his head in a way that someone like Dr McHaffee with all his modern therapy never could. Aaaaaaaaaah!

Of course it didn't end there. These were two Fighting Men, at the very end of their world, at the very edge of existence. If the mute and watching Head lacked blood and flesh, then were plenty of that to be had from the walls in the next minute or so. They... kicked, slapped, punched, gouged, bit, butted, twisted, slammed, kneed, choked, squeezed and scratched. Of course de Mohun targeted de la More's gammy knee; De la More meanwhile aimed more blows at what was surely de Mohun's gammy groin. If it had been a boxing match it would have been hard to call; it would have gone to a points decision by the narrowest of margins. If you like sheer brutality, then you'd have voted for Big John; if it's never-say-die that you admire, then William would be your man.

In the end it was de Mohun who won, and who had the semi-conscious Grand Master dangling from his hands like a raggy doll. Outside, coming in through the high windows, he could hear his two pals and the sound of whips, so they were clearly having some fun of their own. He half-carried, half-dragged de la More toward the door. The poor sod tried to struggle but he was almost past it by this time, yet with his burst eyes he squinted at the Head which had stayed serene and untouched in its box during all that chaos. He was sure it winked at him again.

The very perfect gentle knight that was de Mohun dragged his victim along the stone floor, leaving a trail of both their bloods as he went, grunting and snuffling like a truffle-boar. He pulled open the door to the exercise yard, and the light from many torches flamed into his half-shut eyes, and it was blaze of redness and white, and when he focussed and realised what he was looking at he dropped poor William and used the worst, baddest, most appalling swear-word of them all, far worse to the 14th Century ears than fuck or cunt or shit:

"Jesus..." he said.

*

Lilith was sound asleep now. Curled up on the couch, snoring lightly. Her eyes moving rapidly in dreaming sleep, her red hair flowing out over the arms like a mane. If releasing people made her rival Jenny hungry, then Lilith needed nothing more than a good cat-nap after some good ole American slaughter. Nobody does it better. If Jack hadn't been on a mission he might have thought that she looked rather sweet in repose, almost innocent, with a splay of light upon her face like a cat's whiskers.

He knew what he had to do. He took a deep breath and looked at Yahya. Yahya looked at him. If the latter had had hands he would put his finger to his lips and mouth *Sssssh!* But he did so without hands and for a second it seemed to Jack as though the severed head of

John the Baptist was blowing him a kiss. *Take me*, came the words in his head. The only box available of course was the one Yahya had teleported into at the foot of Cley Hill. Then it was simply a matter of: grab Sacred Head by the sacred ears. Put said Head in box. Place said box under arm. Sneak out the door.

Bizarrely, Jack was reminded of the times when he was a little boy of about 6, and the Social Services allowed him to meet his REAL mother once a month. And little Jack would read to her, because she couldn't read herself, and her favourite stories were also Jack's favourite stories, because – although they weren't allowed to admit it in those politically correct days – her mental age was slightly less than her son's.

The stories they both loved were from the Ladybird Books of the time: *The Amazing Pancake, The Three Little Pigs, The Billy Goats Gruff* – and best of all, *Jack and the Beanstalk*. He did all the voices. And she loved the moment when Jack – the storybook Jack – was sneaking out of the giant's castle with the goose that laid the golden eggs under his arm, terrified that the thing might cluck, or squawk, whatever it is that geese do when they're being squeezed. That was Our Jack then… silently, softly, in some terror. Not fear of Lilith herself, but of what might happen to the world and his Mum if he failed in his mission.

As it was, the rest of the people in the house were too busy giving Shaz a right good Polish seeing-to to notice that Jack had put the box on top of the old garden wall, climbed up the vines, dropped lightly down to the other side and retrieved the box very, very carefully, so as not to bash Yahya about.

He was being watched. He knew that. They would pounce on him or just shoot him down as soon as they were sure of what he was carrying. Skirting the warm stone of the wall he aimed to get as near the main road as possible, and then hi-jack a car. How he would hi-jack a car when he was carrying a box which purported to carry nothing more sinister than an electric kettle, was not something he had thought out yet.

Keep going, said a voice in his head, so he did.

The fact is, he'd probably never have got more than a hundred yards or so if his Guardian Angel hadn't appeared. First, it wasn't easy to run smoothly with a large box containing a severed but supremely sentient head that didn't appreciate being bounced

223

around. Second, it wasn't a Guardian Angel with wings and white dress and halo, but a woman in the last hour of wearing the grey slacks and blue fleece of a Mobile Librarian.

He didn't see her right off: she crept up – or simply materialised. Actually he was starting to feel pissy, coz he was getting no help from The Head. So the first thing he knew about her, as he knelt down behind some bushes and wondered where to go, was the bunch of keys being dangled in front of his face from behind, and a familiar voice:

"These are probably the Keys of Heaven in your own weird mind, but to me they are simply the keys of your beloved Library Van. Which I've parked just down there, round the corner…"

"Jo!" he cried as he turned to see her. "My beloved Van! Come on, let's get in. I am SO grateful."

"Yes. Yes you are."

"But how… why…?"

"It was either this or your P45 and a disciplinary – not necessarily in that order."

They hurried to where she had parked the vehicle, aware that many eyes were watching them, and watching each other, and wondering what to do next.

"God I've missed this!! How are you my beauty…" he said, patting the bonnet with his free hand.

"Get in, grasshopper. I thought you might want to borrow this vehicle of yours. Though today I think it should be Pegasus, rather than Bill the Pony."

Jack looked over his shoulder and saw movement in the long grass, amid the bushes and behind the trees. A helicopter – no two, three of them – hovered in the distance, cameras surely trained on him.

"These are the enhancements you talked about," he said, looking at Jo's hand-painted words in broad white gloss paint on the side of the Library Van: READ YOU BASTARDS! Then he got in, sharpish.

"You can drive," she said, getting out of the seat and giving it to him. "I can't get it out of first gear. My car's buggered. I stole this. It's my last day at work. They're still trying to run a skeletal service back there – ha ha."

He had a dilemma. There was only one other place to sit.

"I have to put this box here," he said, indicating the passenger seat.

"Is it the Holy Grail?"

He looked at her sharpish, too.

"I need to strap it in."

"Worry not, chum. I'll just stand back here and weed your shelves. I see that your Large Print Thrillers have been sadly neglected, though the Romance section seems immaculate. However, the books are still far too tightly packed, and Lynda La Plante should be placed among the L's, not the P's."

Go! said a voice in his head, so there you have it: Jack drove off with the Box strapped safely into the passenger's seat and Jo standing on behind, hanging onto the vertical yellow poles that the van had for unsteady customers.

"Jo, how... why..."

"Did you think I would leave you dying, when there's room on my horse for two?"

"That's a Rolf Harris song!" he said, turning right because the Head told him to, acting like an internal sat-nav. "I used to sing that to my Mum. It was called 'Two Little Boys'."

"Perhaps Rolf Harris was a secret Templar, hmm? The two men on horseback? Hmm?"

If he could have slammed on the brakes to give her a Look and ask Hard Questions he would have done, but cars had appeared from nowhere and were clearly following, though making no attempt to overtake or stop him.

In fact as you'll see, he got no chance to quiz her, so we just have to guess that Jo was like Mrs Loganathan: put upon this planet to discreetly oversee the welfare of her odd chum. In the event he was just glad – so glad – to have her along.

"What twats they are," she mused, looking out of the rear window at a variety of following cars, each one probably at odds with the other, no-one quite knowing what they should do.

"Maybe they just want to return some overdues?" Jack said.

"Then why are all the passengers holding handguns?"

She staggered slightly as Jack put his foot down.

"You know," she added, "I've always felt we mobile librarians are like the SAS of the library service as whole: trained to get in behind enemy lines before they even know we're there, and issue where it hurts. Shouldn't you be doing handbrake turns or something? Isn't that what you heroes do?"

"Jo…"

Two holes appeared in the side of the van's cab, at odd angles. Two beams of light shot through the holes. The van itself was so noisy, and vibrated so much, they didn't realise for a couple of seconds that these were bullet holes.

"Ooh…" scorned Jo. "They are clearly not English!"

"Jo…"

Drive faster, said the voice from the box in his head, and you could tell it had never been part of the library service or else it would realise that on a narrow road with a marked camber, lots of hills and bends, the books, tapes and DVDs would be in real danger of falling off the shelves. Or at least they would have been if Jack hadn't wedged them into place to get as many on each shelf as he could, with no concern for little old ladies with arthritic hands.

Actually, whoever the shooters were, they fired a lot more bullets into the van, but the remaining ranks of too-tightly-packed books absorbed the impact, while the people in the other cars, who had Plans and Orders of their own, shot those other ones to pieces. Plus the road was so narrow that none of them could have overtaken the fat van at the front, and they were all contending with each other as much as trying to down Jack – which not all of them wanted to do.

The side of the van was scraped by the overhanging bushes and trees as he veered from side to side to stop anyone coming alongside.

"Toad's Wild Ride or what!" he muttered, whizzing up and down through the gears.

"It's *Death Race 2000* back there," she noted. "I bet not a single one of them has got a current library card. In fact… I think I know exactly who that lot are!"

"Who?!"

"The dread ones. They Whose Names May Not Be Spoken."

"What… demons? Aliens?"

"Worse, grasshopper – far worse. I fear they are all members of the North Somerset Library and Information Service." They both gave mock spits of disgust at the very mention. "They have always envied, hated and feared the superb service of we their neighbours in our beloved Wiltshire."

"Ah come one... what's going on Jo?"

"Just keep going till you get to the little bridge at Farleigh Hungerford. Take it full pelt. Fuck me, but I feel like a pole dancer back here. It's the best retirement do I've ever had!"

"Jo..." he said again, though it was difficult to say more because of the frantic helter-skelterness of the driving, his head wobbling from side to side with the g-forces. Well you couldn't expect him to get involved in a calm Socratic dialogue, could you, when he was belting across the countryside like Tam O'Shanter pursued by the witches, whose only chance was to cross running water at the Brig O' Doon.

"Where are we going?" he asked, as much to the Head as to Jo.

Cley Hill, telepathed The Head in an English accent.

"To save the world of course," said Jo, who looked like the Long Man of Wilmington as she hung onto the two uprights, and if she'd been able to get to the non-fiction Folklore section she could have found an image of that in *The Modern Antiquarian* by Julian Cope, or else got onto the van's PC and used Google Images, from which she would have found 5800 images in 0.12 seconds.

"Do you know what's going?" he asked, as he saw the broken teeth of Farleigh Castle rising up ahead, on the brow of the hill beyond the narrow humpy-backed bridge.

"I'm a former member of the Libraries and Heritage Department, of Wiltshire County Council. Technically, I have the wherewithal – oops, mind that bastard cyclist! – to know everything."

"Do you know what's in this box?"

"Probably an electric kettle."

Ha! laughed the Head in Jack's head.

Ha! laughed Jack, but then he had to concentrate coz the bridge was coming up fast: down the hill, curve to the left, hedges and trees on either side, and dry-stone walls, the narrow road narrowing even further... He slowed. The cars behind got nearer, still jostling each other for primacy. "Hang on Jo!" he shouted behind him, then when he got to the bridge itself he put his foot to the floor and shot over it, taking off for a moment, and crashing down on the other side with no more damage than a few Talking Books leaping from the rear shelves like poltergeist disturbances.

"Bloody Hell!" cried Jo. She said that because of the jolt on landing, and also because she saw out of rear window the whole following convoy wedging themselves into the same narrow space, one of them going over the edge completely and plunging into the river, the rest just stuck there in a bottleneck of conspirators, if that's the proper collective term. So listen, being chased by members of a Secret Service is one thing: being chased by members of half the Secret Services in the civilised world, each branch with agendas of their own, is probably a distinct advantage.

He changed down a gear and drove up the short hill and stopped to survey the chaos behind. It was obvious to anyone that none of them back there would be able to catch him now, and they were all fighting among themselves anyway.

"Jo, that was–"

"Oh you can drop me off here, thanks."

"What?"

"Now that they're calmed or dead, I'll go back and sort out the rest of them. I read my Lee Child novels you know. I'm au fait with this sort of thing."

"Who are you, Jo?"

"I was once a Mistress in the House of Books."

"Trowbridge library, you mean?"

"No darling... somewhere older and grander that that – although I'm not knocking Trowbridge's non-fiction section, or the work they do with the kiddies."

She pressed the button which hissed open the automatic doors at the rear and paused before descending. For a moment – just a teensy moment – he almost had another of his Funny Turns, and he saw Jo not in the uniform of the Mobile Library service, but rimmed by light, and wearing the sort of long orange dress you might find on wall paintings in Karnak, or Aunu, and she was so very young and very ancient at the once. Then she threw him the precious Wiltshire County Council ID badge, which Jack had once described as being like the badge worn by US Marshals, which empowered him to drive about righting wrongs, doing good, and talking complete shite when he wasn't issuing books to the elderly and housebound. He was touched, could hardly talk. There should have been music playing.

"So I've passed my probation then?"

Jo snorted. She wouldn't go that far!

"Goodbye Jack. Now just remember what you are. Remember who you are."

He went all shivery at those words. What did she mean? Was he a god in human form?

Bollocks, telepathed The Head.

"Quite simply, you really are The Greatest Mobile Librarian in History. But if you don't hurry up, you might well be The Last Mobile Librarian in History. Now get on and save the world."

And then she was gone.

"Who was she?" Jack asked out loud.

She's not an angel. You just saw her Analogue, replied The Head, who still knew everything. *You've all got Analogues, of which you are the lower versions. Sometimes you can merge with them. Often, you go a bit loopy when you do.*

Now Jack would have loved to ask him more, in other circumstances, for it clearly could have opened a whole new world. In fact, he had a Science Fiction novel about this sort of thing in the back. Truth is, though, the sudden disappearance of Jo, amid all the chaos, was quite a jolt. Quite simply, he never saw her again. Whether she just disappeared into another dimension, or stepped out of the line of sight of his rear view mirrors, Jo was suddenly no more. If he'd had time to ape Lilith and do some Googling on his van's PC, then by putting 'Mistress in the House of Books' into the search box he would have come up with 229,000 entries in 0.28 seconds, the very first of which defined this being as Seshat, the Egyptian goddess of writing, historical records, accounting and mathematics, measurement and architecture, with a protective role toward the Pharaoh.

"Bugger me," muttered Jack, driving off fast now because there were three evil looking helicopters in the distance, each one of a different make and so probably different nation. Plus he had an impatient severed head on the passenger seat.

Analogues apart, was Jo put upon this earth to look after Jack at crucial times, as Mrs Loganathan had done for Jenny? Guardian Angel? Or a very mortal member of yet another ancient Order which operated behind the scenes? Was there a mystic Order behind even that once run by Porteous and The Nine? Was the Libraries and Heritage Department of Wiltshire County Council simply a front for the innermost Order behind the Order behind the Orders?

That's the thing with conspiracies: you never get all the answers on a plate, just a few rolling peas and rumbling echoes.

"Get on with it, please?" commanded Yahya, speaking out loud this time, and sounding rather muffled from within the box.

Jack got on with it. For whatever reason, he and his magic van pushed onward and ever so slightly upward toward Cley Hill...

*

If several of the characters have had Damascus moments during the build up to these End Times, then our three Templars from Rockley were having a Golgotha moment some 700 years away.

You could hardly feel otherwise when you've been trussed up on one of the cruciform posts they used to exercise their sword skills, and had half the local populace coming around to beat the shit out of you and your two pals (similarly bound on either side), and all the young smarmy Templar knights watching with impassive faces that you just wanted to tear open. Plus that little twat de Sautré standing next to his battered uncle and looking so bloody sanctimonious that they could have got holy water from his piss. The three of them looked at each other out of scarcely open eyes, and if there was pain there was no self pity. If their lips hadn't been burst, and their teeth shattered, at least one of them might have said something along the lines of You win some, you lose some, eh?

It had all been a trap. William de la More, Grand Master of all England, was not here to initiate his nephew but to find out for himself if his old knights out at Temple Rockley really were out of control, as his intelligence suggested. Young Robert de Sautré was not there to learn about the Order from the other three – especially his hero de Mohun: he was a spy, pure and simple. De la More had arrived not just with a couple of escorts: he had a whole troop lurking outside. The ones who eaten with him during that Last Supper were among his best fighters. The wine supplied them, and them alone, was little more than coloured water. They feigned drunkenness. When de Mohun had left the room with de la More, they had given a signal via one of the servants and the Great Hall was suddenly filled with REAL Templars.

Engayne, however – they all agreed – really was a no-no, a disgrace to the Order in a very different kind of way. They let him and his haemorrhoids ride off into the dawn, which he was more than happy to do.

And that really was more or less the end of the overlap between the doings at Temple Rockley and Jack and Lilith's world 700 years away. Within the next hour, as the sun rose, de Mohun and his two brothers would find themselves thrown into the back of a cart and incarcerated in cells at what was left of Old Sarum, many miles to the south. They could have been put in their own cells, or held at Templar properties in Oxfordshire, but the locals along the Ridgeway near Rockley would never have slept at night in case the monster – de Mohun – escaped. They wanted him as far away as possible.

*

But before then, there were some curious private moments between William de la More and the Sacred Head that you have to take on board....

Imagine the poor old sod: swollen black eyes that he could hardly see out of, nose spread over his face, broken teeth and gasping with the broken ribs, hardly able to walk, yet determined to be left alone with de Mohun's Sacred Head. Of course he didn't know that de Mohun actually made it from a log, never thought that such a lug could have such skill or endeavour. Oh, he knew it wasn't real. But he was certain it had winked. It *had* winked. And my goodness it had an aura about it. That was hardly surprising seeing as it had been linked with currents of consciousness and energy from the 21st Century during its creation.

That was an era when everyone in the God Business was after relics. There were thousands of them circulating or being adored: hair, fingernails, bones, teeth, kneecaps and even foreskins from the Saints. Splinters from the True Cross, nails which had once pierced The Hands of God, shrouds which had once enveloped The Body of God, and stains of every kind on every conceivable item of cloth, which seemed to show The Holy Face. The list was almost endless. So when de la More took possession of that Sacred but very wooden Head, he knew that he had struck lucky and found gold, and felt that it was about bloody time that something went his way.

In the darkness, amid his pain, seeing it through veils of blood, he felt that he was before something holy, though he could hardly ask de Mohun where he got it from, coz Grand Masters should know this sort of thing.

Of course you're wondering again: Was it the same Head that Jenny Djinn took possession of centuries later? Had it been turned into flesh, or did people only imagine it was alive?

The fact is, no-one now can tell.

William de la More, last of the Grand Masters of the Templars in England, closed the little doors on the beautifully carven casket and vowed to his god that no matter what happened to him personally or the Order as a whole, this was one relic that would kept safe, somewhere, for all time.

*

Jack drove through an eerily deserted countryside. There was almost no traffic. Either Lilith or Jenny had put the kibosh on those who caused traffic jams, or made unnecessary journeys. That, plus the fact that the government had declared a State of Emergency which panicked just about everyone left. The fields were empty, except for the occasional tractor, one of which had a greeny-skinned smiling corpse at the wheel, just about to start rotting.

Get that shovel! commanded The Head within his head, so Jack stopped the van with the engine running, leapt out and took the item from the tractor's trailer, trying not to look at the obscenely dead face of the former owner. *Now drive, fast. Cley Hill...*

If there was no traffic on the roads, there were those three helicopters of varying styles that were clearly following him, and – we might suppose – watching each other too. Of course, if this had been one of Jenny's action films, then Jack would have found some convenient tunnel that he could drive into, timing it so that the choppers would crash into the hillside above it. There were no such tunnels, alas, nor even any useful bridges or high voltage power lines anywhere in the area. Besides, Cley Hill was such an isolate mound with only one road going past it, that sneaking up toward the place was never gonna be an option.

"Why Cley Hill?" asked Jack, who still retained his curiosity despite everything else. "Is it to do with the Templars?"

Bugger the Templars, The Head telepathed. *It's because it's a Gateway. There are places like it all over. This is the nearest.*

232

"Bit like a Wi-Fi hotspot, then? I use them on this van when I can't get a proper signal from the regular Vodafone network."

Bugger the library service. Just drive...

So he drove. He drove hard and fast, and the wind made noises like whistling kettles through the bullet holes in the sides of the van. Let's have some music, he thought, wondering what message he would get from the aethers this way. So when he pressed the button and Wiltshire Radio came on and The Dambusters March blared out full volume he had to smile. And when you think about it, if you become certain that the End of the World is imminent, then what else is there left to do but smile and enjoy it. That's the way that Jack's mind worked, anyway.

Cley Hill was now looming across the fields, off to his right, and there was no way he could have sneaked up to the place, so they whizzed along the A36 as fast a clumsy Mobile Library being tailed by attack helicopters can whizz, then positively screamed around the roundabout. If any of his Warminster readers had been there waiting for some spicy Mills & Boon Romances, then they would have been sorely disappointed as he rattled past without a glance.

"What do I do when I get there?" he asked out loud, knowing that The Head heard every word, even inside the box, even before he uttered them. "Just stop in the car park?"

It's Little Cley Hill we want – the low mound to the right of the big one. Drive up to it. Don't stop for anything.

Jack swallowed. "That's a rough track. I'll lose all the books from the shelves."

That might sound trivial given the circumstances, but if you're a Mobile Librarian with a high and narrow van and you get a 'waggle' on the van and the entire stock comes off, then it's no joke when you have to put them back in place again.

Bugger the books. Just drive!

Well, you can see why Yahya had such a big following when he was entire. He was so masterful.

At one point, taking a tiny little side road, he drove past a piggery, and – apart from the stench – that proved such a relief. You see, there were moments when he had been tempted to just drop the box and go back home, because he wasn't sure if the Head hadn't done that thing with the 11 dimensions that Jenny talked about, and swapped locations again, but the moment it was brought within reach of the pigs, well, they just went berserk! The noise! Squealing and grunting, hurling themselves against the walls, in absolute terror. Now there was no way that a 2.4KW clear boil electric kettle with removable locking lid and power-on indicator could make them squeal like that. Whatever was in the box emanated enough unearthly energy that 200 pigs about to be slaughtered could sense it through several walls, and act as if a mini-Chernobyl that was driving past them.

Dogs barked. Men came out to see what the fuss was and Wiltshire accents floated in the air saying things that were slightly stronger than Gosh! and Crikey! – but Johnny Boy moved in mysterious ways and no-one could stop him.

Now logic said that this was Wiltshire farmland he was running through and not some Apocalyptic killing fields. Reason advised that he should stop, and his pursuers in the helicopters would land and turn out to be the most reasonable of men who wanted no more than to ask the simple question: "Excusez m'sieur, but is it that it is the 'ead of God you avez in that box, or a satisfyingly designed kettle from ze Argos automne/hiver catalogue, hein?" But logic is never the best ally when you're involved in something of a Quest, and the Head of St John or the Holy Grail is on your passenger seat.

So Jack drove and jiggled, and twisted the van here and there, the once-beautiful getting scraped to bits so that only Jo's recent graffiti stood proud, and before too long he was turning into the little car park – the same one that Jenny had been squatting and peeing in when it all began, and saw that the gate across the pedestrian footway toward the hill itself was closed.

Of course there was only one thing to do then. It was the ending of the world. He no longer had to worry about scratching his van, losing his books from their shelves, disappointing his readers and getting the sack. He felt that if his boss Jo had still been there he might have been encouraged to give a big YEE HAH! as he drove the van toward the gate like the Lone Ranger or John Wayne – or even that Slim Pickens riding the bomb at the end of *Dr Strangelove*. So he did exactly that:

"YEE HAH!!" he screamed and put his foot to the floor and the big old van smashed right through the big old gate, and you could have heard the noise back in the Library and Heritage HQ if you'd been one of the ones still left alive there.

"Sorry. Sorry girl!" he winced, almost feeling the impact on his own face as his vehicle cracked open the gates.

Now to be honest, the 7½ ton Mercedes Sprinter van might be a superb vehicle when it comes to carrying library books to remote communities across Wiltshire, but when it comes to roaring up a stony track, smashing down a second gate and two fences, and then forging across uneven land around the base of big Cley Hill to get to its smaller companion, it wasn't the most perfect thing. Not while he had to zig zag and avoid any possible air to ground missiles from the helicopters. Still an' all he got there even if his brain was almost shaken loose in its skull, and if he said so himself, that act alone made him the Greatest Mobile Library Driver Ever And For All Time.

Here. Stop here! said The Head within his head, and the fact is Jack didn't have much choice. Unless the van could have transformed into a Challenger tank, there was no way it could go any further up the slope or closer to the summit of the low flat cone which is Little Cley Hill, coz the wheels had spun themselves into the earth and the engine stalled.

"Well done my brave and gallant steed," Jack muttered heartily, patting the dashboard as if it was a horse's head. The van was at such an odd angle that it required a certain gymnastic ability to remove the box from the passenger seat, and then leap down with it.

I want to go home now, said Yahya, in the saddest voice that Jack had ever had inside his head, and he felt that if he opened the box there and then he would have seen The Head weeping.

"So what do I do?" asked Jack as he carried the box up to the flat summit. Looking anxiously at the buzzing helicopters in the middle distance – one, two, three of the buggers – each one keeping as much away from the others as from himself.

Get the shovel and a pile of books and I'll tell you...

*

You haven't forgotten Jenny Djinn and Lilith Love of course. How could you? They were the Death Goddesses of the Age, extraordinary beings who were by this time both more than human and lacking almost all humanity, if that's not a contradiction – although one of them at least still had a current and valid library ticket.

235

So, be astonished to see them in Dr McHaffee's Range Rover, belting across the fields and cutting all the corners, and managing to keep the Library Van within their sight.

And what an atmosphere! You could have cut it with the sort of axe they used to decapitate Yahya all those millennia ago.

Hey, picture it: Jenny – who was by now desperate to see her two beloveds – commandeered Dr McHaffee to do her one last favour. In his urge to bring her back to what he thought was reality, he had agreed, and so they had leapt into his car and gone belting across town to get Jack from the hotel.

McHaffee was mad as hell. Fuming. Inwardly he was probably as much of a headcase as anyone he counselled, but because he had certificates on his office walls and adequate personal hygiene, no-one could really touch him.

"This is the last time, Jenny Grey," he muttered, driving hard, smacking the gears up and down, using her 'old' name as if it might make a point.

Then when they arrived at her rival's hotel-cum-headquarters, Lilith had just sussed that Jack had walked out, and she was standing on the road looking all ways and almost roaring. Walked out on her! Walked out on Lilith Love!!! You could almost feel sorry for her. No-one had ever done that to her. Then again, she had never let anyone close enough to have the chance.

If you'd been neutral, and sure of your immortality, you might have hoped the pair of them would go for each other there and then, and sort out who was the irresistible force and who the immovable object. It would have been like Rocky meets Raging Bull, or Terminator meets the Iron Man. As it was, Love and the Library Man Conquered All, coz the two of them sort of glared at each, kept their powers in check, muttered a few things of the 'Where the hell is he?' type, and then leapt into McHaffee's car when they caught a distant glimpse of the familiar green and white library van livery creaming westward with attendant helicopters buzzing along behind.

"It's all in your head Jenny Grey," McHaffee kept saying, banging on, and it amused Jenny really, because he completely ignored Lilith on the back seat. That didn't go down too well with her at all, but she kept quiet and kept her eyes fixed toward the disappearing Jack.

"Yes it is, Doc! It really is all in The Head. But I'm gonna show you where it all began. Then you might understand. Then you might know about Love and Death and how they're both the same."

If looks could kill...

"Jenny. Come to Tigh Aisling with me. It will be perfect for you."

"What's *tee ashleen*?" asked Lilith with some irritation.

"It's his baby. It means 'House of Dreams'."

"So what goes on there?"

Lilith never got an answer to that because whatever was going on in the sky above them, with the black helicopters, suddenly went onto another level and no-one will ever know, now, what their orders were – if any. That is to say those anonymous pilots from their anonymous countries and highly anonymous security services, decided to take each other out instead of the Van, and it was like Guy Fawkes Night in the afternoon sky – blues and red and purple explosions, and bits flying all over the countryside, and noise like the world was cracking open as the carcasses of the machines fell burning to the ground.

Credit to Dr McHaffee though: he drove on through it like a good 'un, making full use of his four wheel drive to get them off the road and across the fields, shaking them almost senseless so that they forgot to be Death Goddesses for a while and hung on for dear life.

What kept you? said a voice in the women's heads as they slewed to a stop at the foot of Little Cley Hill, next to the Mobile Library, and saw the golden-haired figure of their beloved Jack digging a hole on its summit...

*

"That's my Jack," said Jenny shyly, striding up the slope to embrace him. Or she might have done if Lilith hadn't gone into warp factor 3 and got there first, and before you could say 'Dewey Decimal System', he had a Death Goddess on either side, his arms pinioned by their tits, his cheeks somewhat reddened by their kisses as they both sought to make a point. Any other young fella would have got such a rush of blood out of his head and into other regions that he might have fainted, but our Jack was hugely annoyed instead. He was trying to bury a box containing the severed head of St John the

Baptist; he was trying to save his Mum and the world – or what was left of it.

"Get off!" he shouted mightily, and the two women stood back right sharply – they had never heard him raise his voice before. "And you stay down there!" he shouted further, aiming his shovel toward the approaching Dr McHaffee like some sort of light-sabre.

The good doctor, bless him, might have been as whizzy an analyst as Lilith had once been, but the idea of charging up a hill to confront a madman wielding a shovel didn't have much attraction for him just then. He had never been an Alpha Male: he was in touch with his inner wimp. So he stood back, and he watched, and wondered what the hell it was in the box, and why they were so hyped by it all.

"What is this place Jack?" asked Lilith. And it was weird – really weird – but the little hilltop was encircled by spikes of light, the whole spectrum from infrared to ultraviolet, and maybe it was a visit from the desperate Nine Who rule the World, or maybe they were all producing the sort of aura which comes before an epileptic fit.

"This," said Jenny looking around at the lights, "is where the earthbound souls of the dead go on to heaven." She was very smug as she spoke, answering for Jack like that, and you could tell she had really studied that little book she had once taken out about local folklore.

Ooh, but that really annoyed Lilith. She was half inclined to burst into the van and start Googling on the terminal in there, and get something better than that! As it was, when Jack decided that the hole was deep enough he pushed past them, opened the rear doors of said van and grabbed a handful of the first Large Print Romances that he came to, clearing a whole shelf, then staggering back up the hill with them like an accordion player, dropping some as he went, before tearing the pages out and chucking them into the hole where the box was perched on the edge.

"What are you doing?!" asked the women in some horror. They knew exactly what he was doing.

He's sending me home, said The Head in all their heads.

"Oh why?" asked Jenny softly and lovingly, meaning: *Why would you want to do that?*

"Oh. Why?" asked Lilith sharply and keenly, meaning: *I want an explanation for all this.*

They asked this, but the fact is they were both sort of thrumming, like tuning forks picking up a resonance from The Head or maybe even The Nine.

Listen... if those helicopters and all their missiles and armour-piercing bullets made a helluva noise when they blasted each other, that was nothing to the explosion The Head made when they asked that. In fact, the container burst open at the seams so that Yahya's head teetered there in its rage like an obscene jack-in-the-box. He roared at them. He roared at the world. Two thousands years of pent-up rage.

Actually, you'd need to be an expert in dead languages to pick up everything he said then, though even the dullest Trowbridge Trout or Maine Minger could have guessed that he was swearing in every tongue, from every age, using words that lashed and seared. He sounded in their ears and in their heads, and god knows what McHaffee was making of it all down at the bottom of the hill, because it must have seemed as they were grouped around a ghetto-blaster or something. If you want a sanitised, Anglicised version it went something like:

"Because I want to destroy the whole bloody world! I hate what it's done to me – look at me! I hate what it's become! I want to destroy it with fire and air and earth – because that water baptism shite didn't do me or it a whole lot of good did it? That's why I created you two Death Goddesses, brought down your Analogues. You've nearly done the job for me – bless you both, you stupid cows. Now send me home. Only a life can pay for a life. Only a love can pay for a love. I – Yahya – can only be released by fire and the sacrifice of someone well loved. So get on with it, pretty little Angel Boy cum Damping Rod. The Jenny-bitch has got a lighter. The Lilith-bitch will waft the flames. You can all cover me with blessed earth when I'm consumed. But you have to sacrifice one of them afterward. That's the Law. So choose...!"

Ooh, he was angry. He was in a REAL strop. You wouldn't have wanted to put your finger near his mouth coz he'd have had it.

Lilith looked at The Head and then at Jenny and then at Jack.

Jenny looked at Jack and then at Lilith and then at The Head.

Jack looked at the lights of The Nine which, if spikes of light can seem flustered, were doing that now. Then he looked at the two

239

women. This was the End Time. He had to choose, no fannying about. They all knew that.

"Put me in the ground," came the command, calmer now, but no less irresistible. Jack took him by the ears and did exactly that, face up, the eyes shining with delight and imminent peace.

"Jenny… come on baby light my fires! Light the papers under me." She paused. Only briefly. Turning her lighter to full flame, Jenny did what she was told, so The Head was encircled by greeny-blue tongues.

"Lilith… give me some air time baby."

She did exactly that. This was her Creator. How could she not? She took some torn sheets and fanned the flames around him, which licked up and burned his hair first as if it was the driest and most combustible kindling. He gave a sigh.

"My own Holy Trinity at the last," he said, looking up at the three heads with the sky behind them. "Now Jack… choose. Choose quickly and do what it is you have to do. This only works with the sacrifice bit."

Well, you can see why people flocked to see Yahya in their thousands, years ago, and why some people will walk through the flames or get nailed to crosses for someone like this. Except… Jack wasn't quite like normal people – insofar as martyrs of any kind can be called 'normal', that is.

Lilith looked at Jack.

Jenny looked at Jack.

This was the End Time. They were ready to go. Each one wanted to be the Chosen One. Jack was so utterly beautiful then, surrounded by all the uncanny lights, and had opened such wondrous doors, that it would have been the greatest act of love in their lives, at the end of life, at the ending of the world, to be chosen as The One.

Who did he love best?

Lilith?

Jenny?

There was no doubt in his mind how he had to choose. First he kissed Jenny on the forehead and she gasped with delight. Then he kissed Lilith on the cheek and she sort of swooned.

"Get out the way," he said to both, pushing them aside and striding down the slope toward his Library Van, and there was only one possible decision. This might have been a piece of machinery to them, but in his strange heart and stranger head it had more life and worthiness than either of the two women.

Do it! said The Head in his own head, and with Jenny's lighter and all the paper you could hope to have, he Did It! he set fire to his beloved. He sacrificed Her, there on that holy spot, the smoke reaching to the heavens.

If you were standing where McHaffee was you would have seen the small vertical flame shooting out of the hole in the top of Little Cley Hill, and also the huge vertical flame – its Analogue – rising in parallel, but far higher and wider. You might have heard, too, a cacophony that any writer from Biblical times might have described as a sobbing and wailing and gnashing of teeth that seemed to come from everywhere. Maybe it was the souls of the earthbound that had been queuing up at Little Cley Hill waiting for the chance to 'go on'; maybe it was those two silly women expressing their rage and upset at the loss of their powers; maybe it was the voice of Yahya, his soul released at last, giving a sort of death-rattle.

Or maybe it was simply the pain in Jack's soul as he watched his Magic Steed be consumed by the flames. "Bless you," he said, to no-one and for no particular reason, wiping his tears on his sleeve, the charred bits of his books floating around him like a snowstorm, the mobile library popping and cracking and burning quite merrily.

Mind you, he felt a bit better when he saw his Mum appear as if from nowhere, riding piggy back on K'tan Shui. Somehow, there didn't seem to be anything odd about them being there. Listen... we all have perfectly ordinary days in the ordinary world when, for some reason, nothing makes sense, and the most bizarre things can occur, and we tend to say Oh well! and get on with it. So you can see that in these extraordinary times, when everything was totally uncanny, something like a Mum teleporting on the back of her alien lover wouldn't have raised too many eyebrows. After all, Cley Hill was supposed to contain a homing beacon for UFOs, and the latter had been seen to fly straight into it as if it were an aircraft hangar, so maybe something of that sort was going on.

"Bah!" said K'tan Shui when he looked over the scene through his dark glasses. We might be sure that *Bah!* in his language meant something very different to when we use it, yet he put Maisie down with infinite care and strode up toward that fell trinity. "Pah!" he said this time, looking around the lights of The Nine and then he did something which was odd even by the expanded standards of that lot: he reached out with a "Wah!" and took up the lights of the Nine, just plucked them out of the air – or whatever the medium was they floated in – and plaited them together, his stubby fingers moving with supra-human speed. Then before you could say 'Mysterium', he had them all in a glowing ball between his hands, which he took toward the hole in which The Burning Head lay. "Tchah..." he said softly, dropping the luminous and insubstantial little globe of light into that small grave and then kicking the soil on top of the lot, and though no-one realised it for years, that was the end of the stupid Orders and their arsehole Magi for at least two generations.

Jack, Jenny and Lilith all caught a final glimpse of Yahya before the earth took him: suffused with all the colours of the rainbow from infrared to ultraviolet, but dissolving like sugar in tea, he was crying with relief.

Pax Vobiscum, you lot... came the whisper from The Head in their heads, for the last time on the edge of time.

They stood there looking down at what anyone else would mistake for a molehill. Apart from the crackling of the library van as it consumed itself in much the same way The Head had done, there was only the sound of their breathing and the noise of distant cattle. In fact the only words that any mortal said at that spot then, and for a long time afterward, were McHaffee's:

"Jenny... come away with me. Come to the House of Dreams."

*

Well, that was that. The sudden and massive waves of Death stopped as suddenly as they had begun, and people more or less put it down to some sort of plague, as you know, and the much-trimmed world carried on, limpingly at first but growing stronger as the Japanese made their findings about Zero Point Energy sources freely available to all.

No-one knew what those Japs did with the electric kettle from Argos but its probably in a splendid casket somewhere, and brought out with pomp and tea ceremonies for the lucky ones.

No-one saw Lilith or experienced anything of her Analogue – that is to the say, the Death Goddess Sekhmet – again. For a few years afterward there were rumours of a mad woman in the woods around

242

Cley Hill and nearby Black Dog Hill, but in the New Times which followed, there were any number of those all over the world. She certainly never got back to the US or prime time television. No-one ever read her books after all that.

When K'tan Shui plaited those lights, Maisie had looked on at her fella, chest bursting with pride, as if she understood every word. Which made Jack wonder if in fact his Mum had not been an alien herself, and never had 'learning disabilities' at all, except in Earth-context. After two big hugs she and K'tan Shui just disappeared as quickly as they had appeared, when his back was turned, and he never saw her again either. He felt her presence sometimes though, and never felt that she was far away.

Without another word to those present, Jack walked the lonely miles back to Trowbridge where Keith forgave him for the utter destruction of the van and went off to join the Somerset Library and Information Service without daring to tell anyone, while Mike swung his bollards for the last time and promptly retired.

Jack then became a mover and shaker within the remnants of the still pre-eminent Wiltshire Library and Heritage HQ, giving them hope of starting up services again and becoming a sort of Saint Jack in the process. He might have had a knighthood if the Royal Family had survived, but the fact is a certain Death Goddess with fiercely republican tendencies had put paid to them in the early stages of Her career.

The rest of the disciples, meanwhile, hung around the Old Mill – aka The Sanctuary – for the rest of their lives. Shaz and Tasha became almost venerable, quietly and earnestly telling their stories to journalists and biographers. Along with Felicity, they espoused what was effectively a new religion based upon the supposed Ascension of Jenny Djinn. To everyone's surprise but Felicity's, this took off to such an extent that for a time the remnants of the Women's Institute debated on whether to drop their traditional Jam and Jerusalem policies and follow the shade of the Wiltshire Kali, but that sort of fizzled out, which was probably for the best.

And as for Jenny Djinn, who started the whole thing, it seemed that she had disappeared off the face of the earth too. Perhaps the kind Dr McHaffee had given her a lift somewhere, and helped her start again. Perhaps he had done away with her as a dangerous lunatic. Or, if we go along with the Keep It Simple, Stupid philosophy of John de Mohun, maybe Felicity was right: maybe she really had risen to Kali Heaven and was even now watching down upon her beloved followers, and women and children everywhere. There were rumours of sightings: in Bath, Bristol, Devizes – London even. She had almost become like those celebrities she once had glimpsed in the most unlikely of Trowbridgean surroundings: a hint, a shadow, a parallel or analogue – and possibly a reality.

So now the only thing you can really say that might make any sense after all this death and all this love between the ages and the worlds, is to echo what Yahya said to his trinity that day when the world was pulled back from the brink:

Pax Vobiscum, you lot...

THE END